Juliet Ashton is a bright new voice in commercial women's fiction. She lives in London. Visit her website at: www.julietashton.com

The Valentine's Card

Juliet Ashton

SPHERE

First published in Great Britain in 2013 by Sphere
Reprinted 2013

A CIP catalogue record for this book
is available from the British Library.

ISBN 978-0-7515-4427-5

Typeset in Caslon by M Rules
Printed and bound in Great Britain by
Clays Ltd, St Ives plc

Papers used by Sphere are from well-managed forests
and other responsible sources.

MIX
Paper from
responsible sources
FSC® C104740

Sphere
An imprint of
Little, Brown Book Group
100 Victoria Embankment
London EC4Y 0DY

An Hachette UK Company
www.hachette.co.uk

www.littlebrown.co.uk

Uncle Sam
This book is for you!

Acknowledgements

I have so much to thank people for. I want to thank Matthew and Niamh for not minding when I locked myself in my study. I want to thank Deirdre and Louise and Sara Jade and Penny and Jan and Andie and Kates both H and F for cheerleading/handholding. I want to thank Bogna Rasmussen for translating the Polish sections of the book. I want to thank Jen for babysitting the little one while I got on with my work. I want to thank Emma Beswetherick, Lucy Icke, Tamsyn Berryman and David Shelley of Little, Brown for guiding me safe home to port. And I want to thank YOU for buying this book, because, truly, without you there would be no point to all of this!

Sim's journal

13 February 2012

I need a 'Yes' from you, darling! Gimme a loud heartfelt YES!

Prologue

County Dublin
14 February 2012
7.18 a.m.

Thanks to her eerie superpower for knowing the time the moment she awoke, Orla knew she only had a couple of minutes before the alarm clock let rip. She shut her eyes tight again, mutinously clinging to the night. The bedroom was dark, the world outside still moodily silent except for birds gossiping in the big bare tree outside her window.

Today was, what, a Tuesday? Orla groaned, eyes still closed. Tuesday meant P.E. Thirty-one seven-year-olds, hopping from foot to foot on arctic tarmac, red of nose and knee, whining, *Can we go back in yet, Miss Cassidy?* Orla wound herself tighter in the duvet, deep in denial. From the field at the back of the house a tractor burped and she smiled to herself. *Irish road rage.* She'd mention that to Sim later, when they Skyped. He'd laugh.

Decorative, easy-going, happy to flirt with the plain girls and fuss over the geriatric ladies, Sim laughed easily but Orla felt proud when she made him giggle. She knew the real thing when she heard it, meatier than the polite, diplomatic laugh he employed in his relentless one-man mission to charm the world. Orla loved Sim's giggle. She missed it.

After years of scraping by in Dublin's theatrical circles, her boyfriend's elusive 'big break' had finally materialised when he was cast as the dashing male lead in the BBC's latest costume drama. Not only did the part fit Sim like a glove – he got to wear satin breeches and ride horses, breaking hearts with just his smile – but it also made him the envy of his peers. Orla had been overjoyed when she heard the news. With the Beeb's mighty PR muscle behind it, it was a career-making role. She had jumped up and down, clapped and cheered and kissed him over and over – until she'd learned he would be moving to London for five months.

'Come!' It had seemed obvious to Sim. He never read the fine print of life.

'My job,' Orla had said. 'My home. My family. And, oh yes, my *sanity*.'

She refused to be a spare part and, despite his histrionic pleading, she stood by her decision. Even a woman in love has to be pragmatic and Orla couldn't deny there were advantages to Sim's sabbatical. She didn't miss the schlep to Dublin twice or thrice a week, and she certainly didn't miss Sim's grumbles about the M50 when he drove out to see her in Tobercree. With Sim in London, Orla could plan her evenings to please herself, watch reality TV without standing trial for it, wear the shapeless pyjamas he declared passion killers, and eat toast for dinner.

They were measly, though, these advantages, compared to all the things she missed. The rasp of his stubbly cheek. The beautiful crook of his long brown back in her crumpled sheets. The thwack of his hand on her bottom as he passed by. This last she always scowled at but secretly enjoyed, and enjoyed the faux lovers' tiff that followed even more.

The alarm danced on its bedside tower of books. Orla reached out a hand and hushed it, eyes still obstinately shut. A Canute in floral winceyette, Orla concentrated on holding back the day, stopping it from flooding in and ruining her nest. She wouldn't shower, a saving of ten minutes or so. Coco Pops instead of a boiled egg scored her another five. That was fifteen embezzled minutes to spend dreaming of her upcoming trip.

Three whole days in London with Sim. She would ride a big red bus, visit Buckingham Palace and have a great deal of sex. It would be good, and it would be about time. Orla had underestimated the effects of separation on their relationship. They hadn't seen each other since New Year ... Orla hurriedly shooed away memories of that reunion, turning over onto her other side, only to encounter the cold sheets where, by rights, Sim should be.

She recoiled.

The doorbell rang, with the distinctive sing-song of the postman.

The phone rang.

Apparently the world was conspiring to drag Orla out of bed.

A thought, muddy and indistinct, took shape. There was something about today, wasn't there? She lay still, lashes glued together, trusting her waking brain to sniff it out.

It was Saint Valentine's Day. That cancelled out PE altogether.

Orla opened her eyes.

London
14 February 2012
6.05 a.m.

Never a morning person, Sim had resented being wrenched from his warm, wide bed. The hard edges of the early morning street seemed specifically designed to assault his senses and he longed to rewind, shrug off his clothes and fold himself back in between the covers.

This promised to be a busy day but not the sort of busy day he relished – rehearsing or filming or being measured up for poncey costumes by pretty little things from wardrobe – but the sort of busy day he detested. A meeting with his accountant, a briefing from the PR guy and then a long important lunch with ... oh, someone, Sim couldn't recall who.

Was it normal, the way his thoughts slid away from him like this?

One thought, though, held fast. It was Valentine's Day. Hence his early start. Today's post would seal his fate, one way or another.

He put the confused, flu-like feeling down to his sleepless night, and yawned.

'Ooh.' Sim staggered. He felt nauseous.

Had he drunk more than he'd realised last night? No. It

had been a restrained, civilised sort of evening. He even recalled writing his journal. Orla always rolled her eyes at him for keeping a journal. She claimed it was pretentious (a 'self-aggrandising, luvvie cliché,' as he recalled) but she was just peeved that he wouldn't let her read it and she would eat her words when Hollywood wanted to use it for his memoirs. Anyway, Reece wouldn't let him overindulge the night before a big day, that was practically part of an agent's remit. There had been dinner at Reece's club, just the one post-meal brandy, then home alone. He shouldn't feel this rough, this ... queer. The quaint Irish word fitted the bill perfectly. Sim was an imperfect fit for his own skin.

Limbs shaking, Sim reminded himself of the long professional drought of his Dublin life, his fantasies of landing a high profile television role. Now that his dream had come true (trite but accurate) he mustn't gripe. But giving himself a good talking to wasn't the same as having Orla there to do it for him, with her particular, sexy tone of voice somewhere between disappointed and taking the mick.

This was no time to think of Orla. Today would pan out in one of two ways, and he had resolved to let it take its course without fretting.

Easier said than done.

The nausea passed, giving way to light-headedness. Stopping to lean against a lamp post, Sim blinked rapidly, ran a hand over his face and waited for the sensation to pass.

Tea. Orla always prescribed tea and she was right. It had magical properties that only the Irish appreciated. He'd ask for tea the second he arrived.

It was only when Sim tried to walk on that he realised he

couldn't. The bones in his legs had been replaced with jam. He hugged the lamp post. His scalp was drenched with sweat, yet he felt brutally cold. This was beyond just queer.

A busybody dustcart trundled past and receded into the distance, its lonely roar ringing in Sim's ears. He knew he couldn't shout for help so didn't try. With an almighty effort he took a step, then regretted it as his body rebelled and crumpled.

Reaching out his hands, Sim felt only air, nothing to break his fall. The last, strange noise he heard was the unique gargle startled out of him by the pain in his chest.

His cheek pressed into the pavement.

Sim closed his eyes.

Chapter One

Orla's morning had turned into a horror movie. In slow motion she opened the front door, phone clamped to her ear. Orla stared at the postman the way a Victorian explorer might regard a rhino: he made no sense to her whatsoever. He had been delivering mail to her door ever since she was a child but today it was as if she didn't recognise him. The world had shrunk to obliterate everything except the voice in her ear.

The postman held out a large, very pink, rectangular envelope. 'Give you three guesses who this is from!' God he was cheerful. She'd often envied his *joie de vivre* in the face of early morning starts and Celtic weather.

Orla took the card and read her name and address as if it were Sanskrit. 'I'm sorry, Reece,' she said into the receiver. 'Could you repeat that?'

'I said,' the postman said, misunderstanding, 'no doubt that's a valentine's card from your Sim!'

'Sim,' said the genteel voice from London, 'died fifty-five minutes ago. There was nothing anyone could do. I'm so sorry.'

'Open it!' The postman's voice was all twinkle. 'Open it up and count the kisses! Ah! Young love!'

Orla slammed the door and backed down the hall to vomit on the kitchen lino. From the windowsill, next door's cat glared down at her and walked away; no second breakfast from Orla this morning.

The pink envelope fluttered to the ground.

You can't sit on the floor forever. The thought eventually impelled Orla up off the lino.

Orla looked around her. The world was lit differently. The mugs idling on the draining board, her 'To Do' list on the fridge, the chequered hillock of the tea towel discarded on the table, all dulled. It was as if some celestial being had flicked a switch and plunged Orla into a grey new reality.

She was at a complete loss. *Sim.* She said his name out loud, over and over, like an incantation. She picked up her phone to call him, then dashed it to the floor. She walked from room to room, rubbing one hand up and down the other arm as if seeking to erase herself altogether. Orla wheeled, changed direction, sat down, stood up. Her head shook with the effort of making it true. *So, if I call him he won't answer? If I fly to London right this second there'll be no Sim there? He's gone?*

Her Sim couldn't be gone. He just couldn't be.

She wanted to tear off her clothes, gouge holes in her chest. Surely this was a dream.

With relief, Orla realised that the bed still needed to be made. The bathroom still needed to be put right. Orla dragged the duvet off the floor, fussed with it, neatened it. She wiped the tiles in the shower carefully, chasing every last smear clean away.

She thought about Sim with her entire body. Her mind couldn't pin down any one thing long enough for it to qualify as a thought, but her body, or maybe her being, resonated with him. He was in the dust that floated in the streams of sunlight through the dormer window. He was the soft nubbly feel of the bath mat beneath her feet. He was colour, he was sound.

He could not be gone.

Orla made herself a cup of tea and heard the doorbell ring as if it were under water.

'Howaya!'

Juno stepped over the threshold with the mandatory Dublin greeting and the *droit de seigneur* of an old friend.

'I was on me way to the gym, lady of leisure that I am, and I saw your car in the drive. What's up? Flu? *Love*sickness?' She executed a showy swoon, but straightened up as she took in Orla's face. 'Something *is* wrong.'

'Tea?' Orla passed her, went to the kitchen. She opened the fridge. The food in it was like the food in her childhood doll's house, painted lumps. She couldn't imagine tasting food again.

'Is it this lurgy that's going around?' Juno dipped and weaved around the kitchen, trying to get a good look at Orla as she travelled from kettle to tap to cupboard.

'I had Oreos, but they've all gone.'

It was better, this display of normality for Juno, than the ugly confusion of earlier, and Orla clung to it, fending off the moment when she'd have to say the words out loud.

'I'm not hungry,' said Juno, hoisting herself on to the worktop.

'Your hair looks great,' Orla said to her friend.

Hair. Imagine hair mattering. She caught a glimpse of them both in the chrome of the cooker hood. Juno's hair was fiery ginger, her face bright. Orla's own face was a parchment smudge under black hair. She raked her fingers through the tousles. It felt alien to her. Her eyes were still recognisably her own, though, blue . . . but dulled.

Juno was yabbering, chit-chatting, picking up the salt cellar and pouring some into the palm of her hand. She was so alive it hurt to look at her. Orla returned to her own reflection, a whey ghost haunting its kitchen. She wondered what Sim looked like now. Not his body, but his essence. Up to now he'd *been* his body, now he was . . . Orla had no idea how to finish the thought, and so she plunged back into precious conversational banality, extending it, wallowing in it.

'Don't spill salt, Ju, it's bad luck.' Her lips stuck to her teeth. She squeezed out a tea bag and carried it ceremoniously to the pedal bin. She trod on the pedal, the lid yawned open and the tea bag plunged past it, to the floor.

Orla dropped the spoon. A terrible noise emerged from deep within her, like an animal backing out of a tight space, like something afraid of being burned alive.

'He can't be.' Juno said it over and over. 'He just can't.'

Juno and Sim had been wary of each other, each critical of the other, each resenting the other's importance to Orla, their beloved piggy in the middle.

Orla envied Juno her reaction. It was linear. There were copious tears but Orla could sense an ending. At some point, Juno would dry her eyes, shake herself and attend to things, whereas Orla was a blob on the fabric of time: she had no journey ahead of her, just this sprawling *now*. She didn't say any of this. It sounded melodramatic, and she knew that Juno relied on her for common sense.

'His agent called me. It happened in . . .' This part was

hard to say. In a sea of drear, she hated this detail most of all. 'In the street.'

'But what *is* a pulmonary embolism?' Juno's fifth tissue gave up and she accepted the one Orla held out. Her nose – rather a long nose – was bright red. She was hunched in her tight black sports gear, like a spider. 'He hadn't been ill. Had he? Sim's never ill.'

'I don't know what a pulmonary embolism is. Something to do with the lungs?' It hardly mattered to her. It had killed him. It could have been a bullet or a stroke or a giant custard pie to the face: knowledge wouldn't help here. Even if Orla were Ireland's foremost authority on pulmonary embolisms, Sim would still be dead.

'Have you spoken to your ma?' There it was, that decisive sniff: Juno was rallying.

'Not yet.'

'I'll call her for you.' Juno stood up. 'And the school.' She was brisk again, if depleted. 'You'll get through this,' she said, and it sounded like a threat. 'You have me and you have your ma and your family and your pupils and *everybody*. We'll get you through.'

How? was all Orla could think. Juno was well-meaning but how on earth was she supposed to 'get through' losing Sim without, well, Sim?

'What's this?' Juno stooped to pick up a pink rectangle. 'Oh, it's . . .' She bit her lip, looked apologetically at Orla.

'I'd forgotten about that.' Orla took the valentine and held it reverentially. 'Aw,' she said, a sweet sound, the first un-ugly noise she'd made since the call. 'It's from him.'

*

Housework was a relic of past times, something she used to do. The cottage slumbered beneath three days' worth of dust as Miss Orla Havisham slumped swathed in a blanket, staring blankly at a television screen that yodelled unheard. She saw only Sim, as if her brain were a film projector loaded with old movies.

The troops had rallied. The school was 'brilliant', as Orla put it, offering her as much leave as she needed. The Cassidys pulled together and Orla received all the casseroles and sponge cakes and offers of help she could ever need. The food went in the bin, the offers were forgotten.

The pink envelope, still unopened, had replaced Orla's Ryanair tickets centre stage on the mantelpiece. It was constantly on the move, tailing her from bedside to bathroom cabinet to kitchen shelf. It was a symbol, but of what Orla wasn't sure. She panicked if it was out of sight, yet opening it was out of the question. She knew what she would read. And it would slay her.

If only, she thought, with the sort of histrionics she detested, *if only something really* could *kill me*.

Sim was good at writing cards. Not for him a hasty 'Lots of love', or hurried signature. All his written messages to Orla were careful compositions. She'd kept them all, and had only recently bought a flat-pack container in which to house them. Large, striped in turquoise and cream, it had the presence of an Edwardian hatbox and now sat lidless on the coffee table day and night.

Every so often, Orla dipped her hand inside, as if fishing for tiddlers. His first 'I love you' was there, inside a Hello Kitty card (he knew all her secret vices). That was hard to look at now, yet she read it umpteen times a day, along with the card with Al Pacino on the front that contained an impassioned plea for forgiveness after some argument she couldn't remember, and his ode to the dark depths of her hair as it coiled about her naked freckled shoulders. He'd committed that one to a Snoopy card.

Somewhere in there was the card he'd sent her on his second day in London, a collage of red phone boxes, the London Eye, bearskin-wearing soldiers and a pigeon.

Why the pigeon? (He'd arrowed the bird.) *The flat is AMAZING. You'd adore it. Yes, don't frown, you bloody would. The area is very, very LONDON. Cosmopolitan, vibrant, full of life. Very Sim! And it could be very Orla if you weren't such a stubborn old bat. Lucky that I find stubborn old bats v. v. sexy. X*

This morning's fishing expedition had hooked a glossy reproduction of an old photo of St Stephen's Green, the famous patch of park bang in the centre of Dublin he'd sent her in 2010.

Live with me. Come on! Live with me and be my love. It's cheaper, cosier, with much much more snuggling (you do know what I mean by snuggling, don't you?) I can't have you out of my sight for one minute longer than necessary. I'll clear out a wardrobe and a drawer and an entire shelf in the bathroom. You can cook for me. The fun will never end!

This invitation Orla had declined with wide eyes. 'Are you crazy or what? Me, live in your ma and da's basement? Imagine

what your mother would say. I don't think so, Simeon Quinn.'
Sim had replied on a charity notelet, explaining that he
couldn't do without 'the olds' (as he called them) financial support, but come the big break, come fame and fortune, he and
Orla would buy a big house, he'd pop the question, they'd
waltz down the aisle, do the baby thing and generally be as
happy as any two sane humans could.

The big break had come about – Orla's doubts confounded,
Sim's confidence rewarded – and now here was the valentine
throbbing with its unheard question. Every other missive from
Sim had been torn open and devoured, but Orla debated with
herself whether to read this one. The last one.

Mightn't it *soothe* her? Wouldn't it be marvellous to hear
him again, if only in her head?

No, she'd countered, *it feckin' wouldn't*. Why put herself
through such made-to-measure agony? Why hear a dead man
ask to spend the rest of his life with her? *Just one more day and
we'd have been engaged*. She shuddered, and made a firm decision never to read it, but to keep it within touching distance.
If the house burst into flames it would be the first, only, possession she'd grab.

Wedding days held no appeal. White frocks, aiming her
bouquet overarm at a smartly dressed mob – no. Orla was a
romantic, not a show off. Like many women, she'd been
planning her 'big day' since she could first draw a meringue
dress with a crayon, but when she visualised it, it was the
meaning and emotion she conjured up. Her wedding would be
plain and simple – no theme, few bells and whistles. She had
imagined herself and Sim in nice new clothes, kissing on the
top of the hill beyond Tobercree, having just been blessed by

16

the same Father Gerry who'd married her parents and baptised all five Cassidy kids. There'd be an outdoor lunch on trestle tables. If she could be arsed, she'd hang a few lanterns from the trees. Their friends would carry on drinking and eating pork pies until late. Martha Stewart might throw her hands up in horror but Orla and Sim would be man and wife, wife and man (Orla's feminism could be pedantic). They would be married.

But of course, thanks to a pulmonary embolism, they wouldn't.

Orla tucked the valentine behind the mirror frame as she pinned up her haystack of unwashed hair. She noticed a line under one of her greeny-blue eyes and, hairpins held between her teeth, leaned in to assess it. She peered closer. It had some friends, crowding at the corner of her eye.

Orla had a vivid premonition of her future face, worn and kind and telling its story. Sim, she thought, would never see her old lady face.

Chapter Two

Right from the start, Sim's mother had deemed that Orla was not good enough for her son. Wealthy, connected: not even Ireland's recession could dent the Quinns' bulletproof status. Sim was destined to marry a society gal, someone with long tan legs and a trust fund. Their town house was their castle, and when Lucy Quinn had spotted Orla approaching she'd pulled up the drawbridge.

'Let's avoid the olds,' Sim always said as they slipped down to his basement pad. An only child, he was the fulcrum of his parents' complicated, sophisticated partnership, a marriage so different to the one that Orla had sprung from that it was hard to compare the two. Before her father died, Orla's parents had bickered non-stop, finding loud, creative ways to abuse each other for leaving the dishcloth in the sink, or forgetting to tape *Coronation Street* or backing out of the drive 'like a feckin' head-the-ball'. All was forgotten as soon as it was said, grudges were never held, and dinner-time restored peace over the gammon before war flared again over the arctic roll.

Arguments in the Quinn home centred around ancient wounds, opaque resentments to do with money, other women and broken promises. The miasma in the high-ceilinged rooms made Orla grateful for her family's ordinariness, for the da who taught history and ma who permed hair in the Tobercree salon.

Death creates strange alliances. For the first time in her life, Orla *wanted* to talk to Sim's mother.

They'd left messages. The latest came while Orla lay in a bath, her fingertips wrinkling like walnuts. The sound of that patrician English accent, as redolent of privilege as an ermine stole, had made her sit up from beneath the diminishing foam.

'Orla, it's Lucy. You're not there again. Where do you get to? There are arrangements you should know about. I need to tick you off my list. Call me when you have a moment.'

Moments, thought Orla, wrapping a towel around herself as she padded over to the phone, were all she had. Her future consisted of millions of moments, each a perfect bubble of longing and regret and a fury at fate. She dialled the number.

'Lucy, hello. It's Orla.' It was necessary to introduce herself, she wasn't in the habit of calling her almost-mother-in-law. 'How are you?' She was sick of the question herself, had come close to rage at Ma and Juno and everybody else who asked her, but really, how else could they put it?

'I'm better than I was,' said Lucy carefully. She always spoke carefully, as if picking glass out of her teeth, but today especially so. 'And you? It's a terrible shock.'

The unending understatement. 'Yes. I can't really believe it. I keep hoping there's been a mistake.'

'No mistake. I saw him.'

'You—' Breath fled Orla's lungs.

'I flew over immediately. I went to the hospital.'

'I didn't even—' It hadn't occurred to Orla to do any such thing. She had receded, wormlike; this Chanel-wearing, pearl-toting woman had 'immediately' jumped on a plane. Orla felt selfish, ashamed. 'How did he look?' she asked pathetically.

'What a question!' Lucy batted it away. 'The funeral is Monday. Ten a.m. at St Mary's Pro Cathedral. Afterwards at the Shelbourne. Do you wish to bring anybody?'

'Ma. My mother, I mean. I know she wants to pay her respects.'

'Oh.' Lucy sighed, irritated. 'Very well. I suppose we can make room.'

'Ma was very fond of your son,' said Orla. *Her almost son-in-law*. 'In fact, she adored him.'

'We all did,' said Lucy crisply. 'Any other hangers on?'

Orla swallowed that. Made allowances. Counted to ten. 'My – our – friend Juno. She's on the list, I suppose?'

'Never heard of her. Send me her details. Anybody else?'

'Have you invited Patrick? And Emily?'

'Who are they?'

The friends he kept away from you in case you froze them out or embarrassed him with your pissed carry-on.

'Friends. From drama school. They really should be there. Oh, and his tutor. And—'

'It's not a party!' snapped Lucy. 'It's the funeral of a senator's son. We can't invite just anybody. There are security issues. Now, are you definitely coming?'

The brusque question deftly demoted her. Orla felt her head spin. 'Of course I'm coming.'

'Excellent.'

'Lucy, listen … If you need somebody to talk to. Because we both lost him, didn't we? I don't mean I know how you feel but—'

'True. You can't know how it feels to lose one's only child. So please, no platitudes. Now. I'm sorting out his things in the

20

basement tonight. I'm turning it into a studio. You know how Simon adored my art.'

Nobody else called him Simon. Even Sim's father had got with the programme and referred to him as Simeon. Only Lucy had refused. *You were christened Simon*, she'd told him. *After my father. I don't care if there's already a Simon Quinn in Irish bloody Equity. To me, you're Simon.*

'Oh God, his stuff.' Orla pictured Sim's flat, its exquisite cornicing and high spec finish quite overwhelmed by its tenant's ability to generate clutter. She remembered Ma, back in 2001, dealing with Da's side of the wardrobe, knee deep in sober suiting, sobbing her heart out over a cardigan. 'I'll help.' Orla glanced down at her pyjamas, covered in islets of dripped tea. 'What time?'

'I don't need any help.' Lucy seemed surprised and, as was her habit, insulted. 'The family can manage, thank you.'

'Of course.' Orla was both respectful of the woman's grief and rather frightened of her. Lucy's sharp tongue was legendary. 'But, you know,' she went on, with caution, keeping her voice warm, 'I loved him too and I'd like to help.' She glanced at the valentine.

'If you're worried I will mix his things up with your own, there's no need. I've already whisked through and put your belongings in a bag. You can pick them up any time you want.'

There would be no companionship in bereavement.

'I'm not worried about that at all, Lucy. I just want to do something to help. And honestly, it would help *me* to see Sim's flat again.'

'You'd only hold me up. It's a busy time and everything, *d'accord*, is on my shoulders. I have to sort out the apartment

21

in London, too. I'll send the housekeeper over to do that, I think. Maria's more than capable. I'll see you at the funeral, Orla. I know Sim was fond of you, but please, respect the family's privacy at this time.'

Fond? Orla remembered the rub of his skin against hers, the ferocious and tender feel of him inside her. There had been no privacy between her and Sim. Together *they* were family. If Sim had died just one day later, Lucy would be *unable* to talk to her like this.

'His valentine arrived the day he died.'

This seemed to wrong-foot Lucy. 'Did it?'

'I haven't read it. But I know what it says.'

'All valentines say the same thing.' Ice clinked in a glass.

'It's a proposal, Lucy. Sim and I were going to be married.'

Lucy's snort tapered off. 'Read it to me,' she snapped.

'I can't. I can't bear to open it. But we both knew that when he got his big break he'd—'

'Orla,' there was a discreet gulp and Orla pictured Lucy's well-coiffed head thrown back as she downed her G and T, 'I'm sure your valentine will say some very lovely things. My son was a sweetheart and you were a lucky girl, but as for your little . . . fantasy? Believe it if it helps but my advice to you is, burn the thing. For the good of your psychological health.'

'It's not a fantasy.'

'Orla, I must go.'

The line went dead. No goodbye, no soft word of any kind.

Just one more day, one phone call, one word and she'd have been able to fight Sim's corner and stop his funeral turning into a travesty. She'd have a role, a purpose.

Biting her lip helped keep the tears at bay. Orla was so sick of crying. She let her eyes rest on the portrait of her drawn by Year Two which Sim had framed and hung on her kitchen wall. *They've caught your very special beauty*, he'd lisped. Miss Cassidy had green hair, three eyes and a very, very, very long neck.

She sighed. It was time to get back to work. Year Two wouldn't bother to psychoanalyse Lucy, they'd declare her an evil witch.

As a grown up, Orla felt obliged to be more generous.

She'd missed them, with their skinned knees and their super-tidy ponytails and their general air of wriggliness. Year Two had missed Orla too and let her know with hugs and bouncing and shouted questions about her absence.

'On the carpet! On the carpet!' After a week away, Orla was Miss Cassidy again, using her special teacher voice. '*Now*, please, ladies and gents!'

Thirty-one bottoms collapsed to the rug. Legs were crossed, a *shushing* finger applied to each pair of lips.

'That's better. I'll answer your questions one at a time.'

Orla had wanted to be 'Miss' since for as long as she could remember, following in her father's and grandfather's foot-steps, the third teacher in the family but, as Da had been proud to point out, the first female one. She shied away from the word 'vocation', as she shied from anything pompous or ponderous, but it came closest to describing the fervour she felt for her job, the deep nameless pleasure it gave her.

So her reluctance to leave the house this morning had puzzled her. Her dry mouth and fidgety unease had increased on the short drive over the stone bridge and down the main street.

Now, standing in front of her class, Orla had to concentrate hard to keep frantic negative thoughts at bay.

'Miss! Miss!' The most zealous child in the class, the one who barged to the front in the milk queue and took the tortoise home at Easter *and* Christmas, waggled his hand.

'Yes, Niall?'

'Did your boyfriend really die, Miss?'

Gentle, funny Miss Cassidy, beloved by all the Year Twos that had passed through her classroom, Miss Cassidy who could answer questions about how babies are made with aplomb and was a practised peacemaker in plasticine disputes, was lost for words. Niall's query had confirmed something Orla had suspected since the school bell had rung at nine that morning. It was too soon.

'I'll just be a moment,' she said as she left the classroom. It was the first proper lie she'd ever told the children.

Sim's journal

21 October 2011

Been here a week and feel like a native. All the things I love about this city would make O tut. (She's big on tutting. It's an Irish thing. Her Ma has awards for it.) I love London's crowds, the buzz, its 24-hour, up-all-night energy. Its potential for adventure.

Rum to have Juno on my side for once. 'Go with him, Orla! Wouldn't have to ask me *twice to run off to London,' she said. That woman is ripe for an affair.*

And here's something I can only share with my journal. It's kind of exciting to leave O behind. She's so certain *about stuff, about right and wrong. Without her I can let out my belt and burp.*

Chapter Three

She addressed the valentine.

'This one he sent from a shoot for a butter commercial.' Orla held up a postcard of Ballymaloe. 'He had to say, "It's so golden the leprechauns want it back," and run away from a computer animated goblin he couldn't actually see. On the back he wrote, *Did Laurence Olivier have to go through this? It'll be worth it one day, won't it, when we're married and living in the Hollywood Hills?* And he put too many kisses to count.'

The valentine didn't respond.

'Who are you talking to?' Ma bustled in from the kitchen, yellow Marigolds flapping, apron corset-tight around her black chain store bought-for-the-funeral dress.

'Nobody.'

'Thanks be to God the funeral is behind us. They're heartless, that bunch.' Ma went to the mirror above the mantelpiece to check her iron-stiff curls, not from vanity but because she needed to look neat. 'All the money in the world but not a shred of common decency. They didn't introduce you to anybody and some foolish fecker from the senator's office did the reading! Funerals are part of letting go. Of saying goodbye. They *matter*.' Ma's pointed nose, today's careful powdering worn off with the effort of spring cleaning, shone with indignation. 'A few sandwiches in the kitchen with his best mates would have been more appropriate. That boy had no airs and graces.'

Orla smiled at her mother's loyalty, but airs and graces? Her 'boy' had had plenty. She recalled the critiques he'd habitually make of her mother's hospitality as they drove away from her bungalow. ('Findus Chicken Kiev? I mean, *seriously?*'). As soon as Sim had hit the ground on Saint Valentine's Day his beatification had begun. As far as Ma was concerned, he was now and would forever remain, Saint Sim, Patron Saint of Brilliant Boyfriends. If Ma had been privy to the goings-on in her own spare room last New Year's Eve she might have asked for the halo back.

'That owld bag knows he meant to marry you.' Like a boat loosed from its moorings Ma roamed the room, searching out mess. She rarely stayed still for long, a trait her daughter shared, when not KO'd by grief. 'You should have had pride of place. You're practically a widow!'

'Ma.'

'Sorry. I get meself worked up, I know. But all the same.' Ma punched a cushion into submission.

Orla knew Lucy was hurting, she knew that people in pain don't behave very well, and so she resisted Ma's easy dislike. Orla wanted to believe in essential goodness. She needed kindness and small joys in order to plot a course away from her current state of mind. But most of all she needed Sim.

'You finished with that mug?' Ma held out her hand. She was on a mission to cleanse and scour and improve. Orla knew this to be a symptom of helplessness: Ma's response to the Grim Reaper was to tidy around him. It was a brave retort, in its way, and it made Orla smile. 'When are you back to school? Could you try again day after tomorrow maybe?'

'Mr Monk is very understanding. He said there's no hurry.' Orla chickened out of sharing her plan.

'A job is precious these days. More than ever. That's all I'm saying.'

Fear fizzed through her mother's veins and all her life Orla had fought to resist Ma's pessimism. Jobs can be lost. Colds can be caught. Gloves can be left on buses. People can drop down dead *just like that*.

And planes can crash. Novenas were said throughout the long sleepless night before any of Ma's brood boarded an aircraft. It hadn't stopped Brendan backpacking or Caitlin moving to New York, but Sim had blamed it, in part, for Orla's reluctance to join him in London.

Orla relived those conversations with scalding regret. 'How can you possibly know you hate London when you've never been there?' he'd asked, still grinning, still patient at midnight or later. 'Maybe it isn't dirty and unfriendly and dangerous and ugly.'

'Do I have to visit Hell to prove it's too hot?'

She was clinging to wisps. It disturbed her when a memory changed or went hazy, she was desperate to firm them up and render them as solid as the man she'd loved for three whole years. 'Tell me, Ma, does it ever get better?'

Ma perched on the arm of the sofa, empty mug in one hand, smeared plate in the other. 'It does, hen.'

'Ma, I love you but you're a terrible actress.' Orla carefully replaced the cards, one of top of the other, in the box.

'No, really. It does. Sure, just look at me.'

Orla looked at her. Ma had never regained the two stone she'd lost after her husband's death. She'd given up dying her hair. She was, Orla knew, afraid of solitude and the thoughts it brought, so she filled her days and nights with her children and her grandchildren, often exclaiming how they reminded her of 'my Christie'.

'OK, Ma, I believe you.'

'Trust me. There's always light at the end of the tunnel.' Ma stood up. 'Although sometimes it's a feckin' express train.' She nodded approvingly as Orla fitted the lid on the striped box. 'About time you put the cards away, love. They upset you.' She pointed at the cerise envelope. 'You missed one.'

'No, that's one staying out.'

'Tear it up, Orla.' Ma had a superstitious dislike of the card. 'It'll only bring you unhappiness.' She meant well, Ma Cassidy. She was an old hand at mothering. Orla was her fifth and last and still her baby girl, even at thirty-three years old.

'Ma, you promised not to go on about it.'

'Give.' Ma held out her hand. 'I'll tear it up for you, like I used to with them owld chain letters when you were at school.'

'It's coming with me, Ma.'

Her mother sat back down again. 'Where are you going?'

It had been a po-faced affair, more like a send-off for a statesman than an actor's funeral. Nowhere under the cathedral's soaring dome, in the Latin hymns and the scripture readings, had Orla found a trace of her irresponsible, party-going, people-magnet lover.

He'd once said – leaning back, Guinness in hand, legs apart, back when death had seemed a distant thing – that, 'When I die I don't want you wearing black. Wear your funkiest clothes!'

In her scarlet coat, Orla had been glad of the buffers either side of her, Juno on her right in chic black leather, Ma on the left, frumpily formal. She'd had a whisky beforehand, at Ma's urging, and it had made her giddy and a little sick.

Sitting on the far side of Juno, Jack had squirmed and fidgeted against the pew. Young children at funerals aren't unusual in Ireland, where the old guard respect the rituals of death. Juno, however, was vehemently new guard, free of the heavy hand of Irish Catholicism, and Orla knew she'd only brought him for her benefit. Orla had held her arms open.

'Give him to me.' Orla had taken Jack onto her lap for the rest of the service. He had turned out to be the best buffer of all.

Gravely looking about him, a miniature man in a miniature suit, he'd whispered to Orla, 'You're not really my aunt.'

'No. But I'm as good as.' Orla normally folded Jack up in her arms, blew raspberries on him, but sitting in that church she'd wondered how she ever found the energy.

'Mammy says you're eating your heart out.' Jack sounded fascinated by such an activity. 'Is it all gone yet?'

'Almost,' whispered Orla, peering down at her chest. 'Still enough left to get by, though.'

'I ate a bogey I found once.'

'Jack!' Juno had hissed, eyes flickering around the congregation. 'You never did.' She'd whispered to Orla. 'He makes this stuff up.'

I did, mouthed Jack.

Orla had kept her eyes devoutly on his thumbprint of a face, rather than the wooden oblong in the aisle draped in the Irish Tricolour. The coffin was bulky proof that Sim's life was over.

Orla's breakfast had risen in her throat at the thought of him inside that box. Passing the coffin before Mass began, she'd placed a hand on the wood and left it there, unable to move. Juno's compassionate, 'Come away,' only made her burst into tears.

The first time Sim's ever been mute at a get together. Orla had comforted herself with the absurd. At her feet, in her 'best' bag – a birthday gift from him – lay the valentine.

The service inched on, prayers and responses flying up into the thick air like dry leaves. Orla had recognised nobody, knew none of the hymns. The Mass was an endurance test and she'd found no solace in it. Rather, she'd felt even more keenly her impotence against an indifferent force that could snuff out a person at random, caring little if that person took the hopes and dreams – the very *future* – of another with him.

The disquiet on Jack's perfect little face as he took in her raw eyes and grimly clamped mouth had been perhaps the worst part of the day.

He'd never seen grief before.

'Let's not go to the reception.' Juno had said this casually as they filed out of the cemetery, Ma taking up the refrain with equally strained breeziness. They'd held Orla up, one either side, as ropes lowered all that was left of Sim down into the ground.

'I have to go.'

They'd gone along with her decision believing that she was doing it for Sim, and they were half right. But only half. Orla was on a mission.

In the exquisite hotel function room, Orla had moved among the guests in search of her prey, her coat bright amid the black. Nobody here would *miss* Sim. Their expressions were masks. Nobody here had ever really known him.

On one side of the room, moving among the guests with his customary finesse, Senator Quinn looked tired. On the opposite side entirely his wife's careful make-up couldn't rewind the decade she'd aged in the last twelve days. Orla noticed they never came together.

'Orla.' Lucy had tilted her chignon benignly. 'You're wearing red? How individual.'

'Sim's orders. Lucy, I've been thinking. I want to help.'

'That's kind, but everything's under control.' Lucy had smiled at somebody over Orla's head: she was a tall woman, and always wore heels.

'I recognise that smile. I use it too, since ... since Sim died.'

Lucy had looked puzzled.

'This one.' Orla had mimicked Lucy's expression. 'Nostalgic. Sentimental. Rueful but brave. For a smile, it's horribly sad.'

Lucy took a sip of her champagne. She hadn't demurred.

Orla pressed on, excited that she might be reaching Lucy woman to woman. 'Do you walk into a room, forget why you're there and just say to yourself, *Oh Sim ...* ?'

'All the time.'

'The dot-dot-dots never lead anywhere,' said Orla, quietly.

'I have to greet the Minister for Education, Orla. Excuse me.'

'Hold on, Lucy. I won't keep you long. Like I said, I want to help. I'll go to London for you, clear out his apartment there.'

'Maria is—'

'This feels right. Remember Sim wanted me to go with him, live with him there.'

'And you refused.'

'Yes, and I regret it now.' Orla had hesitated, scared she would expose herself too much. 'This is my way of making amends.'

'Orla, I really must see to my guests. I'm having trouble getting hold of a key for the London property but as soon as I do, Maria will go.'

Orla held up a bronze door key. 'Sim sent me this.' She flourished her ticket. 'And this. My flight leaves at 6.10 a.m. on the twenty-fourth. I *am* doing this, Lucy,' Orla had held Lucy's gaze, 'but I'd prefer to do it with your blessing.'

There was a long pause.

'It shouldn't take longer than an afternoon,' said Lucy. 'He took very little. If you find his grandfather's watch, it's a Longines, inscribed.'

'I know it well. I'll bring it home safely to you. If I find his journal, may I keep that?'

For a moment it had seemed as if Lucy might say no. Orla held her breath. So far Lucy had done everything in her power to deny Orla even the smallest keepsake. The journal had taken on a new significance. Yes she had teased him for his diligence about keeping a diary (a diligence notably absent from any other area of his life), but now it represented a conversation of sorts. The only conversation left to an almost-widow.

'Yes, all right.' Lucy had turned to wave at a new arrival. 'You may.'

Sim's journal

14 October 2011

Ryanair Flight FR112
Mid-air

Watching her grow smaller and smaller as I walked through the departure gate brought on a wintry sadness like when the olds used to dump me back at school for the autumn term.

How can such a soft woman be so HARD? She should be beside me. She could get time off work if she wanted. Like I said to her she's just a primary school teacher. Even I could do that!

Focus, ~~Simon~~. Simeon. I need to focus but nobody touches me like O. I already miss her take on everything. And I'm only on the bloody plane!

Chapter Four

Movement helped. Packing a suitcase, running for her flight, watching the clouds from the window of the plane, all helped with the weight in Orla's chest. The valentine was carefully tucked between the covers of a W. B. Yeats anthology Sim had given her their first Christmas together. The card was retracing its sender's last journey. Knowing this was an odd comfort; Orla was beginning to appreciate odd comforts.

Stepping out of the taxi, Orla double-checked the address.

'Jaysus,' she breathed to herself. 'Really, Sim?'

I love this place! he'd enthused, in email and on the phone. *It's so me!*

In that case, the London Sim was a very different creature. Orla had expected something chic, something louche, not three storeys of sooty brick, sandwiched between a railway bridge and a 24-hour mini-mart. Dublin Sim would have taken one look and bolted to the nearest five star hotel; this crossing of wires made a stranger of him, here where she'd come hoping to commune with him for the final time.

A tube train charged across the bridge, rattling the sign for MAUDE'S BOOKS that swung above the shop on the ground floor. A figure waved frantically through the shop window, as if drowning.

Wheeled suitcase trailing her like an awkward pet, Orla passed a man in a hard hat breaking the paving stones with a pneumatic drill, and negotiated the crawling traffic. She passed the mini-mart with a wince for the death rattle cough of the homeless man downing a can of lager in its doorway. *Ladbroke Grove is the real London, very cosmopolitan*; Sim had conjured up an art deco cocktail bar, not a fluorescent hovel where you could buy Pringles at 3 a.m.

The bell above the door of Maude's jangled and delivered Orla into a place where books ruled. They tottered in piles in the window, stood to attention along white shelves on the bare brick walls, lay brazenly open on the tatty sofa. Hardbacks, paperbacks, cloth covers, massive art tomes, flimsy children's wipe clean stories, new books, old books, raggedy, over-loved books, they almost obliterated the whitewashed floorboards.

The shop was peaceful despite its location on a busy stretch of high road. In the midst of all these stories was a pepperpot of a woman with a bushy white bun of hair and a smile that squashed her eyes into vivid half-moons.

'Maude?' asked Orla.

'And you're Sim's Orla! Every inch the colleen, just as he promised.'

Every elderly lady of Orla's acquaintance crossed themselves and murmured 'Lord have mercy on his soul' at the mention of Sim's name. It was both scandalous and a relief that Maude rattled on at full pelt without paying her respects.

'Look at you with your black hair and your green eyes. You've walked out of a fairy tale! Oh, freckles too, we must count them one evening when we've nothing better to do.' Maude's face beneath her Belle Époque puff of hair was lean and brown and handsome with clever eyes the colour of damp hyacinths. The woman's weathered beauty made Orla shy as she took in Maude's linen dress and rakish velvet scarf. Somehow Maude had grown older without losing any of her juice.

'Thanks for letting me stay,' said Orla.

'But darling the telly people have paid the rent until the end of April.' Maude took an arm; it was as if a bird landed on Orla's sleeve.

'I'll just sort out Sim's stuff and then get home. One night should do it. Then I'll be out of your way.'

'No, no, no.' Stern, Maude was still playful. 'Tonight we talk. All night. With a bottle of wine on the table. And we cry a bit. Probably. You can't make a start on the poor sod's *stuff* until tomorrow at the earliest. So. At least two nights, yes? Agreed?' Maude stopped suddenly and picked up a book. 'Do you like W. B. Yeats?'

'Yes.' Orla could have sworn the valentine bristled in its bookish nest deep in her luggage.

'Have this.' Maude pressed the small, linen covered book into Orla's hand. 'Yeats could be a terrible old fraud at times, but his poems about the agonies of love are right on the button. This way!'

Maude was away through an arch, one foot on the stairs, shouting over her shoulder, before Orla gathered her wits to follow. 'Dare say you need the loo. A nice little wee always sets me up when I arrive somewhere new.'

After the prescribed nice little wee, Orla joined Maude in a pale modern box of an attic, furnished with angular teak and floored in limestone. It was tranquil and impressive and Sim's enthusiasm for his home-from-home began to make sense.

'What a beautiful space.' It looked like the pages Orla tore from interiors magazines.

'It was remodelled a year ago when I had the bright idea to take in lodgers. I wanted arty-farty types, you know, so I thought I should tempt them in with clean modern lines. Here, drink that. Never met a Celt who didn't take their tea strong and often.'

Orla accepted the proffered mug with the first genuine smile of her trip. 'Thank you.' Small kindnesses reared up at her these days, magnified and meaningful. 'Just what I wanted.'

'Sit. Sit. Sit.' Maude flapped her arms. The scent of patchouli flooded the room.

'Gosh. White sofas.'

'Highly impractical but very beautiful. And I might die tomorrow so I insist on beauty.'

Die glittered between them like barbed wire.

'Thanks for the wreath, by the way. It was glorious.'

'I've given up funerals. I thought about him on the day instead. And those anthuriums and heliconia were not a wreath.' Maude held up a bony forefinger and shuddered. 'Such a godawful word. Sim wasn't a wreath kind of boy. It was an arrangement. Ah, you're smiling, dear, why?'

'Hearing you call him a boy. He was thirty-five, after all.'

'Trust me, that chap was destined to be a boy if he lived to, well, my age.'

'True.' Orla recalled her boyfriend's bounce. His hair had been gold and his eyes had been tawny and, yes, he had been a beautiful boy. *Her* beautiful boy.

'Anyway.' Orla slapped her lap. 'So.'

These days she could tolerate other people for a short

while before craving solitude. And then hard on the heels of the need for solitude came the renewed craving for company. It was tricky, this grieving business.

Maude took the hint. 'Ah. You want to be alone, dear. Well, alone with Sim's things.' She stood up, crossed to the door, cocked her head when Orla didn't follow. 'Come on then! I'll take you down to his flat.'

'But . . . oh.'

'I loved the new top floor so much I kept it.' Maude pushed at the door of the flat on the middle landing, sandwiched between the shop and the minimalist garret. 'I feel so Scandinavian up there, wafting through white rooms free of clutter. Whereas *this* flat . . . ' She stood back to let Orla in.

The door opened directly onto the sitting room, which stretched across the front of the house. Trinkets. Gewgaws. Thingummybobs. Shelves of books, tables bearing lamps and glass ornaments and snuffboxes, paintings of doe-eyed ladies and dashing gentlemen. It was hard to imagine Sim in this corner of old lady-ville.

Two sash windows ogled the top deck of a passing double-decker. Orla followed the room as it snaked around the corner, knocked through to create an L shape, with a kitchen, of sorts, in the shorter leg.

'Sim kept the curtains closed *all* the time.' Maude tugged at the moss green drapes with tiny hands, allowing a little February sunlight to elbow through the lace nets. 'Bedroom's at the back.' She pointed to a door at the far end of the defiantly unfitted kitchen. 'Shower room's off the bedroom. The place needs a little TLC. I haven't lingered here since . . . well, since he died.' Maude forced it out. 'Sorry, dear, I can't say he's passed away or gone before or, heaven help us, only sleeping. Poor old Simeon is dead and we must manage the best we can with that fact.' Maude put her head to one side to survey Orla's drooping face. 'Have I offended you?'

'Not at all. I'm no fan of those euphemisms either. It's just,' Orla breathed harder, as if a thumb pressed on her throat, 'I need to be on my own, if that's all right.'

'If that's all right!' Maude seemed touched. She cupped Orla's cheek briefly and left the flat, the door closing behind her with a camp squeak.

Orla waited in vain for quiet to descend, so she could tune herself in to the last space Sim had inhabited. The traffic coughed on, the crossing signal beeped and the homeless man burst into song. Orla went to the back of the flat and sank to the bed, laid her face on the pillow. The longed-for sense of connection didn't come. The pillow smelled of fabric conditioner. Orla let loose a single tear.

The journal would bring him back. Through its pages, she would reacquaint herself with him. That journal would tell her all the secrets Sim would rather have kept to himself.

When she had read that, she would feel free to read the valentine.

Sim's journal

17 October 2011

Landlady's a rum old bird. Cut-glass accent. Weeny. Vague blue eyes, but they'll burn bright in a flash.

41

Street's filthy. Authentic! Wouldn't tolerate it in Dub, but London has its own rules.

Meeting with Reece today. Great bloke. Great agent. From the moment he took me on last year I knew having a London agent instead of a Dublin one would make things happen. 'Be prepared,' he said, 'you're going to be a star.'

YESSSSS!

But also AAAARGH!

There is NOBODY I can confess my UTTER FUCKING RAM-PANT TERROR to except that Fairy of mine. I just tried her and she's not picking up.

Right. Enough navel gazing. What to wear? Reece is introducing me to my leading lady over dinner at his club tonight. So, you're a famed man-eater, are you, Ms Anthea Blake? Like 'em young, do you?

My Dolce and Gabbana suit, methinks.

'What?' Reece's voice was surprised, wrong-footed. 'You're here already? But I would have met you at the airport. Or at least sent a car.'

'Really?' Orla pulled a face at herself in the baroque mirror over the antediluvian gas fire. 'No need. I have two feet and half a brain.' Bereavement had made a beanbag of the other half. 'I'm staying at Sim's flat. I thought I should let you know, as the BBC are paying the rent. I suppose you should tell them or something.'

'That's not a problem.' Reece's voice was assured, confi-dent, measured. Carefully classless in a way that screamed 'public school but works in media'. 'Look, I'm here for any-thing you need. It's the least I can do. Sim is very important to me. Not just as a client. As a friend.'

'I see you're having trouble with the past tense too.'

'Yes. It feels . . .'

'Disloyal? Just breathing feels disloyal. I felt like a murderer when I cancelled his subscription to *GQ*.'

Reece laughed. Throaty. Male. 'He said you were funny.'

'Did he?' Orla liked Reece. He had a light touch without abandoning depth, and he'd obviously been fond of Sim. *So he should be*, whispered the valentine. *He was on twenty per cent.*

'He told me lots about you, Orla. He missed you terribly.'

'I should have come over sooner.'

'Oh look . . . we'd all behave differently if we could predict the future. Listen, Orla, I've got to go. New York's on the other line. We'll have lunch, yes? And call me. If you need anything. Anything at all.'

The candle guttered, making the dark perimeter of the sitting room wobble. The table was cosy as a campfire.

'You made a start, I see.' Maude sloshed red wine into their glasses. A jet choker glittered at her neck. 'First time the place has looked shipshape in months.'

'I folded up his clothes, sorted them into piles. Charity. Bin. Me.' Orla pursued the last smudge of cheesecake around her plate with her finger. Her appetite had raised its head again; Maude's supper on a tray had been welcome. 'Some of them were new to me. There were shirts I never saw him in.'

'He was rather a dandy.'

'I put his books to one side. Perhaps you'll take them for the shop? I'll hang on to this.' Orla reached in to her bag and fished out a copy of *One Day*. 'We talked about this on the phone. He said he should have got the part in the film.'

'Didn't he say that about every part in every film?' Maude swirled her Barolo, making a turbulent sea of it.

'I've put away his glasses.' The ones he never admitted to needing. 'I've *disposed* of his medication, as the containers say. I kept the vitamins. I'm keeping his laptop. It was a present from me last Christmas when he bought me an iPad. I've packed up his passport, his birth certificate, his wallet. I've cut up his bank cards.' That had felt brutal. 'There's one thing I can't find. And it's bugging me. It should be here. He wrote in it every day.'

'The journal? Silly big leather thing like something out of Dickens? It's definitely here somewhere. I often caught him scribbling in it when I nipped down with a little bite of something.'

'You fed him?'

'You make him sound like a guinea pig. He didn't mention it? Oh yes, I fed the boy. Otherwise the stink of stockpiled takeaway containers might have felled me in the hallway.'

'He told me he was learning to cook. Easy things. Like pasta.'

'There was *a* pasta.' Maude grimaced. 'Best forgotten. If I had eyes like Sim's I'd expect the nearest gullible old bat to feed me, too.'

Sim was so fond of fibs. From their earliest days together, she'd learned that a casual, 'Hi, what have you been up to?' was invariably answered with an evasive, 'Oh this and that'. But now details were important.

'I've looked in every drawer, every cupboard. The journal isn't here. Reece – I think you met him, he's Sim's agent? – he brought the personal effects here from the hospital so it wasn't with Sim when he collapsed.'

44

'I'll help you look in the morning. Wine doesn't improve my sleuthing skills. It's here. He was very attached to it. Abnormally so. Oh.' Maude squinted over at the dresser, her eyes on the pink envelope propped against a casserole dish. 'What's this? It's addressed to you, dear.' Maude leaned over to pick it up. 'Did you bring this with you?'

'Yes. It's nothing.'

'Oh good lord, it's a valentine.' Maude put her hand over her mouth. 'You poor girl.'

Fighting an urge to snatch the card, Orla nodded.

'That is hard.' Maude laid it on the table, a hand palm down either side of it. 'Aren't you going to open it?'

'Not yet.' Orla moved the card a centimetre or so, further from the glasses, further from the chaos spilt Barolo could wreak. 'I don't need to.'

'Explain, dear.'

'I know what it says.'

'Happy Valentine's Day, presumably,' suggested Maude. 'Did Sim sign them or just put a question mark? I always put question marks.'

'Sim always signs them. *Signed* them. He's – he *was* very good at cards. Made them special, you know?'

'I can guess.' Maude's eyes, though tired, were set to optimum twinkle.

'The valentine contains a proposal.' Orla sucked her lips, then carried on. 'So, really, Sim asked me to marry him before he died.'

'Are you sure?' In the candlelight it was hard to tell whether Maude's expression was one of delight or horror.

'As sure as sure can be.'

45

'I do love that accent. Even the four minute warning before a nuclear apocalypse would sound charming in a light Irish accent.'

Orla obliged. 'Attention. The end of the world is nigh.'

'Exactly!' They were both silent for a moment. 'What would your answer have been?'

'The loudest yes in the history of yesses.'

'Then why not read the proposal, answer it in your head, and tuck the card away somewhere safe?'

'Maude, I can't break my heart twice in a month.'

'You *will* read it.' Maude was all action and energy, sweeping away the tray to the sink and returning with another bottle. 'Shall I tell you when?'

'If you like.' Orla was tired, deep in her bones. Never a massive drinker, she found the second bottle of wine awoke a frightening thirst.

'When you're happy.'

Orla spluttered. Maude continued.

'Happiness creeps in by the window if you lock the door. Trust me. I've been as sad as you but look at me now. Cheerful as a, well, I'm no good at similes. Cheerful as a postbox. Right now you're certain that you'll never again giggle till you break wind, but I solemnly promise you will. Look.' Maude lifted her profile and raised her glass. 'This is me. Solemnly promising.'

'I'm normally better company than this.' Maude was trying so hard with her dreadful audience.

'Dear, you're at sixes and sevens. Is this your first bereavement?'

'No. My father died when I was twenty-one.' *Jaysus, twelve*

46

years ago. Daddy was already a decade out of date; he'd never heard of Barack Obama, never seen *Avatar*, nor met four of his seven grandchildren. 'That was different, though. Daddy was ill for ages. I moved home. It was calm.' The family popping in and out. Tea in the pot. Father Gerry hovering. Jim Cassidy had died a traditional Irish death. Nothing left unsaid. By the time he let go of Ma's hand one dawn the poor man was worn out from *I love you*s. 'With Sim, it's been too fast. I can't take it in. How a man so healthy can just . . . ' Orla tailed off, reluctant to inflict her incessant inner chorus on Maude. 'So much is left unsaid. Sorry. Like I said, I'm not normally this odd.'

'I've lost many people I was mad about,' said Maude, her high cheekbones saucily red from the alcohol. 'It's vile. Different every time. You have my permission to be as batty as you like for as long as you're here.'

'That won't be long,' said Orla hastily. 'I'll be gone the day after tomorrow at the latest.' Discreetly, firmly, she reclaimed the valentine. 'As soon as I've found the journal.'

Sim's journal

10 May 2011

It's still sinking in. I got the part. I am the Comte de Caylus in The Courtesan.

I hope you can keep secrets, dear Journal, because at long last my life is going to get INTERESTING.

Chapter Five

'Orla? It's Ma. Can you talk?'

'Howaya Ma?'

'So. A week already.' [Pause] 'I *said*, love, a whole week already.'

'Yes, Ma. A *mere* week. I'll be home soon. It's this journal. It's bugging me.'

'His owld diary? Sure why does it matter so much?'

'Ma, we've been through this.'

'Yeah. Sorry, love. But I worry about you.'

'Please don't, Ma. Worry about one of your other kids for a change.'

'They're all grand. Deirdre's grand. I'm looking after her little ones while she's at work. And that Caitlin's tearing up New York. Hugh is after getting a promotion and hasn't Brendan only gone and bought a llama for the smallholding. A feckin' llama! Sure, they're all grand.'

'Except for your pesky youngest. Did you look in at my place?'

'It's still standing. I turned off the immersion. Picked up the post. All bills. *Phelim! Stop hitting your sister with the Lego!* They have me heart crossways. Four at once is too many.'

'Deirdre can afford a nursery, surely.'

'Ah no, she shouldn't waste her money on them places

49

while I'm here. Some school leaver who doesn't know her arse from her elbow bathing *my* grandson? I don't think so!'

'Give them a kiss for me.'

'I ran into the supply teacher who's standing in for you. Pretty thing. Looks about twelve. Her great-aunt was second cousin by marriage to the one-legged woman who sold eggs to your nana.'

'Practically family. Is she getting on OK?'

'Apparently the kiddies love her.'

'Nice try, Ma. I'll be home soon. Promise. As soon as I find the journal. London is *not* my cup of tea.'

'Orla, you don't look like you,' complained Juno, her kohl-rimmed eyes enormous on Sim's computer screen as she peered into the Skype camera.

'Sit back a bit, you eejit. That's better.' The screen showed Orla an underwater Juno, moving with an eerie delay, her outline bleeding into the background. 'Sim never mentioned he had it fixed,' she muttered. 'It conked out a few weeks ago but it seems OK now.'

'I think I prefer just phoning. You seem to be sitting in the middle of a badly lit jumble sale. And oh God is that the feckin' valentine I can see?'

'Yes it is and this flat's nicer than it looks.' Orla's need to defend the three small rooms surprised her. She was sleeping better with the tranquil bookshop beneath her and Maude's pitterpat above. 'The clutter grounds me.'

'Rather you than me.'

Juno was a lover of all things modern. She was fast-forward all the way, leaving others – her husband in particular –

panting in her wake. The modernist eruption of white concrete that was their house had been built to her design, right down to the last light switch. He had fancied something Georgian.

'Listen,' she continued, 'a place that size doesn't take a week to search. It's not the diary keeping you in London, so what is?'

The friends never fibbed to each other. Jack's sudden howl saved Orla from answering. She couldn't share the unformed but insistent questions about Sim's last few months that snagged at her thoughts like a rusty anchor at the ocean bed.

'Shush! Jack! Shush now! Mammy'll be there in a minute!' She returned to Orla. 'He's hungry. I sent Himself out for a curry. Told him I was too tired to cook.'

'I'm shocked. You? Wriggling out of housewifely duties? Never.'

'I'm scared of that new cooker. It has fourteen dials! Men flew to the moon with fewer knobs. If you pardon the expression.'

'Jack sounds so sweet when he cries.' The envy was new and unwelcome. Orla had never coveted Juno's clothes, bags, shoes, husband, space-age house or photogenic child before. 'He sounds like a sleepy kitten.' Grief coloured her emotions with broad crayon strokes: she wanted a baby. She missed the baby she might have had with Sim.

'Listen to it all day every day and it's not so sweet.'

'Say something nice about him, Ju. He looks like a mini George Clooney but you never big him up. You're unnatural, you are.' Orla echoed Juno's mother.

'Shut up, you. You know what I'm like. I don't do gooey,

51

but I'd throw myself in front of a train for little Jackster. And I'd do the same for you. You know that, don't you, lady?'

'I do.'

'I have a favour to ask.'

'I can't babysit tonight if that's what you're after.'

'Listen to me, Orla. Please stay in London and have an adventure on my behalf. Use this feckin' journal as an excuse if you need to, but don't come home and decompose in Tobercree like the rest of us.'

'Isn't Jack an adventure?'

'Of course, but he's not a reckless, dirty, filthy one like the one you should have. You've had freedom forced upon you, may as well not waste it.'

'It doesn't feel at all like *freedom*, Ju.' More of a cell. 'I'm not like you. I don't have your courage.'

Juno chafed against the manifold luxuries of her life, even though she'd chosen them. A rising star copywriter in Dublin's incestuous advertising fraternity, Juno had turned her back on her career the instant it became clear that her boss was falling for her. The relationship had accelerated – with all the speed of Himself's Porsche – from a casual drink after work to an epic wedding. A honeymoon baby had been a step too far even for him but, lo and behold, Jack turned up a mere nine months later. Still Juno refused to learn domestic skills, railing against her adoring, indulgent husband as if he were a tyrant.

'You're a feckin' tigress, Cassidy. Being with Sim blunted your nails. He was so . . .'

'So what?' Orla said, sharply.

'Well, you know, he didn't take criticism kindly.' Juno said it archly, as if it was code for something more damning. 'He

52

was the star, wasn't he? No room for two of *them* in a relationship. Now you can be, well, *you*.'

'Seriously? You choose this moment in my life to go all self-help on me? If you so much as think about telling me to feel the fear and do it anyway I'll be on the first flight home and throttle you.'

'*Coming, Jack!* Listen, hon, I have to dash. Call me whenever you want. Dump on me. My shoulder is there for the weeping on. But do not come home!'

Juno was right to be suspicious. The journal, although important, was a red herring. London's faults and failings, all accurately prophesied by Orla, were what kept her there.

Every morning when Orla awoke in the floral papered bedroom with its view of the bins she murmured to the valentine on the bedside table, 'We're not in Kansas any more, Toto.' London was Sim's adopted town, and she felt closer to him here than at home. Sim had told her he felt real in London. Trying to understand the place – and in so doing, to understand Sim – Orla shared her observations with the valentine.

London's filthy, she told it. It struck her anew each time she stepped out of the front door to wade through apple cores, fag ends, empty cans and abandoned newspapers. *It's noisy.* She and the valentine listened to tube trains thunder over the bridge like an inexhaustible invading army. *It's unfriendly.* Tobercree people bade each other hello. They nodded, winked, squandered pleasantries. Sure Orla wasn't naive enough to believe that their hearts overflowed with love for their fellow man, but she would trust them to fetch a bucket of water if she screamed 'fire!'; the sloe-eyed man in the mini-mart, on the other hand, barely even acknowledged Orla as he took her money in his dry hand, counted the coins suspiciously into the till and handed her a receipt. *He'd let me burn*, she told the shocked card.

Homesickness she dealt with briskly, with Juno cheerleading from across the sea. Orla missed the grassy smell of the lane in the morning and the clean grey roofs of the town stretching away down the hill; but it wouldn't help to leave and go back. Nothing was as simple as that in Orla's new life. She was homesick for Sim, and Ryanair didn't offer time-travel.

'The torture of being in the place that killed him distracts me from the torture of doing without him,' was how Orla had explained it to Maude earlier, as she'd helped her alphabetise biographies in the shop. 'It's sick, I know.'

'Why, pray, do you despise London?' Maude held Oscar Wilde to her heart for a moment before shelving him.

'For starters, it's too big. How'd you get to know people in a place this size? And nobody looks happy. And there are too many cars. Everybody's from somewhere else, it's like one massive bedsit. It's cold. Cold cold cold.'

'Me, am I cold?' The thought seemed to amuse Maude as she aimed a Kerry Katona at the bargain bin. She was in layers of sludge-coloured cashmere and oatmeal linen.

'No. You're a one-off.'

'Here.' Maude had handed Orla a sheet of lined paper. 'Be a darling and pick up a few bits and pieces for me.'

Out on the street, Orla scanned the list. She'd noted that every so often the kindly little dear would turn imperious and farm out a chore to the nearest human. Customers found themselves popping to the mini-mart for a bottle of milk. Maude never waited for a yes or no, she simply expected obedience.

Into Greggs for a Danish pastry, then to the ironmonger for a packet of fuse wire; Orla made her way up the street, visiting every shop she passed. Almost as if Maude were forcing her to interact with common-or-garden Londoners.

At home, popping into the chemist could be perilous; Orla cringed at the memory of meeting a brother-in-law with a packet of maxi panty pads clamped to her chest. Here, there was no likelihood of seeing a familiar face. Orla picked out a jar of Pond's cold cream, as per the list, and joined the queue at the counter.

False eyelashes winked from a shelf. Orla smiled – not the low calorie smile of the past weeks, but a glorious full fat grin.

It was 2009.

Dublin is the world capital of parties. The 'little gathering' at Orla's new flatshare had snowballed, as friends of friends and enemies of friends knocked at the door, flashed a bottle and were admitted to the tiny space in the shadow of Christchurch. Conversation, loud and loose, battled the music. Bodies swayed, leaned, embraced, fell down. It was either a nightmare beyond imagining or the best party ever.

'I blame *you*, Davey.' Orla poked a finger at the vast chest of her landlord, a rugged black-bearded character with a bottomless pit of goodwill for mankind. 'All your bloody actor friends. One whiff of a free drink and they're there.'

'*Mea culpa*.' Davey held up his meaty hands. 'It's like a feckin' Fellini film in the front room. The entire cast of that new revue is here and I don't know a single one of the feckin' feckers.'

Orla hadn't seen the revue in question, but she'd read the gushing reviews. 'One of them's dressed as a badger.'

'I caught him widdling in the umbrella stand. Thought I was feckin' hallucinating.' Davey rubbed his head. 'I feckin' think I might be feckin' drunk,' he said morosely.

'I feckin' think you feckin' are.' Since moving in she'd had to put Davey to bed a few times, but his charm and her good nature were such that it didn't feel like a chore. 'Have a little sit down.'

Orla shouldered through the assault course of arms, shoulders and arses that was her hallway. When the Valentine's Day party had been mooted, her knee-jerk response was to rant about the degrading commercialisation of romance in the modern world, the idiotic annual pressure to conform by being in 'a relation-ship' (clawing air quotes around the words), eating an overpriced meal in a pink-lit restaurant, buying a rose from an uninterested oik touring the tables with freeze-dried Kenyan blooms, declar-ing love for the nearest halfway acceptable male.

'It'll be an anti-valentine party,' she'd asserted.

'I take it nobody's ever sent you a valentine card?' was Davey's reply.

'Shut up. And no.'

With the party at full throttle, Orla had reached her tipping point. The lively atmosphere became claustrophobic, the music was just noise and the faces around her looked freakish in their animation.

'Hey.' A hand shot out from the scrum and caught Orla's wrist. 'I've been looking for you.'

'And you've found me.' Orla peered closer at the man she'd flirted with earlier. His pupils, black as liquorice, blotted out his irises. A film of sweat sat on his upper lip. His too-tight striped blazer was ridiculous. In the hour since they'd made eyes at each other he'd taken something and she'd sobered up. 'Can't stop!' she mouthed as the music soared.

'I'm not letting you escape again.'

'Oh, but you are!' smiled Orla, trying to pull away.

'No, come on. You're shit hot. Stick around.'

The paucity of the compliment depressed Orla profoundly in a way it wouldn't have if she had been sober or the music less loud. Modern men expected modern women to feel flattered by a fusion of expletives and Paris Hiltonisms – it dashed her spirits. She didn't say this. She just looked at him.

A partygoer behind Orla butted in. 'Is this lout bothering you?' The voice was deep. and accompanied by an arm that snaked over her shoulder and reached down to unfurl the fingers around her wrist.

'He's fine,' said Orla, taking in the red lacquered fingernails on the strange hand.

'Oi, Simeon, back off. Me and this lady are getting on like a house on fire.'

'Consider me the fire brigade.' Sim held Orla's arm, leaned in close and whispered, 'Come with me.' The accent was a silky mixture of romantic Ireland and moneyed England.

Half turning, Orla saw tiger eyes, locked on hers like a sci-fi tractor beam.

'You and I,' continued Sim, 'are going somewhere quiet to kiss.'

'Hang on.' Orla looked haughtily at the hand on her

shoulder. 'We're certainly not going to kiss. I don't know you. And besides you're . . . ' She looked him up and down.

'Dressed as a woman?' Sim kicked open a door marked KEEP OUT YOU BASTARDS! with one gold stiletto. 'After you.'

'I'm only going in here,' said Orla, 'because it's my bedroom.'

'I see. Not to do this?' In the darkness Sim bent and placed his glossed red lips on Orla's. He kept them there, not breathing, not moving, for a strange, lovely moment. Then he leaned back, his backcombed wig brushing her face. 'You look like a fairy,' he whispered. 'A rather cross fairy.'

Orla wasn't sure what to say. This stranger was many things. Six foot four with a high forehead, a straight nose and a classically square chin; broad shouldered, narrow hipped; wearing an emerald green sequinned gown slashed to the thigh, and as outrageously presumptuous as she'd expected the revue's much-discussed star to be. She blinked, and pulled away from the arms wrapped around her. Orla was no groupie.

'Out!' She used the tone she'd perfected on Year Two.

'You couldn't be so cruel.'

'Are you for real? You drawl,' she noted, wonderingly. 'You actually drawl, sexily, as if you're acting the part of an actor.'

'I am quite quite *quite* real.' Sim infused his words with animal desire that lit something inside Orla. This close, in this light, his eyes were amber. Even heavy with false lashes they were provocative and clever, and they reflected Orla back to herself: she was no fairy. She was his prey, and she didn't struggle as he ate her up.

Sim's kiss started slowly – barely a touch – but the tempo built, naturally and inevitably. Greedy, his mouth played with

Orla's lips, until he parted them with the expertise of a virtuoso and they were locked together. The rhythm picked up, became more urgent, charging along like the dance tune banging through the walls.

With an effort, Orla pulled away. Her face was smeared with lipstick and blusher. In a moment of clarity she saw this for what it was: a small woman apparently kissing a glamorous giantess. 'This isn't me!' she said, a piece of dialogue she would regret ever after and which Sim often quoted with a hammy hand to his brow.

'Sweetheart, this isn't me either.' Sim stepped back and curtsied in his figure-hugging gown. 'Is it the frock that's bothering you? I can take it off.' His hands went to the zip.

'No!' As a child, Orla had struggled with telling right from left. As an adult, she appeared to be having similar trouble with yes and no. The thought of this strange man naked but for green tights was at once wondrous and absurd. She turned away, her hands over her face.

Self-control was important to Orla. She always thought of herself as a mature, poised woman who chose her path with care, who never said 'squee!', who didn't Google kittens, who wouldn't cry in front of others. Above all, she was level headed about men: snogging trannies was a no-no.

Now in her late twenties, Orla had notched up only two relationships worth the title. She'd liked Man A a lot but he'd moved to Belfast; she'd believed herself in love with Man B until the petty irritations piled up and she'd neatly ended the affair. Neither lover had provoked this feral response. Orla wanted to devour this man. Instead she bit her knuckles, eyes shut in the darkened room, hoping he'd just dissolve in the same way he'd just appeared. Orla's response to all things sexual was largely head-led: now her loins were in charge and they were in party mode.

With a flash of insight that wasn't entirely welcome, Orla realised that she'd never truly fancied the pants off anybody before. That was quite a revelation for the drunken small hours, and it made her uncomfortable. She wheeled round.

'Tell me something about yourself.'

'What do you need to know?' Sim pulled off his wig and rubbed his scalp. 'Jesus, these things are itchy. Um, I'm Simeon Quinn. Call me Sim. I'm thirty-two. I'm unattached. You?' She nodded. He continued. 'Good. I'm an actor. I came straight here from the Canal Revue and yes, I was singled out in the reviews thank you for asking. I'm allergic to penicillin. My favourite flavour crisp is smoky bacon. And my feet are killing me.' He kicked off his platforms. 'That's better. How do you women cope? Although,' he looked down at Orla's black satin heels, 'they do *great* things for *your* legs.'

'Is this just, you know, a random collision in a bedroom at a party? Or is this something more,' asked Orla, bold with the urgency of lust.

Beneath their unwieldy lashes, the cat eyes blinked. 'You get heavy awfully quick, Fairy.'

'If I write my number on your arm, will you use it?'

'Yes,' said Sim, not skipping a beat.

Orla grabbed a pen from her chest of drawers. She wrote, in large and legible numbers, the magic formula of her mobile phone. 'Right.' She bit her lip, enjoying this new non-ladylike self. 'Come on then.'

Sim's face split into a smile. It was not quite so handsome

60

as the previous ones and therefore, Orla suspected, rather more genuine.

'You're a funny little onion,' he said approvingly, before enfolding her again and impressing that autocratic, expert mouth of his on hers.

They toppled down onto the bed. Sim seemed surprised by the passion of Orla's response. 'Oh *yes!*' he murmured against her neck as she bit at his ear. Surprise registered once again when she resisted all attempts to rearrange her clothes too fundamentally. Rolling about, dislodging pillows and snarling up the duvet, their clinch was as much quarrel as embrace.

'Please, oh *please*,' begged Sim, his voice hoarse.

'No. Get off. Come here.' Orla was in charge, holding him back, giving him some slack then reining him in. A lusty terrier, she pawed him and played with him, but retained enough of her Polaroid self to refuse to give in to either his pleading or her own. There were kisses, there were touches, there were gasps and mews – but there were limits. She anticipated a next time with this man, this big strong stallion of a specimen who was as fired up as she, who was as stricken, who would, she sensed, loom large in her life.

Finally they dozed, entwined. The room solidified in the cold light of early day. Sim yawned, a big leonine roar that drew cords in his neck and was at odds with the remains of his diva make-up.

'Sounds like the party's still going.'

Music drifted from the sitting room. A handful of people debated drunkenly in the kitchen. Somebody somewhere was crying uninhibitedly.

'They're maniacs,' said Orla fondly. She was fond of everybody this morning.

'Look. I'd better shoot off.' Sim leaned on one elbow and looked down at her. Even sleepy and hungover, his eyes were like laser beams. Orla felt naked. 'I've got this,' he said, pointing at the scribble on his arm.

'Bye then.' Orla felt shy.

Sim didn't. He kissed her a last time, hard and fast. 'Bye, Fairy.'

Orla knew he'd ring. She promised herself that when he did, she wouldn't be coy. This was big, and she must embrace it honestly. She fell asleep to the lullaby of house music and that insistent sobbing.

'I said, is that it?'

'Oh. Sorry. Yes. There you go. Oh, hang on. That's a euro.'

Tears welled in her eyes, the coin bounced to the floor.

'I, sorry, I'll leave it.' Orla pushed past the resentful queue, out onto a road she didn't know.

'Oh Sim,' she said.

Sim's journal

14 February 2009

Fluffed my first line. Stage manager cocked up Act II props. Again. Frosty audience, had to work double hard to seduce them.

Speaking of seduction – party afterwards at some beardy guy's place and met the most gorgeous creature. I mean, really fucking off the scale fabulous. Mane of hair like a cavewoman.

Elusive, though, led me a right merry dance through the party.

Got bored of pursuit, went off-piste, and found myself in a clinch with a little sweetie. Lovely kisser. Fell asleep together in her titchy bedroom.

And whaddyaknow? Cavewoman was still there in the morning. Boohooing over some cad. I drove her home, showered, and we had a private party à deux.

Chapter Six

4 July 2012
17.14
From: junogirl1@yahoo.com
To: orlacassidyfairy@yahoo.com
Subject: Two things

1. Himself has been promoted. Cue cheers, cannons firing, glitter confetti etc etc. This means more money, bigger car, second baby (so he thinks – good luck with that one, boyo) and EVEN LONGER HOURS. So, my bestie is in London and my other half is in the office. Honest to God, some days the most intelligent conversation I have is an earnest discussion with Jack about whether Superman has a willy.

2. What are your summer school students like? Any hot eighteen-year-old Latin studs you can have a little rebound fun with while you teach them English? Ooh, I can hear the storm of tutting from here.

3. (Yes, I lied, sue me, there are three things not two.) HAVE YOU TORN UP THAT SPOOKY VALENTINE YET? You'll be guessing I'm after a 'yes' on that one.

Right. I'm off. To the park. Or the fucking park, as I like to call it. AGAIN.

Miss you.

But don't you dare come home.

J xxxxx

Orla felt the heat on her bare arms, clingy as a new lover. Propelled by snatches of music from the cars stalled nose to tail along her route, she strode jauntily like a catwalk model.

'I love you!'

Orla wheeled at the shout and rewarded the grinning black teenager in a Renault Clio with a look that was all shock but probably translated as toughness.

'Sorry babes! Don't shoot!' He held his hands up.

Orla walked on, strut cancelled, mortified.

'Evening Sheraz.' The familiar flat bang of the bell over the mini-mart door brought the shopkeeper up from beneath his counter. 'Just a bottle of milk tonight.' With one hip Orla slammed the chiller shut, mentally pixellating the sell by dates on the scotch eggs.

'Why semi-skimmed, silly girl?' For Sheraz it was all one word, *silligirl*. 'Buy the full fat. Put some meat on your bones.'

'Pay you Friday?'

'Pay me Friday. Here, missy.' Sheraz was peremptory. Months of selling Orla her semi-skimmed milk gives a man certain rights. 'Take this for Maude.' He held out a pair of pop socks in cellophane, bright purple and covered in dust. 'Last packet. Nobody will bloody buy. And they will suit Maude.'

'Ooh, thank you. They're just her thing.' Orla took the pop

socks. 'Is her order ready?' Maude eschewed the BOGOF bait of the supermarkets to give Sheraz her custom.

'Yes. I'll drop it in later.'

'I can take it.' Orla held out her hands.

'No.' Sheraz looked injured. 'I deliver. *He* can watch shop.' He flicked a thumb in the direction of his son, an elongated male of indeterminate age who never spoke, never smiled and loped up and down the aisles of his father's fiefdom day in, day out. 'New hair?' Sheraz queried.

'Yes. D'you like it?'

'No.'

'Thanks. *You* look stunning, by the way.'

'Get out, silligirl.'

The phone hopped up and down inside her bag. Orla paused on the pavement to scrabble for it.

'Orla Cassidy? Please hold. I have Reece Dodds for you.'

'Orla? Hi sweetheart.'

'Reece, howaya?'

'Are you in the street? Or are there roadworks in your bedroom?'

'I'm just outside my flat. The delightful music of London is what you hear.'

'Come on, Orla. There's something about this town you like. You're still here.'

'True.'

Time had still not recovered its equilibrium. It dragged its heels, only to break into a sudden sprint, or appear to loop back on itself, but its most impressive trick by far was to turn Orla's 'couple of days' in London into a staggering five months.

She'd never been a foreigner before and to Orla's surprise she relished it. London – flawed, grubby, relentless, just as she'd prophesied – had turned out to be an easy date. She owned the street just the same as the next incomer.

It brought her closer to Sim, walking the same route to the tube he'd walked, waking up in his bed, hearing the ping of his microwave. Like him, she had fallen hook line and sinker for London and at some point – though she couldn't pinpoint when – she had decided to stay.

'How, you know, how *are* you, Orla? Really?'

'I'm doing better, Reece. And you're very kind to ask.'

'No. I'm a git. I owe you a dinner. I'm neglecting you.'

'*Whisht*. You spoil me! How are *you*? I know you feel it too.'

'I'm busy. Which is good. Weirdly, though, at the moment I'm busy with our boy. You know *Courtesan* starts in October, don't you?'

'Yup.'

'Listen. Dinner must happen. What are you to up to a week from today?'

'Hold on while I consult my PA.'

'Very funny.'

'*Hey Emma Posh-Totty! Am I free to dine with a top London agent next Thursday?* She reckons we're good to go, although she's not the sharpest knife in the box. Inbred, doncha know.'

'I think I know her.'

'By which you mean you think you slept with her.'

'By which I mean I think I slept with her. Will my club do?'

'Reece, your club will do.'

Snapping her phone shut, Orla squinted at her reflection

in the plate glass of Maude's Books. Sheraz was a peerless mini-mart proprietor but he was no stylist: the fringe was a triumph. Sim had been right when he'd nagged her to cut one in all those times.

Beyond the glass, Maude stood on a decaying tapestry footstool, reaching for a book on a high shelf. Her cotton wool bun wobbled in its customary half-collapse.

Not a customer in sight. The sums didn't add up. Maude's Books' clientele, although devoted, was tiny. It ran on enthusiasm and its proprietor's deep pockets. Catching Maude's eye, Orla executed a quick mime she hoped would translate as *see you upstairs later*.

Even with all the windows open, the flat was torpid. With the velvet curtains, the fringed sofa and the conga line of ornaments, Orla could fancy herself madam of a New Orleans brothel were it not for the incessant squawk of the crossing signal and the wheeze of slowing buses.

She switched the radio on. Sim's death had made silence intolerable; Orla's life had a constant soundtrack now, be it radio or television or iPod. Unwelcome thoughts barged nearer in the quiet.

'Hello sweetheart.' Orla picked up the valentine on her way to the fridge to deposit the milk. 'Miss me?'

The valentine was showing its age. It had lived a little since February. It had been cried over, stuffed in handbags, taken out again, screamed at in the darkest dip of the night. Now it was resting by a vase of roses the colour of dried blood, sent by Reece.

'Work was so-so, thanks for asking,' Orla called over her shoulder as she fixed herself a baguette of leftovers. 'Gan disrupted the class again but I dealt with him.' Orla recoiled from the mouldy polka dots in her mayonnaise. 'We were so worried about taking this summer school job, weren't we? Remember me saying I couldn't handle adult students? Well,' she paused, knife in mid-air, 'I *say* adult, but they're late teens which is still a kid in my book. Anyhoo, they're no different really to Year Two back home. Bigger, granted, but all the same gripes and excuses and tics.'

Banging the fridge's tiny door, she muttered, 'Remind me to get that seal fixed,' before collapsing onto the sofa with a grateful sigh to wind down from the sweaty tube journey home. Orla had baulked at the tube when she'd first arrived. It had seemed incredible that anybody would choose to stand on a crowded, reeking platform waiting for a train that screamed in like a dragon. Now she barely noticed the smell or the noise or the fact that she was pressed hard against five people she hadn't been introduced to. The tube was simply the most efficient way of travelling to the repurposed Victorian primary school in Hammersmith where she taught overseas adults to speak English like a native – better than a native, in a few cases.

Orla had allowed Maude to bully her into taking the job.

'I am starting to disbelieve your *one more day then I'm off* routine,' Maude had said, handing Orla the small ads. 'Your students would be immigrants too. You'll have plenty in common.'

Orla had prevaricated.

Maude had made noises about rent.

Orla had capitulated.

It turned out that helping privileged teens from China,

Russia and Europe vault the language barrier was satisfying, but Orla wasn't just a stranger in town, she was a stranger to contentment, to the everyday fulfilment of ordinary life.

There had been progress. Her emotions were warming up. She could laugh at jokes. She rediscovered a pleasure in small things – the softness of a new towel, the green smell of chopped chives. Maude noted each trifling improvement and celebrated them as 'another step on the road to recovery'. Orla couldn't see it. Only the valentine truly understood.

'It's like a funky United Nations in my classroom. All chinos and great hair.' Orla swivelled round to get a better view of the pink envelope. 'That Italian fella is doing his level best to flirt with me. You'd laugh. I give him the full-on Cassidy freeze. Fair play to him, he doesn't give up. Oh, and listen to this. The deputy head – you know, the one with the perm – at least, Jayzus, I *hope* it's a perm – asked would I be interested in applying for a full-time post in September. I said I'd get back to her.' She put her sandwich down. 'What do *you* think?'

Sim's journal

18 April 2009

Another terrible party. Halfway out of the door a girl caught my eye. Coal-black hair. She half turned and I thought HOLY SHIT (yup – capitals). It was the fairy. I tiptoed away backwards but she turned and looked straight at me.

Nothing.

Nada.

Not a flicker.

The old ego took a moment to reboot. I mean, we kissed. I'm good at that stuff. She turned away, calm, a little bored. She wasn't half as cute as I remembered. I'd exaggerated the tilt of her nose, the Snow White-ness of her skin. And where was the mischievous half smile? I approached her, asked if she forgets all the men she snogs at parties.

Fairy looked irritated.

Then another smaller woman came over, made to the same basic design as the first, but . . . Oh Jesus. She was the fairy! Not her friend, no wonder I'd been blanked. Fairy was soft, and she was blazingly pale, and she was all woman and she made me think that things might be simple and people might be kind.

Turns out she was with her sister Caitlin over from New York (NOTE TO SELF: ask C if she knows any agents in NY). 'I wrote my number on this bastard's arm,' she says to her, right there in front of me, 'and he hasn't found a gap in his busy schedule to call me in two whole months.'

Orla was in bed, correcting coursework, but memories were making it hard to concentrate. She took off her glasses.

'Truth please. No bullshit,' she'd said to Sim at that crappy party in that manky club when he'd sworn he had a good excuse for not calling her.

He told her later her 'no bullshit' had stopped him in his tracks. He'd ditched, so he said, the usual guff and plumped for a simple, *I washed your number off.*

Orla had shrugged, told him she couldn't care less, but secretly she'd hoped he'd stick around. He had. The less encouragement she gave him, the more he followed her. It was a powerful feeling, having this magnificent lump of maleness tail her all evening, desperately trying to get back in her good books.

He'd had her at hello, as the quote goes.

Why didn't I ever tell him that?

Caitlin had been disapproving but Sim had persevered, and when Caitlin was safely on the last bus back to Ma's, Orla had agreed to a coffee. She was wearing the most hideous bobble hat in the history of hideous bobble hats and decided if *that* didn't put him off, perhaps they were on to something. 'Come to mine,' he'd said. 'I'm on Fitzwilliam Square.'

'Aren't actors traditionally poor if they're not famous?'

That winded him. He was accustomed to women going weak-kneed at his flashy address. He'd been disappointed, too, with her reaction to discovering his father was a senator.

'Ah,' she'd said wonderingly. 'You're one of *those* Quinns.'

'Nothing,' Sim told her a few months later, 'about the way you said it suggested you were a fan of Dad's.'

Inside his flat, Orla maintained a strict six-feet rule. She sat on the far end of the sofa, and when Sim inched closer, she stood and relocated to an armchair.

'You honk when you laugh,' he told her, and she honked at that.

The coffee never appeared: wine, a good bottle, was poured instead.

'As we're on the subject,' Orla told him. 'You have a *great* laugh.'

'That's my real laugh. The one my agent tells me never to use. The one that shows my back teeth and makes me look, and I quote, "like a masturbating baboon". You make me laugh, Fairy.'

Orla relaxed the six-feet rule.

Frustrating, then, to discover that Sim was implementing it on her behalf. He hadn't wanted to conquer or compromise her. A personal first.

About two in the morning the chat dried up. They were both tired, and looked it.

In Ladbroke Grove, a changed and wiser woman, Orla closed her eyes and lay back beneath the juggernaut of memory as she recalled the next part in vivid, comprehensive detail. She had put her glass down, closed the six feet between them, straddled him on the sofa and kissed him.

There followed, in Sim's words, 'the most amazing sex ever to occur in this postal district.' Fast, hungry, Orla tore at his shirt and he pulled her Lurex top over her head. She peeled off his jeans and he lifted her out of her little cord skirt. Joined at the lip, they kissed the whole time, as if wary of a heavy fine for persons caught not kissing.

It was good. It was filthy. It was wholesome. They sighed, sated, and wrapped themselves around each other like kittens. Falling into a dazed sleep, Orla had felt able to say, into Sim's chest, 'Something real is happening, isn't it?' She couldn't help but sound amazed.

Dazed, Sim had agreed. 'I rather think I've sealed my fate.'

Chapter Seven

'Settle down, everybody. Including you, Fabio. In fact, especially you, Fabio.'

The class laughed. A fortnight in and cliques had formed, characters emerged. Orla was proud of their progress, and she had her pets already, the shyer ones: a gangly Chinese boy, a bruise-eyed Russian girl.

'Who's up for a bit of role play? OK. Fabio, seeing as you're so chatty, you're taking a pair of trousers back to a shop. They don't fit. Ning, you're the shop assistant.'

Ning looked bemused.

'The shop worker. The person who works in the shop.'

'Ah!' Ning grinned.

'I return this trouser,' said Fabio. His narrow eyes slid back over to Teacher. 'They are too small for my girlfriend's bottom.'

The class laughed again. The hive mind had decreed it was too sunny to study.

'Concentrate, people!' Orla surreptitiously clocked her reflection in the glazed book cupboard. The grief diet had erased her pound by pound with frightening speed, but now she saw her bottom was back, and she was glad.

'Ning! Remember your pleases and thank yous.'

Turning away food had been a denial, one that bound her

to Sim who would never eat again. It was something she could do for him. Orla appreciated the faulty logic, yet couldn't quell the prickle of guilt that she was able to eat again.

'Sick, I know.'

'Not at all, darling.' Maude was setting the shop to rights. 'A strange fancy, yes, but understandable. I'm just relieved your appetite has returned. The leftovers made me weep when you first arrived.'

Helping out with Wednesday's late closing had become a ritual. Maude always anticipated a rush. None ever came, and tonight was no exception.

Orla gathered together some Irish playwrights to make a window display. 'I'm one of your lame ducks, aren't I?'

'Don't know what you mean.' Maude was brisk as she repositioned the standard lamp. Ambience was important in the shop. Her conceit was that it should feel like a comfortable sitting room, tempting the customer to lounge on the sofa with Will Self or Jackie Collins.

'You collect us. I've seen you giving Sheraz's hopeless son pep talks when he delivers the shopping. You're letting that girl with the frizzy hair pay for those amazing books on the impressionists in instalments, even though she's always behind.'

'She's an art student. She's had a difficult life and her hair is curly, not frizzy.' Maude switched off the lamp. 'It doesn't feel right here,' she murmured and lugged it across the white floorboards.

'Here. Let me.' Orla took the lamp. Everybody jumped to help Maude, despite her spindly strength. Five foot nothing, with arthritic fingers, this woman had deftly remoulded Orla into something resembling a human again in the past weeks. 'Don't make another duck of the student who's coming for a job interview with you tomorrow, Maudie-pops. She's far from lame.' Bogna, with her pointy nose, straightened hair and smart mouth, did not fit the rich kid profile of her fellow summer schoolers. 'She's a little toughie.'

'Good. Women need to stand up for themselves.' Maude shook her head, irritated, as Orla placed the lamp. 'To the left. More.'

'Do you really need an assistant?'

'Don't rehash old conversations, Orla dear. I know my business. Try it nearer the counter.'

'Like this?'

'Yes. Right there. The light is kinder. And now,' smiled Maude, 'switch it off.' She turned the handwritten sign on the door to SORRY, WE'RE CLOSED and moved gently around the shop, patting a book here, righting a rug there.

Outside was London-dark, a milky navy that never approached the dense ink of a Tobercree night. The busy street had a different ebb and flow by night than it did by day. Orla looked out on it, and felt, tentatively, that she was starting to belong.

She'd been resuscitated. This feeling of rebirth had circled for a while, teetering on the edge of her consciousness, but each time the thought had begun to take shape, Orla had batted it away: to flourish was disloyal. It was not the behaviour of a woman in love, nor a woman in mourning. Five months ago, Orla had wanted to leap on Sim's funeral pyre yet now here she was, in a new job in a new home with a new friend. Listing her small accomplishments – her little acts of bravery – made Orla want to take the stairs three at a time and press the valentine to her chest.

Two years ago – or was it more? – as they'd walked back to his place with the makings of an omelette, he'd asked her about marriage.

'Are you horribly feminist about marriage? Do you think it's patriarchal shit? Or do you think you might marry me some day?'

What she'd thought was: *you mean you want to marry me? Me? The actual me married to the actual you?* What she'd done was take the bait, home in on his deliberate misreading of feminist attitudes to marriage, and explain that, 'If some chap I loved *madly* wanted to enter into a contract with me and call it marriage then I'd join him.'

Orla cursed her priggish younger self. Couldn't she have allowed herself a little soppiness? Given him something more?

'You look tired.' Maude had crept stealthily to her side. 'There are lovely little lines gathering under your eyes, like cracks in the ice.'

Only Maude could romanticise wrinkles.

'Mmm, I'm knackered.'

'You Irish and your poetry . . .'

Orla laughed good naturedly. 'I didn't sleep well. This morning, the five-second horrors came back.'

'Oh *Orla*.' The word was steeped in empathy. 'I thought we'd done with them.'

'Apparently not.'

Early in Orla's tenancy, she'd described for Maude how she felt at the start of each day. How she awoke underneath the duvet, limbs all warm and heavy, senses shaky, and how, for five whole seconds, Sim wasn't dead and everything was more or less right with the world before the room's edges shifted and firmed up and Sim would disappear, leaving her alone all over again. The five-second horrors.

And then one day – no terrors. Then another day without them, then the terrors again; then three days off. This halting progress had continued until Orla had dared to believe she was cured.

'It's a one-off, dear.' Maude sounded confident as she tucked a pen into the cottage loaf of her hair. 'No wonder you're looking a little washed out. That new job of yours is demanding.'

'But I love the demands.' Being needed was one of the things she missed most. 'Most of my class plan to live here, get a job, so they need to brush up their language skills double quick. One of the Russian girls – Jaysus, what's her name? Tasha, I think, she's from Georgia – is struggling. I stayed behind, gave her a leg up. Because not everybody has a Maude to look out for them.'

Deep in the lower strata of Orla's bag, her mobile cheeped. They exchanged glances.

'Wednesday night,' Maude checked her delicate gold wrist-watch, 'eight p.m. Bang on time.'

'I'll see you up there.' Orla wandered to the back of the darkened shop, digging out her phone.

'I'll have the wine open.' Maude retreated.

'Orla? It's Ma. Can you talk?

'Ma. Howaya?'

'I'm grand. Mustn't complain. Awful quiet here today. I was

just thinking of how you used to drop in some days on your way home from work. But, sure, amn't I an old, old woman and haven't you youngsters lives of your own?'

'Deirdre texted me this morning.'

'She did, did she? Oh, she's gone *very* technological since she got that new Blackcurrant.'

'She texted me just after she left your house. She said she passed Hugh on the doorstep.'

'He painted me shed. A horrible colour, but what can you do?'

'Not so lonely after all, for an old, old forgotten woman, eh, Ma?'

'You'd make a grand detective. For your information I *am* lonely for my youngest child. When are you coming home?'

'Soon.'

'Still on the trail of the long-lost journal?'

'I've more or less given up. Unless he plastered it into the walls, it's not here.'

'They won't keep your job at the school open forever.'

'Ma, I feel bad enough about leaving my class to end the school year without me, don't pile on the guilt. There's a bigger picture. Sim's death threw all the cards in the air. I love Tobercree Primary but now ... Anyway, they've given me one more month to decide.'

'What's to decide? You were only meant to be gone for two feckin' days! It's time to get back to normal life. I don't want you to screw your life up because you're upset over Sim.'

'I'm not *upset*, Ma. I'm altered. Listen, any goss?'

'Hasn't her next door got herself a new fella? And him a big bald bastard with a beer gut you could trampoline on!'

'Ma!'

'Musha?'

'I do miss you, you know.'

'She's wrong about screwing my life up,' Orla told the valentine as she towelled herself off after her shower. 'And yes, before you say it, Ma's wrong about a lot of things. She was right about you, though.'

Ma Cassidy had developed a soft spot for Sim. She'd sat him down in her dead husband's chair, plied him with sweet tea and homemade cake, cackled like waterfowl at his every joke. *Quality*, she'd pronounced him, marvelling that a senator's son should be sitting in her conservatory eating her éclairs just like a normal fella.

'You always said I was too close to Ma. She feels threatened by my independence, I guess. Hey, Sim, lookie here. My bum's back!' Orla dropped the towel to show off her newly reclaimed asset. She wiggled it. The valentine remained silent.

'Please yourself.' Orla pulled on a pair of large white knickers that Sim would have reviled. 'I know, I know; Bridget Jones pants. But men have no idea how excruciating thongs are.'

Padding up the stairs, Orla wondered if she'd simply exchanged one old lady for another. Maude's point of view was more worldly, less Tobercree-centric than Ma's. Perhaps that was why Orla had listened when Maude had exhorted her to stay all those months ago.

Orla had been keen to fly back to her coop. 'I'm not up to London,' she'd told Maude, tearful yet again. 'I'm a small-town person. I thought a change of scene would help but all

it's done is prove that nothing can help. I mean, look at me!'
She'd dabbed her eyes with an exhausted tissue. 'I keep
thinking, surely that's all the tears one woman can drum up,
but somehow I produce more.'

'Such impatience,' Maude had said and produced a linen
hanky. 'Did you really expect London to be a magic cure?
Where's your courage, woman? Sim faced his own challenges
here, remember. Yes, it was his dream come true, but it was a
mountain to climb as well.'

'His big break.' Orla had found the ironed hanky comforting.

When I get my big break, so do you, Sim had told her countless
times. *I'll be my own man then. And you, Fairy, will be my woman.
All legal and above board.*

'But, Maude,' Orla had parried, 'my job. My house.'

'If your employers value you they'll hold your job. If they
run out of patience, there are other jobs. That big family of
yours can pitch in and store your personal belongings and
advertise for a short-term tenant.'

'I suppose ...' Unbidden, a memory emerged of Sim's
reaction when she'd put in an offer on the little home Orla was
so proud of.

What are you trying to say? He'd struck postures from his
Richard III. *That you don't see a future for us? Or you don't think
I can get a mortgage? Why not cut off my balls and be done with it?*
The location of the house had perplexed him. *Why buy out in
the bloody sticks?*

Explaining to a man who lived rent-free on Poshington
Square that the sticks was all she could afford had taken a
while. The cottage was an investment in their future, she told

him. She needed a toe on the property ladder, needed a room of her own; she did not intend to be a kept woman, flashing a film star boyfriend's Platinum card.

More easily dealt with was the issue of his balls: she was far too fond of them to chop them off.

She thought of her cottage often, on its lane where the woods met the edge of town. She thought of Sim's strop less often: it still provoked a sensation of being stifled. Posthumously she could admit how disappointed she'd been that he didn't try to understand.

'Fear is something quite separate from what frightens you,' Maude had said, as Orla wept, irresolute, over a half-packed suitcase. 'It's a distorting mirror, Orla. Why not face down dirty old London and try to discover what Sim saw in it?'

'Perhaps the journal will turn up,' Orla had said, 'if I stay.'

Orla knocked on Maude's door and let herself in.

'Come in, come in, it's wine o'clock,' laughed Maude.

Orla was glad she'd taken Maude's advice. Across the divide of death she and Sim shared the thrill of re-invention in a new city.

And London is the perfect place to be lonely.

Chapter Eight

Bogna shrugged. 'Sometimes, yes, people make joke about seaside when they hear name, but I don't give toss.'

'I bet you don't!' Sunshine bounced happily off the shop's white walls. Maude, standing on a box behind her counter, was entranced by the self-confidence of the skinny-jeaned, stud-nosed nineteen-year-old job applicant. 'Orla says you're a lively addition to her class.'

'That's not what I said,' said Orla, leaning against some bookshelves where she was pretending to read *Mansfield Park*. 'I said she spent all yesterday morning throwing Polo mints at Ning's head.'

The dark-haired man on the shop sofa gave a strangled laugh, verifying Orla's suspicion that he wasn't engrossed in his book but eavesdropping.

'Orla was saying boring things,' Bogna appealed to Maude. 'And Ning has big head, so . . .'

'I'm sure I can trust you not to throw sweets at the customers.' Maude was indulgent: the job was already Bogna's, much to Orla's dismay.

'Who's your favourite author?' asked Orla, putting aside *Mansfield Park* and all pretence of uninterest. She saw nothing in Bogna to suggest she'd make a shop assistant. Orla felt responsible: she'd offered the job to Tasha, and Bogna had overheard the Russian girl's *niet*.

With a withering look Orla recognised from class, Bogna said, 'I don't need job, you know.'

There was a growl from the sofa, making Orla jump. The dark man turned the page of his book like a cracked whip.

'OK, I *do* need job,' snapped Bogna. 'Because mean brother makes me pay rent for apartment he bloody owns. Me. His sister.' She unleashed another withering look, this time aimed at the sofa. 'He is beast.'

The beast shifted, head still bowed over his book.

'He looks rather nice to me,' said Maude mildly. 'Now, can you do Wednesday evening five to eight p.m. and all day Saturday?' Maude, mistress of snap decisions, crumpled up the list of questions Orla had written.

'Hmm.' Bogna turned her mouth down. '*All* day Saturday? I like to have big bath and get ready for night out.'

Another, louder, growl from the sofa. '*Bogna . . .* '

With a martyred air, Bogna conceded that yes, she supposed she could do all day Saturday. 'How much you pay me?'

'Eleven pounds an hour.' Maude ignored the frustrated *tsk* from Orla, who'd suggested ten.

'Not enough.'

'Oh.' Maude was flustered. 'Well, I suppose I could—'

'Wait, please.'

The man stood up, wearily. In this feminine domain he was emphatically dark, in black jeans, black shirt, with black hair. His skin, however, was emphatically white, giving him the appearance of a fairy tale prince.

'Bogna.' He turned to her and spoke in a rapid undertone,

his voice as dark as his clothing. '*Musisz pracować. Ta pani jest przyzwoita, dobra i bedzie ptacić uczciwe wynagrodzenie. Powiedz "dziękuję" iwnos się stąd.*'

With downturned mouth, Bogna said, 'OK, Maude, eleven pounds is fine.'

'Marvellous.' Maude clapped her frail hands.

'And?' The man looked expectantly at Bogna.

'Thank you,' said Bogna robotically.

'What did you say, just then, in that lovely language?' Maude asked the man towering over her. He was un-summery, a bracing blast of East European winter, and Orla could tell that Maude had taken to him as much as to his sister.

'Nothing. It doesn't matter,' he said.

'My evil brother said,' said Bogna, eager to go against his wishes, 'that I need a job and you are decent and good and will pay a fair wage and I should say "yes" and we should get out of here and leave you to get on with your day.'

'And does your evil brother have a name?' Maude was coquettish. Orla turned away, keeping her smile a secret. Across a ravine of forty years, her landlady was flirting with the tall dark foreign stranger.

'I'm Marek.' He got there before Bogna: it was obvious they vied for the driving seat. 'And we're very grateful that you see potential in Bogna. She'll work hard for you, I promise.'

'It's wonderful to see a family pull together.' Maude's wistfulness made Orla realise she had never met any of Maude's family. It shocked her that it had taken months for this to register. Was she so wrapped up in her own grief that she had stopped noticing other people's?

'My sister enjoys your classes,' Marek said to Orla, from the doorway. 'She'd never admit it in front of you, but she talks about you.'

'Oh dear . . .'

'It sounds as if you don't take any nonsense. I love the girl but I know what she's like. Bogna's much younger than me, she's my half-sister, although we don't talk about halves in our family. Now my father's gone, she's my responsibility, so thank you for taking an interest.'

Maude had drifted off to the Romantics section and Bogna, hand on a car door handle, impatient.

'You don't need to thank me,' said Orla. 'She's bright, she's capable. And she's a character,' she added, carefully.

'English understatement,' said Marek. 'It comes in so handy.'

Orla laughed. 'All right, she's a nightmare, but there's a sweetness there too.' They both looked out at Bogna, rattling the car door and scowling. 'Deep, but there. And it wasn't English understatement. It was Irish understatement. They're similar.'

'Ah. I didn't recognise the accent.' Marek had eyes so brown they verged on black. They were intense: Orla felt scrutinised.

'Your English is perfect,' she said, taking a step back.

'I've been here a long time.' Marek looked off to the left, remembered. 'Almost twenty years.'

'You must like it here.'

'Marek! *Pospiesz sie!*' Bogna could growl as darkly as her brother.

'Like?' Marek considered, as he turned away. 'London can

86

be a lonely place.' He threw his car keys into the air and caught them. Over his shoulder, his dark eyes met her blue ones. 'But every so often, something happens. Yes, London is a place where things can happen.'

Orla didn't wait for them to drive off. She went to the sofa and reapplied herself to *Mansfield Park*.

'Interesting chap,' said Maude from the counter.

'Hmm,' said Orla. Later she'd tell the valentine about him. *I met an 'interesting chap' today,* she'd say. Or maybe she wouldn't. She didn't have to tell the valentine *everything*, after all. No need to bore it.

The stationmaster's clock above the bar, a quirky piece perfectly at home among the other quirky pieces dotted round the Soho members' club (a headless gold statuette, a stuffed parrot, a kimono), showed Orla that Reece was forty-three minutes late.

Again she consulted the menu, a list of twenty-first-century restaurant staples she could now recite by heart.

Sustainable cod and chips.

Pork belly.

Classic burger.

Reece could be stuck at work, under a train, or have plain forgotten about her. Essentially law abiding – a trait Sim had deplored – Orla didn't feel bold enough to check her messages, because of the handwritten notice prohibiting the use of mobiles in the club.

'More water? Or d'you want to start on the hard stuff?' The waitress, mixed race with a buoyant Mohican, was chummy. All the staff were chummy but professional, as if your best mates had conspired to sit you down to a nice meal, but for their own reasons refused to sit down with you.

'Umm.' Orla wondered what the correct thing to do was. Her halter-neck sundress had felt 'right' in her room, but among the bordello reds and golds of this zeitgeist-nailing interior it felt 'wrong'. 'Maybe a glass of wine? The house red?'

'Sure.' Mohican crinkled her eyes. 'Go mad.'

The red was suavely smooth, but Orla refused a second. An hour late now. Perhaps Reece wasn't coming? When should she leave? And then he was standing over her table, tie askew, pale face a portrait of grave dismay. 'Orla. This is unforgiveable. I hope you ordered some – ah, yes, good, you did.'

London people kissed. Orla had witnessed much kissing in the hour she'd waited. She stood just as he bent, and their kiss became a bruising collision of Reece's teeth and the top of Orla's head.

'Sorry. Jaysus. I'm a klutz, Reece.'

'You're a vision.' Reece sat down, leaned eagerly over the table, studied her. 'Sim would love that dress.' They shared a complicit look. The first mention was over. 'Tonight you look just like he used to describe you. Black and white and pink, Sim said. With join-the-dots freckles and your own microclimate of fresh air and damp sunshine.'

'He said all that?' Orla laughed, shy in the face of Reece's rugged handsomeness. His hair was a bright and roaring red, cut short and tufty, accentuating the fine design of his face. Everything about his face was lean – long slender nose with flaring nostrils, a wide thin mouth, and inquisitive, catlike blue eyes that creased to slits when he smiled.

'Apologies for the formal attire. I lunched an LA lawyer. Those guys judge a man by his suits.' He loosened his tie. 'That's better. Are you starving? I am.' He snatched up the menu. 'Sim reckoned you were the only girlfriend he'd ever had who admitted to an appetite.' He paused. 'I'm letting him down, aren't I? It's weeks since we met. He'd want me to look after you.'

'Don't be silly.' Orla hesitated, then put a hand over Reece's. It was pale, red at the knuckle, a strong hand for a creature of business, raw looking. 'You've been very kind to me.' He was special. He'd seen a gaggle of people around a man lying on the pavement, sauntered over to investigate and found Sim dying. Reece had watched as Sim's last breaths escaped from his body. Touching Reece's hand was a bridge to that moment. He could have no idea how important he was to Orla. 'I'm not a child. You don't have to babysit me.'

He looked down at Orla's hand, then up into her eyes. She withdrew her fingers. 'Fishcakes,' said Reece, emphatically. 'Hope they're better than my old school dinner ones.'

'Boarding school, I bet. No, *public* school.'

'How'd you guess?'

'Sim was exported to one in Yorkshire. Fishcakes loomed large when he banged on about the terrible deprivations of a ten-thousand-pounds-per-term education.'

'Knowing Sim, he charmed the bloomers off Matron and had a whale of a time.'

'The older ladies always fell for him.'

'Actually . . .' Reece pursed his lips, slowed right down. The red hair and scrubbed skin gave him a youthful burnished look which made him difficult to age accurately: Orla felt he could be her contemporary or twenty years her senior. 'There's something I need to ask you. To do with Sim and *Courtesan*.'

'Oh?' Sim's posthumous success was a tricky subject for Orla. She sidled towards it, unsure. He would have been delirious at the wall to wall PR, but it made Orla feel hollow, as if she were at a surprise party where the guest of honour didn't show.

'Do you read *OK!* magazine?'

'Officially? No. But truthfully? Yes, Reece, of course I read it. Cover to cover. Sim used to joke that one day they'd photograph us in our Malibu beach house. We planned what we'd say. He went for "this is my time to be me", but I plumped for "we want to give something back to society".'

'They want to interview you.'

'Me? Feck off!'

'Seriously.'

'Why? Feck off!'

'They want to talk to you about Sim, how you got together, how you're coping without ...' Reece faltered, 'Bad idea. Sorry. I'll tell them to, what is it, *feck off*?'

'The *Courtesan* thing's not even on telly yet.' Orla's heart pumped harder. Anonymity suited her. Sim was the one who'd wanted to be in *OK!* and now here she was in a London members' club discussing interview requests while he lay in a coffin. The cosmos had cartwheeled.

Their food arrived. Both were glad of the distraction, but as soon as the fishcakes were tasted, judged, pronounced better than school's, Reece returned to the subject.

'I want you to be, you know, prepared. The Beeb spent a fortune making *Courtesan* and they're spending another fortune promoting it. They want awards. And syndication. Sim's a gift to them. They're running with the whole "dead before his time" thing, "young star cut down in his prime", all that bollocks.' Reece leaned back, looked at the ceiling. 'Trouble is, the little bastard was so handsome.'

'Wasn't he though?' Reece had told Orla about the panic straight after Sim's death, when the BBC had sounded out the Quinns about retaining their son's performance. With some rejigging of the storyline and the use of a lookalike in longshot, they'd been able to salvage the production without recasting the Comte de Caylus. Orla would have liked to hear it from the Quinns themselves: another small hurt she'd had to bear.

'Are you going to watch it?' Reece asked.

'Not sure. Seeing Sim walking and talking and wearing fancy breeches. Being *alive*. It would be voodoo.'

'It might help.'

'It might kill me.'

'I should shut up.'

'No. You should say—' Orla held up her glass, '—happy birthday, Orla!'

'What?' Reece looked aghast, held up his glass automatically and clinked it with Orla's. 'You're kidding. Why are you here with boring old me and not with your mates?'

Confessing that her landlady was her closest friend would sound bizarre to an arch networker. Orla could have explained that she'd chosen not to seek out new people, that company exhausted her, that a septuagenarian fulfilled all her needs, but said instead, 'My friends are all in Ireland.' There had been cards from the family and a Skyped, out of tune round of

Happy birthday to you / you look like a poo from Juno and Jack. Orla hadn't told Maude, hadn't wanted any fuss. Now, in this tipsy room lively with laughter and gossip, fuss seemed desirable. Another green shoot, Orla guessed, unfurling and stretching towards the light.

'Happy birthday, Orla.' Reece looked sobered. She hoped – very much – that it wasn't pity in his eyes. 'Sim would have taken you somewhere splendid. I'm a poor replacement.'

'No, you're—' Orla was cut off by a shriek from the doorway.

'REECE! DARLING!'

Reece swivelled, half stood, 'Look what the cat's dragged in!' he cried.

The room swelled, the lights brightened, as heads turned to see the newcomer. Petite but long limbed, with a dancer's prancing step, the woman approached their table, singing good-humouredly, 'YOU'VE BEEN AVOIDING ME, YOU CUNT!'

As the actress neared them – and it *was* an actress, Orla would have bet her house on that – the years stacked up. She grew older with each step until she enveloped Reece in a bear hug, and Orla could plainly see how the shoulder-length hair rebelled at decades of red dye and how the eyebrows aimed for the ceiling at an improbable slant.

'I'm so rude,' she said, noticing Orla. 'Interrupting your tryst like this.' She held out manicured fingers to Orla. 'I'm Anthea.'

Well, of course she was. Orla kicked herself for not recognising a household name.

'Hello.' Her voice small, Orla was dismayed to discover she

could be star struck. She shook the lily-like hand. Anthea's grip was as strong as a docker's.

Anthea Blake trained her attention on Reece once more. Orla was able to study her, as extravagant endearments and the fruitiest of four-letter words ricocheted off the walls. Feminine without a hint of submissiveness, Anthea elicited a heightened, almost erotic response. Orla wondered if she was reacting to the woman's fame, or to something intrinsic, carried on the fog of perfume and riding the flicked tendrils of mermaid hair. She was smothered by Anthea's charisma, but happily so, and awaited the moment when Reece would announce their common denominator and this star would shine on her.

The fact that Sim had been filmed naked alongside her, Orla preferred to sidestep.

Tapping his Blackberry as if waking a tiny animal, Reece nodded at Anthea's convoluted complaint about her current director. 'I'll call him tomorrow. It's a simple misunderstanding, darling. I made it quite clear – no weekend filming.' He turned to Orla, ushered her into the charmed circle (which was the focus, discreetly, of the room) by saying, 'Ant, darling, this lovely creature is Orla, our gorgeous Sim's beloved. And Orla, this is the incomparable Ant Blake, the courtesan herself.'

'Oh.' All Anthea's vivacity stilled, as if somebody had pulled out her plug.

Orla accepted the awkwardness with good grace. She'd become expert at ignoring such tongue-tied reactions. When Sim died, Orla had become 'poor Orla' – and it was bad casting.

'Hello Anthea,' she said. 'I've heard so much about you.'

'And I you.' Anthea's hand went to her throat, a dramatic gesture that seemed natural; perhaps it had become second nature after a working life spent making it to order. 'I'm so sorry. About . . . ' She waved the hand, as if referring to something too awful to name. Her eyelids fluttered. 'God. It was so . . . ' All of Anthea's fifty-plus years marched back over the line in the sand drawn by her plastic surgeon. 'A talented man. A great loss. You must miss him terribly.'

'Yup.' Orla felt hot, ambushed by grief again. In the actress's eyes she read real distress – which was a surprise. 'It gets better,' she heard herself say, dismayed at her own banal heartlessness.

'He's bloody marvellous in *Courtesan*. He'll blow me off the screen.' This was safe footing, and it revived Anthea; her face glowed once more. 'But I've disrupted your meal. Do carry on. Lovely to meet you.' She threw Orla a kiss. 'And as for you . . . we'll talk tomorrow, Reece.'

The merest shadow of a 'look' passed between client and agent. Orla felt it was more than dismay at this shared encounter with grief; it felt as if Anthea was planning a ticking off.

'That wasn't meant to happen,' said Reece in an undertone as a phalanx of staff shepherded Anthea upstairs like a visiting potentate. 'Ant's a love but she's very full on. Are you OK?'

'Of course!' Old-fashioned good manners, drilled into Orla by Ma, meant she strived to be the least troublesome bereaved woman in the world: it was her job to save Reece, *everybody*, from any discomfort on her behalf. 'The chips are good. Want one?'

'Ant finds it hard to talk about him.'

'Me too, sometimes. And you.' The droop of Reece's red head told Orla a lot. He and Sim had shared a genuine friendship, not just the necessary professional intimacy.

'I don't want to talk *about* him,' said Reece. 'I want to talk *to* him.'

'You want to know a secret? I actually do!' laughed Orla. She could tell Reece about the valentine. He wouldn't laugh at her crazy widow's weeds. 'I tell Sim how my day went. I ask his advice about what to cook for dinner. I tell him jokes, I moan – sweet Jaysus, do I moan! About the tube, the weather, money. I treated him to a ten-minute riff on my fat ankles this morning. He used to stick his fingers in his ears and sing the national anthem, anything to shut me up, or shut me out; but now he has no option but to hang on my every word.'

'Do you imagine him?' Reece was intrigued. And touched. 'Or do you talk to a photo?'

'This is where it gets truly loony. Honestly? I talk to a card.'

'A card? What do you mean?'

'A valentine's card. The last one he sent.'

Reece sat back, put down his fork.

'The one that arrived just as you were telling me about ... just when you called with the news.'

'It's unopened, right?'

'Yup.'

'Good.'

'I know what it says.'

'You do?'

95

'You probably know too!' Orla hadn't realised this before. 'Sim told you everything.'

'Um, not everything.' Reece was uncomfortable, his bon-homie withered. 'What do you think it says?'

'I *know* it's a proposal.'

'Of marriage?'

'No, of caravanning in Wales. Yes, Reece, of course of mar-riage!' Her attempts to lighten the mood were doomed; Reece was sombre.

'I had an inkling,' he said.

'I can't open it. You understand ... Reece!' Orla assayed a light laugh which fell on its face. 'Don't look at me like that.'

'Seriously, darling, this is morbid. Wrong. Get rid of it.'

'I never thought I'd say this, but you sound like my Ma.'

'Keeping hold of it, *talking* to it, but never intending to read it? That's not healthy. It's odd, Orla.'

'I didn't say I'll *never* read it.'

'If you want my advice—'

'I don't, but go on.'

'Burn the bloody thing.'

Orla took the card to bed with her that night. She kissed it, having carefully wiped the ruby stain off her lips first: the card was deteriorating now, and she treated it with respect.

'As if I'd burn you. You're never going in the fire, matey. Do you remember Valentine's Day 2010? It was our first anniversary. The actual card's back in the hatbox under my bed at home but I can quote it to you, if you like, *aren't* I clever?'

Dearest Fairy,

365 days and counting. I love you! Is that old hat yet? This shouldn't work. You're a buttoned up schoolmarm and I'm a star struck eejit. I should be with some glamour-puss as shallow as I am. You should be with somebody solid and solvent who nods approvingly when you talk all clever and doesn't tease you about your arse. But the stars will have to realign. The rule-makers will have to start again from scratch. Orla and Sim are doing it their way. I'm hanging on for ever. Please tell me you'll do the same.

Happy Valentine's Day.
Sxxxx

P.S. Hear that? In the distance? That's my Big Break circling nearer and nearer . . .

'You didn't have to bang on *quite* so much about me being a buttoned up schoolmarm.' Orla kept it light when she complained to the valentine, just as she had with its sender. 'And maybe I'm not a glamour-puss but I scrub up well.' She'd always bristled against his caricature of her, but never carped: the resulting row wouldn't be worth it.

'Goodnight, darling,' she said, and switched off the light.

Sim's journal

14 February 2010

Do you know what I'd like? Once – just ONCE – to order a meal <u>for which I am bloody paying</u> without a Greek chorus of disapproval from my girlfriend. Valentine's Day is a big con / the set meal is better value / you don't even like foie gras.

One year in and O can get my goat more efficiently than any other living person. Take tonight, for instance – the restaurant was <u>too nice</u>.

Yes. Too NICE.

Very loudly, I told her, 'But darling, nothing is too good for you, you moany cow.' And that made us laugh. And it's game over when we laugh. Everything set us off after that.

Orla Cassidy is exasperating. But I love her. Not like I did a year ago. This is deeper. I love her like . . . I can't even find a comparison. I love her like I love her. She's the nicest person in the world and I don't deserve her.

Chapter Nine

'I've always liked her on TV but she sounds hideous in real life.'

'I'm making her sound grotesque. She's nice, honestly. Very charismatic.'

'Fancy being called Ant. I'd rather be Thea. Bet she fancied the pants off old Sim.'

'Juno. That kind of hurts.'

'Sorry. I'm being flippant. But everybody fancied your fella, Orla. And you loved it!'

'I kind of did. I kind of didn't.'

'She wouldn't have had a hope in hell. I mean, even if he'd been single. She's decrepit.'

'Weirdly ageless, actually. Like a sprite. Very slender, very feminine. Not girly. *Feminine*. Dazzling presence. Now I know what the term *star quality* means.'

'Sounds like you fancy her yourself.'

'Are you growing your hair? The screen's so blurry it's hard to tell.'

'Himself hates it. We had a sit-down to discuss the state of the marriage.'

'Sounds ominous. What was the outcome?'

'The state of the marriage is that the marriage is in a state.'

'No, really.'

'Really.'

'*Really* really? I've missed a few episodes, haven't I? So bloody wrapped up in myself.'

'I don't mind.'

'Well I do.'

'Himself and me'll work it out. We always do. If only he'd keep something in reserve for *me*, not use up all his sparkle on client lunches, you know? He came in the door tonight and before I even opened my mouth he held up his hands and said, *Go easy on me, it's been a long day.*'

'His voice isn't like that. You make him sound like a eunuch chipmunk. I suppose he has to work hard to keep you and Jack in your, er, high standard of living.'

'You're trying so hard to be nice when you want to shout, *you greedy bitch, you want the moon on a stick and then you're annoyed because the poor man is tired*. My mother just says it right out. That's a direct quote, actually.'

'I don't think you're a greedy bitch.'

'Don't you? I do. Listen, how's the valentine? Still in one piece? Hasn't fallen into a shredder by mistake?'

'Why doesn't anybody get it? That card is my lifeline.'

'If you were here, we'd go out for a Thai curry, cure my marriage and drown that card in the Liffey. What's this Reece like, then? A possible?'

'A what? You mean, Jaysus woman, a possible *boyfriend*?'

'No, lover. They're much better value. Or do you plan to wall yourself up with your old biddy?'

'I don't hop from man to man.'

'Unlike me, filthy tart that I am, eh? You didn't say it, but you thought it now didn't you ...'

'Ha! Well, if the tarty hat fits ...'

'I was a bit of a one, wasn't I? God, it was fun. So, anyway, Reece isn't a possible? Are you truly telling me you're in London, capital of the known world, and you haven't met one single solitary man who's piqued your interest? Who hasn't made you feel, well, *womanly*?'

Marek, she thought – and almost said it out loud.

'No.'

That unusual name with its soft opening and its whiplash final syllable had popped up like a mole from her subconscious, after just five minutes' exposure to a dark and quiet man who should mean nothing to her.

'Who sent you flowers?' Bogna circled the roses on the counter, popping her gum.

'None of your beeswax.' Orla played with the long-stemmed beauties, trying to muss them up, failing. Such haughty blooms could do nothing but look stiff and expensive. Reece's tastes were grand: Sim had known to send her posies.

'Arthur used to send me roses,' said Maude, halfway up a ladder, dusting the foreign language section. 'Always red. Like those.'

Arthur! Orla pounced on the unsolicited nugget of Maude's autobiography and squirrelled it away. That there'd been a Mr Maude was obvious: according to the post Orla picked from the mat each morning, Maude was a Mrs, and double-barrelled at that, but her husband was never mentioned, nor alluded to. If a conversation threatened to trespass on Maude's romantic history, however obliquely, Orla felt the air between them thicken and become gelid.

As an Irish woman, Orla was accustomed to the special atmospheres generated by her elders. Weaned on Ma's trademark atmospheres surrounding menstruation, intercourse and homosexuality – Breda Cassidy's holy trinity – she knew when and how to step away from discomfort.

Another one of Maude's no-go areas was any conversation about her financial set-up. Coming from a family that had always lived close to the bone, Orla was fascinated by the wealthy. She'd been perversely impressed by Sim's ability to spend money – his unerring choice of the most expensive items on any menu, be it a Harvester's or the Ritz. Likewise, Lucy's habit of arranging for the tiniest pot of Crème de la Mer to be delivered from Brown Thomas, instead of popping it in her handbag, had left her dumbstruck.

The economics of the rich was beyond her. How, Orla had puzzled, did a job – even one as high profile as Senator Quinn's – generate sufficient money to fuel a Dublin townhouse, an underground garage quivering with cars, a dependant son and a high-maintenance wife? And mistresses don't come cheap.

Similarly, though, how could an elderly woman with no visible means of support own three floors of central London real estate? Orla was savvy enough to know that even in this edgy postcode, flanked by pound shops and bookies, Maude's house was the financial equivalent of an entire street in Tobercree. But still, the middle flat was let out at a cut-price rate, and the shop was a drain, not an asset. Presumably Maude had what Ma referred to reverentially as 'old money' – cash that had tumbled down the generations to land in her pocket.

'Arthur?' asked Orla warily, concentrating on the roses.

'Orla's flowers are from a friend to celebrate a wonderful development in her life.' Maude turned to Bogna, dropkicking Orla's timid cross into the long grass.

'Yeah?' Bogna was careful not to look interested. She hoisted her bra strap with her thumb, manoeuvring one breast so it sat up and begged beneath her slash-necked tee.

'She's accepted a full-time job at the college.' Maude beamed: her plan had come together. 'From September the tenth Orla will be a TEFL tutor to adult students. That stands for Teaching English as a Foreign Language. Her contract's for one year. After that,' said Maude mysteriously, 'we'll see.'

'Why does she do this?' Bogna looked disgusted, as if Orla had belched. 'College is rubbish and boring.'

'Not to me,' said Orla patiently. 'I love teaching.' She noticed that the roses were stripped of their thorns.

The bell above the door sang and Maude scurried over to greet the customer, wafting talc in her wake. Orla leaned on the counter and recalled the latest Wednesday call from home.

'Orla? It's Ma. Can you talk?'

'Howaya Ma?'

'Grand. Grand. Lookit. I had a queer owld conflab with your headmaster outside the butcher's.'

'Oh.'

'Yes, madam. *Oh* indeed. Says he, Orla's staying on in London. Says I, No no no, Orla wouldn't make a decision like that without telling me.'

'Ma, I'm sorry.'

'So am I. That I raised a chit with no manners.'

'Ma! No, don't cry! Please, Ma.'

'What makes you want to be so far away, amongst strangers?'

'You don't say that to Caitlin. Or when Brendan went backpacking.'

'They weren't bereaved. Grieving. Half mad with—'

'Ma! I can cope.'

'You're half dead, Orla!'

'I know! I bloody know, but we mustn't say it.'

'Oh, love. I've made you cry.'

'I hate crying, Ma. Eighteen days tear-free and now I'll have to start at day one again. How's everybody?'

'Grand. Deirdre's suing the man who put up her conservatory.'

'Good for her. She hasn't sued anybody for ages.'

'And her little Roisin is after winning a prize for reciting poetry.'

'She sent me the clip. It was almost as long as *Titanic*.'

'Don't. We shouldn't laugh. But Jaysus, there's only so many times you can watch a child recite a Viking saga. You're coming home for Christmas, aren't you?'

Maude's reaction to the job offer had been to toast Orla's burnt boats. It had troubled Orla, who preferred to imagine a serviceable bridge behind her rather than a flotilla of burning wrecks. True, she thought as she checked an old edition of *A Sentimental Education* for marks and scuffs, this new job was to her liking. The students would be more motivated than the summer schoolers, less privileged, champing at the bit to embed themselves in UK society. To enable them would be satisfying. Yet despite it all, a little line of seven-year-olds snaked through her thoughts, with all their credulity, their enthusiasm, their *need*. They were in the boats she'd torched.

The bell above the door sounded again; this was a busy Saturday by Maude's standards.

'Not you,' snarled Bogna.

Orla looked up, a tut springing to her lips: three times today she'd had to chastise Bogna about her people skills.

'I don't finish until five, Marek.' Bogna was scowling at her brother. 'Come back then and drive me home.'

'I have no intention of driving you home,' said Marek. 'Orla, come for a coffee with me.'

Maude looked up from her accounts, ears pricked, like a dachshund who's heard the fridge door squeak.

'Now?' Orla stalled.

'Yes.' Marek held the door open. He regarded her squarely. He didn't elaborate.

'OK.'

'Bloody hell,' said Bogna loudly as the door closed behind them.

'I've never noticed this place before.' Orla took a corner seat in the unpretentious café two streets away, with its fluorescent lighting and a beehived proprietress.

'It's Polish.'

Marek sat opposite, slid a laminated menu across the checked plastic cloth.

'Ah.' Orla smiled. 'Good. I've never tried Polish food.' *Shut up*, she counselled herself. *Don't fill the gaps*. The walk to the café had proved that Marek didn't do small-talk; a bonus, in Orla's view. There was too much small-talk in the world, filling up each nook and cranny, leaving no room for contemplation. She scanned the offerings, stumbling over G's and S's and Z's.

'Do you like biscuits? Cake?' asked Marek.

'I do.'

'OK.' Marek stood. 'What sort of coffee do you like?'

'White, thanks.' Orla had withstood the siren call of coffee chains, and stuck to 'old-fashioned' coffee.

At the counter, Marek ordered in Polish, his deep bass voice rumbling over the hard edges of his mother tongue like a tank. Orla watched him, noted that he didn't turn and smile at her. She wasn't sure he'd smiled at all on the way, just strode on as she scuttled to keep up. She wondered why she'd acquiesced. She put it down to the opiate quality of that dark voice with its merest tang of an accent. As Sim would attest, Orla was not a natural yes-girl: Celts are suspicious and she tended to respond to direct invitations with 'maybe', 'why?' or 'feck off', and yet here she was, in a corner, watching a tall black-haired man bring her a chipped plate of little sugared crescents.

'They are *rogaliki*,' he told her. 'Try one.'

Orla did as she was told. 'Delicious,' she said, licking sugar from her lips. 'I've never come across them before.'

'In Poland they're everywhere.'

'Right. Mmm. Lovely. Yum.' *Stop. Stop filling the gaps.* She chewed on.

Marek sipped his coffee, which came in a doll-size teacup and was as sticky as tar.

'So,' said Orla, when the silence had lost its elasticity. 'D'you come here often?'

He got the reference, as she knew he would.

'Actually yes. My first job was around the corner. I still come here every Thursday for lunch.'

'What do you do for a living?'

'I am a cliché.' He nodded his head in acceptance of the fact and his shiny fringe fell across his eyes. Orla noticed that his hair needed a trim: neither one style nor another, it flopped, glossy as a Georgian front door and charming despite its neglect. 'I am a Polish builder.'

'Hmm. There's a lot of you around,' smiled Orla.

'Or I used to be. Now I have builders working for me. Men from home. I am a developer.'

'Is that a tricky way to earn a living? In the recession?'

'Not for me.'

He wasn't bragging, she knew, he was stating a fact. Orla took in the cut of his black velvet jacket, the heft of his watch, and realised that Marek was a man of means. A self-made man of means.

'What kind of property do you develop?' *He asks me out; I ask all the questions.*

'Nowadays, I concentrate on building from scratch. Mixture of social housing and high end. You understand this?'

'Sort of. You get permission to build expensive houses if you agree to sell some of them to people who find it hard to get on the property ladder.'

'Exactly so,' said Marek, pleased. Not pleased enough to smile, she noted, and wondered what it would take.

'It must be satisfying. To give people a home.'

'It is.'

Another silence, filled with more *rogalicki*, doughy and comforting.

Marek said, 'So, when do you go home? To Ireland.'

'Oh, I'm not. I'm staying on.'

'Good.' Marek nodded, looking directly at her, his blackish gaze steady. 'Good. Why?'

'I've accepted a full-time job at the college where I taught Bogna.' She left it at that. The silence lay between them on the red and white check. When she couldn't stand it any longer, she carried on, like a drowning swimmer coming up for air, and gabbled, 'I've given up my old job at home, decided to give London a proper go, stopped pretending it's a temporary thing or a stopgap, accepted I've made a quantum leap and that I've changed.' Orla stopped herself, shocked at what she would blurt out to neutralise a silence: she'd never admitted out loud that this was such a gigantic prospect for her. 'Listen to me!' she fluted, embarrassed at answering questions he hadn't asked.

'I am.' Marek pulled a biscuit apart. A tinny tune sounded from the breast pocket of his jacket. Taking it out, he frowned at it. 'Work,' he said.

'Take it,' Orla sat back, 'I don't mind.'

'Of course not.' Marek was stern. He silenced the little machine with one fleet stab.

'You're not a slave to your mobile phone, then?' smiled Orla. It pleased her that at least one modern human had the psychological strength to leave a call unanswered. Sim had been welded to his iPhone, allowing the world and his wife access all areas.

'No. Otherwise the tail wags the dog, and life is the wrong way round.'

'Just a lump of metal, after all,' said Orla vaguely, as she flushed at her treason in comparing Sim, unfavourably, to this stranger. Her quantum leap was going a little far, and a little fast.

The weather, huffy since the start of September, finally collapsed into a sulk.

'Looks like rain out there. I should get back.'

'Yes.' Marek stood, his chair scraping on the lino.

'What do I owe you?' Going Dutch would convert this potential date into a simple coffee between two consenting adults.

'Nothing.' And, tickled by her disgruntlement, Marek smiled at last. 'You owe me nothing. I paid already.' The smile was wide, artless, pitched his face into a whole different gear. He had even white teeth, except for his pointed canines. The fairy tale prince could also play the wicked wolf, it would seem.

'Thanks. It was lovely. Thanks.' Orla scolded herself for her effusiveness. *It was coffee and a damp biscuit. Just go!*

Reaching the door first, Marek held it open for her, squinting up at the foaming sky. 'Don't like the look of that.'

'It's going to pour.' Orla dipped beneath his arm, out into the street, turning to him with a genial look of farewell. She didn't get to say her goodbyes, because he began to talk rapidly, steadily, eschewing punctuation.

'We are a cliché, talking about the weather like two old people. I know this didn't go well. It was dull. I was boring. But I think we should meet again. I know what has happened in your life to make you sad. I'm sorry about it. I've lost people. You're coping well, I think. I'm going to persevere, Orla, I warn you. I won't rush you but I see something in your face, something that I recognise, and I can't ignore it.'

Orla blinked.

Without allowing her time to speak, Marek said, 'Here, take this,' and draped his scarf, grey and soft and musky, around her neck. 'It's turned cold and you're dressed for summer. *Pozegnanie*, Orla Cassidy.' He turned and walked away.

A fat blob of rain stained the pavement. Orla held the scarf to her nose. Cashmere, she guessed. She turned and ran back to Maude's Books.

The rain chased Orla, falling harder with every step she took. By the time she turned the corner onto her stretch of the high street, her hair was plastered to her head and her sandals were ruined.

She squelched to a halt.

Across the road, a man teetered on a ladder against a hoarding, pasting down the last corner of a huge poster of a twenty-foot-tall Sim in a frock coat. Airbrushed, his face was smooth and perfect, with a heart-shaped beauty mark pencilled above his top lip. His eyes, greener than she remembered, looked straight down at her. Impish, sexy, and not at all dead.

Sim's journal

11 December 2011

It was a fib by my rules, but Orla would file it under 'lie'. Whatevs. With my best my-puppy's-been-run-over voice I told her the Skype camera is broken. And it isn't. So. No Skype sexiness tonight. She was

devastated. Who'd have thought she'd take to it so enthusiastically?
But if we Skyped, if she saw my face, she'd know everything, in a flash.
   That's the way it is with fairies.

'You're loving this, aren't you?' Orla took it out on the valentine as she nibbled her fingernails, hunched by her window in a darkened sitting room tinged a seasick yellow by the street lamps. A glass of wine sat neglected, as, somewhere on the floor above, did Maude, whose offer of company Orla had spurned, preferring to sit on her own at the window and contemplate Sim.

'Bastard,' she whispered, holding the valentine to her cheek. This was a luxury she allowed herself only now and again, knowing it could age the envelope. 'How many other widows have to put up with a gigantic cardboard clone of their deceased other half leering down at them?' The universe – which had excelled itself of late – demonstrated yet again just how nasty its sense of humour could be. Orla treated herself to a kiss, a chaste one, on the card's flat pink front. 'I love you.' She enjoyed the words, enjoyed meaning them. 'I do, I love you Sim.'

The beauty spot mesmerised her, perfectly placed on the curve of his lip at the exact point where Sim's smile changed from innocent to knowing. That curve had incited Orla to devilment on countless occasions. It had brought her back to bed when she should have been jogging, made her miss the last episode of a favourite serial, had promised much and then delivered. And there it was, for all the world to see. Pimped out on the high street. *Those lips are mine, dammit!*

With a slug of wine that both anaesthetised and warmed

her, Orla reminded herself that Sim was just acting for the camera. 'But you meant it when you looked at me,' Orla told the valentine, 'I could always tell when you were faking it.'

Not that *he* could always tell when Orla faked it. 'You twit,' she said fondly to the valentine, laying it carefully on her lap. 'You really thought I enjoyed sitting like an eejit in red lingerie and saying I'd been very naughty and please would you slap my bum. Jaysus, Sim, I can tell you now that I am not the woman for a peep-hole bra. It dug right into me. And the crotchless panties struck me as hilarious. But you pleaded – don't deny it, you feckin' pleaded – and once I'd got over the embarrassment it was just like any other household chore.' She stroked the valentine, sighed. 'It wasn't the real thing. It wasn't like having you in my arms.' She choked a little at that. She capsized against romantic language these days. A platitudinous pop song could catch her unawares. 'Do you remember ...' Whispering now, this was personal. 'Do you remember how it was for us?'

Orla did. She had been unlocked by Sim. By her own lust for him. By his insouciant sexiness, his readiness to play. Being rugby tackled and ravished by Sim Quinn was a memory that would warm her all her life. Orla's sexuality was direct, wench-like, *fun*. She liked to jump on the bed, then jump on him. Before him, she'd acted and reacted, taken some pleasure with her lovers, but she'd never dived down to the depths, never luxuriated in passion.

It's pure with you, Sim had said, early on. He'd likened her to a milkmaid, called her that for a while. It became shorthand: *Any chance of my encountering a saucy little milkmaid on the way home from this pub?*

Every chance, koind sir.

'So, you see,' she told the valentine, 'the sexy underwear, dirty talking thing never did it for me.' She had been relieved when the Skype camera broke down. Orla had no dark streak, sexually. She tried not to wonder whether Sim had found his milkmaid too wholesome. 'I wore that nurse's uniform whenever you asked,' she admonished the valentine, huffily.

Across the road, Sim's eyebrow arched, daring, provocative. Orla swallowed. Her hand felt the soft jut of her tum. She cupped a breast, braless and heavy in the folds of her dressing gown. Orla put the valentine to her forehead as if it could cool her. The breathless denouement of tussling with herself beneath the covers wasn't worth the crushing sadness of the long night afterwards, when she had to admit that her lover was a phantom, his words of desire script-edited by herself.

Across the road, Sim's eye was unblinking. Orla wasn't reflected in it. She drew the curtains, ran a bath, lay in it too long. Damp, marshmallowy, her thighs peeped through the bubbles. She wondered if love was over for her.

Allowing another man to study her flesh, her familiar dips and gullies, felt fantastical. What if he was cruel? What if she felt mocked? What if he pounced, and she felt violated? And where would she find the energy for all the legwork of a new relationship, the two steps forward, one step back of sexual discovery? All those men out there, naked under their clothes, each one a different planet, requiring its own etiquettes and language. The thought exhausted her.

And what was Marek like under his black clothes? The leap to him was instinctive and shocking. Why jump from half an hour in a Polish café to sex?

Orla's soapy sponge slalomed down a calf.

It had been an odd half hour. Something else had gone on, parallel to two strangers sipping coffee and trading polite comments. Like spies, they had communicated beneath the surface. They had been working up a code.

Marek's declaration in the street remained undigested, usurped by the *Courtesan* poster. She'd been blank with shock and admiration at his candour and his courage, even if she did reel at the importance he attached to her on such short acquaintance. And then a few steps around the corner – *Pow!* As messages from beyond the grave go, that poster was a doozie.

Orla dropped the sponge, lay back, closed her eyes. Ma would say it was a sign.

Sim's journal

13 November 2011

Poor Maude. I've worked it out. It's obvious, once you realise. I want to help but . . . There shouldn't be a but. I'm a shit. I just don't have any energy left over from dealing with my own mess. Reece doesn't hold back. 'You're screwing up,' he says. 'Fucking idiot.' If O was here, none of this would be happening. So it's her fault, too, in a way. Poor Maude. Poor me. And although she doesn't know it yet, poor Fairy.

Chapter Ten

'That's a unique problem. I don't know what to say. And I always know what to say.'

'I can vouch for that, Ju. Remember that flasher by the swings? You said to him—'

'*I won't scream because I don't want to make a fuss over nothing.* I have fond memories of him and his little purple Hoover attachment.'

'I don't *want* a unique problem. I want nice obvious problems. But there's no agony aunt in the world who's had a letter that starts, *Please help me. There is a twenty foot high picture of my dead not-quite-fiancé staring in at my window.*'

'Ha! We shouldn't laugh.'

'Yes, we should. Please let's laugh.'

'Tell me about college.'

'It's good. Great, really. I have a lovely Russian girl and a fabbo African girl, Abena, who I'm just in love with. I have no idea why the Japanese guy is in my class. He speaks better English than what I do.'

'Teach him to say feck and eejit. God, Orla, if Sim was alive, I'd kill him.'

'I was so glad,' said Orla, interrupting herself to kiss Reece on the cheek, 'to get your text. It's been a horrible morning.

You're just what the doctor would order if he had any sense.' She settled into a plush Regency-style chair; stained and frayed, it seemed faintly surprised to find itself furnishing a tatty wine bar in Hammersmith. 'But what brings you to this neck of the woods? I thought you could only breathe the rarefied air of Belgravia or Soho or ... ooh, my knowledge of posh London has let me down.'

'Meeting. Money men. Just up the road in a re-purposed brewery.' Reece, his overcoat a tribute to the worsening weather, pushed a bowl of nuts towards her. 'Tell me about this horrible day, then.'

'Abena, she's one of my students, from Ghana, is having problems with her visa. I've been on the phone to various bastards who don't give a you-know-what, and I'm speeding on the adrenaline.' She crossed her fingers. 'Abena is not going home. Not while I'm here. I'll lie down in front of the aeroplane if I have to.'

'Arguing with officialdom has brought colour to your cheeks.'

Orla smiled, blushed. Was he flirting? She peeked at him over her glass. No, he wasn't. He was being gallant. He was being protective to his dead friend's almost-fiancé. She was relieved: she liked Reece in that role.

'Ooh, for me?' She took the stiff, creamy envelope he proffered.

'For you and a plus one. It's an invite to the Reece Dodds Artists annual party.'

'Hmm.' Orla read the invitation, felt the bumpy embossing of the logo, savoured the quality, went cold with dread. 'I don't know ...'

'No excuses accepted. It's the end of October, three weeks away, so plenty of time to get used to the idea. It's always enormous fun, if I do say so myself. All my clients, the great and the good, will be there. Sim fell in the pool last year.'

'He rang me when he got home, blind drunk, hooting. He'd wanted me to fly over for it.' A poignant tune reprised; something else she'd do too late to please him. 'Yes, of course I'll come.'

'Good.' Reece's shoulders dropped. 'Mission accomplished.'

'Is it dressy?'

'Yes, country mouse, it's dressy.' Reece was amused. 'It's *posh*, as you would say. My place in Sussex. Flunkeys everywhere. Teddibly teddibly lovely little nibbles to eat. Champagne flowing like, well, champagne. And when you finally collapse I put you up at the hotel up the road.'

'I'd better buy something new to wear.'

'You'd look lovely in a sack, but yes, do buy something new and wear your highest heels. And use your plus one. Why not?' Reece rebelled at the face she pulled. 'Sim would want you to.'

'Not you too.' Orla shook her head. 'Everybody says *Sim would want you to be happy*. Ma. Maude. Even Juno, my mate. But you and I know better. He'd rather I jump in the grave after him, sobbing and rending my garments. He'd like me in a black veil and matching chastity belt for the rest of my life.'

Early on in their relationship, Orla had detailed her few love affairs; the non-starter, the stately plodder, the out of character but kind of nice one-night stand in Ibiza – her entire love life dealt with in half an hour. *I was waiting for you*, she'd said. How he'd loved that.

She'd never found the right moment to ask about Sim's past and now he was gone, her imagination filled in the gaps, peopling his past with lithe-limbed actresses, older women, slutty fans, friends' sisters, foreign exchange students, cheeky-eyed waitresses, bendy teenagers, every female in his year at drama school plus his mother's friends.

'If Sim had his way I'd be in a convent.'

'It's up to you.' Reece spread his hands, palm up, as if she were a lost cause.

'I'll fly solo.'

'In that case, here's a thought.' Reece leaned in, thighs wide, leaning towards her over the low table. 'Bring the valentine.'

'As my plus one?'

'No,' said Reece with mock patience. 'Bring it and we'll … deal with it.'

'Read it?'

'We could do that. Read it together.'

'Well …' That felt exposing. Orla squirmed.

'It might be cleansing. You needn't show it to me but I could be there to support you while you read it, and then we get back to the party, have another glass of shampoo, maybe push each other in the pool.'

Such flippancy. The valentine was precious, not a boil to be lanced.

'Or,' Reece clattered on, 'we could burn it. Ritually. Let the ashes float into the sky. Take some of your sadness with them.'

'Will Anthea be there?'

'Well, yes.' Reece frowned. 'Is that a problem?'

'No. Why would it be?' Orla frowned back.

'No reason, just the way you asked.'

'To be honest, I was trying to steer you away from the card, Reece. I don't need another lecture.'

'But you do. You obviously do. Because you're a woman in the prime of her life whose primary relationship is with a pink envelope.'

'Were you this bolshy with Sim?'

'At all times.'

They both grinned. There was a sibling aspect to her relationship with Reece that was missing from Orla's relationship with her actual brothers. They were alike, Orla and Reece, on some level; they *got* each other. She understood why he found her devotion to the valentine unsettling and why he periodically tried to cure her of it. Flattered that he found time and energy to care, she was gentle with her rebuttal.

'I'll work through it in my own way and shush!' She leaned over, placed a finger on his lips. 'I won't necessarily read it. But for now, and for the foreseeable future, that card is Sim. So indulge me.'

The movie was famously complex. When Orla slid the disc into the DVD player she'd thought she was in the mood for time shifts and dystopian futures but half an hour in and she wished she'd opted for something starring Jennifer Aniston and an animal.

On the adjacent armchair, Maude had given up all pretence of following the plot and was emitting dainty snores, her eyelids shut and fluttering slightly as she dreamed old lady dreams.

Turning off the television, Orla fast-forwarded to Reece's

party. She'd agreed to go, she was going, but the scene playing out in her head was terrifying: a glittering do worthy of Jay Gatsby, every bejewelled guest beautiful, coiffed and sneering at the newcomer with no conversation and a high-street frock.

With Sim, parties had been easy. That lighthouse charm of his drew people to him, while she'd stayed slightly behind, clasping his hand, feeling cool and safe in his shadow.

Mundane girliness of the sort that manifests as yabbering about hair and nails and Brazilians bored Orla, yet she was presently hostage to a shrill voice that squealed at her daily. It said, *What'll I wear?* She missed Juno keenly: her friend had an eye for what worked, and could gently steer Orla away from the sudden enthusiasms that assailed her in Top Shop.

She thought that if she knew Anthea better, she could call her up and ask her advice. It would give the actress an opportunity to overcome her awkwardness about Sim's death. Orla glanced at the curtains that shut out Sim's coquettish smile. She stood and pulled them apart, unable to wreak even this petty disloyalty. 'Why can't you be my plus one?' she asked him, and promptly tumbled down a rabbit hole of memory.

He would always pick up on the third ring.

Orla's own voice, sugary with sleep. 'Ah, sweetie, there you are at last!' After several unanswered calls, this one from deep beneath her duvet would have been her last attempt before giving in to sleep.

'Yup.' Sim was tired, and taut. 'Here I am.' There'd been an abrupt noise, like a door banging shut.

'You just getting in?'

'Yup.'

Laughably wide of the mark, she'd imagined his London flat all teal and taupe, with lacquered surfaces and the purr of central heating. 'Are you worn out, poor thing?'

'Very.' A strained grunt told Orla he was tugging off his shoes. Trainers, probably.

'Put your dressing gown on. That's why I bought it. So you'd be cosy when you were tired and far from home.'

A loud yawn, like a lion after a three-course meal, had forced Orla to hold the mobile away from her ear. 'You *are* tired!'

'Sorry, Fairy. You calling to say goodnight? Too knackered for cybersex tonight, naughty knickers.'

'Darn it. Never mind.'

'Nothing to eat in this bloody kitchen,' grumbled Sim over the thud thud thud of cupboard doors opening and slamming.

'It's too late to get in,' sympathised Orla, switching off her bedside light, relishing his voice in the dark. 'How come they kept you so late?'

'Oh no you don't. No no no.'

Confused, Orla assumed Sim was talking to somebody else. But no, he was addressing her and his voice didn't sound tired any more.

'Don't start, Orla.'

'Eh?' She laughed uncertainly. She could tell he was serious. 'Start what?' She wasn't riled. She was too puzzled to be riled.

'I know that tone. *How come they kept you so late?*' His impersonation was high pitched.

'I don't sound like that.' Orla clung on to her good

humour. 'Look, sweetheart, you're worn out. Let's say good-night and—'

'No way.' Sim was fired up, as if they were already deep in a bitter altercation. 'We sort this out here and now.'

'Sort *what* out?' All ambrosial snooziness dissolved, Orla sat up.

'You know how long I've worked for this, waited for it. This is my big break.'

'Yes. Absolutely. We agree. So far so good. Now could you tell me what the feck we're arguing about?'

'We're arguing about the fact that I do *not* need to hear that bloody tone in your voice.'

They were getting somewhere. Kind of.

'What tone?' Orla switched the lamp back on; this was shaping up to be a long one.

'You know.' Sim was rudely impatient. 'The sarcastic one. Suspicious. Like you're laying traps to catch me out.'

'There was no tone. I asked why you were late. I was being *sympathetic*.' Orla slapped the bedclothes for emphasis.

'I know you better than that. I haven't forgotten the face you pulled when I told you who was playing the female lead.'

Opening her mouth to protest, Orla clamped it shut again. He was right about that. She turned her horse and trotted down from the moral high ground. 'Well, in my defence, Anthea whatsername has a bit of a reputation. And it was just a face. It was a joke, really. Remember jokes?'

'I bet you skimmed the script to see if I had a sex scene with her.'

Orla's conscience – diligent, puritanical little pest that it was – wouldn't let her say *Ha! That's where you're wrong!*

'Most women would do that.'

'I don't go out with most women.'

There was a pause. Orla willed herself to hold back, not to share with him how hard it was to read stage directions for her boyfriend and a famous *femme fatale* to lie naked together on a fur rug.

The heat had burned itself out when Sim spoke again. 'I'm pining, Orla,' he said. 'I'm far from home. And I miss my fairy.' He sighed. There was a squeak as he sank on to the bed. 'Plus I'm a prat, which doesn't help.'

'I'm pining too.' Orla welcomed the ceasefire. 'So much. But while we're on the subject . . . ' Time to risk a joke? 'Why *were* you so late, you filthy philanderer?'

Sim laughed wearily.

'Seriously, though, O, I *have* picked up on something when you ask about Ant. As if you suspect something's going on.'

'Rubbish.' Orla was vehement: this was not a fair cop. 'I know how bad you are, and I know how bad you aren't. I have nothing to fear from Anthea.'

'We have to nip this in the bud.'

He wasn't listening. 'But I told you—'

'No. Hear me out. When I make the leap to movies, and that's soon now, I'll be acting alongside world-famous sexy women. It comes with the territory. We can't have this kind of row every time I get my kecks off on camera.'

Useless now to point out that 'this kind of row' was entirely of his own making.

'Orla, you're either with me or against me.'

'Can you hear yourself? You're an actor, not a rebel leader

124

rallying the troops.' The silence scared her. 'Say something!' she bleated eventually.

'Are we cool? Can I get on with my job without worrying about you?'

This was, apparently, all about her. Orla swallowed. This dish could be served later, cold.

'We're cool, darling.'

The dish was never served.

Some west London wag had drawn a moustache under Sim's nose.

Chapter Eleven

Orla took in Bogna's laddered black tights and denim short-shorts.

'Aren't you cold?'

'Yes.' Bogna looked down at her legs, turned an ankle. 'But is worth it to be gorgeous.'

Bogna *was* gorgeous, in a hard-edged, flick-knife way that found expression in her Doc Martens and her eyeliner. 'We need women like you,' Orla told the sullen teen, 'to balance out the WAGs.'

'What's a WAG?' Maude looked up from where she knelt by the cookery corner.

Bogna explained. 'Silicone boobies, hair extensions, stripper shoes and rich boyfriend.'

'I believe my learned friend has covered the basics,' said Orla.

'Sounds ghastly,' said Maude with feeling, pressing a hand on one wobbling knee to raise herself.

Putting down her book, Orla rushed to Maude's side but was beaten to it by Bogna, who helped her to her feet.

'Thank you, dear.' Maude smiled sweetly at her newest, most unlikely slave. 'Gather up that pile of food titles, will you? Arrange them in the window. You're so good at that. Try and tempt all the huddled masses hurrying by in this horrid rainstorm to come in and plan a hearty meal for their poor little selves.' She turned to Orla. 'How's Abena? Any progress with her visa woes?'

Typical of her to remember the name. 'Not really. The UK Border Agency is slow, and the process is very complicated. She's working so hard in my class, not knowing if she'll still be here at Christmas. I'll keep you posted.'

'Do.' Maude put a hand on Orla's arm for a moment, then was off again, rearranging, titivating, stroking a book here and there as if they were pets.

'Bogna,' asked Orla tentatively as Bogna slammed down a Delia. 'Is bright blue still "in"?'

'In?' Bogna sounded contemptuous.

Oh Jaysus, I don't even know the trendy word for 'trendy'.

'I mean, um, fashionable?'

'Why do you ask?' Now Bogna sounded amused, which was far worse than contemptuous.

'I'm going to a party and I need a new dress and that electric blue colour was all over the place a while ago and so ...'

'Black,' said Bogna emphatically. 'Black. Short. Big hair.' She shrugged. 'Always.'

'Hmm.' There would no doubt be plenty of black at the party, much of it Armani. 'Maude ...'

'Yes?' Maude gave her her full attention, face angled like a flower leaning towards the sun.

'Would you pop round the corner with me later?'

'Why?' Maude looked suspicious; the flower drooped a little.

'To check out a blue dress in a shop that I pass on the way to the tube. It's sort of like this,' Orla drew a line across her pectorals, 'and down to here.' She tapped her thigh above her knee. 'I want to try it on, but there's nobody I can trust for an opinion.'

'I'm ancient, dear. My opinion is no use to you.' Maude pressed a button on the till and a drawer shot out. She peered into it, and sighed.

'You're not ancient, you're ageless. And you have style.'

The elders in Tobercree favoured manmade fabrics and elasticated waists but there was something poetic about Maude's outfits.

'I'm not the right person to ask. Bogna will help.'

'I don't have time,' said Bogna hurriedly, positioning a wooden spoon in the window display.

'I don't have anybody else to ask,' said Orla. In a world where even the village idiot has a hundred Facebook friends, this felt a shameful thing to admit. 'It's two minutes' walk, tops.' She shadowed Maude as she crossed the shop. 'Please?'

'No!' Maude wheeled and they almost bumped noses. 'If you like the dress, buy it. If you don't, don't.' Speeding towards the back room, she threw a belated 'dear' over her shoulder, too late to soften the impact of her tone.

'Who blew raspberry up her fanny?' asked Bogna.

'Bogna, that's not a real expression.'

'Is now,' said Bogna.

'*It* is now.'

'Exactly.'

Today should be my *turn to have raspberry up* my *fanny,* thought Orla, borrowing Bogna's sulkiness. Nobody had grasped the significance of the date.

When Maude returned, her habitual good humour had

been restored. She made tea for everybody and read aloud from T. S. Eliot and Tina Fey, one of her 'Keep Out' signs hammered firmly over the incident.

Upstairs, alone, Orla lay on the sofa, her mind a blank, curtains drawn against the giant Sim. A knock on her door brought her upright, as if hinged at the waist.

'Come in!' she shouted, then jumped to her feet as Marek entered.

'Oh,' she said, curling her stockinged toes. 'I assumed it was ... I didn't hear the front door.'

'I came to the shop,' explained Marek. He stood at the threshold, unsure of his welcome. 'Maude said to come up, but if you are ... '

'Nope. I'm not.' Orla shrugged, aware that she was being a bit bristly and rude but unable to help it. He was so tall and his clothes were so dark. Marek was a big male slab in her chintzy bower.

'I want you to come to dinner tonight,' said Marek, adding, 'with me.'

'Really?' Orla wondered why the poor man bothered. She was dull. She was heartbroken. All her manners had atrophied. Couldn't he see she was of no earthly use to him?

'Really.' When Marek was amused, two flat dimples puckered his cheeks.

'Well then. Yes.' Dragging up some grace from somewhere, Orla threw him a 'Thanks, that'll be nice.'

It would get her through the evening, jostle her past the dread hour.

'Good.' Marek backed out of the door.

'On one condition,' Orla hastened.

He looked at her questioningly, patiently, like a dutiful father visiting a child in a Wendy house.

'This isn't ... romantic, OK? It can't be a date. Because I'm not dateable, Marek. I know what you said, and it was lovely, and I'm flattered, but I'm not the real deal. I'm not all there any more. I'm not worth the effort. This isn't, by the way, a plea for a compliment. I really am not worth the effort.'

'It's dinner. Two people. A table. Some food. Dates, anyway, are what Bogna has with those spotty sods who turn up for her. But we'll be just a man taking a woman to dinner.' He bowed his head, double-checking. 'That's acceptable to you?'

'Absolutely.'

'I'll come back at eight, in a cab.'

'You're picking me up?'

'Of course.' Marek was surprised by her surprise. 'That's too early?'

'That's perfect.' By 9 p.m., when people all over the country were settling down to watch the first episode of *The Courtesan*, Orla would be eating restaurant food and negotiating silences with Marek.

There were no silences. Little about the evening panned out the way Orla expected.

The restaurant was sleek, hushed, with heavy cutlery and unimpeachably white linens. A contrast to the café, and a contrast to Orla's comfortable cords.

In black again, Marek fitted in nicely. His looks were democratic, altering to his surroundings. Tonight the dark swoop of hair was glamorous, the long slender nose reminiscent of Nureyev. Orla noticed for the first time how full his lower lip was, how it pouted in repose. Perhaps he caught her staring; he smiled, and was an eleven-year-old. 'Wine?'

'Please.'

Marek read the list, pondered it. He had a brief conversation with the sommelier before tasting the wine and sending the first bottle back. Firm, polite, sure.

'So,' he said after they'd ordered, after they'd covered the weather, her week at work, Bogna's performance at Maude's Books. 'Let me tell you some things.'

A covert look at her watch told Orla that it was ten minutes to *The Courtesan*. In Tobercree the Cassidys were gathered *en masse*. Juno was taping it. Lucy ... with a start, Orla realised she had no idea what Lucy was doing on this momentous evening. Beyond a curt acknowledgement of the Longines watch, Orla had heard nothing. Even though any interaction with the Quinns left her feeling two inches tall, Orla had called and left a message, and even sent a postcard. Orla felt that Sim wouldn't have wanted them to be so perfectly estranged. *Talk, Marek!* she willed him.

It was as if he heard her thoughts.

'So,' he said again, hands folded on the table. 'You should know about me. You should know that I am sane, solvent.' He paused, allowing the waiter to set down their food. 'I'm forty-one. I have all my teeth.' He bared his teeth, white, strong, like a healthy animal's. 'I own a company that does well and so I have a house in Chelsea and another in Skwierzyna near my family and another in Devon because it's beautiful there. I like to ride horses.'

131

Orla could imagine him on a horse. The image prompted a sensation, deep inside, like a door swinging open. She coughed, swigged some wine, and the door thudded obediently shut.

'I like to walk but not in town. I work too much. I need new clothes but shopping bores me. My parents are both deceased now.' Marek made an unhurried, discreet sign of the cross. 'I support my stepmother, Bogna's mother. And as you know I do my best with Bogna but I still worry that she'll end up a stripper. I don't normally talk this much but I'm not normally as dull as I was the last time we met, either. You make me a little nervous and I'm not used to that. I like it when you blush like that, by the way. I'm allergic to coriander. I'm bloody good at table tennis. I have a scar across my back from the time I fell off a wall when I was fourteen and landed in barbed wire. I used to smoke but now I don't. I drink sometimes; I get drunk sometimes. I never go to the gym and I secretly dislike people who do. I have three friends, the rest are acquaintances. My friends can expect a lot from me. I expect a lot from them, but mainly I expect them to make me laugh and not let me down. I make snap decisions. I can be arrogant and if that happens please hit me on the nose with a rolled-up newspaper. That's what my mother used to threaten me with, because it worked on our dog. And I am married.'

'And you're what?' Orla, grateful for the flood of information and the way it washed away the minutes, sat up straighter.

'I married very young,' said Marek carefully, holding her gaze. 'You and I have something in common, Orla. Perhaps that's why I fool myself I know you better than I actually do. She died, you see.'

'I'm so sorry.' Orla knew it didn't help. 'That's terrible.'

'It was a long time ago. Fourteen years. Bogna – good God, this never occurs to me – Bogna was only five.'

Orla knew time was immaterial. 'Were you living over here?'

'Yes. I had come over first, then Aga joined me when we could afford it. I really only came to England because of her. She wanted a different sort of life. Better. I came here to . . .' Marek smiled, with little mirth. 'To make my fortune. A Polish Dick Whittington.'

'Am I being condescending if I comment on how good your English is?'

'Yes, you are,' said Marek, and he laughed with her. 'But so it should be: I've been in this country for what feels like a hundred years. Poland was very different back then, just emerging from the Soviet era. It was grey, like porridge. I remind my sister of that sometimes, how lucky she is. When I was her age we had nothing.'

'Bet she loves that speech.'

Marek looked to the ceiling. 'She's not my biggest fan. I'm the only person in the whole world who says no to her.'

'Sounds to me like you're very good to her.'

'Sure. But that's an adult opinion. Bogna still sees everything through the eyes of a twelve-year-old. I want. I get. Gimme gimme gimme.'

Marek looked down at his plate for a while before looking up at Orla.

'My wife, Aga, was this type. She was not happy with her life. She wanted *things*. But when we looked around us in Skwierzyna there was no way to improve our situation, and accumulate these modern luxuries. We were twenty. Imagine. Twenty and married.' Marek shook his head, as if to dislodge a vision of his younger, naive self.

'I gave up my law degree. My father was furious. I came over here. I'm not one of the recent influx,' he said, underlining this with a wave of his butter knife. 'At first I was a unicorn, the only one of my kind. There were no kabanos for sale in Sainsbury's, no Polish clubs. Just the one café I took you to in Ladbroke Grove. No internet either: I spoke to my wife once a week, from a payphone in the hall outside my bedsit. I worked on building sites, I knocked down walls, I learned how to build extensions – learned how much the British love extensions – and I sent every penny home. It was a tough time, and I would have loved to have the support of the kind of Polish network we have now. So, teacher lady, that's why my accent is good. Because there was no option. I had to fit in. I needed camouflage. And once I hit my stride,' Marek raised a charcoal eyebrow to acknowledge his easy use of colloquialism, 'I discovered that I love this city. It's …' Marek grasped for a word, held out his arms as if holding a beach ball. 'It's elastic! There's room for anything and everyone. Exploring it kept me sane, because it was a while before I made friends. My focus was my wife, bringing her over. Because, you know, I was crazy about her and I am a romantic man.'

He paused, looked intently at Orla.

She coughed, and fussed with her side salad. This was the longest Marek had spoken since she'd met him; her pasta was neglected.

'Sorry. Where was I? I save. I buy a little flat. Tiny. My wife comes over. We buy a bigger flat. We buy a house. We try for a baby. No baby.' Marek's matter of fact words were undermined by his jaw, which clenched. 'I work harder, longer. The housing boom is wind in my sails. Aga discovers more and more things that we need. That becomes what we talk about. Things. Never how we feel.'

'It's easily done.'

'No, it's not.' Marek was adamant. 'We should have fought it. We should have taken more notice. I've had a long time, too long, to go back over those years in my mind, and, seen from this distance, our marriage was strangely old-fashioned. I was a bread-winner. Aga was a housewife.' Marek held his fork like a caveman's club. He put the fork down, interlaced his fingers to illustrate what they were not. 'We weren't partners. We had *roles*, instead of personalities. I still wake up at night and regret I didn't say, *let's get away, just you and me, somewhere windswept where there are no shops and no telephones*. Even when we *escaped* it was to villas with private pools. We choked on luxury.'

Marek sighed.

'We'd had another of our stupid rows, that day. Oh, by the way, this is something you should know about me. I have a temper. I am a passionate man.'

The flutter in her tummy was unexpected. Orla hated arguments.

'I'll remember that.'

'I rarely give in to it, and it's over very quick, but every now and then, *kaboom!*' Marek mimed a mushroom cloud, nudged the sommelier, apologised. He and Orla shared a conspiratorial smile, before he returned to his subject and his face became sombre.

'I yelled at Aga, that morning. She yelled back. We hurt each other where before we would have held back. Yet neither of us would walk out on the marriage.'

'There was still some love there,' suggested Orla.

'That's not the reason. We were far from home and clinging together. We didn't want to let our families down, but I didn't look forward to seeing her and I could feel her disappointment in me. Any fool could sense the lack of happiness in our house.'

'That's so sad.'

'And then she's gone. Cardiac arrhythmia. I won't go into it but basically, the rhythm of her heart was interrupted and Aga was snuffed out. I found her. She'd been on the floor of our new conservatory all day. She was so proud of that conservatory.'

The simple way Marek presented such heartbreaking details touched something in Orla, like a finger plucking at a harp.

'Sim, my boyfriend, he died suddenly too. It's hard, isn't it?'

She was sick of the pain in the world. The loss.

'Very. But, Orla, in other ways my loss is unlike yours.'

'How?'

'I didn't love Aga.'

There it was again, that searing frankness. Orla frowned, sorry for the dead woman who inspired such an epitaph. 'What, not even a little?'

'Not like I should have. Not like I'm capable of. We were bitter, like animals chained together in a cage.' Marek waited a moment before saying, 'If Aga was still here, we wouldn't be together.'

Ouch. Was this insistence on calling a spade a spade an east European trait, wondered Orla, or simply Marek. 'How can you know that?'

'Because I am clear-eyed.'

'If Sim was alive we'd be together.' *We'd be married, entwined in our jimjams on the sofa, watching him on TV.*

'I envy you.'

'Really, don't.' Orla snorted caustically.

'That give and take, that companionship, I've always wanted it. I've found other things – desire, good times – but there's no substitute.'

'Like marge and butter. I Can't Believe it's not Love.'

'Sorry?' Marek floundered.

'You know, the spread? It doesn't matter.' Sim would have got that. 'I'm being glib. Ignore me. I wasn't brought up to talk about emotions. Even though I'm Irish I have a stiff upper lip.'

'You don't have to be English to have one of those.' Marek broke a bread roll freckled with caraway seeds. 'Poles have a stiff upper body. Eat, Orla, eat,' he exhorted. 'I don't say any of this to depress you, or to ruin our – whatever this is, not a date, definitely not that.'

'You haven't depressed me.' The bogeyman Death was a regular guest at Orla's table. 'It's all part of life.' She intuited why Marek had gone into such detail. 'It brings people closer, talking about the big stuff. Life. Death.'

'Yes!' Marek seized on that, glad to be understood. 'Since Aga's death I only bother with the real things. I try to be honest. I try to connect. When I want to,' he added.

Ignoring the compliment, Orla said, 'It's a way of honouring her, I suppose. Of taking something, some little thing, that's positive from her death.'

'Perhaps.' Marek looked above her head. 'Yes.'

'After all,' said Orla, 'we do have to recover, somehow.'

'Yes. We recover because we have to.' Marek's raisin-dark eyes were sombre. 'It has hardened me. I'm a different person. I expect less. I hope it doesn't do the same to you.'

'I think it already has.'

'Fight it. You don't want to be like me. Forty, scarred. I only embark on relationships that have an obvious fault so that I won't be hurt when they inevitably finish.' Marek slid to a halt. 'That would make the worst ever profile on a dating site.'

Glad of the ray of light, Orla laughed. 'GSOH, likes long walks and log fires goes down better.'

'I've always hoped I'll find somebody I want to be nice to. Somebody I can be myself with. Spoil a bit. Know.' He considered that word. 'Yes. *Know.*'

His gaze was frank. Marek was a clean arrow of a man and when he looked at Orla she felt examined, but gently, as if her frailties would be excused.

It was ten o'clock.

The Courtesan was over.

Orla held her watch up to the valentine. 'See? Just gone eleven. Not late at all.' She unwound her scarf. It was Marek's, she realised. She'd meant to return it. Tugging off her jacket, she toppled to the sofa like a felled tree. 'You'd have approved of the restaurant,' she told the card. 'Classy. And there was squid on the menu. You'd have ordered the squid, wouldn't you, darling?' She smiled at the pink shape on the mantelpiece; she knew it so well. 'No, it wasn't a date. No need to scowl. Worry lines, Sim, worry lines – so very ageing! I made it clear it was just a friendly meal and Marek was cool with that.'

No need, thought Orla, feeling her lips tentatively with her fingertips, to blab about what happened on the doorstep. He'd lowered his head, she'd panicked, she'd dropped the key, she'd bent to retrieve it, he bent with her, she'd bumped her head on his chin as she straightened. They'd giggled. He'd backed away, hands in pockets, head dipped, eyes on her. 'Goodnight, Irish,' he'd said, the words heavy with reluctance.

'Goodnight!' she'd said, the word bright with relief.

Chapter Twelve

'Orla? It's Ma. Can you talk?'

'Howaya Ma?'

'Grand. Grand. Apart from me hip. I'm going all clicky. You'd think I have a machine gun in me knickers when I get off me armchair.'

'That bloody hip. Is Deirdre running you to Tesco like she promised?'

'Yes. She's a good girl.'

'Girl?'

'You're all girls to me even if you live to be a hundred. So. Anyroad. We watched it.'

'It? Oh ... And?'

'Janey Mac, Sim was magnificent. You'd swear he was French. And the gear on him! Satin. Frills. You couldn't see him for lace. But oh he's a bad lot, Orla. A right sod. Nearly killed a poor servant girl because she dropped his claret. How did he remember all them lines?'

'I'm glad you liked it. It's all over the papers here. Seems like the whole country sat down to watch it. By the time it was over, Sim was a star, just like he wanted – just like he knew he would be. Did you hear he's up for an award? Best newcomer. Posthumously. Lucy was interviewed in the *Daily Mail*.'

'Let's hope she didn't burp gin all over the journalist. I'll watch the next episode, but Jaysus, it's hard. I had a little cry on me own, like, in the kitchen afterwards. What did you do while it was on, musha?'

'I went out to dinner with a friend.'

'Oh. Reece?'

'No, um, yes. Reece.'

'You haven't even noticed, have you?'

'Noticed what, Ma?'

'Me cunning plan. I'm employing reverse psychology. I haven't asked you if you're coming back for Christmas for at least three weeks and you haven't even bloody noticed.'

'Sorry, Ma.'

'If I had a euro for every time my childer said "sorry Ma" I'd have enough for a diamond hat by now. So.'

'Am I coming home for Christmas?'

'Yes.'

'I don't know.'

'*She doesn't know*. Charming. And what about New Year? You can't miss me big party. It's tradition.'

'I'm not a fan of New Year, Ma.'

'Since when?'

'Since ... I'm just not, Ma.'

'Still looking for that diary?'

'It's somewhere. It'll find its way back to me.'

'Careful about reading it, love. You know what they say about eavesdroppers.'

'I know. They never hear good of themselves.'

A celebration was called for. Not because of the ecstatic *Courtesan* reviews, but because of the expression on Abena's face when she walked into the chilly classroom with its high banks of Victorian windows and announced, 'I can stay! I can stay in this wonderful country!'

Orla took everybody, all eighteen of her global tribe, out for coffee and cake. 'It's role play,' she told them (and herself). 'We're role-playing people who are thrilled about their friend's happiness.'

'Now all I need,' said Abena, leaning in close and confidentially, so that the fabric elaborately knotted about her head touched Orla's fringe, 'is a man to love.' She wiggled her shoulders. 'I am ready for him!'

'Plenty of men in London,' murmured Orla, sipping her latte.

'Yes, but I don't want just man.' Abena scowled. 'I don't want lazy, bloody rude type. I want a special fellow.'

'Me too.' Javier, across the table, overheard. His Spanish accent was deep and guttural. 'I want *real* man. You know what I mean?'

From the cheers and snorts it seemed that everybody did.

Orla, still finding her way as teacher to a crowd of adults, didn't know whether to join in or hold back. Javier jabbed a finger at her and gave her no choice, demanding, 'Orla, do you have a lover?'

To a backdrop of delighted whoops – and Abena's outraged, 'Javier, you are cheeky boy!' – Orla felt herself blush. The truth would upend a bucket of freezing water over the party. ('My lover is dead' is such a vibe-killer.)

'I was taken out to dinner a week ago. By a man. Not lazy, Abena, nor bloody rude. There are some decent men in London if you look hard enough.'

'Ooh,' said Sanae, a doll-faced Japanese girl whose penchant for long socks baffled Orla. 'Does he call you all day? Does he beg for next date?'

'Well, no, actually.' Orla shrugged at their disappointment. 'Sorry, but he doesn't.'

'I think,' said Abena, chin up, regarding Orla with grave disapproval, 'you do not enc ... enc ...'

'Encourage?'

'Yes. You do not encourage the gentleman.' Abena lowered her fleshy chin, clamped her round brown eyes on Orla's. 'Sometimes I think you are like a nun. What are you saving it for?' She paused for effect. 'The worms?'

It was obvious, really. The food laid out on Maude's coffee table, the candles lit on the mantel, the wafting Cole Porter, was all a ploy to usher Orla painlessly past episode two of *The Courtesan*. Maude claimed it was spontaneous, but Orla had heard the phone call to Sheraz specifying *nice olives please, big fat ones, proper hummus, pitta bread, decent tzatziki*.

'I like a themed meal as much as the next woman,' said Orla, raising herself from a white cushion on the floor. 'But Jaysus, Maude, I can't take another sip of that retsina.' Lips puckering, she crossed to the fridge for the cold bottle of white wine she'd brought.

'Bogna made me smile today,' said Maude, legs crossed on the floor, defying Orla's notions of what the older generation should be able to achieve with their nether limbs. 'She said to me, *what my brother wants, my brother gets*.' Maude let out a tinkling, synthetic laugh.

'How was that funny?' asked Orla. 'Could you possibly be angling, Ms Maude Roxby-Littleton?'

143

'Yes!' said Maude emphatically, the tinkling laugh curtailed. 'What happened last Saturday? You've been silent on the subject, Orla. It's very cruel of you.'

Just like Ma, thought Orla. *One's posh, the other's as Irish as a pint of Guinness, but they both live vicariously through me.*

'I've been quiet because there's nothing to tell.'

'Oh I *hate* it when you do that!' Maude slapped down her pitta bread and crossed her arms petulantly. 'Why must you downplay everything, as if you're not made of the same flesh and blood as the rest of us? Good lord, that man puts his balls on the line coming to your door, humbling himself in front of his sister and me – and you can tell it doesn't come easy to a proud specimen like Marek – and you still insist it was just a meal.'

'Maude, you know why I can't get—'

'No, no, let's not make this about dear Sim.' Maude took up the pitta again and smeared it with garlicky goo. 'At some point, my precious girl, you have to stop making him the centre of everything.'

'A little soon for that, no?' muttered Orla, not liking the turn the conversation had taken.

'I don't think so,' said Maude. 'Women who put men at the centre of their existence often find it's a mistake.'

'I've never done that. Ever. If anything I didn't make Sim important enough.'

'Is that how you see your relationship with Sim?' Maude sounded intrigued.

Orla felt a surge of empathy for butterflies she'd seen impaled on collectors' pins. 'You sound as if you disagree.'

Maude hesitated. 'This is none of my business,' she said,

with an air of finality. 'Please, dear, forgive me. You needn't talk about Marek if you don't want to.'

'*Everything* is your business.' Orla surveyed the feast in front of her, every morsel of it evidence of Maude's care and sensitivity. 'There truly is nothing to tell. It was what it was.'

It was a source of guilt, and a source of pleasure. It was vivid, a gemstone in her pocket. After prolonged prodding from Juno, Orla had finally confessed that yes, she found Marek attractive and not just physically; he was an elegant, intriguing thing both forthright and veiled. There was much more to learn about Marek.

'I've met him a couple of years too soon,' she'd told Juno. 'The timing is wrong.' Orla had agreed with Juno that yes, sure, the timing is *always* wrong, but disagreed that she should encourage him.

'See where this leads.' It could lead nowhere, because Orla wouldn't let it. Emotionally speaking, she'd backed into a cul-de-sac.

'Never mind *my* gentleman followers, Maude,' said Orla, arch. 'What about George? Hmm?'

'You and Bogna are very very naughty.' Maude's long, thin, faded pink mouth was tight with the effort not to smile. 'The poor chap is just a customer.'

'Customer, my arse.'

En route to Sheraz's that afternoon, Orla had been ambushed by Bogna and manhandled out to the back room. Twirling Orla around to look back at the shop through the bead curtain, Bogna had hissed, 'Look!'

In the shop an old man loitered by the poetry and a

schoolboy pored over an aged *Beano* annual, drinking a can of Coke.

'Him!' Bogna jabbed a finger at the elderly man. 'Maude's stud!'

The stud wore a raincoat over tweed trousers and an old pair of shoes so polished they shone. Balding, colourless, with pince-nez teetering on the bridge of his nose, he wasn't reading the book he held, Orla knew, but was peering over the top of it at Maude.

'Explain.'

'He comes in every Saturday. Always buys a book. And always stares.'

'At Maude?'

'Yes. Like sheep. *Look!*' Bogna's appetite for scandal, and her bony-fingered prodding, reminded Orla of her female relatives back home.

'I'm looking,' she assured Bogna, sidling away from her. 'He's agog.'

'What is gog?'

'He's entranced. Can't stop looking at her.'

'He is mad for it.'

'As mad as a pensioner can be for it, I guess. How does Maude react to him?'

'Watch. He's going over!' Bogna jumped up and down, her customary nonchalance forgotten. 'Grab her, man!' she hissed. 'Kiss her!'

Orla strained to hear the conversation. Stud asked the price of his weathered poetry omnibus; Maude replied that it was eight pounds but as a regular he could take it for six. The customer beamed, paid up, hesitated, turned away with his paper bag full of poetry, turned back again, opened his mouth, closed it, left hurriedly.

'He's got it bad,' crowed Bogna, delighted. 'He's called George.'

'Does Maude know she has an admirer?'

'Look at her face.'

A self-satisfied smile broke Maude's customary serene expression.

She knew.

Sim's journal

11 February 2012

When I was three, so the family story goes, I put my hand in the fire. 'I wanted to see what it felt like, Mummy.' Head hurts. Hair hurts. Ego hurts. Driver had to hammer on front door to wake me this morning. Maude not quite so charming as usual when woken at 5 a.m. Late to the location shoot. Pretty little make-up girl (she's <u>dee-lish</u>) bemoaned the circles under my eyes.

'Richard Burton boozed,' I reminded Reece. 'Oliver Reed. Peter O'Toole.'

'You are not Richard fucking Burton,' he said.

I've chosen the valentine card. Perfect image. I'm drafting and redrafting the words. I've got to get it just right. O tells me I'm 'good' at cards but the significance of this one is paralysing me.

Ant is worrying me. She's being odd. Around the crew I can trust her to be discreet but today she was mouthing off, saying, 'I can't wait to meet your Orla. We'll have SO MUCH to talk about,' all sarky. I grabbed her wrist. Left a mark. The pretty make-up girl had to cover it up.

Fairy, Fairy, trust me on this. Trust me to know what's right for us.

Give me a heartfelt YES right from your toes.

I'm not three any more but I can't keep my hand out of the fire. At least when you burn yourself you know you're alive.

Chapter Thirteen

'Tonight's the night.'

The valentine had watched Orla go through the rituals of hair washing and styling, anointing with body lotion, the business of eyelash curling. Buffed, sheened, primped, Orla put her arms into the blue dress, slid it over her head, snaked the zip up her side.

'Will I do?' Orla waited for the card's response then thanked it. She was generally uneasy with compliments, distrusting them, but Orla knew she looked striking. She'd *made an effort*, as her Ma constantly exhorted her to. The dress fell to mid-thigh, showing an expanse of leg Orla didn't normally share with the world. Her hair had behaved and lay straight and heavy and shining around her discreetly made-up face.

Sim would have stood in front of the door. He would have told her she wasn't going anywhere. He would have kissed her lipstick off and they would have been late for Reece's party.

The valentine was a poor substitute.

Lipstick. Phone. Small mirror. Fresh breath spray. Keys. They followed each other into the evening bag, another new purchase. Beaded silk, it drooped like pretty chain mail. A larger tapestry bag, borrowed from Maude, stood packed and patient by the door. 'Toothbrush!' exlaimed Orla, bolting for the bathroom and sucking the bristles dry before tucking it into her washbag.

Knees together, Orla sat on the edge of her bed, waiting, careful of her alien glossy self, nervous to move too suddenly in case her eyelashes drooped or her fringe collapsed. The valentine waited with her, on her lap.

'No falling in the swimming pool this time, got it?'

The doorbell propelled her off the bed, sent her skittering around the room, looking in the mirror before grabbing the invitation and cramming it and the card into the small bag.

New shoes turned her dash to the sitting room windows into a hobble. Orla pushed aside the lace curtain and looked down into the dark street. Beneath the towering picture of Sim (now with graffiti genitalia) a long-nosed car crouched at the kerb. On the pavement, Marek stood looking up at the window. He saw her and smiled.

Snatching up the overnight case and shouting a goodbye up the stairs to Maude (who replied, 'Do everything I wouldn't do!'), Orla hurried down to the front door, bandy with the effort of keeping her heels under control. She paused and held the bag to her face. The beads were cold on her lips. 'He's not really my plus one,' she whispered. 'You are.'

Sim's journal

13 February 2012

She'll open it in about ten hours. I feel like death. Nerves? Or the brandy I had after dinner? Midnight already. Time flies when you're shitting yourself. Must sleep and stop fretting about tomorrow. I have plenty of tomorrows and after this particular one, the others will have the rosy glow of a fresh start.

Floor lanterns lit their path over the gravel to a rambling shingled house, each window amber, radiating civilised good times. Orla suddenly despised her outfit, realising too late the bag didn't match. The valentine, inside the bag, made itself as heavy as lead. Awkwardly, she took Marek's elbow, then dropped it as if it were too hot to handle. The valentine would not sanction elbow holding.

Fairy lights peeped out of the box hedges standing to attention around the door. The scene was picture perfect. Sim would have loved it. He'd have been champing at the bit. Looking up at Marek she saw a smooth mask take possession of his features, a level, almost corporate stare that hinted this was more of an ordeal than a pleasure. Then he felt her gaze, met it, and grinned, shunting his eyes into crescents.

The door opened before Marek's hand reached the bell pull, and they entered a wide hall that managed to incorporate a suit of armour, a Sam Taylor-Wood photograph of a weeping Daniel Craig, a venerable oak staircase and quite a few famous people. *It's dreamlike,* thought Orla, *to recognise people you've never met.* A good dream or a nightmare she had yet to decide, as she held up her chin, a sign of insecurity that Sim would have recognised and answered with a squeeze of her hand – or, possibly, her buttocks: parties brought out the devil in him.

Orla exchanged a furtive look with Marek as a young actress, more famed for her beauty than her talent, strolled down the stairs, glass in hand. A singer Orla had once queued to see trotted past, chirruping, 'Off to the loo!' over her shoulder to a languid man who fronted a prestigious BBC4 series on the renaissance.

'It's like,' Orla whispered to Marek, as they weaved through the scrum towards a tray of champagne, 'those dreams when you meet the Queen and you've got no knickers on.'

Marek's expression revealed that he never had such dreams.

Debonair in a dinner jacket, foxy cap of hair glinting, Reece descended on them and twirled Orla out of her coat, handing it to an anonymous serf who manifested at just the right moment. 'You've made my night,' he said in an undertone before greeting Marek. Orla detected the faintest trace of reserve as he said, 'I'm so glad she used her plus one. She needs looking after.'

'Does she?' The comment seemed to amuse Marek as much as it irked Orla.

'Come on, chaps.' Reece ignored the question and turned, his hand on Orla's back to guide them through ceiling-height double doors. 'Let's throw you in at the deep end.'

The party pulsed with conversation so animated it verged on the manic. Orla felt an adrenaline rush, as if she were standing on tiptoe before a bungee jump. The room was generous in its proportions and venerable in its decoration (Louis XIV flirting with Andy Warhol against Chinese papered walls), and lit by countless tea lights and candles: Orla pitied whoever had stooped and stretched to light them all.

'Did you bring it?' Reece murmured as they followed the magic path that opened up for them through the guests.

Orla opened her bag to afford him a peek of pink.

'So, you really are ready?' Reece's eyes seemed sad.

'I am. I turned a corner out of the blue.'

'Is it to do with ...' Reece inclined his head minutely in the direction of Marek, who was tailing them. 'I couldn't believe my ears when you said you were bringing somebody.'

'It's nothing to do with him.' Orla saw Reece didn't believe her and let it lie: she didn't entirely believe herself. 'It's to do with me.'

'Here's a cosy perch to people-watch.'

Reece motioned to a high-backed velvet chair the colour of rotten plums, seating himself on the arm when Orla sat down. Marek stood to one side, weighing Reece up with a sidelong glance.

'Now,' he said discreetly, bending his head to Orla's, 'what's the plan? I hope, darling, you've decided against reading it.'

Orla nodded.

'May I be there? In case you need me? I don't want you facing it alone.'

Reece seemed intent on disappearing Marek. 'OK,' nodded Orla. 'I'd like that.'

'It's a privilege. And Sim would want me to make sure you were in one piece afterwards. Shall we say in one hour? Do it with some ceremony?'

'Sure. Is Ant here?' Orla couldn't talk of Sim tonight. She was far too brittle, far too riddled with doubts about every aspect of this evening.

'She's somewhere, getting off with the help, feeling up a producer. I'm sure she'll break from the undergrowth at some point.'

Reece must surely be tipsy to talk like that. Orla took a

closer look at his brilliantly cold eyes and reconsidered: perhaps he was on something. She was vague about what that might be – she was the kind of woman who took Calpol with misgivings – but she'd endured enough veiled references to 'naughtiness' and suchlike from Sim to intuit that there had been some drug-taking during his last months. She'd always despaired of his weakness, noting his feigned nonchalance when Charlie's arrival was whispered at parties. She also noted his animation, his altered pupils, his energetic chattiness and his maddening sniffs soon after. Orla had allowed him this subterfuge, but alarm bells had insistently rung about him running wild in the fleshpots of London without her.

'What's your strategy?' asked Reece, baffling her. 'I mean, do you want me to introduce you around? I can get you to some key people, let them know you're Sim's lady. Even though he's not here, everybody's talking about him. He's the biggest star at this party, which is, as we well know, just how he'd want it.'

'Oh no, no, don't introduce me to feckin' *key people!*' Orla found it funny that Reece didn't find it funny: this was where they diverged. He was an agent to his fingertips and she was, well, she was a *civilian*, as Sim called non-actors. 'Just let me prowl around incognito.'

'Food,' snarled a deep voice. Marek's white fingers found Orla's and tugged her up from the velvet throne. 'There,' he pointed to a long table obliterated by dainty nibbles and nuggets arranged on platters and stands like an edible Caravaggio, 'I'm starving.' He inclined his head to Reece with a curt, curiously Ruritanian nod. 'Excuse us.'

'Remember!' called Reece, after them. 'Midnight. Find me.'

'Marek!' Orla shook her hand free. 'That was our host.'

'He's not my type.'

'Reece has been a saint to me.' Orla, nearing the buffet and feeling her spirits lift a little at the sight of all those carbohydrates, admitted, 'Although, I have to say, he was chilly with you for some reason.'

'Not chilly. Rude.'

'OK, rude. I don't know, perhaps, you know, Sim's best mate and everything, he's feeling ... conflicted.'

'You're not being unfaithful. Sim isn't here. I am,' said Marek, a little too passionately for a man standing over a row of quiches.

But Orla's conscience felt differently. It told her she was being unfaithful and that love doesn't end with a piffling thing like death. She had lost her appetite. Was she the only romantic left on earth?

'It's boiling in here. Can we just go ...' Orla looked longingly at the plate-glass extension that ran the width of the house, peeled back to reveal a purple night hanging over the garden.

'Sure.' Marek turned regretfully away from the food. 'You know, you shouldn't get between a Polish man and his dinner,' he grumbled. 'I'm very tetchy if I'm not fed regularly.'

'They're just the canapés. According to the invite there's a hog roast. That'll be outside, surely.'

Marek picked up the pace, his hand on the back of her neck. Orla sped up too, to escape the hand. Its casual pressure had made her skin fizz. Outside on the stone terrace, the roast hog, with its primitive, stimulating aroma, was the belle of the ball, but Orla barely nibbled at the squashy roll Marek fetched for her.

'I'll have it – if you don't . . . ' he said, hopefully.

'I don't.' She handed it over as they settled down on a wrought iron bench a little distance from the house.

'I was very surprised by your call,' Marek despatched the pork roll in a three bites.

'I needed a plus one,' Orla said, shrugging.

'All these compliments. How does my ego cope around you?'

Checking to make sure he was joking – the pout was set to maximum – Orla thudded her palm to her forehead. 'I'm sorry, Marek. That was so bad mannered.'

She remembered the car journey, his jokey, *This isn't a date either, right?* Orla steeled herself to tell the truth and hoped the card wasn't listening.

'I did want a plus one, but I wanted it to be you. Marek Zajak. Because . . . ' She was uncertain how to phrase it. 'Because you're kind,' she ended lamely.

Marek's sooty brows descended. He looked as if she'd hit him. 'Kind? That's . . . a good thing but – *kind*? Is that all I am to you?'

'No. I wanted to get to know you better,' she said, all in a rush, as if confessing to murder. 'There. God. Am I bright red?'

'Like a tomato.'

There was that transformative smile again. Marek looked so glad it made Orla smile too. The soppy delight of smiling back at a man who's smiling at you had been forgotten during Orla's purdah.

'I think we are a good fit.' Marek said this so quietly that she had to draw her head nearer to his to hear.

'Are we?' She could only be evasive and non-committal.

Orla was a fiancée *manquée* and one of the things that drew Marek to her, she knew, was how seriously she took such commitments.

'Yes, we are.' Marek seemed sure about their fit and its goodness.

The hubbub receded. The night air made the tiny hairs on Orla's arms prickle. She touched her throat, where a pulse leapt. Marek kept his eyes on hers.

A woman passing on silver platforms stumbled in the grass and gate-crashed their bubble, apologising as she nudged Orla's hand and spilled her wine.

'Sorry, oh look at you, I'm such a—' Anthea's solicitous babble ceased when she recognised Orla. 'Good god,' she said, 'the little colleen.'

The actress wore a turquoise scarf tied as a headband and Orla had time to think two disparate thoughts concurrently – *A headband? Jaysus!* and *She looks amazing* – as she said, 'Hi, Ant.' The nickname came out tentatively and Orla immediately felt a fool.

'You look lovely,' said Anthea. 'And who's this handsome creature?' She held out a hand to Marek, who shook it firmly, and dropped it decisively. 'You don't hang about, you dark horse,' she said, admiringly, to Orla.

'What?' Orla flinched.

'Nothing, nothing, please don't take fright and bolt like a wounded deer.' Ant tapped Orla's chin with a fan. (*A fan!* thought Orla. *A feckin' headscarf and a feckin' fan. And still she looks better than me.*) 'I didn't expect to see *you* here. You're much too wholesome and Oirish for Reece's annual debauch. I assumed it was client list only.'

'Well, I guess, because of Sim . . . ' Orla tailed off. She felt her cheeks burn. She was Irish, not Oirish, but she couldn't protest; Anthea's celebrity had such force that it left her thwarted and powerless.

Not so Marek. 'Do you work in Reece's office?' he asked, very, very politely.

Anthea treated Marek to a glare Orla recognised from her mid-eighties biopic of Elizabeth I.

'No?' Marek pressed. 'Then are you perhaps his moth—'

'*Do* tell me you've brought the famous valentine's card!' Anthea barged across Marek's question.

'Famous?' Somebody had turned up the volume of the speakers in the trees and the lanterns flared. 'Did Reece tell you about it?'

'Yes and I disapprove wholeheartedly.' Anthea leaned in, sombre suddenly, her breath perfumed with gin. 'Are you trying to keep the poor bastard alive? Let him rest!' She swayed. 'We all loved him,' she said, blinking rapidly, 'he was lovable. Lovely lovely Sim. So easy to love.'

The tribute sounded like an insult, the way Anthea said it. She looked up at Marek, who stood as straight and tense as a soldier. 'Did you know your little girlfriend talks to an envelope?'

'Orla is not my little girlfriend.' Marek had leeched every ounce of good humour out of his face. 'She can talk to a toilet seat if she wants to.'

Anthea ignored him, turned back to Orla. 'Give it to me, darling, and I'll tear it up for you.'

'No. Really.' Orla took a step back from this whirlwind of offence.

'Is it in there?' Anthea eyed the beaded bag.

'Look, it's – can we just drop the subject?' Orla heard herself jabbering. In her mind's eye she saw herself punch Anthea – a cartoon *kerpow!* that would launch the actress into the koi pond – but ingrained good manners and a peculiar fear of what might come out of Anthea's mouth next kept her polite.

'You're absolutely right, none of my business.' Anthea shook her head and the scarf's tassels danced. 'But you're a fool, Oirish, if you read that thing. And Reece? Well, the man's a fucking vulture and I shall tell him so. Now. Where was I?'

She looked about her, then broke into a vivacious grin, waving her hand high and giddily in the air. 'There's the controller of BBC2. I *must* rescue him from that dreary bint.'

'What a witch,' said Marek with feeling when she was out of earshot.

'She's tipsy.' Why she defended her, Orla couldn't say.

Marek said nothing.

'More grub?' suggested Orla.

'She interrupted us. We were talking about—'

'Loo!' interrupted Orla brightly.

With a sigh, Marek accepted the glass Orla pressed on him. 'OK. You don't want to talk about us. I get it. Go. I'll wait here.'

Inside, a small door in the panelling gave on to a spacious room papered in *toile de jouy*, impossibly pretty, with a mirror so cunningly lit that it doubled as a time machine and offered Orla an airbrushed vision of herself ten years ago.

Closing the toilet lid, Orla sat down heavily. She took the valentine out from her bag.

There was chatter outside the door, the jangling laughter of women on their umpteenth spritzer. A tentative knock. A giggle.

Orla held the valentine in front of her face. 'Tonight isn't the end. We can't have an end, you know that, Sim, don't you?'

A vision of Sim scuttled crab-like under her defences. Carrion, with earth pressing down on empty eye-sockets. Orla whined and squeezed her eyes shut, holding her stomach as if about to vomit.

'You all right in there?' An estuary accent more intrigued than concerned.

'Fine. Won't be long.' Orla held the valentine to her cheek, swooning with need, wishing it were warm and real. She caught sight of herself in the mirror, a woman canoodling an envelope on a toilet.

This, she thought, *is the shore that grief washes you up on*.

Orla peeled the valentine from her cheek, confronted it.

'Listen, we have to talk about Marek. I know you think I fancy him. Well, I do.' Orla cleared her throat. 'But it's not just about that. Marek's a good person. Strong. He allows things to have meaning. I feel he might honour what we had. Oh God, Sim, I'm getting hopelessly wanky here. Do you understand what I'm trying to say?'

Lately it took more effort to conjure up the valentine's retorts. The card was quiet. Sullen perhaps, even disapproving: *just a piece of paper*, she thought with terrible clarity. Orla worked her finger under the flap at one end of the envelope and pushed it across. The edge was ragged now, like a wound.

'Excuse me? Hello?' It was a different voice this time. Male. The estuary girls had fetched help. 'Is everything OK?'

Before the disembodied voice got any closer, Orla stuffed

the card back into her bag, unlocked the door and pushed through the little crowd on the other side of it. On the far side of the room she saw Marek stepping in from the garden. Orla took a pace towards him, then paused and observed.

He fitted right in. His tuxedo was as black as his hair and as elegant, its cut emphasizing the emphatically male proportions of his shoulders and the length of his legs. Yet his masculinity wasn't bullish: there was a grace to Marek that was all of a piece with his colouring. *He's a panther*, thought Orla, surprising herself with such a simile at a time like this, *and he's perfectly at home here, just like he's perfectly at home in Maude's Books or a café that smells of cabbage.*

The girl talking to him was familiar. Hair a paint-box red, breasts surely not as God made them, she was a soap opera stalwart. She was laughing immoderately, and Marek was grinning back.

Orla felt jealous. She didn't like that, stowed it discreetly away. After her insistence that this wasn't a date, it was absurd to be possessive. *All the same*, she thought, squaring her shoulders, *I'll see off that pile of fillers and botox.*

'There you are.' Reece put a hand on her arm before she could move. 'It's been an hour. Are you standing me up?'

'No, not at all.' Orla lifted her chin. 'I'm ready.'

The phrase landed between them.

'I didn't think I'd ever hear you say that.'

'You're not the only one.' Orla took a deep breath. 'Let's do this, Reece, before I change my mind.' She let Reece take her hand but dug her heels in as he dragged her away. 'Hold on. Marek.' She pointed at him. God, he was laughing loudly with that girl. What was so feckin' funny?

'No. Never mind old Dracula. We'll do this together.'

'Don't call him that.'

Reece, shouldering through the crowds, ducking from puckered lips and outstretched hands, didn't catch her tone, and laughed.

'Really, don't.' She wasn't Oirish and Marek wasn't Dracula.

'Through here.'

A heavy door swung shut behind them and the party was on mute. The walls of the darkened room shivered as if they were alive, abstract blue ribbons snaking up and down them.

'I've made this off limits after Sim's party piece last year.' Reece led her along the side of the pool, through the pearly blue in the gloaming, past ferns and grasses in pots, to a small round table with two café-style chairs. 'Sit, darling. Gather yourself.'

The air was sticky and tropical, cut with the discordant tang of chlorine.

'Let's see it,' said Reece.

Fumbling in the bag beneath the table, Orla was conflicted at this eleventh hour. A surge of certainty galvanised her into a decision and she put the envelope on the table. 'There.'

Reece bent down and took a ceramic plate from beneath a potted plant with fat succulent leaves. 'This'll do,' he said.

Inert, sitting back, Orla was grateful for his forward motion. She was tired of the endless advice about the valentine, weary of sifting through muddy motives and loaded comments. She sat up again when Reece produced a lighter. Platinum and yellow gold, it was very slim, very Reece.

'Put the card in the saucer,' said Reece.

Doing as she was told, Orla put the pink envelope on the plate. She nodded to Reece and he lowered the lighter until the flame lapped at one corner. They watched, their faces golden, as the blaze drew a black swath across the pink. Ash drifted on the drugged air.

'It's done.' Reece's face was bluish again as the tiny bonfire subsided. He was whispering, as though they were in church. 'Are you OK?'

'I am.'

'Sure?'

'Sure. Thank you. For being with me.'

Reece's face looked full, as if crammed with feeling. 'This is such a relief. I don't want you to go under, Orla. Sim really loved you, you know,' he said, with a downward inflection.

'I know he did.' Orla allowed the past tense to sit, uncorrected. 'D'you know what, I think I'll go now. I'm whacked.'

'Of course.' Reece stood, took her hand unselfconsciously as if she were a child. 'Did you find Ant?' he asked.

'Unfortunately, yes.'

'Why so?' Reece stopped, his face alert in the glitter-ball shimmer of the pool.

'She was odd. Kind of aggressive. I thought I liked her but tonight she was, well, she was bitchy, actually. No other word for it.'

'It's not you.' Reece seemed keen to impress this on Orla. 'It's fashionable to have demons these days and Ant has more than most. She drinks a little too much, partakes of Columbian marching powder a little too much. And she doesn't get enough love, if you want my opinion. Ignore her, really. Just ignore her.'

'There are bigger things going on in my head, to be honest.'

'Good. Stay away from Ant. She's not your type.' Reece opened the door back to Narnia. 'Wait outside with Dracula and a car will whisk you off to the hotel just up the road. Separate rooms, as sternly requested.'

'Why do you call him Dracula?' Orla had spotted Marek's dark head among the mob and, as if he'd felt her gaze alight on him, he'd turned and was making his way over.

'Just a nickname. You know, he's pale and intense, with that rumbling Transylvanian kind of voice.' Reece saw Orla's expression, looked chastened. 'Sorry. I'm still a public school boy at heart.'

'You look washed out,' said Marek, before he even reached her. 'Are you all right?' He put a hand to her brow, an oddly mammy-ish gesture from a tall dark handsome man in a dinner jacket.

'I'm fabulous,' smiled Orla, taking his arm. She telescoped out, saw a fetching couple, the woman casually taking the man's arm. 'Thank you again,' she said to Reece, 'for having me.'

Chapter Fourteen

The view was, deservedly, the hotel's pride and joy.

Slowly, shyly, an untidy line of trees had emerged in the deep trench of the valley as the night drained away. After some hours in the cane lounger, bundled up in a hotel dressing gown, Orla was as familiar with the trees' outline as she was with the view from her Tobercree bedroom.

The veranda served the back of the inn, a communal space on to which all the ground floor rooms opened. The adjacent pair of French windows were Marek's. The light around the edges of his curtains had clicked off about 2 a.m. An invisible thread between the figure in the lounger and the doors, until then quite tense, had slackened.

The purplish mist was dissipating: today would be bright and clear.

They hadn't spoken on the ride to the hotel, looking obdurately out of opposite windows as the taxi bumped over potholes. Her hand had lain curled on the seat beside her and Marek had put his hand on top of it, gently, like the mist landing on the trees. Orla remembered looking down at the strong fingers, the splash of dark hair on milky skin, the blue slender ropes of veins over finger bones.

The air in the cab had become denser as she sensed him playing chicken with her, waiting to see whether she would pull away. Or not. Orla had chosen to leave her hand beneath Marek's, drawing comfort from it, feeling safe the way she'd used to when her father took her little paw in his bigger one on the way to Mass, letting her know she was his favourite.

The other hand, however, she'd kept on the valentine.

It had been easy enough. She had already opened the envelope, so when she realised at the party, with absolute clarity, that she did want to read the card – and she wanted to read it alone – she had simply removed it from its pink carcass under the table. Only the trappings had gone up in flames.

As lies went, she hoped it was a white one.

In the hotel corridor, outside her door, Marek had broken the silence to wish her a polite goodnight. He walked to his own room, then strode back and kissed her, very hard, on the lips. This was not the gentle caress of mist on tree: when Marek pulled away his face was so troubled that he looked almost angry.

'I had to do that,' he told her before marching to his own room and slamming the door behind him.

Orla hoped he was asleep by now. She hoped everybody in this corner of England was asleep. She was about to have her last conversation with Sim.

No drum roll. No Master of Ceremonies calling *pray silence ladies and gentlemen*. Just the surround-sound of waking birds for the moment when all the speculation would end and she would hear him ask, and she would give him her response.

Yes.

Orla turned the valentine over on her lap. The image on the front of the card was a line drawing. A simple, fuzzy charcoal heart, black on white. Very simple. Quite unlike anything he'd sent before.

'Still surprising me,' she said fondly. 'Sorry about that business back at the party. I felt as if I needed to satisfy Reece. He's been so involved, so worried. Plus I needed to get him off my back. Oh, I know you loved him, Sim, I do too, but if he knew I'd decided to read this he'd have been all over me for details.

'You remember you used to say he was like a mother hen? Well, I don't need a mother hen for this. This is between you and me. You and me,' she repeated. She liked how it sounded.

She opened the valentine.

So. There you are. My darling, my beauty, my beloved, the sun, the moon, all the poetry in my ugly world, certainly all the cleverness. I imagine you reading this (I imagine you a lot when we're apart, as you well know, some of it X-rated . . .) and I imagine your face concentrating as you take in what I'm saying.

You've been with me forever. Or that's how it feels. You know every nook and cranny of me, physically and mentally. Especially emotionally. Very quickly, and rather late, I grew up with you, in you. I'm the man you made.

You know me so well. I wonder if you know what I'm about to say? I wonder if you've guessed what I'm about to ask?

Orla paused for a while, collecting herself. Here was the authentic voice of a Simeon Quinn card, that careful, honest gravitas so unlike his scattergun conversation. It was all so precious to her. Each new word glittered, making her so happy that she hated the thought of reaching the end, even though she yearned to gobble it up.

Taking up the card again, Orla read on, then leant back on the lounger, eyes closed, as quiet and as still as a stone martyr on a tomb. She stayed that way for some time, before leaping up, all action. She strode, bare feet slapping on the wooden decking, towards her French windows. Ajar, they showed her a glimpse of her room lit by lamps whose efforts were becoming redundant in the dawn light. She paused, her hand on the handle, then turned and closed the space between her windows and Marek's in three strides, tearing off her dressing gown as she went. Naked, she rapped urgently on the glass.

'Marek! It's me!'

He opened the door, his sleepy gaze sweeping up and down her. The sight of Orla's pale body woke him like a sentry startled out of rest by an alarm.

'Orla?' he whispered.

'Please kiss me again.' Her voice was choked, but had a rising undercurrent of heat, that Marek immediately responded to.

His arms went around her, pulling her body close to his and away from the veranda. Marek kissed her, as ordered. His pout was a cushion against her lips, moving then to her throat.

'You're so white,' he said, wonderingly.

'Marek,' she said. It was a plea of some sort. Orla kissed the top of his ruffled head as he bent, dragging his lips across her breasts, holding her close with the strong splay of his fingers.

'Is this real?' she asked, knowing it to be an echo, knowing he wouldn't recognise it.

Marek straightened up, bending his face to hers. 'This is real, *moje złotko*.' He kissed her with an unexpected ferocity, like a cat making a sudden pounce.

And Orla responded, really responded, with all the pent-up energy of her grief. All the loneliness, all the fear, all the clenched attempts at coping motivated her body as it welded itself to Marek's.

Mouths attached, they wheeled and whirled towards the bed. Marek whooped as they fell on to it and Orla tore at his striped boxers, forcing them down before returning her hands to his hair – so thick, so grabbable.

Avid, eager, they matched each other for passion. Orla, flung back in the disarray of smooth hotel sheets, felt his hands lock on her wrists, pinning her down. She wriggled, then stopped as she saw the glint of his eyes intent on hers from above.

'Orla,' he said, as if it were a new name, and the most beautiful name he'd ever heard.

'Marek,' she said, and gasped as he plunged into her. Her throat arched, her head was thrown back, she was overboard and falling and loving the fall, keenly alive to the ends of her fingertips. She screamed so loudly that he broke his rhythm, surprised, presumably by her abandonment.

She screamed again, like a feral girl. And then it was done, and they were both panting, astonished.

'You're amazing.' Marek was half laughing. He covered her body with his own, kissed her forehead, her cheeks, her nose, then collapsed beside her. 'You're going to kill me. My God, Orla . . .'

She turned away from him, waited for his breathing to subside into the shallow regularity of sleep and began to cry.

I wonder if you know what I'm about to say? I wonder if you've guessed what I'm about to ask? I wonder I wonder I wonder I wonder if I should just kill myself now and be done with it because I can't bear to say it but I HAVE TO.

You always say I'm selfish and, well, here is your proof: I want you to let me go. I'm in love.

You know the woman I'm talking about, but you don't know her. *She's not like you. Your lives are as different as can be, one lived in the glare of showbiz, one lived in the back of beyond. Let me go to her, and live that other life, because oh God forgive me, darling, I am not in love with you. And I don't think I ever was.*

Chapter Fifteen

The high hedges flashing past the car were twiggy and bare, all their summer pomp dissolved. Orla stared out at them, low in the seat like a child. Beside her Marek shook his head wryly, his grin confirming that he too was experiencing flashbacks of the night before. He turned and caught her eye, letting out a muted '*aww*' when Orla dropped her chin. Reaching out, he playfully nudged her nose with his knuckles, as if he found her modesty adorable.

He misread her reticence, just as he had on waking, during breakfast and as they checked out.

The car was luxurious, a Jaguar. 'Not new,' Marek had been at pains to point out. He was proud of its sleek silhouette, its period sophistication. Carefully chosen, it suited him, in much the same way as his worn-in velvet jackets.

Stopping at a petrol station, Marek smiled at her as he returned across the forecourt. Orla smiled back: even from her vantage point at the bottom of a deep dark well it was a smile that deserved an answer. Clambering into the driver's seat, Marek tossed a Crunchie bar into her lap with a wink. Grateful, Orla undressed her snack. She believed that all men should know to bring back sweets to the car after paying for petrol. Da had always done so, and so had Sim. Although Sim had known to bring a Bounty.

As their tyres spat pebbles and rejoined the A3, Orla clamped down on that thought. So Sim had known which chocolate bar she preferred. So what? The time for comparisons had passed.

It was so obvious, falling for your co-star. Orla suppressed a shudder, closing her eyes tight shut against the desire to howl. She'd promised herself to keep it all in until she was back in the flat.

Marek whistled along to the radio. He tapped his hand on the steering wheel, not a care in the world, a perfect picture of the post-orgasmic male.

Orla urged the car on, as if it were a horse she could gallop to safety. She scrunched up the Crunchie wrapper and poked it into her bag. Earlier she'd scrunched up the card, ripping it into confetti and leaving it in the wastepaper basket of her hotel room. One reading had consigned the whole passage to memory.

I am not in love with you. And I don't think I ever was.

It was that final jab, almost an afterthought, which tormented her.

What a Judas the card had been, squatting on her mantelpiece, listening to her prattling on, clutching its sour message to its bosom all this time.

Humming along to an inane R&B track, Marek swung them round a roundabout. He drove suavely, with a light touch, as if the Jag were an extension of his personality. Orla studied him. He was a catch. Other women's reaction to him at Reece's party had proved that. Only a Teflon coating of grief could have blinded her to his allure.

Sensing her gaze, Marek's pout deepened as he tried not to

smile. *He's so happy*, thought Orla, both envious and nervous. Only feet apart, their morning-after-the-night-before experiences were very different.

A wash of heat warmed Orla's limbs as she remembered their lovemaking. It had been wild and even magical and she had wanted him.

That wasn't the reason she went to his room, though. Not the main one. Reading the valentine had provoked a sensation of dropping over a precipice. The instant she'd read, *I don't think I ever was*, Orla was in freefall.

She had gone to Marek because she needed a soft landing. And because, in that moment, all sense of *shouldn't* and *can't* had vanished. Orla had given herself permission to touch Marek.

Marek was strong but he had been so gentle with her. She remembered his long lean legs, so well defined, and the rude sudden curve of his buttocks. He was beautiful. And Orla had responded like a wild thing.

It had been so different to sex with Sim.

Again, she clamped down on the comparison.

Marek had stopped whistling.

The landscape had changed, hedgerows giving way to gum-spattered pavements and rows and rows of windows. 'London,' murmured Orla, sitting up.

'Are you OK?'

'Yup. Yeah. Of course.'

Marek turned the wheel, turning abruptly off the main drag. He scanned the clogged side road for a space and parked the car. He turned to her, taking his seat belt off, the venerable leather of the seat creaking musically. 'What's up?'

'Nothing. Honest.' Orla shrugged, with a smile she was sure was horrible. 'Let's get back.'

Marek switched off the radio. 'This is Sim, yes?'

'No. Well, yes.' She looked down at her lap.

'Darling,' said Marek, and the word blazed in Orla's head. 'I understand. Or I try to, you know that. Listen, listen to me.' He tugged her chin up, pointed her gaze towards him. 'You burned the card. That's a chapter closed. Not forgotten, of course not. But—'

'I didn't, Marek. Burn it, I mean . . . I read it.'

Marek, mouth still open to continue his previous thought, stared.

'I read it and it wasn't a proposal.' Orla heard tears thicken her voice and blinked. She mustn't cry in front of Marek. The poor man didn't need that. 'He told me he was leaving me for Anthea Blake. And he said he didn't love me. He never had.'

Like ripping the plaster off a scab, admitting it left Orla gasping.

'Oh God,' murmured Marek. He put his face in his hands.

'It's better to know.'

Through his fingers, one brown eye looked her way. 'Really?'

'Well, no, not really.' Orla's laugh was dry as a dead leaf. 'It's all horrific, whatever way I look at it.'

Marek recovered. 'When did you read the card?'

Orla hesitated. 'On the veranda. After you went to bed.'

'Ah.' Marek's face altered, hardening into a likeness of itself. 'So, last night, that was, what? Rebound sex?'

'No, of course not.'

Gripping the wheel, Marek stared straight ahead.

'But I'm confused, Marek, I—'

'I am here,' he interrupted. 'I am alive. I won't let a dead man order me about and neither should you. I never met this Sim.' He thumped the wheel with a closed fist and Orla jumped. 'This is about you and me!' Marek turned the key, and pulled out as if getting away from a bank heist.

They didn't speak the rest of the way home. As Marek fetched her overnight bag from the boot, he said, 'When a man and woman lie down together it means something, or it means nothing. I don't believe last night meant nothing.'

'I'm sorry,' she said.

'Is that a goodbye?' Marek held on to the bag, wouldn't let her take it.

'No, it's a sorry. I'm leading you a right old dance.'

'I like dancing.' Marek held out the bag. 'Actually,' he reconsidered, 'I don't. But, you know, I'll dance with you if I have to.'

Orla waved him off, grateful he hadn't asked to come in, sorry to see him go.

Tiny though she was, Maude held on to Orla with remarkable strength as Orla sobbed and gulped out her story on the sofa.

'There, there.' Maude rocked to and fro, and Sunday afternoon crept past as her lodger snivelled and raged and finally subsided.

Lighting lamps, Maude prescribed wine and food and brought both, laying it out on the coffee table.

'I've got no appetite,' said Orla, cramming a bacon sandwich into her mouth.

'Just when you'd turned a corner ...' muttered Maude. 'Wish I could get my hands on the boy.'

'He wasn't a boy, he was a grown man.' Orla talked with her mouth full: legions of Cassidy women spun in their graves.

'I still can't believe he'd—'

'Believe it, Maude.' Orla crashed through her landlady's attempts to rewrite the past. 'He dumped me. With a valentine's card.'

'I knew he had his faults but—'

Interrupting again, Orla voiced a sudden sharp and unwelcome apprehension. 'Did you know, Maude? That he was seeing somebody else?' Orla quivered with the need for Maude to shake her head.

But Maude was taking a deep breath in, carefully composing herself before saying, 'I knew something peculiar was going on but I didn't know it was *this*. He became secretive. Closed off. And the drinking ...'

'But you didn't know about *her?*'

'No, dear, I didn't know about this hussy, whoever she is.' Maude was definite. She tucked an escaped tendril of white hair behind her ear, and Orla noticed how her earlobe sagged. She loathed spotting new signs of old age in Maude. Maude must live forever.

'Are you kidding? You don't know who ...' Orla spluttered into her wine. 'It was Anthea. He left me for Anthea Blake. The bitch. The fucking bitch.' She closed her eyes and groaned, her hand to her forehead.

'We'll allow you one *fucking* and that's it,' said Maude evenly, patting Orla's lap. 'Early bed or sit up all night? Your choice, dear.'

One look at the tartan criss-crossing of veins in the whites of Maude's eyes meant Orla could make only one answer. 'Early night, please, Maudie.'

Sleeplessness, her old foe, made its triumphal return. Orla saw a future of tormenting wakefulness, of twenty-four-hour days spent contemplating the squalid truth. Laid out on the sofa, she stared at the muted early-hours television and chased her thoughts round a circular track.

She had been wrong. The central certainty in her life was a lie. She had believed in Sim's love the way she believed in two plus two making four – it just *was*. The belief had sustained her, and only now was she realising just how much – even after his death.

Lucy had been right to exclude her at the funeral. Orla wasn't Sim's girl. Death hadn't been the thing that tore Orla and Sim apart: it was another woman.

Some calamities diminish as they sink in. *Everything looks better in the morning*, Ma used to say, but the more Orla dwelt on the confession, the worse it got. Her feelings had to execute an about turn in a cramped space. Loving Sim was redundant now.

There were huge gaps in her knowledge. Blanks that bugged her. When had it started? Had it been a bit of fun that snowballed? Or was it a *grande amour*, unstoppable, such as she'd thought their own had been? Times, places, dates. Orla was rabid for detail. But there was nobody to ask.

The room grew cold and Orla dragged herself off to bed, stopping for a peek between her curtains at the poster. An advertisement for Fiat, its colours dulled by the cold early hour, towered above the street. Sim had gone.

178

Sim's journal

17 October 2011

I turned, and saw a look. It was a secret look, one I wasn't meant to see.

I wish I could un-see it. All my future was mapped out in it. I saw the ruins of my present life in those expressive, lovely, lonely eyes.

In this business the people who are envied, who are adored and confident, can betray themselves with a look. Then they're vulnerable. Then you're drawn in.

I wish I hadn't turned around.

Didn't call O tonight.

Chapter Sixteen

The class was quiet. Their tutor was in an odd mood. They felt abandoned, like motherless chicks, and didn't stick up their hands to supply answers or ask playful questions.

Abena, the last to take her copy of their homework questions, asked in a husky undertone, 'Did something bad happen in the weekend, Orla?'

The name sounded lovely in her sluggish accent. Slow moving, broken in the middle – *Or-la*.

'No, nothing.' Orla, by contrast, was brittle, like certain aunts back in Tobercree who sucked the oxygen out of family gatherings. 'Just a bit under the weather. That means not feeling well, feeling low.'

'Ah.' Abena patted Orla's shoulder maternally, even though she was a good ten years her junior. 'Sanae say it is man trouble. But I know you are too smart for that.' Her chuckle saw her to the door, and the classroom was quiet.

Orla's feet walked her to the Piccadilly line, not the Hammersmith & City line, of their own accord. Soho's tangle of streets was confounding and she was on the verge of giving up when she finally found the address, walked up the narrow stairs to a bright room above a restaurant and introduced herself to the receptionist as 'a friend'.

'Orla!' Reece's office was handsome, its panelled walls almost obscured by movie posters, theatrical playbills and a framed gallery of his clients. He stood up behind his desk, a wide blond wood trestle almost invisible beneath a landslide of paper: Orla guessed he knew the whereabouts of every document on it to the nearest centimetre. 'Darling, how nice!'

'You knew.' Orla stood on the patterned rug in a superhero stance, feet apart and hands on hips.

'About?' Reece looked quizzical. By his expression he was holding out for this to be a prank.

'About Sim and his affair.'

A brief war raged on Reece's face before he jettisoned the look of incomprehension. Resigned, sad even, he moved to a chesterfield the colour of olives and dropped heavily on to it. 'Sit with me, darling. Tell me what you've heard.'

'What I've *read*.' Her face was hot, but Orla's words came out coolly. 'I didn't burn the valentine.' She clocked Reece's surprise and moved on before he could take her to task. 'It's all there in Sim's own words. And you knew and you didn't tell me.'

'Whoa, Orla. Don't go scattering accusations. Sit down.' Reece patted the seat beside him. 'Come on.'

Orla knew what it was like to sit by Reece, how safe it felt beside such a fierce watchdog, but she didn't sit down.

'He left me, Reece! He walked out on me for *her*!' She gestured at a framed glossy photograph of Anthea.

'Ant?' Reece rolled his eyes. 'Good God, is this about *Ant*? You think he was—'

'I know he was!' Orla began to pace. If this was how stroppy, volatile people behaved she could see the attraction.

181

She felt powerful, uninhibited. 'And don't feign innocence, Reece. You knew everything about Sim. And there was me thinking your advice to burn the card was for my benefit! You covered up for him, like you do for all the lousy adulterers on your walls!'

That term was unfashionable, but it was *true*. She wondered if Reece could see through the steam of self-righteousness to the soft pulpy hurt beneath. Apparently he could. He patted the seat beside him again. 'Come on. It's me, Orla. Let's talk.'

After the merest hesitation she sat. 'Don't bullshit me, Reece. You knew.'

'Yes,' said Reece. 'I did.'

'Bastard!'

'I deserve that.' Reece dipped his head. His ginger crop was freshly shorn; short needles of hair littered his collar. 'Sim was doing a lot of stuff he was ashamed of. Stuff he knew you wouldn't tolerate.'

Tiring of her role as conscience of the world, Orla muttered, 'You make me sound like a headmistress, not a girlfriend.'

Reece put out his palms, too weary to debate it. 'He needed your good opinion just to get out of bed in the mornings. Without you, he was a kid let loose in a shitty candy store. The boozing was chronic.' Reece winced at some memory. 'I did my best to keep him away from drugs, but the streets of London are paved with coke these days.'

'We could have got through that.' Drinking, snorting – such minor infractions in the shadow of Sim's unfaithfulness. 'How could you let me cart that card around? And how could you introduce me to Anthea? That was low. You made a fool of me.'

'Listen.' Reece was grave. 'Sim would have come back to you. I know it in *here*.' He struck his chest. 'I lied to protect you, not him. I don't think anything went on with Ant, not really.'

'Real enough for him to leave me. He fooled us both, it would seem.'

Orla spotted a familiar face on the opposite wall and got up to study a black and white Sim, grinning winningly, holding a clapperboard with *The Courtesan* written on it.

'That job was the end of us,' she murmured, admitting at last that she hated it, that her fingers had tingled with cave-woman apprehension of danger from the moment the mammoth script had arrived. 'Oh, and look who's in the next photo along.' Orla tapped the framed colour shot. 'Cosy.'

'That's the latest shot of Ant. Her and the director the day she got the *Macbeth* gig. She likes that photo, thinks she looks young. She'd just had her latest shot of Restylane.'

'It's too late to slag her off like that,' said Orla. She folded her arms, stared at the image. Ant was smiling widely, leaning in to the portly director as if she'd been waiting her whole life just for this moment. 'Actors are dangerous,' she murmured. A detail caught her eye. She leaned in, looked closer.

'Come away. This is unhealthy.'

'Reece, I want an apology from her. I need her to be straight with me.' She was tired of the doublethink of these sophisticated, scuzzy people. 'It's time for some honesty.'

With obvious reluctance, Reece said 'Have you been completely honest with yourself?'

The question twisted tighter a knot already snarling Orla's gut. 'How do you mean?'

'You *truly* had no inkling at all? No intuition that Sim was flailing? He needed you, Orla.' Reece looked away, as if he'd seen something on her face he couldn't bear. 'Sorry. You said you wanted honesty.'

Winded, Orla, whispered, 'Of course I knew. After New Year only a fool could pretend, but I must be a fool, Reece, because I managed to carry on as if nothing had happened. I chose to believe it would all come right, like it always did for us. I thought we were impregnable. That we'd bend but never break.

'So, clever old you for sussing me out when I've been hiding behind my own back all this time. I'm not innocent in all of this.'

'Yes, you are.' Reece rose and put an arm around Orla, then the other when she didn't repulse him. 'When Orla was just a name, a girl in his anecdotes, it made sense to help Sim keep his hell-raising from you. But now that I know you – and love you – it's tacky and I regret it.' He let Orla lean in to him: her anger had left the building. 'Promise me though, darling. One thing. Don't approach Anthea.'

Orla's head came up. Two hands on Reece's chest pushed him firmly away. 'Protecting your clients again?'

Reece went to his desk and perched on the corner, explaining with a sigh, 'It's my job. And my duty. We have no proof. We don't really know what happened.'

'I rather think I do.'

'There's a vast list of suspects to choose from, Orla. Make-up girls, producers, runners, assistant directors, some girl at some party.'

'No. Sim wouldn't leave me for a girl at a party. I could tell from the card that this wasn't just anybody, it was a *somebody*.' She harrumphed mirthlessly. 'A somebody who could help his career if I know Sim.'

'No need to demonise him. Let's just say we don't know who it was and leave it at that. No point in dwelling on it.'

'No point?' Orla was dumbfounded. 'No point in knowing who the love of my life left me for?' She stood up, her feet suddenly sore in the ankle boots that had always pinched, her jacket dusty and cheap in this moneyed room. 'I've been dumped from beyond the grave,' she said shrilly. 'I'm one of a kind. I'm unique. A dead man has jilted me. Of course I need to know who it was for. And I do know.' She lowered her chin, glowered at Reece. 'And you know too. At least give me that, Reece. Please.'

Sucking his cheeks, Reece didn't answer for a long moment. He sat forward, hands entwined between his open legs, head hanging. 'Orla, you can't approach Ant. Or accuse her. Think of the scandal this could create.'

Orla stayed silent (she was, in fact, dumb with disbelief at this new slant). He continued.

'They're co-stars in a smash hit. He's a hugely romantic figure to thousands of fans. Have you seen the Facebook pages devoted to him? Full of poems and prayers and fan art.' Reece looked abashed at Orla's stony face. 'No, no, of course you haven't. Sorry. As far as anybody's concerned, Ant is just his co-star, a dear friend, somebody who encouraged a younger rising talent. There'll be a sequel to *Courtesan*, and Ant'll be in it. If you were to kick up a stink about this, tell anybody, it would be excellent tabloid fodder. Notoriety sells these days, but not this sort. Can you imagine? *I stole sexy younger man from lovely girlfriend and then he dropped dead.* The Beeb would go mental.'

'Why am I supposed to care?'

'You must care about Sim's legacy.'

'Not as much as you care about Anthea's fee.' Ugly, but inescapable.

'I'm her agent. Every aspect of Anthea's life is my responsibility.' Reece hesitated as if weighing up whether or not to go on. 'Look, Orla, truth is, Ant's a little bit . . . fragile.'

'Fragile! The old cow's made of cast iron. She strode in, saw my boyfriend, tucked him under her arm and strode off.'

'Her life hasn't been easy. Ant's always looked after herself, always been on her own.'

'What about the lovers? Including ones already spoken for?'

'All part of it. She chases unattainable men.'

'She feckin' attained mine.'

'If this is all true – and it's a big if – imagine how Ant must feel, knowing Sim died leaving you in the dark. As it is, she drinks too much, employs an astrologer, a numerologist, a nutritionist, and a different therapist for every day of the week. She's troubled, Orla, and it could tip her over the edge if you approach her. Why prolong the pain for both of you?' Reece hesitated. 'In some ways, surely, the revelation makes it a little easier to move on?'

'Easier?' Perhaps words had alternative meanings she was ignorant of. 'I need closure, to use an irritating phrase. I want somebody to say they're sorry. To tell me I'm right. And I don't appreciate you making me responsible for Anthea's mental health. I owe her nothing.'

'That's true, but don't expect closure or an apology from

Ant. Even if she is the other woman. There's no happy ending here, just the usual ugly aftermath of an affair.' Reece sprang up, straightened his shoulders. 'Believe me, I know. Showbiz isn't famed for its ability to keep its cock in its pants.'

'I thought the valentine would be the end of it. A soft-focus ending.' Orla slumped. 'Instead it's another sordid beginning.'

'It doesn't have to be. I mean, what about Marek?'

'Dracula?' asked Orla sardonically. 'Oh. Right. After being a figure of fun at your party, suddenly he's the answer.'

'I was rude. I've been in the business too long and I get jumpy around civilians. He seemed charming. And very tasty.'

'Tasty.' Orla laughed at the word, and how it failed to do justice to Marek. 'He is that. He's quite special, I think.' She could say so now. 'But,' she swerved back on course. It was unsettling to linger on Marek. 'He's not the point.'

'No, Fairy, you are.'

'Don't call me that.' Orla was Miss Cassidy suddenly, admonishing a seven-year-old caught drawing boobies in his maths book. 'Only Sim called me that and if he was here I wouldn't let him.'

'Dinner. That's what we need.' As Orla huffed and puffed her refusal, Reece picked up the phone on his desk, pressed a button and said 'Ange, you can use my ticket to the National tonight if you like, and get the Ivy to squeeze me and a guest in at,' he looked at his watch, 'in about an hour. Talk to Fernando. He'll sort me out.' Replacing the receiver, he spoke over Orla. 'No arguments. I want to keep you near me for a while. I feel so bad in so many different ways about what happened. I want to repair us. That's my job, yes, but not with

187

you. This is personal. So please, shut up and let me take you to the Ivy.'

'I've never been less in the mood for a swanky restaurant. Things *are* OK between us. Let's have a coffee, or something, soon.'

Orla almost felt sorry for Reece. He lived in a world of shifting reality, where everybody pretended to be something else and all that mattered was how things looked. Orla's insistence on tearing away the mask had unsettled him.

'Has this helped?' Reece's face was so pained it verged on the comical.

'It has.'

She'd learned far more in this room than Reece could imagine.

Orla had proof.

'Orla? It's Ma. Can you talk?'

'Ma, what you and Da had was real, wasn't it?'

'Eh? Real? What do you mean, *what we had*?'

'You loved each other?'

'God bless us and save us, Orla, what kind of a question is that? Didn't I live with the man and feed him and wash his clothes and put up with that feckin' pipe for thirty-five years?'

'Yes. Sorry. Ignore me.'

'I haven't seen a single Cassidy this blessed day. You have your own lives, I know. Can't be hanging round the neck of a has-been like your owld ma.'

'You're surrounded by family so much they get on your nerves. You almost killed us all last Christmas lunch.'

'See, Orla, that's what I miss. Your sensitivity. You *noticed* I was upset.'

'You were screaming and revving the electric knife at us, Ma.'

'Have you watched any of Sim's thing at all? It's getting very exciting. Too rude, though, Lord have mercy on us. I can take a bosom now and then – I'm very with it, as you know – but men's arses is a step too far.'

'Hmm.'

'I did love your Da, pet, if that's what you meant. And he loved me.'

'Good.'

'And all of youse. God, that man loved youse lot.'

'Thanks, Ma.'

Chapter Seventeen

'She's late again.'

'Traffic's always bad on a Saturday.'

'Bogna gets the tube.'

'Hmm. Well. Same difference.'

The shop helped Orla to focus. Perhaps it was the books, standing around her in their hundreds, all testament to the power of organised thought. Perhaps it was the calm of a customer-less oasis in the midst of pound stores and betting shops. At work she hadn't had time to examine the nugget Reece had unwittingly handed her, but here, in the dusty silence, broken only by Maude's incessant, distracted monologue, Orla could turn it over in her hands, and hopefully nurture her grim excitement until it spawned a plan.

Since Sim's death, her mind had returned to the valentine whenever it was at rest, like a silver ball rolling down the grooves of a pinball table. Now, with the valentine in a hotel bin, the silver ball rolled down to rest against the journal.

Thinking about the journal was, Orla knew, a respite from thinking about what Sim had done to her. The role of victim didn't come easily to her, and Orla smarted and struggled against its tight confines. She wanted to *do* something, not sit bemoaning her lot, mourning all over again the loss of a love. There had been plenty of sitting and bemoaning in the past months, and now she pounced on the journal as a solid objective.

The journal would explain, explicitly and unselfconsciously, everything she needed to know. It would be honest, it would name names; it would detail Sim's estrangement from her in chronological order. It was the key to peace of mind. Her desire for it bypassed want for pure need.

And now she knew where to find it.

Orla had not been studying Anthea Blake's eerily smooth forehead in the photograph hanging in Reece's office. She'd been transfixed by the leather-bound book in Anthea's arms.

Maude turned at the ding-a-ling of the bell, a broad polite smile on her weathered, delicate face that became secretive when she recognised the first customer of the day. 'Why, George,' she said pleasantly. 'Good morning.'

'Good morning, Maude.' George tipped his hat and Orla wanted to cheer. Why didn't men tip their hats any more? It was so civilised, and such a compliment. She edged far enough away to give Maude and George privacy, but close enough to listen in.

'Any luck with finding that book for me?' asked George, rocking back and forth on shabby, polished shoes.

'*Ancient Rome* by S. J. Virtue? I'm afraid not.' Maude sighed prettily. 'It's awfully rare. Shall I keep trying?'

'Oh, do, please. I'll have a little browse, if I may?'

'Browse to your heart's content.' Maude turned away, humming, with a quelling look for Orla's thumbs up from children's fiction.

Selecting an odd little book about Yorkshire, George fished out his wallet, handing over the exact money. 'Thank you,' he said, taking the candy-striped paper bag from Maude, on her plinth behind the till. 'Has anybody ever told you,' he said, 'that you have a look of Katharine Hepburn about you?'

'Never.' Maude patted her flossy white bun, which she'd admitted to Orla she'd modelled on the actress's.

'She's one of my favourites,' said George, turning for the door. 'Quite the beauty.'

'Not one word,' warned Maude as the shop door closed behind him. Her weathered face was putty pink.

'But he's crazy about you,' said Orla, delighted that a sharp-elbowed world could still supply romance. 'And he's adorable.'

'He's a man, not a soft toy. Look, dear George is a perfectly nice chap, I'm sure, but I don't have time for the lovey-dovey stuff.'

No, thought Orla, *you're too busy keeping an eye on me*. She saw how Maude watched her, wary like the keeper of a volcano scheduled to blow. The knock on the door last thing at night, the constant supply of eggy invalid food, the soft look of concern when Orla, as happened all too often, lost the thread of one of their meandering conversations.

'You'd have plenty of time for lovey-dovey stuff if you stopped worrying about your lodger. I'm all right, you know. I have to be.'

'I'm not worried. I care. There's a difference.'

Not a difference the Cassidys had ever discovered.

'You know I appreciate it, don't you?'

'So stiff!' giggled Maude. 'I thought the Irish were profligate with emotions. You lock yours away in a safe. It's all right to cry. It's all right to rend your garments.'

'It's not!' Orla was suddenly vehement. 'I've done it already. I can't do a second lap. I thought I was over the worst of it but no. Fresh shit hits fresh fan.'

'Nibble away at the pain. Manage it in bite-sized pieces.'

'If only it wasn't such a . . .' Orla groped for the appropriate adjective, 'such a *stupid* heartbreak. I mean, come on, to be jilted posthumously. To be dissed by a man who's already feckin' dead. There are no support groups. There's no self-help guide. It's funny, goddamn it, and I'm the only one not laughing.'

'Dear me, the well of self-pity is deep today.' Maude pointlessly tidied the counter, moving paperclips and rubber bands to little effect. 'Nobody's laughing. Everybody is appalled. Even Sheraz. He asked after you when he delivered my groceries this morning.'

The door opened.

'Ah! Bogna. At last.'

'Don't have go at me.' Bogna streaked past, shrugging off a yeti fur coat. 'I have migraine.'

'Don't have *a* go.' No such thing as an ex-pupil for Orla. 'You have *a* migraine.'

'No, she has *a* hangover.' Marek caught the door before it banged in his face. 'She called me for a lift. When she finally got up.'

He found Maude first and said a polite greeting, then saw Orla and said nothing.

'Always he follows me and nags me and UGH!' Bogna threw her hands in the air with an angry chin jut, a teen archetype.

'Hi Marek,' said Orla, with acute self-consciousness.

193

'Yes,' said Marek, baffling her. He left the shop, went to the kerb and got into his car.

'What goes on with you two?' Bogna called as she sought out the kettle beyond the beaded curtain. 'Did you mess with his head? He never is in bad mood about woman but my God this week. He is like bear with sore bum.'

'Head, dear. Head.' Maude, on tiptoe, squinted over the window display. 'He's waiting for something. Or somebody.' Her eyes swivelled towards Orla.

'Get out there!' shouted Bogna irritably, slamming down the Kenco. 'Stop being like little virgin!'

Joining Maude at the window, Orla saw Marek's fingers drum on the wheel. His outline seethed with energy even when he was still. She saw his fine nose, the round of his definite chin, the slant of his dark eyes. It astonished her that this man should be waiting for her, a man she'd barely thought about in the past few turbulent days. Orla wondered at her priorities, and reminisced about the good old days when she'd recognised a good thing when she saw it.

'He'll get a ticket,' murmured Maude.

'I should go. I can't let him get a ticket.'

'No,' said Maude. 'Heaven forbid.'

The sight of Marek had transformed the day for Orla. Marek was like nobody else. And he kept coming back. Like a goat, he gobbled up the rubbish she strewed in his path, and kept on coming. She sauntered out to the car and bent to look in through the open passenger window at his profile.

One of their characteristic silences ensued. Marek broke first, leaning back on the headrest, looking at the ceiling and asking, exasperated, 'Are you getting in or not, woman?'

With a smile, a proper one full of glee, such as Orla assumed she'd never crack again, she climbed into the passenger seat and Marek drove off through the knotted traffic.

A few streets away, in an industrial estate that housed DIY warehouses and tile depots, the car slowed and stopped with a sexy grunt beside a skip.

'Scenic spot,' said Orla.

'I like it.' Marek's dimples flared. 'Nice for picnics.' He turned, took off his seat belt and took her head between his hands in a motion so fluid it seemed rehearsed. He kissed her gently but confidently. 'I've missed you.'

With nobody to betray any more, she could admit it. 'I've missed you too.'

'You have?' His voice soared girlishly high with surprise.

'Just a bit.'

'It's a start.' By lowering the pitch of his voice, Marek created a bubble within the car, one that contained only them and their recent history. 'I can't stop thinking about that night. Your heart told your head what to do for the first time since we met. Perhaps you should shut up and listen.'

His finger trailed along her nose.

'That's the sweetest nose I've ever seen,' he whispered. He kissed it, and something unfolded, like a flower opening on fast forward, within Orla. His hand fell to her shoulder, trailed down her arm and when his fingers met hers they snaked together. 'I see your face everywhere now. I think you're in every crowd. But you never are.'

'Marek, I'm damaged, I'm—'

'No, no, no.' He overrode her fledgling demurrals. 'Listen. This is you and me. It isn't about Sim or ... or Anthea Blake.

195

It's about Orla and Marek. Orla and Marek are going on a date. Like two normal adults. Because, *moje słotko*, that's what they are. Normal. And lucky.' He kissed her, urgently this time. He meant business.

Marek's lips on her neck, one hand scooping the peach curve of her bottom, Orla whispered, 'Your sister said you get what you want.'

'And I want you.'

Something in obstinate, obdurate Orla responded to his forthrightness, and admired his expectancy.

'A date, then.' She pulled away a little, delighted when his hand, thwarted from exploring her bottom, immediately moved to the buttons of her blouse.

'A date.' Marek sat back, dishevelled, happily dissatisfied. 'Oh Orla, you'll drive me mad. Tonight?' He saw her hesitation. 'Are you busy?'

'No, but—'

'Then it's a date. We're normal people and normal people go out on Saturday night. Yes? Good. You pick the place. I'll meet you there. Be quiet. I know you're an immigrant and you hardly know any restaurants – that's what Google is for. Pick somewhere nice because tonight I'd like to get a little drunk with my new girlfriend. Because,' he registered her start, 'I think that's what you are.'

He dropped her home. He always would, she knew. Male gallantry could bring out her haughty side but Marek didn't make her feel patronised. He made Orla feel like a woman.

Chapter Eighteen

'I knew Sim was thick. I knew he had a shady side. But this!'

'Ju.'

The pig. The revolting, grotty, underhand, piggy little pig man.'

'*Ju!* Enough. And stop jiggling, stay near the camera.'

'Do you know who he was shagging?'

'Anthea Blake.'

'Oh come *on*! She's a hundred years old.'

'Fifty and two months.'

'Do you hate him?'

'If I do, if I give in and loathe him, then that's the best three years of my life made pointless. Her, I hate, though. That's easy.'

'Why? She's nothing to you. Why does the woman get all the flak?'

'Please don't say it takes two to tango. She burrowed in between me and my man, like a tick. Thanks to her I'm just the little colleen he toyed with before he found the love of his life. You've got the wrong idea about her. Anthea's clever. She's written a book. She has a degree. She collects Jane Austen first editions. And there was me in Sim's other ear, jabbering about Year Two's nativity play. She's met Obama, for Christ's sake.'

'I'd love to meet Obama.'

'Well, there you go. You run off with her too.'

'Never. She can't hold a candle to you. Sim was crazy. Please, please don't let this set you back. You were just coming to life again.'

'I'm doing my best. But it's hard.'

'You're crying! Lean closer to the camera. Are you crying? Oh, Orla, I wish I was there to hug you.'

'Me too. I'm not crying. My eyes are wet, that's all.'

'Mind you, maybe Sim was right. To get out, I mean. Maybe he was brave.'

'I don't follow.'

'We all hang on, don't we, after the love runs out? Or lust, or whatever the feck it is.'

'Sim was *not* brave, Ju. He dumped me by valentine card.'

'But he did it. He took the leap into the unknown. If he'd lived, you might be thanking him by now.'

'Big if, Juno. Big huge ma-*hoo*-sive if.'

'I'm just saying that—'

'Please don't. Don't just say that kind of thing.'

'So I'm not allowed to call him names but I'm not allowed to suggest he might be right.'

'Look, I've got to go. Marek's treating me to dinner and I've to choose the restaurant.'

'Marek? When were you going to tell me about this?'

'I just did.'

'Yeah, offhand, as you're signing off.'

'Sorry. Next time I go through a heart-breaking trauma I'll make sure to send you a bulleted memo. But for now – good-bye.'

'Hang on, don't—'

'Bye, Juno.'

Know thine enemy.

Orla wouldn't recognise General Sun Tzu if he fell on her head, but his 1,600-year-old maxim rang in her ears as she opened her iPad to research restaurants.

Anthea had the journal. That was greedy: stealing Sim's heart wasn't enough for her. Anthea's memories of him, although sad, were uncomplicated: she'd lost him in the first flush of love and now she danced on through her gilded life with the journal in her hands.

The injustice burned.

She has everything, thought Orla, scanning the Wikipedia page dedicated to Anthea Blake. *And I have nothing*.

This lady Tweeted. Infrequently, impersonally, with a reliance on exclamation marks.

Trying 2 learn lines. Mr Shakespeare I love you!!!

Orla had assumed that Anthea was the wrong vintage to work up any interest in Facebook, but a page existed in her name. Written in the third person but seemingly 'official', Orla guessed that some assistant in the lower echelons of Reece Dodds Artists kept it fresh.

'After filming a new advert as the face of Royal Blend instant coffee, Anthea will take a few days' well-earned rest before rehearsals for her Lady Macbeth in the forthcoming prestigious Globe production of the Scottish Play. Time, maybe, to get down to some serious baking and turn out one of her famous cakes!'

Orla recalled the cake she'd made for Sim on his birthday. It had refused to rise, but she'd persevered and iced it, producing, in his words, 'a cowpat with candles'. She'd laughed at the time, but now it was just another memory smudged by Anthea's grubby fingers.

More clicks, more haphazard fact-finding. Orla felt vaguely squalid. *Enough*, she thought to herself, and set about searching for somewhere to eat. 'Nice + restaurant + London' was no help. Every restaurant in London thought it was nice. This was more Juno's territory; Juno could sniff out a hipster hangout blindfolded.

Juno's bad-mouthing of Sim earlier was very characteristic. All her opinions were brightly coloured and loudly expressed. Orla cherished Juno's outspokenness, and forgave the occasional bruise it caused. They were bonded. When she thought of her best friend, she still saw a gap toothed seven-year-old with nits. She knew Juno had to poke Sim in the eye for his offence, just as she'd done to the class bully in Juniors when he'd grabbed Orla's skipping rope.

Even so, it didn't help to hear Sim torn to shreds. For this reason, Ma must be kept in the dark a while longer. Telling her would spark off an eruption of abuse that would make Juno sound like an amateur.

But Juno's assertion that Sim was somehow brave had irked. Orla should thank him for taking a hammer to every sweet memento she had of him? No.

A website for a chi-chi bistro claimed the screen, all purple walls and zinc tables. 'Nah, wrong end of the road,' she concluded, wandering virtually to a Greek taverna, garnished liberally and tastelessly with plastic lemons and portraits of

Archbishop Makarios. Checking it out on Google Street View, she declared it 'perfect' and texted Marek with the address, adding a small 'x'.

After pressing send, Orla took a moment to do something unthinkable a week ago, but now a must. With two jabs of her forefinger she deleted Sim's number and all his messages, including his last, sent at midnight on the thirteenth of February.

> Tomorrow's a big day for both of us, Fairy. Brace yourself. X

A soft rap at her door startled her and made her throw down her iPad, as flushed as if she'd been caught masturbating in John Lewis. 'Come in, Maudie!'

'Dear?' Maude stood, nonplussed, on the threshold. 'Shouldn't you be getting ready?'

'I've bags of time. It's only—' Orla looked at the ormolu clock on the mantelpiece and her hand went to her throat. 'Shit!' she said.

'Quite,' agreed Maude.

The entire afternoon had been eaten by the internet.

'Jump in the shower,' ordered Maude. 'Chop chop.' She clapped her hands for emphasis. 'And then I want to talk to you.'

Damp, smelling of ylang ylang, Orla sat on the bed and rubbed moisturiser strenuously into her face as if waxing a car.

'Slow down, dear. Not washing your hair?' Maude disapproved.

'Not enough time. I'll backcomb it.' *And make it look worse,* thought Orla. 'Shall I wear the black dress with the bits on the shoulders or shall I, hang on, no I can't wear the new dress because he saw it the other night.'

'Black with bits.' Maude was decisive enough for Orla to suspect her of shutting her up. 'Now. Listen.' Maude sat on the end of the bed, clear of the pile of tubes and brushes and goo that Orla was applying as she squinted into an inadequate hand mirror. 'I have something to tell.'

'Yes?' Orla's hand stalled in mid-air, one eyelid only half anointed with liner.

'Don't stop, dear.' Maude settled her full velvet skirt around her. 'I haven't talked about this, well, *ever*, so forgive me if it sounds a little rusty. I need you to know you're not alone, not unique. Well, not in one important aspect at any rate.'

The mascara wand swooping in and out of her vision, Orla waited while Maude cleared her throat, uncharacteristically hesitant.

'Very well. Here we go. Arthur and I were married in 1961. I was twenty-two. To save you counting on your fingers, that makes me seventy-four. You might imagine I had long ironed hair and miniskirts, but the swinging sixties never reached our corner of the home counties. I dressed like my mother, in neat suits and stupid hats and always, always stockings.

'Arthur was destined for great things. In my parents' world, the one I happily and unthinkingly inherited, great things meant a powerful job with the Foreign Office. That was just the icing on the cake, because Arthur was handsome. The first time I saw him he was in tennis whites and I thought he was a young god.'

202

A lipstick lolled forgotten in Orla's towelled lap.

'We were happy. He's the only man I've ever gone to bed with. And no regrets there. I adored him. And he me. He was proud of my looks. Forgive the boast, but now that I'm just a mass of wrinkles and bones I feel I can say it. He also applauded the way I kept house. A lovely big rambling thing, on the edge of the village. We had a duck pond and a paddock, with a fat little Shetland I just loved.

'I'd been trained to be a wife from the moment I could walk. I was required to look pretty but not tarty, run the homestead and churn out babies. That last was beyond me.

'Arthur wanted a son to carry on both barrels of the family name, but we shared a cheery philosophical outlook. "Never mind," he'd say. "We've got each other." That helped when I gave in and cried into my pillow. I used to imagine what our baby would look like. His eyes. My hair, God help it. It would have – but listen to me rattling off on a tangent, dear, that's quite another story.

'He said it over and over. "We've got each other." We were close. I wanted for nothing. And then, after thirty-four years of marriage we were blighted by serious illness. Oh, Orla, it was hard. Eighteen months of hopeless agony for Arthur, who fought all the way in the certain knowledge he couldn't win. I nursed him, read to him, slept at the foot of his bed. I knew he'd do the same for me. Goodness gracious, girl! Don't gawk like that – finish your face!'

'Oh. Yes.' Orla hurriedly returned to her features in the mirror. Rubbing in blusher felt too banal an activity while listening to Maude's never-told tale. She wondered where it would lead.

'After he died, Arthur left me very comfortably off, but the lion's share of his legacy went to a woman in the next village, a woman I knew rather well. Or thought I did. Arthur had fathered four children with her. Set them up, supported them, sent them to the best schools. Spent every Wednesday night there when I thought he was up in London on Her Majesty's service.'

Orla gaped. In idle moments she'd fleshed out a past life for Maude but never had it sounded like this. She slung her make-up into the bag, stood up and grabbed a pair of cranberry jeans; the black dress with bits felt too dressy.

'Four children, Maude?'

'All girls.' Something like the first cousin of a smile flitted across Maude's features. 'So I too was *dumped from beyond the grave.*' Maude attempted a comedy horror intonation, but she was wan and couldn't pull it off. 'You're wrong, Orla: one *can* survive such exquisite betrayal. I'm living proof. People say this all the time but I know how you feel.'

'Yes, you do. I wish you didn't.'

'Pish. It made me the woman I am. I can't disown a single hour of my life, even the truly horrid ones. And nor should you. I imagine, if you're anything like I was, you had an initial period of denial when all your senses told you that your beloved Sim could never be so barbarous.'

Orla nodded.

'Then there was flaming anger, the kind that makes you want to punch things or even people.'

'Quite a lot of that,' admitted Orla.

'I smashed a lovely Meissen bowl when I got home from my solicitor's office. Been in the family for yonks. I wanted to roll up to the woman's house and have it out with her. Can you imagine?'

Only too well. 'Yup.' Tartly, Orla zipped up her jeans.

'I restrained myself. Spilt milk and all that. What could she say to me that wouldn't hurt me more?'

'I guess.' Orla's face was in shadow as she reached into the wardrobe for a blouse patterned with swallows.

'And now I suspect you've moved on to the next phase – deep deep sadness. Am I right?' Maude's voice was liquid with compassion.

'Yes,' said Orla briskly, pulling on the blouse, before bleakness overwhelmed her and she froze in scarecrow pose, arms stretched through the sleeves. 'Tell me how I get past this, Maude.'

Maude considered for a moment, eyes on the worn rug. 'I know each generation thinks they invented the idea, but probably I loved Arthur just as much as you love Sim.'

'*Loved!*' snapped Orla, all action again, attacking the fiddly buttons.

'Well, I used the past tense as I swept up the Meissen shards, but I found my way back to loving him. It was tricky, but I did it for my sake as much as his.'

'I don't want to love him. Only a fool would love a man who did that to her. If I'm to survive, I have to hate him,' said Orla miserably. 'How can they do it, these men?'

'Couples are cruel to each other. Arthur and Simeon weren't the worst. We loved them and that love had meaning. Ring fence it. They can't defend or explain their actions in life from beyond the grave. We have to find our own way back to loving them, and leaving them behind.'

'What did you do?' Orla hoped for a map, with explicit instructions. The route she was planning was not sensible.

With a sigh and a creaky readjustment of her legs, Maude said, 'I started again from scratch. It wasn't just Arthur who'd lied to me. My family knew. As I hadn't been able to fulfil my side of the contract, they understood that Arthur must have an heir. I found myself looking at my mother and wondering how many times she'd sat with me, chatting about this and that, choosing not to warn me about the great calamity in my life. No, I didn't *understand* and I still don't. Love has certain rules. I don't mean morals, the made-up sexual dos and don'ts. I mean things such as treating each other with respect, telling each other the truth, whether it's a marriage or mother and child.'

Maude slapped her lap, happy to have reached the turning point in her tale.

'But you asked, what did I do. I sold up, lock stock and barrel, and walked away. All the way to London, where it's noisy and modern. I had friends here but I didn't look them up. The puzzle of working out who knew and who didn't was too painful. Simpler to sever all ties.'

'Your mother?' asked Orla, watching Maude's childishly slight seated figure in the wardrobe mirror as she tucked in the blouse and pivoted to check out her back view.

'We never spoke again. She died in 1999.' Maude's hands moved, one over the other, over and over, as if she were washing them.

'I immersed myself in a new kind of life, among all kinds of people. I went into business – not the done thing in my circle, I assure you. I was my own woman, rather late in life, and it felt marvellous, Orla, like taking off one's corsets after a ball.'

Never having worn corsets, and certain that the Tobercree Church Hall Disco didn't qualify as a ball, Orla smiled.

'I fitted in, snug as a bug in a rug, as Nanny would say. Who'd have thought?'

'Me,' smiled Orla. 'I'd have thought. You'd fit in anywhere.'

'I wish I could offer you a helping hand through the sadness, dear, but it's something you have to face, endure, and then let go.'

'I know.' Trouble was, Orla was on her second lap. She was trapped in an emotional Groundhog Day, facing, enduring, letting go and then meeting the same old feelings again.

'Trust me, child. This is the worst of it. When it clears you'll be filled with energy and you'll break into a run. That's when I opened the shop. If I can do it . . . ' Maude left that lingering in the air as she stood, with some effort, and advised, 'Perfume, dear, on your hair. That gets a chap going.'

Chapter Nineteen

The meze kept coming. One smiling moustachioed man after another approached their table to deposit platters of hummus, feta, mushrooms and stuffed vine leaves.

'I hope you're hungry,' said Marek, sitting back, surveying the feast.

'Ooh, ow, the peppers are hot,' Orla fanned her mouth, regretting her bravado. She *was* hungry: she'd forgotten to eat. This was yet another symptom of her return to the recent bad old days and she determined to do the starter justice. 'Do you like Greek food? I should have checked.'

'I like food. I am a Polish man. We don't turn anything down. But yes, I love Greek food. Have you ever been to Greece?'

'Never.' She had hardly been anywhere. Orla was a champion of the staycation long before desperate tourist boards coined the term.

'Then I must take you,' said Marek. 'I've been to Santorini, and the mainland. We could explore the islands together.' Without looking at her, concentrating instead on marrying up a pitta and a meatball, he asked, 'Would you like that?'

'Yes,' she said, rather enjoying the subjugation of being 'taken' somewhere. She wouldn't, she knew, have to look up deals or organise passports for a trip with Marek. 'You have excellent meze manners.' She steered the conversation away from a putative trip, shy of projecting their rickety partnership into the future.

Marek questioned the phrase with a look.

'Some people have the *worst* meze manners. They just dive in and vandalise the hummus, drop feta in the olives. You're approaching things calmly, you're not double dipping, you're not nicking all the best bits.' Orla enjoyed the glimmer of enjoyment in Marek's dark foreign eyes, and warmed to her playful theme. 'And you haven't tried to feed me. That always ends badly, usually with taramasalata in my eyebrows.' His hic-cupped laugh rewarded her. 'My friend Juno – I've mentioned her before – almost gave up on the man she married during their first date because of his meze manners. *He* tried to feed her.'

'I would never dare.'

'Good. It's a messy old business and neither side really enjoys themselves.' Orla refilled Marek's glass and her own from the bottle he'd chosen. He'd eschewed both the straw-covered house carafe and the ouzo, promising her that the lemony notes of the chenin blanc would complement their food perfectly.

'This wine is nice. I mean, memorably nice,' said Orla. Left to her own devices she ordered the cheapest, and left to his, Sim had ordered the most costly. They'd mocked wine buffs. *Mmm! A fine bouquet with hints of dirty knicker and the merest whisper of Formica!* 'It actually tastes like you said, as if we're on a summer beach, and not in rainy November London.'

'I'm glad you like it. I'll remember that.'

From somebody else that could sound suave, part of a trite

209

seduction, but Marek meant it. Orla's hand hovered over the food. She knew Marek was watching her, had been since the moment she'd arrived, as if he were at an invalid's bedside. He was watching for signs of relapse.

Sim hadn't come up in conversation. There was no mention of the valentine and no solicitous enquiry about how she felt. Sensing this was a plan, and not an empathy deficit, Orla applauded Marek's tact.

He was happy. Orla made him happy. She didn't need to be witty or profound or even, Lord knew, well coiffed; Orla made Marek happy by sitting opposite him and sharing a meal. This was empowering stuff for a spirit as gaga as Orla's. And, in the middle of a main course of unctuous lamb, she realised *she* was happy, too – and her happiness wasn't to do with the meat. It was to do with Marek.

'To us!' she said suddenly, holding up her glass, going with it, being, as Marek had optimistically described them, *normal*.

'To us!' Marek's glass shot up with alacrity. 'To Orla and Marek,' he said, more quietly, lowering his chin so that his upturned eyes were trained on hers.

'To Orla and—'

A commotion outside distracted her. The dark wintry street turned to apocalyptic day as a battery of lights snapped on. Parting fronds of plastic ivy Orla peered through the window.

'What is it?' Marek rose in his seat to look over the dusty greenery. 'They're filming something. Look, there's a guy with a camera on a sort of trolley thing.'

'Those lights are dazzling.' Large globes on a high scaffold lit the street like a stadium, illuminating a beetling herd of purposeful figures in padded body-warmers jabbering into walkie-talkies. It was as if a small army had laid claim to the parade of shops opposite.

'Do you think it's a film?' Marek sat down again, not as interested as the waiters who all gravitated to the windows, arms crossed, mouths open.

'Could be.' Orla wondered if she looked shifty.

Concentrating on his lamb, Marek said, 'Or a commercial maybe.'

'Yes, I think it's a commercial,' said Orla carefully, on boggy ground. Her raised fork empty, she held open a peephole in the ivy with her other hand.

'Commercials these days,' said Marek, 'seem to be in one of two camps. Either they're shouting *buy this cheap sofa!* or they're sophisticated mini movies.'

'Hmm.' A small trailer, parked a little way down the road, had become an object of interest for the body-warmer pack. It exuded a pregnant sense of something imminent, as individuals hurried towards it and away again, vaulting up the steps to knock on the door, conversing with the unseen occupants, pressing their earpieces, talking into their handsets, making hand gestures at colleagues nearer the cameras. The stark lights were trained on the window of a café, but Orla could sense that the small utilitarian trailer was about to burp out something important.

'You don't like your main?'

'No, I do, I just ...' Orla smiled mechanically, then her eyes slid back to the trailer as the door opened and Anthea Blake emerged on the top step. 'I'm just distracted, that's all,' she said thinly, as a solicitous hand shot out to guide Anthea down three steps.

211

'Is it *that* fascinating out there?' Marek seemed bemused by his date's inability to focus.

'Kind of.'

Orla's breath was trapped somewhere deep in her diaphragm. Like a doting lover, she couldn't look away from Anthea's progress towards the spot-lit café, the crew parting for her as if her charisma walked two steps ahead clearing the way. Dressed in nondescript bourgeois style for her role in the coffee commercial, Anthea nevertheless gleamed with the result of professional attention to her hair, her face, her outfit. Her benevolent smiles for the worker ants seemed assumed to Orla, the tic of a person who knows they're the centre of attention.

Marek, seeing Orla's mouth fall open, half stood to look out. 'Ah,' he said in a chalky resigned voice. 'I see.'

The spell broken – Orla had been unprepared for the physical effect of seeing her nemesis – Orla belatedly set about her food. 'Fancy seeing her here.'

The attempt at wryness fell on stony ground. 'You planned this.'

For the briefest of moments, Orla considered a wide-eyed rebuttal. Ashamed of the impulse, she laid down her cutlery. 'I did,' she conceded, bowing her head but keeping her eyes left; Anthea was being positioned in the café's pseudo daylight at a window table. The cynosure of many eyes, the actress was a petite monarch accustomed to her power and casual about it.

'I'm over here, Orla.'

'Sorry.' Orla tore her eyes away to focus on Marek. 'Don't look at me like that!' Orla hoped the protest was playful. She didn't like his frank disquiet, nor his disappointment.

212

'Anthea Blake is why you chose this restaurant. Why you changed tables.' Marek balled his napkin and dropped it on the remains of his meal, nodding at a waiter who hurried over. 'Did you want to see me at all?'

'Of course.' Orla realised, a little late, how this looked. 'I did, I mean, I do. Honestly. But I need to see *her* and it seemed obvious to, like, dovetail the two.'

Orla wasn't entirely certain she could explain it to herself.

'Why do you need to see her? Surely she's the last woman on earth you want to be near!'

Marek's brief interchange with the waiter asking for the bill, immediately, gave Orla time to formulate a reason that didn't reflect disastrously on her judgement, her state of mind, her manners. She couldn't.

'I'm sorry, Marek. It's hard to explain.'

'Look at you!' Marek's voice rose. 'Even while we're arguing about it you can't keep your eyes off the street!' Marek stood, his chair falling back.

Other diners looked over and at each other, covertly curious.

'She has something that belongs to me!' hissed Orla, aware that they were the floor show.

His wallet wouldn't cooperate, refusing to emerge from his breast pocket. Marek swore under his breath, yanked out the little leather envelope and plucked a fan of notes. Flinging them on the table without counting them, he headed for the exit.

After a second's shocked inaction, Orla rose and followed him, gathering her jacket and bag with hunched speed as if fleeing a burning building.

Across the road, Ant sat at a table, serene in the midst of industry. A man in a baseball cap perched on the table, talking to her, eliciting nods and a tinkling laugh that Orla believed she could discern through the noise of the crew, a gathering crowd and Marek's hasty footfall as he stalked to the corner. He stopped dead a little way ahead of her, shoulders suddenly falling, and wheeled to face her.

'We'll go home,' he said calmly. 'Start again. Yes?'

Orla relaxed a little: she hadn't scared him off utterly. When Marek held out his hand she took it eagerly, enjoying its warm strength in the cold night air.

Her outstretched hand in his outstretched hand, Orla was dimly aware that the dynamic between her dawdling self and the brisker Marek was that of busy parent and reluctant toddler. She looked back at the surreal hub of light and purpose about to be eclipsed by the corner they were turning.

Craning her neck, unwilling to lose sight of it, she stopped dead, resisting the tug of Marek's grasp. The journal might be back there, in the Portakabin.

She has everything, thought Orla.

'Oh no no *no*.' Marek sounded exasperated. His fingers closed tighter around hers. 'Look at yourself, woman.'

He didn't say it unkindly. In fact, he said it with compassion. And Orla looked at herself.

She saw a woman who shouldn't give Anthea Blake and her latest romantic scalp another thought but who nonetheless longed to stride across the road, elbow through the guardians assigned to exclude mere mortals from the filming of such a holy thing as a coffee ad and confront Anthea about theft, about love, about right and wrong.

Marek kept his hand in hers and when her body lost its readiness to spring his grip relaxed, and he closed his eyes with relief when finally Orla turned around and said, 'Let's go home.'

'Would you have stopped me if I'd pulled away? Physically stopped me, I mean.' Orla looked down at the arm wrapped around her, its dark hairs vivid against the snowy chaos of the bedclothes.

'No. You're a big girl. You can do what you want.'

Marek and she were entwined, pretzel-like, a Siamese twin fashioned by a mutual need for skin against skin. He kissed the top of her head, squeezing her as he did so, and she enjoyed how virile his body felt against hers, full of male strength and potential.

And she enjoyed that she enjoyed it, without checking first with the dead to see if they minded.

'Wouldn't you even have stopped me a little bit?' Orla was disappointed. Never prone to Tarzan and Jane fantasies, she nonetheless found the image of Marek throwing her over his shoulder a provocative one.

'No.' Marek was on to her. 'Perhaps you'd like me to wear a fireman's helmet next time we make love? Or I could pretend to arrest you.'

'I love your house.' Orla changed topic, her mind pleasantly at ease after a prolonged period of kissing and stroking and charging around each other's erogenous zones like delighted tourists newly arrived in a resort.

'You said that.'

'I know. But I do. I *love* your house.' Mews buildings had

always fascinated her, commanding huge fees for what was essentially a horse's dormitory. In this squat, compact space tucked in behind an august Chelsea street, Orla finally grasped the point. It was cosy and it was luxurious, but it was playful too: Marck had inserted a high-end kitchen in a stable. The juxtaposition of exposed brick and chrome pleased her, as if she'd stepped into a magazine article about how the other half, the half with all the taste, live. And the spiral staircase delighted her with its whimsy, although she could attest to how uncomfortable it was as a venue for lovemaking. 'You've got lots of books.'

'You approve.'

'I do.' Orla unapologetically judged people by their bookshelves. Juno was still in the naughty corner for a Jeffrey Archer compendium, and Sim's meagre library – Orla's thoughts skidded to a halt, shook themselves and changed direction.

It didn't matter what Sim had or hadn't read.

'I'm getting to know your body,' said Orla shyly, picking up the arm that lay across her and brushing it with her lips.

In response, one part of that body perked up a little, bumping the top of Orla's thigh like an insistent Labrador angling for walkies.

'Ooh,' she laughed.

'Sorry,' said Marek, not sounding in the least penitent. 'Your body is like ...'

'Steady.' Orla had received many clumsy compliments and didn't want the moment tarnished.

'Like an ice-cream. Like a big sweetie just for me. Like a bank holiday.'

'*Okay.*'

'Oh God.' Marek, who seemed to like ice-cream, sweeties and bank holidays a *lot*, groaned as he nuzzled her closer, that Labrador becoming more insistent. 'You've bewitched me, Irish.'

This soppiness, allied as it was to his need to feel her naked against him, to touch her breasts wonderingly with his strong hands, to feel her bottom as though he were blind and the meaning of life were written on her buttocks in Braille, thrilled Orla. Particularly as she could answer it with equal portions of desire and interest.

In one respect, however, they were mismatched.

Orla wasn't as crazy about Marek as he was about her.

After years of being the catcher, she was suddenly the catch. It was exhilarating: had Sim felt like this? She reversed up that dead end abruptly, chiding his ghost for intruding yet again. She doubted, anyway, that their reactions would match; Sim had felt entitled to admiration, whereas his legacy had left Orla grateful for it.

Marek's guileless honesty about just how much he liked Orla was at odds with his measured, adult, alpha male approach to life. She made a kid of him, bouncy with happiness; he was, she'd found, an enthusiastic flinger of ladies across beds. He made her feel young in return, if optimism and glee and belief in good things finally happening to good people can be said to be young.

But these feelings were finite, trapped within the walls of his stylish mews house, or at least the walls of their togetherness. Orla couldn't immerse herself the way he did; there was unfinished business elsewhere, and it was tacky stuff, gum on her shoe, and on her soul.

When Marek leaned across to kiss her as he dropped her outside Maude's Books at a bleached and early hour, he said, 'So. No Googling you-know-who. Yes?'

'No Googling you-know-who.'

'What time tonight?'

'*Tonight?*' Ignoring the insolent parps of impatient drivers trying to manoeuvre past the Jag, Orla paused, one foot on the pavement. 'You crazy fool!' she laughed.

'I can't wait any longer than that!' Marek said it as if it was obvious. 'I'll cook for you. Get to mine for eight.'

'Yessir.' Orla blew a kiss to the departing car, liking the swathe it cut through the traffic.

Sim's journal

28 October 2011

I used the word 'love' today. I said, 'If you lined up all the people in the world in order of who I thought I would or should fall in love with, you'd be at the end of the line. O wouldn't even believe me if I told her I was in love with you.'

But here we are. In love.

Chapter Twenty

Pushing away her plate, Orla stretched her arms above her head. 'That's the third meal you've cooked for me now,' she said.

'And?'

'Yum.' She looked longingly at the remains of the roast chicken over on the worktop. 'Seconds?'

'Where does it go?' asked Marek, rising to persuade another plateful out of the carcass, its bare ribs sticking up like the remains of a bombed-out cathedral.

'No mystery about that.' Orla slapped her thighs, which were becoming more slappable by the day. 'Right here.'

'Then have thirds,' said Marek, his deep voice colluding with his accent to render the suggestion naughty as he set down a chicken leg in front of her. He watched her eat, chin on his hands, ignoring her '*Marek!* Get off!' until he stood and began to load the dishwasher.

'I'll do that.'

'You're my guest.'

Orla wondered when she'd be elevated (or would it be relegated?) to non-guest status and permitted to do something, anything, for herself. She was growing accustomed to his house, could bend the sound system to her will, knew which cupboard door hid the fridge, but Marek's notion of hospitality was courtly: he topped up her glass, brought her food, passed her a towel after her shower with the swift discretion of a valet. None of this dented his manliness; if anything it enhanced it. He was exciting to be with, smelling of a citrus aftershave and prone to spinning her into his arms as she passed.

'This kitchen is lit like an old Hollywood movie.' There wasn't a mirror in the house which Orla had to approach sideways. It was the most thought about, considered property she'd ever been in. 'Even the dirty pots by the sink look like a renaissance painting.'

'I get the best guys in. A perk of my position.'

Not all the homes Marek built came with wrinkle-reducing lighting and bespoke cabinetry; Orla had seen folders of his pet projects, the social housing where space per family was limited and budgets were tight. Neat, pleasing, well planned, they looked like somewhere she could live. He built honest houses, warm and welcoming.

'Are you rich?' asked Orla abruptly, surprising Marek into halting a ladle halfway to the dishwasher.

'Rich? That's a child's word. Nobody's rich any more. Nobody has gold under the bed. Money is abstract, virtual.'

'Quit stalling, Rabbit.' Since learning that Marek's surname, Zajak, was derived from the Polish for hare or rabbit, Orla had coined a new nickname, pleased with how much it didn't suit him. 'You're rich or you're not. To give you an example – I'm not.'

'I'm comfortable, I suppose.' Marek smiled, dimples deepening. 'To say *I'm rich* sounds all wrong. I work hard is how I prefer to put it.'

'Do you think you would have done so well without Aga spurring you on at the start?'

Aga could be mentioned, unlike Sim. There was a particular face Marek assumed when her name came up, one of formal blandness that nevertheless spoke of pain.

'Possibly not. I wasn't ambitious until I got my first taste of success and that was all down to pleasing her. Then I found I was good at making homes, and I enjoyed it. So I have a lot to thank her for.'

Poor old Aga, thought Orla. She didn't live long enough to outgrow her greed. Perhaps she and Marek would have made a go of things if she'd survived. Perhaps they'd still be together and Orla would be sitting all alone bathed in unflattering lighting. This glimpse of an alternative present made her cough, shift position, boot the thought away. Her feelings about Marek often manifested indirectly. Orla could imagine the hurt she'd experience if she suddenly lost him, yet had difficulty admitting how she felt with him right there in front of her. She sighed for her romantic two left feet.

'I like that you call it "making homes",' she said. 'Sounds so much nicer than property developer.'

'Your mother preferred property developer.'

'Don't remind me, Marek. You got the full Cassidy third degree. Da wouldn't have asked you a single thing. He went on instinct. Ma likes information. Lots of it.'

'Hmm.' Marek was smug. 'I think she likes me.'

'It's safe to say she does.'

Orla remembered Ma's gulping, squawked summing up.

'Janey Mac, Orla, you fell on your feet there! You kept him quiet, you little madam, and me eating me heart out with worry that you'd be a spinster like your Great Aunty Peggy, you know, the one with the funny foot. Doesn't he talk lovely? He's like an aristocrat, with that lovely accent and he reckons he's a property developer and he looks after his sister so he has a good heart and he says, so nice, so proper, "You raised a lovely daughter, Mrs Cassidy," imagine hearing that from—' Ma had stopped short of her first criticism of Saint Sim.

Orla hadn't meant to introduce Marek to Ma that evening; such events had to be planned with care and approached with caution, like a zookeeper introducing bashful pandas in the hope they might mate. Marek had simply mouthed 'Your mother?' at her and taken the phone.

As Orla died a thousand deaths she heard Marek's responses to Ma's quick-fire interrogation. 'Yes, once, I'm afraid I'm a widower, Mrs Cassidy . . . I'm about ten years older than your daughter . . . I have my own business . . . Poland . . . yes, I'm a Catholic! . . . more than twenty years ago . . .' At this point he'd looked puzzled but ploughed on with 'My favourite Eurovision winner would be Dana with "All Kinds of Everything", I guess.'

'I like your *Ma*.' Marek drawled the word as he ran water into the sink. 'She is a proper mother. She doesn't try to be your friend. Now I must meet Juney.'

'Juno,' Orla corrected him. 'She's busy with her little boy.' That was glib, and Orla divined from Marek's silence that he knew she was stalling. Juno would fly to London in a heartbeat, Jack on her hip. 'She already likes the sound of you, anyway.' *For starters*, thought Orla, *you're not Sim*.

During a hurried Skype over breakfast that morning,

mostly dedicated to complaining about the camera, Juno had said, all in a rush, 'You know these conversations hold me together, don't you? You wouldn't give up on me, O, would you? Not even if I did something terrible?'

Orla's toast-crunching had ceased at Juno's tone. 'Have you murdered somebody, Ju?'

'Not yet. Although if Himself falls asleep in front of *Newsnight* again I don't hold myself responsible for my actions. I miss you sitting on my shoulder. You're my conscience.'

'I am *not*,' Orla had roared, her outrage only partially mock. 'You're an Irish Catholic, proud owner of the most highly developed conscience in history. You don't need me to tell you right from wrong.'

'S'pose not.' Juno had sounded miserable.

Back in the moment, the delicious moment, with seconds of roast chicken in front of her and an easy-on-the-eye man rinsing dishes a few feet away, Orla murmured, 'Perhaps I should see her soon.'

But Juno would know. She'd take one look and *know* that Orla was planning something toxic.

What was it about London, wondered Orla, that made people do things they had to hide from the ones who knew them best?

Back when Orla's worst vice was biting her nails, Ma would come at her with the Stop 'n' Grow; seven-year-old Orla would dodge around the kitchen table, shrieking with laughter.

As we grow more sophisticated, so do our bad habits. Orla's colleagues were addicted to gossip: the current hot staffroom

224

topic was the burgeoning dalliance between the office manager and the newest tutor. Orla, busy withstanding the lure of her own habit, left them to it on the central lagoon of sofas and folded her legs beneath her on an islet built for one, an uncomfortable chair upholstered in nubbly material by a radiator. Beneath her chair, her iPad dozed in her bag, its wonders dormant. She'd made a promise to Marek; it was off limits.

Ruddy red cheeks, flattened nose and an upper body that threatened to rip through the constraints of his M&S machine-washable suit told the most casual onlooker that Cal was a rugger-bugger. His Irish forebears made natural allies of him and Orla in the staffroom, but it wasn't the only reason he sought her out this lunchtime. His crush on Orla was common knowledge amongst the staff and the main reason soft-hearted Orla always greeted him warmly even though he bored her rigid. Cal's passions were rugby and beer, and they were pretty much all he talked about.

'Not feeling sociable today?' Cal dragged over a section of the low-level modular seating that sat like toy furniture in the massive room whose Victorian bone structure was mocked by the college's preferred laminate and plastic. 'Usually you're in the thick of it.'

'Not today,' said Orla grinning toothily, overcompensating for her real response to Cal – boredom.

'Man,' groaned Cal, unwrapping a Mars Bar lustily, 'I was wrecked yesterday evening.'

Ninety-nine per cent of Cal's stories began this way, just as the denouement always featured him falling out of a minicab with a traffic cone on his head.

'Were you?'

'Yeah. I was out of it. Fell asleep in the kebab shop. My mates covered me in ketchup. Woke up and thought I'd been stabbed. Classic.'

'You're a crazy bunch, all right.' Orla chatted on automatic pilot, her thoughts catching on her bag, out of her sight but pulsing beneath the chair. 'Early night tonight, then?'

'Nah. Hair of the bloody dog!' Cal held up his polystyrene cup of machine coffee in salute to his own recklessness before describing, in meticulous detail, his contribution to his team's victory prior to the kebab shop hilarity.

Cal droned on, Orla interjecting with an 'ooh' or 'really?' at intervals. She shifted on her chair, fancying she could feel the rounded rectangular outline of her iPad through the seat; 'The Princess and the Pea 2013'.

'I took off down the left. Shoulda seen me!' Cal's face shone as if he'd glimpsed God.

'Hmm.'

'I saw my chance and yes! C'mon! Get out! Thirty twenty-seven!' Cal bounced on his seat, a toddler with pneumatic thighs.

'So you scored a goal?'

'Well,' Cal's pity mingled with tenderness for her adorable feminine ignorance. 'We call it a try.'

When Cal was summoned to the kitchenette to open a jar (he was lionised among the college women for his jar-opening abilities), Orla sat on her hands. When alone, she existed in a fog of need. That such a miraculous answer to her prayers as the journal should exist, and yet be denied her, was surely the work of some malign spirit with access to the control knobs and levers of Orla's life.

How odd that nobody seemed to notice Orla's yearning – she felt it so keenly. Didn't Marek sense it? And as for Maude – nothing! And she would notice a single misplaced pin from space.

Without expressly deciding to, Orla bent down and whipped out her iPad. She worked the gadget dexterously and with studied intent, trying to drown out her promise to Marek. He hadn't mentioned it since, an omission due more to discretion than forgetfulness, she knew.

She launched Twitter.

Lazy morning in Blake Towers! Charity ball tonight for #nspcc! Honoured to be involved!

Lazy morning? Rightly or wrongly, Orla felt she knew Anthea well enough by now to guess that no morning at 'Blake Towers' was lazy: she imagined the Tweeter on the phone to Reece, complaining, cajoling, demanding, then suffocating him with an avalanche of compliments.

Hopping nimbly from link to link, Orla polished her defence manifesto, hoping she'd never have to test it on Marek. *Everybody does it! Throw a stone into any crowd and you'll hit someone who's feverishly tracked an ex's relationship status on Facebook, or written cryptic messages on a colleague's wall, or checked out Tumblr snaps of the party they weren't invited to.* Yes, the internet offered a thousand exquisite ways to self-harm: Orla was only human to join in.

By the law of averages, this cyberstalking must surely present Orla with a fabulous nugget sooner or later: it would eventually highlight a spot in Anthea's crammed diary when the actress wasn't at a premiere, a rehearsal, a first-night party, a charity dinner, a dear chum's birthday bash, or supper with somebody higher up the celebrity food chain. And then Orla could find her, accuse her, hear her confession and demand the journal.

Reece wasn't the only one shy of scandal: Orla didn't want her name linked in perpetuity with Anthea Blake. This was where the internet came in handy: it was like having a brash, fearless private detective on the payroll. It would tail Anthea and alert her to the perfect, discreet moment to challenge the woman.

Until then, Orla would pick at the scab that kept trying to form over her damaged self-esteem. She would put up with the squalid sensation that lingered like a head cold after chasing Anthea through the internet.

All of a sudden, an article caught her eye, sending a frisson of excitement up her spine. It was a two-year-old piece, on an interiors website, all about Anthea's home.

'Orla?' Cal stood over her. 'The bell went ages ago.'

Stop 'n' Grow hadn't worked either. Orla still bit her nails.

Sim's journal

1 November 2011

Set was tense. Have the crew noticed? What if we just said, sod it, and ran away together? Mum would DIE. Dad . . . I can't dress this up: Dad would disown me. He'd have to. The Irish press would go to town on the scandal of the senator's son and his 'unsuitable' beloved.

Maude – Maude might understand.

Chapter Twenty-One

'Admit it, old lady,' said Bogna, 'you like George in sexy way.'

'Hey!' Orla couldn't let that pass. 'We don't call Maude *old lady*.'

'Ugh.' Bogna sighed at the tedium of political correctness. 'All right. Admit it, senior lady.'

Bogna was no longer Orla's precocious, surly, mini-skirted in all weathers ex-pupil, she was Orla's boyfriend's little sister. Marek was now outed as Orla's boyfriend. That Rubicon had been crossed. Before she'd read the valentine, the formality of that statement was freighted with baggage and she'd wondered if she could ever confer the term 'boyfriend' on a man again. Now it was the obvious, indeed *only* description for a man who cooked her meals, made regular and exquisite love to her, sent her texts that began, 'Good morning beautiful'.

'But I *am* old,' said Maude mildly. 'Have you catalogued my French classics yet, Bogna?'

'I hate Flaubert,' said Bogna. 'And Zola gives me dry heaves.'

'Try not to mention it around the customers.' Maude sniffed, possibly in recognition of the redundancy of her rebuke: the street outside heaved with humanity, but none of them turned their toes towards the shop. 'And I would have thought it bloody obvious that I like George very much.' Her face was wry as her sparring assistants turned to her, united in amazement. 'Old though I am, I have not quite withered yet. George is well turned out, polite, cheerful and his eyes are a particular grey I've always admired. Like pebbles,' she said, looking past Bogna and Orla. 'Like pebbles at the bottom of a spring.'

'Bloody hell,' said Bogna loudly, slowly.

'I don't intend to act upon my feelings.'

'Why not?' Bogna was outraged. She always acted upon her own romantic impulses: many times Orla had begged for fewer details of a social life which involved much WKD and what Maude termed 'heavy petting' by nightclub bins. (Marek, Orla knew, was ignorant of the WKD and the petting, preferring to believe that his sister was 'saving herself'. She rather admired this wilful fiction, adhered to against all the evidence.) 'This is twenty-first century!'

'I'm aware of that, dear. I'm happy as I am.'

'Nobody is happy alone,' grunted Bogna, and Orla could hear Marek's obstinacy in her tone.

'We're not all the same, thank goodness,' said Maude. 'If we all liked pistachio ice-cream the world would run out of the stuff. Luckily, some of us prefer chocolate chip.'

At the noise of the bell, all three of them turned, ready to greet a customer. 'Only me!' beamed Sheraz, staggering under a large cardboard box. 'I've run out of Toilet Duck.'

'We'll survive,' murmured Maude.

'Orla? It's Ma. Can you talk?'

'Howaya Ma. Wednesday already!'

'*December* already.'

'Yeah.'

'Aren't the years getting awful short?'

'Kind of.'

'And here we are in December. Well, well, well.'

'Well, well, well indeed.'

'Don't pretend you don't know what I'm getting at, ya little feck!'

'Ma, such language and me only thirty-three.'

'Orla Cassidy, are you or are you not coming home for Christmas?'

'No, Ma, I'm not.'

'Great. Fabulous. Right. I'll cancel the turkey. I'll spend the day in bed. On me own.'

'Ma, you'll have the usual full house.'

'This could be my last Christmas on this earth.'

'You've been saying that since 1990, Ma. You're fine. Aren't you? You'd tell me, wouldn't you? Ma?'

'Yes, I'm feckin' fine. I wish I had a nice fatal illness to tempt you back with but I don't. If your father was here—'

'He'd tell me to do what I wanted to do, Ma. And this year I want to be in London.'

'What about New Year's Eve? We're always together on New Year's Eve. It's better even than Christmas. I'll do me special coleslaw again. It'll be a riot. Just like last year.'

'Hmm.'

'Don't *hmm* me, madam.'

'Just give me this year off, Ma, and maybe I'll be there for next New Year.'

'Ah, sure, couldn't we all be dead by next New Year?'

*

Orla rounded up her class on the steps and explained the academic director's reaction to the news that their classroom ceiling had collapsed.

'They were swear words. If he'd spoken more slowly you would have understood.' Her flock were fluent cursers.

Shivering but demob happy only an hour into their Thursday, a day that usually delivered an oral test and grave looks from Teacher, the students smirked at one another.

'Now, there's no room available for us today because ...' Orla didn't really understand her boss's reasons. 'Well, anyway, admin promise they'll sort us out with a corner later today or tomorrow. Until then why don't we all simply set up a temporary classroom in a café or – hey!' By then, she was talking to their backs, as her students dispersed like spilt mercury.

'Lazy buggers,' said Abena fondly.

'Abena, if you like, you and I can—'

'Are you kidding me?' Abena hugged her, blocking out the winter with the sunny smell of the oils in her hair. 'Bye bye!'

So Orla was at home, stretched out on her sofa, iPad throwing out light and colour on her lap. Orla had sworn off it that morning, awaking, horrified, to find the tablet cradled in her arms like a beloved pet. But here she was again.

Orla rapidly whizzed through the forums on Digital Spy – nothing on her subject since the rumour commented on and debated by fourteen members, that Anthea was to go into EastEnders – and on to Sleb Snap, where she skidded to a halt. There'd been a sighting that morning.

As a return visitor, Orla had no right to sneer at the tackiness of a site that published candid snaps of celebrities submitted by Joe Public, but curling her lip helped her to feel a little less soiled as her cursor hovered over the thumbnail of Anthea.

The blurry image bloomed to fill her screen. Wraparound sunglasses gave Ant the look of a fugitive fly as she sped past the lens of a mobile phone camera, head down, hair held out of her face with a scrunchie. Orla read the caption.

SHE'S TINY IN REAL LIFE QUITE RUDE
JUST PUSHED PAST ME AND HUBBY. LOVE HER
IN THE CORTESAN. DIDNT SHE GET HER
KIT OF IN SOME OLD FILM?!!

Indeed she did, madam. Orla knew the title (*Sing Me No Songs*), the year of release (1974) and the critical reception ('A turgid fable of gangland London enlivened by its young stars and much talked about nude scene. Two stars.') She knew that Anthea herself had referred to it in a 2011 *Empire* magazine interview as 'tame low budget nonsense. Just a flash of boob and a bit of bum. Nothing like the graphic nudity young actresses are bullied into these days'. Orla had seen the fuzzy stills, studied the out-of-focus pointed little breasts that were nothing like the impressive contents of The Courtesan's corset.

Helpfully, the fan had snapped Anthea passing a shop called Primrose Hill Antiques, placing her accurately in a small area of town. The untidy hair and lived-in sweats led Orla to conclude that the actress wasn't far from home.

This shot of adrenaline was familiar by now. Orla was amassing data (a highfalutin' word that conferred near-respectability on her hobby) and each fresh factoid brought her nearer to pinpointing Anthea's address.

The address held a special power. With Anthea's address, Orla could plan the final act, the *tête à tête* that would bring the journal home.

Her virtual day got better and better: after following the shaky lead of an offhand mention of Anthea Blake as a collector of rugs, Orla happened on the very interiors site she'd found and subsequently lost a week ago. Learning from that day's frustration, Orla now collated all her finds on Sim's laptop with a cross-referenced accuracy her students would recognise.

A gallery of eight interior shots: rich pickings indeed. The first shot – *Ms Blake's elegant exterior* – divulged information straight away. The house number, normally obscured in such articles, was there for all to see. Orla lived at number forty-nine, something street.

Orla lay back on the sofa and wandered at leisure through Anthea's home.

She favoured Christmas colours. Red and green and tangerine, the house was moody and seductive. And dark: Orla had to squint at some of the pictures to discern the highly decorative scheme.

It was a night-time house, theatrical yet artless. A shot of Anthea on the stairs, sending a come hither look over her shoulder, triggered the self-criticism that teetered in the wings during these forays: *I'm seventeen years younger than her but I wouldn't look that good in a v-backed dress.*

Her phone chirruped. *Marek*, she thought, with a rush of warmth, only slightly corrupted by her guilt. Thank goodness, she thought, that he's safely far away and can't see what I'm up to.

I'm just around the corner.

Orla let out a small mew.

Make the best of your unexpected day off and JOIN
ME! I'm in the Polish cafe. I'll feed you rogalicki until
you burst. X

Of course, it's Thursday. Marek, a man who did what it said
on the tin, ate at the café every Thursday: Orla loved, even
wallowed in, his reliability. She typed out

See you in five mins!

But the words ate themselves before they were sent, disappearing as Orla backspaced over them. She looked at the
photo gallery. *Next: Anthea's boudoir.*

Would love to, but busy! Sorry! Later? Your place?
Kissing 'n' that? Xxx Miss you

That was true: she did miss him. Orla had divided herself
so neatly down the middle that she could miss Marek and
forgo seeing him at the same time, just as she could bewail the
stupidity of cyberstalking and indulge in it at every opportunity.

Shame. I MIGHT kiss you later. p.s. I WILL kiss you
later.

Anthea's bedroom leapt out at her: Orla hadn't thought to fortify herself against it. It was, she had to admit, the perfect setting for Sim. She pictured him sprawled, naked as a baby, on the Chinese silk bedspread, his impertinent arse happy under the gilded stars on the purple-tented ceiling.

In her tear-stained imaginings, Orla had often strayed into this bedroom. She'd never had the décor right, though, as she forced herself to watch Sim kiss Anthea's neck and move down to her shoulders. (She knew his routine well.) Orla had clearly heard Sim's milky sighs and groans of pleasure, seen his look of joyous surprise as Anthea bent to leave a trail of kisses down his torso en route to her goal. Their orgasms had kept her awake as if they were in the next room.

Orla scanned the text like a scholar, alert, nose twitching for data. The author of the piece, no doubt bewitched, used superlatives like a drunk buying shots for everybody in the bar. Anthea was 'screen temptress and fine classical actress, Anthea Blake'; the house, apparently, reflected her 'passionate nature' and echoed the 'timeless quality of her beauty'.

Yes, thought Orla, *and the Duralit toaster on the worktop reflects her passionate nature. As does the toilet brush just in shot in the marble en suite.*

'An Olivier award sits on her mantelpiece, perfectly at home in this theatrical house. "As soon as I saw this place in the estate agent's window I knew I had to have it," Anthea tells me over a glass of her favourite rosé champagne. "I believe in fate."'

Orla broke off to snort unattractively. *You believe in copping off with other women's blokes.*

'"How could I pass up a house on a street named after the

237

very first Shakespearean heroine I played? The part that won me the Olivier. I've been very happy here and I can't see me ever moving out."'

Orla's zest for codifying paid off at last. She whizzed through her dossier, tracking down a note she'd made a while ago. This was fun; a similar thrill to untangling a Sudoku. Clean and contained, her spreadsheets were removed from the messy confrontation they would enable.

Orla lifted her head. As if a migraine had cleared, she was suddenly blessed with perfect vision. *What the* feck *is wrong with me?* She leapt up, the iPad tumbling, and punched her arms into the sleeves of her hooded rain jacket. Running through puddles, she didn't stop until she reached the crossing opposite the café.

He was leaving, pulling his collar up, hastening through the deluge.

'Marek!' Orla's shout couldn't compete with the cantankerous traffic. A bus obscured her view as she battered the traffic signal button with a flat palm. She jumped up and down on the spot until the green man appeared, but the bus still squatted on the crossing, forcing Orla to dart around it. She hit the other pavement running and didn't break step, dodging shopping bags and dog leads, reaching the side street just in time to see the low, distinctive, chocolate brown car pick up speed and grow smaller.

Chapter Twenty-Two

'It's disappointing,' said Orla as sternly as she was able, which wasn't very sternly at all. It was hard to attain maximum sternness in a Starbucks, aware that she and her multinational assembly had taken over most of the available seating yet spent as little as possible on coffee. 'I know it's a Monday and we all hate Mondays and we're disappointed that we *still* don't have a classroom, but I expected some effort from you. Learning English is the biggest favour you can do yourselves. Abena, are you listening?' Her pet, round and brown and sparkling Abena, was behind with her coursework. They all were. They were as bad as she was, it transpired, at dealing with unexpected free time.

'Sorry. My eyes cannot resist *cake*.' Abena made a diamond of the simple word, polishing it with African vigour until it shone.

'Mmm, brownies,' said Dominika.

'I like best lemon cake,' offered Javier, looking expectantly at Orla.

'What? Jaysus.' Orla tutted but was already on her feet. 'Shut up, shut up!' She flapped her hands at their sudden volubility. 'I'm not taking orders. I'll buy a selection of lemon cakes and brownies and nutty bastards and you can fight over them.'

Queuing by the glass display case, Orla decided to pop into admin after this disastrous tutorial and beg again for access to some tiny corner of the college. Her students were lagging behind, and she was fearful for their results.

'All of them, please,' said Orla pointing to the straggling brownies left on a tray. 'And seven lemon things. And four of *those*. Eat in.'

The course needed to get back on track. And she needed to escape her iPad. If she'd joined a gym at the start of these unexpected three days of leisure she'd be part-way to a presentable arse by now. Instead, she'd drunk cup after cup of tea and tunnelled ever deeper into the underground seams of the internet.

She hadn't Googled all of Friday away; Marek had sneaked away from work to take her skating.

'I've never done this before,' she'd warned him, her ankles buckling like Bambi's knees the instant she stepped out onto the ice.

'Lean on me,' he'd said.

Marek was good, his style economical but graceful. Orla was bad, even worse than she'd worried she'd be, managing only a crouching mince. She knew her nose was cranberry and her knees hurt from a spectacular fall, which had made Marek want to guffaw. He'd held it in as he helped her up, but those dimples gave him away.

'Here.' Marek held out one arm, glided up behind her so that she leaned back on it, and took both her hands in his, wide, cruciform. 'I'll support you. Just lean on me. I can take it.'

Off they went. She stumbled. Recovered. His body was

long and hard and hinted at reserves of strength he didn't bother to use, but could call upon. Orla was too busy trying to stay upright to steal a look at his face but she knew it would be serene, with that pout that stopped it being severe.

What scares you? she'd wondered. *And would you ever show it?*

'*How* much?' she squeaked at the girl in the Starbucks apron. She pulled a couple of notes from her purse, swept a beady eye over her students, all happily impersonating the way she pronounced their names. They were worth it, she supposed.

'I'm afraid I'm off out again, Maudie-poos.' Orla peeped apologetically around the door of Maude's eyrie.

'Afraid?' Maude's neck lengthened at the word as she muted the television. She made barely a dent in her nest of sofa cushions. 'Why afraid, dear?'

'I haven't been around much this week.'

'Good!' Maude laughed at Orla's dismay. 'Now, now, no gurning. You know I cherish your company but truly, I'd need a heart of stone to begrudge you your new romance.'

Orla stepped into the room, coat on, scarf wrapped, already halfway to Marek's in her mind. 'You sure you'll be all right?'

'I'm not a china doll.' Maude turned up the television again.

'Why don't you nip out somewhere? A bit of fresh air would do you—'

'What would do me good is for you to stop wittering on.' The look Maude gave Orla was blank, her hyacinth eyes cool. '*Shoo*,' she added deliberately.

Worrying about Maude, fretting that the woman never

seemed to get out these days, consumed Orla for the whole of her tube journey.

It was impossible, however, to brood with her bare bottom hard up against a kitchen cabinet and Marek inside her. A white bowl, a spiral of artful ridges, crashed to the floor. Neither noticed.

'I love you,' said Marek afterwards, as they stood clinging together, like survivors of a shipwreck. He pulled back far enough to see her eyes. His were weary and happy. 'I really do, Orla. I love you.'

Orla opened her mouth but found herself silenced by his finger on her lips.

'You don't have to answer,' he whispered, and kissed her unhurriedly. 'I just had to say it.'

'The students will have a field day if I go in wearing the same clothes tomorrow.' The mews was still and grave in the dark, its merry trellises grey. Orla hopped from foot to foot. 'Go indoors, Rabbit, you'll catch your death.'

'I'm fine.' Marek shivered in a tee and boxers, arms folded, shoulders hunched. 'Bring a change of clothes next time. Promise? This feels like an excuse to run away.'

'Why would I want to?' Orla leaned in to him, bent her head back, offered him her lips, an offer he took. 'I love your bed hair.'

'Christ.' Marek put a self-conscious hand to his Keith Richards pompadour.

'I like you ruffled. I like knowing it was me who got you that way.'

They kissed again, swaying.

242

Orla knew her fringe was in her eyes, her mascara had bled Rorschach blots on to her cheeks, her nose was cherry red. She was suffused with feelings of gratitude towards Marek for loving her, just when she felt her most unworthy, her most discarded.

But, thought Orla, how could the enchantment last? For enchantment it must be. Orla was a reserve. Sim had known her inside out, thoroughly road-tested her and concluded, *Nah*.

A metallic purr announced the taxi rounding the corner of the mews.

'Text me when you get inside your flat.' Marek made a guttural noise in his throat. 'You should have stopped me having that third glass. I could have driven you.'

'The cabbie doesn't look like a murderer to me, Marek.'

'They're the worst ones.' He leaned in and gave the driver Maude's address. 'Do you have cash?' he asked Orla, straightening up, patting his top and underwear as if there might be a stray tenner lurking somewhere.

'Yes, yes, stop fussing and get back to bed. I'll text you. Goodnight.'

She saw him decide not to say it again as he kissed her chastely on the forehead and waved her off, but as the taxi jolted over the cobbles before joining the smoother, fleeter road, Orla knew he loved her.

The cab stopped at the lights. She imagined Marek picking his barefoot way back to the rectangle of light stretching from his open front door, like a beachcomber hopping across hot sand. She leaned forward and tapped on the glass dividing her from the driver.

'Actually, change of plan,' she said, and named a road in Primrose Hill.

Chapter Twenty-Three

'It's about time, don't you think? My mum'll take Jack for a couple of days. Is this line funny? You sound as if you're in the middle of the street.'

'I'm having problems with this phone.'

'Speak up! Why are you whispering? Nice if I could rely on Himself to look after his own son but he's needed at the office yada yada yada.'

'He's a big high-up important bloke, Ju. Look, can we do this tomorrow? I'm a bit frazzled and—'

'I can hardly hear you. So, which weekend is good for you? I want to come on a weekend so I get full value out of you. Don't worry, I won't kip at yours. I'll treat myself to a hotel. You can come and jump on the bed, pillage the mini-bar. I'll take you somewhere fabulous for din-dins. For me, next weekend is *perfect* for all sorts of reasons.'

'Not for me, I'm afraid. I'm away.'

'Away? Where? You never said. Oh, is it Marek? Is he whisking you away?'

'No, it's a college trip, to ... Whitstable.'

'Weekend after?'

'Um, no, I'm looking after Maude.'

'In what way?'

'She's not well, and she's having a little operation.'

'What sort of operation?'

'A little one, on her, um . . .'

'You can just say you don't want me, you know.'

'Calm down, missus. I'm just busy, that's all.'

'Too busy for me? You're never too busy for me. Or you never *were*. I need to talk to you, Orla.'

'Juno, let's please sort this out tomorrow. I have to go. We'll sort a date. I miss you too, you know.'

'Do you?'

'I do. Good—'

Orla cut herself short as the porch light came on in the house next door. Ending the call, she ducked, hoping that her black outfit would be swallowed up by the dark hump of the hedge. A *trat-trat-trat* of claws conjured up a small dog preceding its owner out into the tiny, bin-filled rectangle that London estate agents describe, straight-faced, as a front garden.

Leaning further into her hide, Orla's soft cheek encountered a hard sprig and she stifled her *Ow*.

'Poo-poo for Mummy!' A stage whisper floated from an invisible figure in the porch. 'Poo-poo! Come *on*! It's freezing. Poo-poo for Mummy!'

Shrinking, eyes squeezed shut, Orla froze in case the brittle hedge's indignant crackling gave her away. Too late, she cursed herself for not conjuring up a cover story. If Mummy's poo-poo was not forthcoming and the woman looked her way, Orla had no valid reason to be standing in the hedge of a vacant house. Police might be called. At the very least the woman would jump out of her skin.

Thankfully the dog's ablutions were swift and Orla was soon alone again, focused once more on number forty-nine,

245

the house exactly opposite. Beatrice Gardens was leeched of colour in the weak light of the street lamps and Orla was cold, her gloves not up to a December night.

She could be in Marek's bed right now.

They always (already they had an 'always') began the night entwined, before each would sleepily loosen their limbs until they were companionably side by side. As morning crept across the room, so they'd curl back in to each other. She would wake up smelling him, feeling the softness of his hair and the slumbering vitality of his body.

This is what you've brought me to. You and your bloody journal. Talking to Sim was no longer a symptom of missing him. To miss Sim would be so wildly inappropriate that some remorselessly logical department of her heart had simply closed the relevant section down.

This was about claiming what was rightfully hers. This was about justice, and answers, and peace of mind. Tonight was the culmination of her virtual vigil, the reason she'd stashed away each clue, each crumb.

Twitter had alerted her to Anthea's unusual plans.

Crikey! Quiet night in on my own! I must be losing my touch! LOL ;) x

Orla had already divined Anthea's address, helped by the carelessly un-blurred house number and the clue embedded in the quote about living in a street named after an award-winning role. Orla's archive of Anthea facts – useless in any other situation – had thrown up the Olivier for *Much Ado about Nothing*, a play that Orla had studied at school. She'd had a soft spot for the firebrand heroine and now, all these years later, had punched the air when a street map of Primrose Hill had thrown up Beatrice Gardens.

And now Orla was there, and could stride across the road, ring the doorbell and light the blue touch paper with a calm, *I know about you and Sim*.

She'd do it by midnight. Orla had promised herself this when she'd alighted from the taxi and stood, irresolute, in the middle of the road. She had imagined storming up the steps, but the house was so tall – and so broad, and so complacently expensive – that it had cowed her and she had retreated to the handily sited empty property to regroup.

Excavating a spyhole in the dusty hedge was easy. The house behind her was for sale following what looked like a speedy renovation of white paint and stripped boards that had run out of steam or cash before it reached the jungly front garden. Through the untidy gap, Orla could see number forty-nine perfectly.

Two storeys over a basement, broad steps up to a handsome front door, Anthea's house was as well presented as its owner. Repointed bricks sat as straight and correct as a computer-generated image, yet the property had all the character of its vintage. Early Edwardian, confident and wide, semi-detached from a less groomed twin, it had cost, according to Zoopla, a figure well north of what Orla expected to earn in her lifetime.

The hall light shone through the fanlight above the door. The sitting room curtains were closed, but not pulled quite together, allowing an uneven slither of warm lamplight to escape.

Anthea was in there. Possibly on the moss green sofa Orla had admired online, possibly on the rug brought back from filming in Peru. Maybe Anthea was reading the journal, a book she only figured in towards the end. At will, she could flick through the intimate ins and outs of the early days of Sim and Orla, or she could skip to the finale and its car crash of lies.

It was almost midnight. Orla restrained her thoughts, keeping them from scurrying sideways. She must be strong and certain: right, after all, was on her side.

The soft swish of traffic circling Regents Park was like distant surf. Orla yawned. She'd assumed folk stayed up all night in these boho media byways. Only a handful of upper windows were still lit on the street, and apart from number forty-nine, one sole ground floor window attested to hardy types still up and watching a flickering television.

In Tobercree, the Cassidys regarded early nights as lily-livered giving in. There was always another round of tea to be drunk, another topic for in-depth discussion, another family member to lightly roast. *Lightweights*, thought Orla, as a light died in a loft to her left.

Eyes trained on Ant's front door, Orla pictured Sim skipping up those steps, a beribboned champagne bottle in his paw. He'd fit right in. She could practically hear the confident tune he'd bash out on the brass lion's paw knocker. The heavy lantern hanging in the porch, the bay trees flanking the door, the antique boot scraper on the caustic tiles, all these House Beautiful accoutrements would combine with Sim to create a visual medley of poshness.

When he'd visited Ma, bounding up to her hacienda-style bungalow, sidestepping the miniature concrete donkey with its panniers of geraniums, he'd taken great sarcastic delight in the doorbell that played 'Waltzing Matilda'. All the curtains in the cul-de-sac would twitch, and Her Next Door would brazenly emerge to get a look at 'the senator's boy'.

Home yet?

If she ignored his text, Marek would call. Orla's finger dithered over the letters on her phone before she barked at herself to get on with it. After tonight there'd be no need to lie.

Just got in. Goodnight. xxx

Orla downgraded *lie* to *fib*. Standing this side of an untruth, she saw how it shape-shifted. Presumably Sim had played similar games with the dimensions of his own lies.

She shied away from an estimate of how many times he'd misled her and she'd cheerfully accepted it, jolly and innocent, a mug.

Goodnight, Orla. And I meant it. I love you. X

Had Sim blanched when the lie worked and the other party carried on loving? Marek's simple message should have turned her heart over with happiness but instead it made her feel like a cur.

Across the road, the slit of light from Anthea's sitting room died. Seconds later, the hall went black. Anthea was climbing the stairs, the stairs carpeted with seagrass. Orla stiffened. This was it. She had to strike before Anthea retired. She felt as if a great pressure was pushing down on her head, pounding her into the hard earth like a tent peg.

The light in what must be Anthea's en suite snapped on: Orla could see marble walls above the louvre half shutters. The glass misted up. The lady of the house was running a bath, or a shower. No point, thought Orla, giddy with the reprieve, in knocking on the front door while Anthea was naked and wet. Let her finish. And then, then Orla would have no option but to end this peculiar duet.

There she was! The bedroom, at the front of the house, was sketchily visible in the leaking light from the en suite. Anthea stood in front of the windows, arms up like an angel to pull the heavy curtains which Orla knew were a deep Cadbury's purple. Anthea looked out into the dead street, looked straight at the house opposite, looked, or so it seemed, at Orla.

With one jerk, the curtains closed and the silhouette disappeared.

Five minutes to Orla's self-imposed deadline. After, she could delete the careful biography she'd amassed with all the loving care of a number one fan and stay up all night reading Sim's candid words after years of being spoonfed the careful compliments in his cards.

Prepared for the grenades hidden in the last few pages, Orla also hoped that earlier entries would prove that she *had* known the real Sim back then. That he *did* like chocolate chip ice-cream; that he *had* loved her once.

The en suite was pitch black. Fear made Orla's body weightless. A quote popped, unbidden, into her head, from *Much Ado about Nothing*. Benedick, Beatrice's lover and adversary, had boasted, '*it is certain I am loved of all ladies*'.

If Sim had lived, he'd have been perfect casting for Benedick. He was loved of all ladies, and the last two of them were arranged neatly opposite each other now, just about to merge, before flying apart for good.

Without warning, the clouds grumbled and Beatrice Gardens was drenched. Orla staggered under the rain, her hair plastered to her forehead in an instant, her nose dripping, the back of her neck wet.

She left the garden and stood in the street, watching the one window still lit in Anthea's house. Inside her gloves her fingers were numb. This wasn't the clean rain of Tobercree, that floated leaf boats down the lane: this was hard-assed London rain, swilling fag ends along the gutters.

A church bell, muffled by the downpour, tolled glumly.

Move!

Orla couldn't cross the road: it was as wide as the Serengeti.

Move!

Sim's last two loves were metres apart. One was indoors, pampered, warm, bath-fresh and sweet smelling, about to lie down beneath a jade bedcover; the other was out in the dark, blinded by rain, cheated out of her paltry legacy.

Move!

Orla's obstinate feet wouldn't obey.

The light in the upstairs window died.

Chapter Twenty-Four

'Every cloud has a silver lining, even a cloud that involves a ceiling falling on the heads of charming young people,' said Maude. 'I'm rather sorry you're back in your classroom tomorrow. I shall miss you at elevenses.' She placed a plate of toast slathered in honey on the shop coffee table. 'There. Eat it while it's hot. I heard you sneak in at all hours. Out carousing with your Polish hussar again?' Living vicariously through Orla had lit Maude from within: she was like a geriatric supermodel – *because I'm seventy-four and worth it.*

'Yeah,' said Orla. It wasn't entirely a lie. But, like so many of her recent exchanges with the people closest to her, neither was it true. She watched Maude tootle around her little empire, nibbling toast and tucking a book in here, turning one the right way up there. When Maude touched her books she was communing with a vast breadth of human experience, yet she couldn't sense the turmoil going on just feet from her where Orla sat, eating toast, gazing out of the window.

It had foundered, the simple plan: *cyberstalk Anthea – discover a time when she's alone – approach her to inform her that I know about affair with my man – take the journal – read it – collapse in heap – recover – live happily ever after – (with Marek?)*

A barrier of her own making had kept her in the rain at Beatrice Gardens until after 2 a.m. The gulf between herself and Sim's lover had opened up like a ravine that yawned, unbreachable, in the short space between the parked cars and Anthea's gate.

As each minute ticked by, it had seemed increasingly unlikely to Orla that she could ever confront Anthea. She had no voice, just a squeak of fear and unhappiness. She would cry, she knew, and say the wrong thing – a string of wrong things. She couldn't compete with Anthea's power.

Anthea held all the cards. Anthea had been the one Sim loved when he died.

At some point, watching a darkened house had become too absurd even for Orla's new state of mind and she'd trudged home, ignoring taxis' flirty orange lights, to climb into bed just as the night gave way to dawn.

'He seems awfully keen.' Maude sat on the arm of the sofa, all the better to fish. 'As does a certain young lady not a million miles from me.'

'Mmm.'

'Bogna's never seen him like this. Said he's had plenty of girlfriends but nobody special. Not until you.' Maude stood and walked behind the sofa to slot a slender volume between two leviathans. 'According to her, you've brought him back to life.' She frowned at a Marian Keyes in among the foreign titles. 'He's certainly repaid the compliment.' She leaned over the back of the sofa to say into Orla's ear, 'It's rude to ignore little old ladies who are trying to make conversation.'

Orla laid her head back on the sofa, and regarded an upside-down Maude, glad of her, sorry to be shutting her out. 'He told me he loves me.'

Maude clapped her hands together. 'Of course he loves

you! He has taste.' Bending into Orla's hair, she murmured, 'I know you're not as whole as you appear, dear. I know better than to trust this miraculous recovery. Remember I'm here.'

Startled by Maude's clairvoyance, Orla tensed. She stood and watched Maude drift away, humming, swaying her barely there hips under her voluminous skirt.

Maude would save her. Maude would say the one pithy thing that would keep Orla from her shameful internet scavenger hunts and her battles with self-worth in Primrose Hill; kind, clever Maude's clarity would nail Orla's folly so that it could never be taken seriously again. Maude would save Orla from herself.

'Maude, listen,' she began.

'Customer!' trilled Maude, looking over Orla's shoulder. 'Good morning George,' she said, her voice sprightly as a lark's.

'May I have a word?' George turned a tweed cap over and over in hands that were as gnarled, Orla noticed, as tree roots.

'Of course. Is there a problem?' Maude's brow lowered as she approached him.

It was hard to harbour bad thoughts about George; he was old and gentle and mad about Maude. His timing, however, was regrettable. Orla's secret buttoned itself back up.

'Not at all.' George dropped his voice – a pleasing voice, genteel with a slight crack that earthed it and reminded the listener that beneath the carefully pressed clothes George was a man. 'Maude, I promised myself that today would be the day I finally told you something.'

'Yes?' Maude was encouraging, but Orla caught the shift in tone, as if the old lady's toes were pointing away, ready to carry her off.

'I enjoy visiting this shop. You should be very proud of it.'

Go George! Orla bit her lip, willing him on.

'I *am* proud of it. Thank you.'

'But really I come here to see you.'

George's gulp was audible, and hopefully camouflaged Orla's gasp.

'Do you?' Maude was carefully non-committal, in waiting mode.

'Yes. As I'm sure you must know. I would like to get to know you better, but I don't flatter myself the sentiment is returned.'

Don't be cool, Maudie! begged Orla, head down, crunching her toast *very quietly*.

'Do flatter yourself, George,' said Maude firmly, and Orla could picture the glint in her blue eye.

'That *is* good news!' George forgot to keep his voice intimate, so Orla didn't have to strain as he said, in the manner of one proclaiming good news, 'In that case, Maude, please do me the honour of coming out to dinner with me. Tonight!' he added, speeding on the confidence she'd given him.

'Why not let me cook for you?'

Celebrations on hold, Orla knew that George wasn't versed in Maude-speak and might not recognise the question mark as rhetorical.

'I wouldn't dream of it. Just get your glad rags on and allow me to show you off.'

'I'm a very good cook.'

George, read the signs.

'I have no doubt of that, Maude. But I want to—'

'You want to boss me about.'

Clang. There it was, the change of mood that Orla and Bogna and even Sheraz dreaded. George had provoked the one bum note in Maude's shimmering range.

'No, no, no.' George sounded as baffled as Orla had been when she'd first ridden Maude's switcheroo. 'Not at all. But a nice restaurant, of *your* choice, wouldn't that be a delightful way to spend an evening?'

'No. It would not.'

Garlanded with icicles, Maude's announcement had no response and Orla risked a peep at the couple. George had stopped kneading his cap. In fact, he'd given up all movement, standing like a statue.

'Perhaps I should . . .' George motioned at the door with his cap.

'Perhaps you should,' agreed Maude. After the bell's hollow laugh she headed for the back of the shop, saying over her shoulder, 'I don't want to hear a word, not one word, about that ever again.'

Maude roughly pushed apart the beaded curtain and lingered in the back room for the rest of the morning. And Orla went upstairs, to seek out her iPad and her laptop.

'Is it your dream, to be a teacher?' Perhaps it was because English was Marek's second language that he could say stuff like that without it seeming pompous. Or perhaps it was because he spoke as if he'd weighed the words and found just the right amount. He was naked, unconcerned about it, sitting up in Orla's bed and eating grapes. They popped and died between his teeth.

'Dream? Don't know about that.'

Why was she denying it?

'It's one of the most important jobs in the world,' said Marek, perfectly serious. 'When you have very little, education is riches. You're responsible for little minds, Orla. Well, not so little minds in your present job. But you'll go back to little minds one day.'

That was insightful. Until he'd said it, Orla hadn't quite realised it herself, but yes, she would return to the bizarre world of interfacing with seven-year-olds. If he could see that, perhaps he could see other things. Orla stood and pulled her dressing gown tighter around her: she didn't care to be transparent this morning, not when she'd risen early to trawl Sleb Snap while he was still asleep.

'No, don't.' Marek pulled at the cord of her wrap and it opened. He moved and tugged her to him, so that his arms were on her skin beneath the dressing gown. His head nuzzled her stomach.

Orla put her hands in his hair: she felt invested with power as if she'd tamed a lion and made it come to her. She was tearful, unexpectedly. A great surge of tangled emotions rose in her. She wanted to speak but she didn't know what she wanted to say. Anybody who has ever kept a secret would recognise the 'stoppered up' sensation that kept her mute.

'Christmas.' Marek let go, flopping back on to the bed, arms over his head. 'What are we doing?'

Letting her hair fall over her face as she reknotted her dressing gown cord, Orla said archly, '*We?*'

'Yes, hard-to-get bloody Irish, *we*. I know. I'll cook a traditional English turkey for you and Maude. And Bogna. Unfortunately. Here. Yes?'

'Yes please.' Orla felt a jigsaw piece click into its place.

'And let's plan New Year's Eve too,' said Marek, patting the bedclothes beside him. He patted harder when she ignored him. 'Come here, woman.'

Woman came there, settling her face into his chest. 'I'm not a fan of New Year,' she said. 'It's maudlin.'

'I've never been to Trafalgar Square at New Year,' mused Marek, as if she hadn't spoken. 'Always looks crazy on TV.'

'Oh Jaysus, Trafalgar Square!' Orla shuddered. 'Imagine it. Surrounded by drunks, freezing cold, everybody roaring, and then a schlep home in the small hours.'

'In short, something you'd never dream of doing?'

'No siree.'

'But it kind of excites you?'

'Sort of. In a *thank Gawd I'll never have to do that* way.'

'That's decided, then. We'll kiss at midnight in Trafalgar Square.'

'No way, Rabbit!'

'It's perfect. A new experience for both of us to kick off the new year. *Our* new year. I'll do this to you at midnight.' His pout found her lips and flirted with them a little.

'If you do that,' whispered Orla, 'I'll have to do *this*.' Marek's eyes widened. 'And in the middle of Trafalgar Square, that'll get us arrested.'

Marek moved on top of her. 'Worth it, though.'

*

Abena was out of breath. Her face, peeping around the class-room door, glowed with excitement. 'It is a man for you!' she gasped, euphoric. 'He is handsome!' she added throatily, her face promptly disappearing.

Glad to escape the smell of fresh paint in their patched-up room, Orla gathered together her books and pads, aware that her cachet among her students had just rocketed. She tugged on her coat, glad that Marek had turned up, as if he knew she needed him.

An urge had been tugging at her hem all afternoon, like a precocious child. There was no need to go to Beatrice Gardens now that Orla had proved she couldn't follow through and liberate the journal, but her subconscious disagreed. Orla was struggling to resist a pull she didn't understand, the pull to stand and watch Anthea's house, even if Anthea wasn't in it.

And now here was Marek, saving her from herself.

A pack of students clustered around Abena. They straightened up and attempted to act normal as Orla's heels rang on the tiles of the entrance hall. Abena pointed through the door marked ADMIN where a man lounged on an office chair, watching her approach. He stood, pulled at his lapel, shrugged his shoulders into position.

'Hello you.' Orla's greeting stood firmly in the featureless no-man's-land between friendly and unfriendly.

'Time for a coffee?'

'Sure.' Orla threw a disapproving look at Abena's gang, but the kissy noises only got louder, following her and Reece out of the building.

*

At a table of a family-run Italian café which took its coffee seriously and sprinkled oregano on the all-day breakfast, Orla defrosted slightly.

'You and I had a deal,' said Reece, sad and disapproving.

'Still mates, we said. Keep in touch, we said. But you never pick up my calls. And you never get back to me.'

'I've been busy.' Orla waited a moment, sipped her coffee. It was hot and thick and strident. 'I'm seeing somebody.'

'Marek? It's . . . ' Reece cast about for language that would be acceptable to her. 'It's going somewhere, then?'

'It might. It's good. He's nice.' Marek would smile, she hoped, at such understatement. Marek knew how she felt about him . . . didn't he?

'That's so good.' Reece smiled indulgently. 'You deserve it.'

Orla didn't want to discuss this with Reece. The scales had fallen – or been ripped – from her eyes. She missed her old confidant. 'Don't get overexcited. I'm not in love.' Somewhere a fairy fell down dead; there'd been no need to say that.

'It'll be ten months this day next week.' Reece turned his cup round and round on the saucer.

'I know.' Orla always noted the fourteenth. 'A long ten months.'

'An age,' agreed Reece.

They sat quietly for a while, companionable but absorbed in private thoughts. Reece bent to extract something from his briefcase and when he spoke it was impersonal, and rehearsed. 'Take a look at this still, Orla.'

He watched Orla lean over the A4 print-out. 'Would you say that woman looks like you?' In grainy black and white, a blurred figure filled almost the entire page. 'It was taken by Ant's security camera. Spooked her. I didn't say so to Ant, but I thought it looks a bit like you.' He watched Orla scrutinise the picture. 'Can't be you though, can it?'

Orla stared at herself, captured in the eerie palette of a night lens, sodden, shoulders slumped, zombie-eyed. 'No,' said Orla slowly, sitting back, facing Reece squarely. 'It can't be me.'

Not really a lie: Orla *didn't* recognise the desperate woman in the picture.

'Good,' said Reece deliberately, crumpling the picture. 'Because if it were I'd be worried.'

Clever, how he wedded warning and solicitude like that.

Chapter Twenty-Five

'Hi, it's me! How's Whitstable? I looked it up after you told me you were going there and did you know it's where Dracula arrived in England after his voyage from Transylvania? Well, of course you did. You're the clever one in our set-up. Guess you're busy with your pupils or whatever you call them. Call me when you're home and you have a minute. I want to run something by you. And I don't want you to judge me, Orla. OK? Bye. Ooh, and watch out for tall dark strangers in capes.'

'This is nice,' said Marek, in a murmuring voice she loved, barely moving his lips, as if too sledgehammered by bliss to speak.

Orla, lying back against him on the sofa, her head on his shoulder, their hair mingling, every limb heavy, agreed. The film was almost over and she dreaded having to shift; the position they'd found was as perfect as that position she always found in bed just before the alarm sounded.

'I'm going to Poland on Friday,' said Marek, in the same low honeyed tone. 'The fourteenth.'

'What? No!' Orla sat up. 'Oh Rabbit, for how long?'

A laugh was startled out of Marek by her distress. There was pleasure, too, at this little proof of her attachment to him.

His eyebrows moved together in a V of kind concern. 'Darling, I won't be long. It's business, family stuff. My stepmother likes to make a fuss. I have to go.'

'Yes, of course.' Orla, with some effort, reset her expression. Panic ticked in her chest, though, and it coloured her next question. 'How long will you be gone, exactly?'

'Two days. Three at the most.'

'Three. That's not long, is it?'

'It's seventy-two hours. I'm flattered. You're going to miss me, aren't you, *moje złotko*?' He held her tightly to him, his chest firm against her bouncier one and Orla keenly felt how perfectly their differences complemented each other. When he let her go, she dipped her head but he dipped his too to look at her face. 'Tears? No! Orla, is something wrong?'

'Something's *right*,' mewled Orla, glad to feel this way, glad to have pushed through the dam of debris between her and Marek.

'I should have asked you to come with me.' Marek scooped her up so she was sitting on his lap. He kissed her, laughed, and said, 'I was scared to ask in case you pulled a face.'

'Me?' said Orla in mock amazement. How could she have such power over such a man, yet fail to make an idiot like Sim happy? She kissed Marek, enjoying her right of way over his sculpted lips.

'Well?' Marek shrugged a question. 'Why not? Come. Meet my family. See Skwierzyna.'

'But . . .'

'You and your buts,' roared Marek, suddenly loud and exasperated.

'*But*, college, Marek! I have to be there in front of the class when they all shuffle in.'

She remembered Sim's *you're just a primary school teacher!* when she'd cited her job as reason not to come to London.

'Then fly out after me and come for the Saturday and Sunday.'

'I don't know ...' Orla *did* know. A weekend without him would give her time with the other towering figure in her life. As was her habit these days, she expertly smothered the thought. 'It's a bit ... soon.'

'If you think so.' Marek budged Orla off his lap. 'Film's over.' He nodded at the screen and stood up. 'I've got calls to make.'

If the mews had a cave Marek would have retreated to it, but he had to make do with his office. Orla heard the door click shut and aimed the remote control at the screen, bouncing from shopping channel to panel games to sitcom.

It would be easy to go with him. Just go and, maybe – crazy idea, this – *enjoy herself*. But the other Orla, that selfish greedy twin with an appetite for voyeurism and self-flagellation, couldn't pass up such an opportunity. Perhaps it would all go her way. Perhaps the internet would roll her straight sixes and deliver not only an opportunity to face Anthea but the courage to go through with it.

Orla could read the journal while Marek was away. She could be a fresh clean new person when he returned.

An old *Antiques Roadshow* flashed past. The next channel offered her a documentary about New York. From inlaid writing desks to skyscrapers to, bang, Anthea Blake with a heart-shaped beauty spot and foot-high white hair. Orla had stumbled on a repeat of *The Courtesan*.

Finger frozen, Orla watched Anthea, her powdered face and sly eyes part visible behind a fan. Anthea snapped the fan shut with a flourish and Orla jumped.

'Madame, do not cross swords with me.' Anthea advanced on the camera, her lips a bloody red. 'I eat pretty upstarts like you for breakfast.'

'Isn't that . . . ' Marek was behind her.

'Yes, it is.' Orla pushed buttons at random, muting Ant and reducing her in size before finally managing to banish her.

Marek said nothing.

Rather loudly.

It gave Orla pleasure to creep to the glacial outer reaches of Marek's bed, shiver there for a moment, then shimmy back to his side and arrange her limbs over him, feeling the warmth he radiated. Marek was easy-going about her tendency to treat him as a climbing frame, happy in her koala-grip. Naked, they'd drawn a line under the grotty atmosphere that had lingered until bedtime.

Now Marek shifted in his sleep, a dozy mumble on his lips. Suspended between sleep and wakefulness beside him, super-comfortable and about to dribble, Orla's thoughts roamed in a non-linear fashion, alighting in no particular order on Juno's peculiar defensiveness, her own need for a new bag, whether to have porridge for breakfast. And then Maude popped into her dozy head.

I'll treat Maude to something nice while Marek's away, she decided. *A nice meal in town, maybe?*

Orla's sleepy brain discovered something that had been hidden in plain sight all along. It raced along a trail of breadcrumbs and reached a conclusion that jolted her into a sitting position.

'*Kochanie, jestes OK?*' Marek sat up with her, but his spine was still asleep and he collapsed back on to the pillows, pulling her with him. As he burrowed back into sleep, his head on her shoulder and his hair tickling her neck, Orla burned holes in the ceiling with her eyes.

It was so obvious, she chided herself. So bloody obvious.

'Orla? It's Ma. Can you talk?'

'Howaya Ma. Actually, I'm just about to—'

'Listen, there was a murder! An actual murder in Tobercree!'

'No! Who was murdered?'

'Well, they didn't die. The man who runs the electrical—'

'If he didn't die it's not a murder, Ma.'

'Don't spoil it!'

'Ma, can we talk another time? I was just about to—'

'The eejit who lives over the chip shop is *helping police with their inquiries*. It's the best thing that's happened in Tobercree since – ever!'

'Ma, I have something important to do, so I'll—'

'Young lady, what's so important that it can't wait until after the one conversation I have with me daughter every week?'

'Sorry, Ma. Ma?'

'Yes, musha?'

'Was I a coward when I was a kid?'

'You were lovely. The easiest one of the lot. Never a frown. A breath of sunshine.'

'But did I run from things? Was I a sissy?'

266

'Are you kidding me or what? You were my little tigress.'

'That's the word Juno used.'

'If you were in the right, you'd stand up to anybody.'

'Ah. Listen, Ma, I really do have to go.'

Orla cut off her mother's splutters and dashed out to the hallway, apprehending Maude on her way to the top floor after shutting up shop. 'May I have a mo? It's important.'

'Of course,' said Maude immediately. She preceded Orla back into the flat, tinsel fragments in her bun: Christmas decorations had gone up that day. Ordnance Survey lines zigzagging beneath her eyes gave the game away about Maude's age in a way her steady blue gaze never would. 'What's wrong, dear?'

'Nothing. Not with me. Well, no more than the usual.' Orla's light-hearted grin came out as a death's head grimace and she saw Maude recoil as they seated themselves at the small square kitchen table.

'I can sense you working out how to begin. Just talk to me.'

'I was going to ask you something.' Orla forced herself to sit. Her legs wanted to stride, but she must rein herself in, keep this small. 'But that would be false, because I know the answer. I've done a little research, I've thought very hard and I know, Maude, that you're agoraphobic.'

Maude went very still, the only movement a tightening of her lips that sent a sunburst of lines radiating outwards.

Orla carried on. 'You haven't stepped outside the door since I arrived in London ten months ago. All your groceries are delivered. You shop online. The only times you ever lose your good humour – your *lovely* humour,' she amended, in hopes of

267

softening Maude's facial expression which ossified with each word, 'is when somebody badgers you to go out. You won't come shopping with me, you turned poor George away with a flea in his ear. So I looked up agoraphobia on the internet and you're a classic case, Maudie.'

It felt important to keep Maude's eye: the old lady seemed determined to stare her out. Eventually it was Maude who looked away, and stood up, patting inconsequentially at her dress, angling her body towards the door.

'You have no notion of what is your business and what isn't, do you, Orla?'

Refusing to be stung, Orla stayed clamped to her seat and said, 'Maude, we know each other too well for that to wash. You made me your business the moment I appeared on your doorstep. I drew boundaries and you stepped regally over them. You have stuck your admittedly very elegant nose into my every nook and cranny, and I didn't hear you say "please". Now it's my turn. Sit down, Maude.'

When Maude scowled her face lost all its whimsy. 'Don't boss me about. Arthur was the last person ever to do that and now I allow nobody the right.' She trotted to the door, yanked it open.

Hoping to pin Maude to the spot with her words, Orla rattled through them. 'I have every right, because I love you, Maude, and because I need to repay you. Now,' she said, more calmly, glad that Maude's hand had paused on the doorknob, 'I hope you'll find it a relief to sit and talk about it. Because whether or not you like it, I *know*.'

'You weren't the first to rumble me.' Maude spoke low and ruefully, as she slowly closed the door and turned to face Orla, her face her own once more. 'Sim tried what he called an intervention.'

'Sim guessed?' Sim, so recently rebranded from Saint to Satan?

'Yes.' Maude sat down with the mien of a woman who didn't expect to get up for some time. 'I fobbed him off easily enough. He didn't have your grit.'

'Never mind Sim. This is about you.' Orla's mouth was dry. She didn't feel qualified to tackle such a problem, but their mutual understanding was both exquisitely nuanced and light as air: only Orla could persuade Maude to open up. 'Maude, you're afraid to go out, aren't you?'

Maude was silent. She stared at her fingers bent crabbily from the middle knuckle.

'It's a recognised condition. You can get help. I'll be involved every step of the way. You're not unique, you're not alone. You have me, and we can call on a whole host of resources.'

Still nothing from Maude.

'We can go as slowly as you like, so long as we make a start. These four walls aren't big enough to contain the likes of you. Imagine, Maude, how it would be, if you could just walk out of the front door and—' Orla halted as Maude's hands balled into fists. 'I won't force you into anything. But it's time you rejoined the messy old human race you're so fond of.'

More silence. Orla was encouraged by the relaxing of Maude's fingers. 'Come on, Maudie. Don't leave me to do all the work here!'

A wet blob appeared on the scrubbed wood of the table, followed by another. Maude's head sank lower.

'Oh Maude, no,' whispered Orla, bending her head so that it touched Maude's. 'I didn't mean to make you cry. I want to help, that's all. Maudie, please.' That whining tone wouldn't do. She sat up again. 'Have a little weep. As you've told me many times, it helps. But then, Maude, *talk to me.*'

Still the flossy white head remained resolutely down. Orla crept her hand over, fearful of being brushed away, but when she cupped her fingers over Maude's she felt the older woman's resonate at the touch. 'We'll just sit here for a bit,' she said.

Eventually Maude spoke, a mumble quite unlike her usual vocal authority.

'What was that?' Orla squinted as she strained to hear.

'I'm too ashamed to talk about it.' The words fell out painfully, like stones, each one separate and ugly.

'Not with me,' insisted Orla, glad to have some signs of life from the bowed figure. 'You'll always be my heroine, whatever happens.'

That did it, kick-started Maude. With a short-tempered snort of derision her head flew up. 'I'm nobody's heroine. And you of all people don't need one.'

Striking while her iron was hot, Orla lobbed a question. 'When did it start? How long have you been . . . ' – she hardly knew how to describe it – 'how long have you been *in*?'

There was surrender in Maude's sigh. 'About thirteen years.'

The gasp forced from Orla was regrettable; Maude flinched. 'As I said, dear, it's disgraceful.'

'How did it start?' Orla squeezed the hand still prisoner in her own. 'Just *talk*, all around it, any direction you want. I've got all night.'

270

'Marek?'

'He's in Oxford, looking at a potential project.' And Anthea, she thought, is probably sitting in front of an open window, reciting Sim's journal. The other Orla was powerful, but her powers had limits: Maude was in need. 'I'm all yours. Where did you go the last time you went out?' prompted Orla, standing up to put the kettle on.

'That's easy. It was a short walk to the cobbler by the tube station. Is he still there? I had a favourite pair of red shoes that needed new heels. I never saw my shoes again, because I closed the front door when I got back and I haven't been through it since.'

'What happened between the shoe repair place and home?' Orla leaned against the cooker, arms folded.

'Nothing untoward, if that's what you mean. I remember how sharp and chilly it was, a really fine winter's day without a hint of damp. It was the last day of nineteen ninety-nine, the dregs of the old century. And as I came up the stairs the phone was ringing.'

Maude looked around, as if realising something.

'It was ringing in this very room. It stood on that dresser there. Next morning I was up bright and early. I decided to celebrate the millennium by walking all around the neighbourhood I'd chosen for myself two years earlier. A victory lap, if you like. I planned to look in on Sheraz – he'd be open of course – and go as far as the playground, ring in the new century. I put on my coat, and a scarf, and I looked out a hat.'

Maude looked past Orla, miming the donning of these accessories.

'Gloves. As I walked down the stairs I slowed. Slower,

271

slower until I was creeping along with my hands on the wall, feeling my way. And my breath ... ' Maude's hand flew to her neck. 'It was stuck somewhere deep inside, as if I'd been bunged up. My mind popped like corn, with no coherent thoughts at all. Foolishly, I remember thinking, *when I get outside I'll be fine, some fresh air will sort me out.* I wondered if this was what going insane was like, or was I having a heart attack and a stroke all at once. I put my hand on the latch and all became clear. It was *outside* that was causing the uproar.'

Swilling the teapot to warm it, Orla was glad of something to do. Silent, she was loath to break the spell of this second tale of Maude's that had never been heard before.

'As soon as I retreated and turned around, my breathing evened out and although my heart was still thumping I could gather my thoughts. To test it, I turned again, approached the door – it was just a door, Orla, the same old door in need of a lick of paint that I'd nonchalantly passed through a thousand times – as soon as I turned, my whole self went into revolt. I knew then that even if the house were on fire I'd have walked back up the stairs. Something unnameable and vile waited for me outside.'

Life, thought Orla. She poured two cups of treacly tea and sat back down. 'What was the phone call about? The night before?'

'They're not connected. Please, dear, don't turn amateur psychologist.'

'Who was it?'

'It was my solicitor.' Maude played with the handle of her cup. 'He informed me my mother had died that afternoon.' Maude gave a shallow laugh that sounded like something breaking. 'Just to reaffirm my non-heroine status, Orla, I must add that I'd refused to visit her while she was mortally ill.' She looked up suddenly, her expression a mixture of defiance and supplication. 'How d'you like me now?'

'I like you,' said Orla, 'just as much as I did five minutes ago. And that was better than I like just about anybody else.' Orla was all softness, all warmth. She had never envisaged a moment when their roles would be so neatly reversed. 'It's time you forgave yourself, don't you think?'

'I should have visited.' Maude brushed away Orla's sympathy with a motion of her hand, as if shooing a fly. 'It wouldn't have hurt me to say goodbye, tell her I understood.'

'But you didn't understand,' Orla reminded her, determined to be Maude's advocate as she'd obviously abandoned her own defence long ago. 'It would have been false and that's something you never are. With hindsight you feel differently, but hindsight holds all the cards and we mortals don't. If you'd behaved differently, I mightn't be sitting here now. Imagine that. I'd have missed out on my Maudie.'

'And me my Orla.' Maude hesitated. 'My Orla-ie,' she added, the first sparkle in her eye since the start of their conversation.

'There seems to be an obvious and direct link between that phone call and your attack.' Was that an appropriate word? wondered Orla. Maude didn't recoil, so she guessed it would do. 'However much you want to shy away from that fact. I suppose you don't want to believe that your mother and your old life still have that much influence over you.'

'They don't,' said Maude. 'I never looked back once I left.'

'But she was your mother,' pressed Orla gently, hating to lead Maude down a path overgrown with brambles and thorns but certain that she must. 'Maybe if you confronted your guilt about—'

'I am NOT guilty!' Maude had never spoken so loudly before. True, it didn't qualify as a shout to somebody brought up in a house where Ma summoning them sweetly to the dinner table sounded like Boadicea's call to arms, but it shocked Orla.

Backing off, however, was out of the question.

'You don't *want* to be guilty,' Orla acceded. 'Some stern, strict part of you insists you did the wrong thing, whereas I think you did the human, fallible thing. And as a wise old woman once told me, we're all allowed to make mistakes.'

'She sounds like a silly old coot,' muttered Maude.

'Sometimes,' said Orla darkly, 'she's exactly that. But most of the time, she's, like I said, wise.'

'And very old.'

'That too. Although she wears it well.' Orla sipped her tea. It was, as her father used to say, strong enough to trot a mouse on. She let the silence flower, rewarded for her reticence when Maude spoke.

'I didn't just leave it at that, of course. I tried again later that day. When it got dark, I thought, *aha! maybe now*, but no. If anything the physical symptoms grew worse. More beastly still was the way my mind fell apart. It was a terrible sensation, as if my thoughts were made of jelly and I could feel them melting. Nothing was fixed, nothing was sure.'

Maude's speech sped up as she relived her terror. It crossed Orla's mind to stop her but she watched and listened instead, confident of the healing power of full disclosure.

'The only thing that helped was crawling back upstairs on

my hands and knees. By the end of January the first I'd capitulated.'

Suddenly brisker, as if on firmer ground, Maude said, 'I set about arranging everything so that my new way of life flowed as easily as possible, given the restrictions. Sheraz was happy to deliver; he's such a gent. I already had a computer and I acquainted myself with the vast array of, well, *everything* one can order online. I found the numbers of all the businesses I patronise around here and with the help of a fabricated bout of the flu they all agreed to deliver. Once that was in place it was easy to keep the deliveries going. There are advantages to having a head of white hair and liver-spotted hands.'

'They're freckles, surely,' interjected Orla, grateful for Maude's rejuvenation but suspicious of it too. Maude was styling her descent into solitary confinement as a splendid jape.

'Holidays are impossible. I'm glad I travelled before. Friendships, well, many fell by the wayside.' Maude blinked away some memories.

Orla had never wondered why such a gregarious, life-enhancing broad had so few friends. *Too busy thinking about your damn self.* 'Is that the real reason you rented out the flat? To get people into the house?'

Maude looked startled. 'Good God, you've hit the nail on the head!' she squeaked. 'Well I never. I did that quite behind my own back but you saw through it at once. Bravo,' she said, with an approving nod. 'We've been sitting here for ages, dear, and my elderly bottom is suffering. May we reconvene another night?'

'Well . . . ' Orla was inclined to thrash out the subject in one go. 'One more thing. What next?'

Maude shrugged, rearranging her clothing, patting her hair. 'I get by perfectly well. Especially now I have you. And I flatter myself that you might come and see me when you move on.'

'That goes without saying. But it's not enough. You should be out there, in the real world, Maude. I want to take you out for tea. I want to feed the ducks with you. I want to share with you the chamber of horrors that is Sheraz's chilled cabinet.' Maude's chuckle emboldened her. 'May I ask your GP for a home visit and take it from there?'

The chuckle was cut off abruptly. 'Absolutely not. Are you listening? No.'

'*That* Maude only rears her head when this topic comes up.'

'I know, I know.' Maude groaned, her face distraught, all its polite perkiness dissolved. 'You don't deserve it. You're trying to help but I'm beyond help.' She put her hands to her face and when she re-emerged her expression had reasserted itself, like a conjuring trick. 'The truth is, I've made the best of my life. And fate hasn't abandoned me: it sent me you. If you truly want to help, let me be.'

'No can do.' Orla had never said that before, but it fitted the bill.

'You're the one we should worry about,' said Maude as she stood up, knuckles leaning heavily on the table.

'Me? Why so?' Maude's fairy godmother powers could easily stretch to mindreading; Orla readied herself to repel charges of cyberstalking.

'Because this new relationship with the devilishly handsome Marek is precious and vulnerable. And you look to me like a girl swinging a Ming vase around in a string bag.'

So she didn't know. Good. 'I see what you're doing, sneakypants. This is about you, not me. I won't force you to do a single thing you don't want to, Maude, but imagine the roles were reversed for a moment. What would you do?'

Maude gave Orla her best gimlet stare, but relented, threw her hands in the air. 'You've got me there, dear. You've got me there.'

'Maude! Hang on.' Orla intercepted her at the door and wrapped herself around her as if Orla were a mother and Maude her best beloved child. 'You mean so much to me,' she said.

'I know,' said Maude.

Chapter Twenty-Six

Orla checked her watch as the students bent their heads over their regular Friday morning assignment. Marek's plane would be in the air. Their leavetaking outside his house at a blearily early hour had been sweet. He'd held her hands to his lips and kissed them.

The only person who knew of her craving was now out of the country. There were no constraints on her. The anticipated euphoric surge of release didn't come. Her stomach was full of acid.

'Abena!' she admonished, as the girl leaned towards her neighbour.

Abena looked ashamed, resumed sucking her pencil.

Absurd, to rely on a man after so short an acquaintance. Absurd, maybe, but Orla did rely on Marek. He looked so swashbuckling yet came with a John Lewis guarantee: a combination attractive to her. Their physical communication was intense, lusty but respectful with no awkwardness (or nurse's uniform), and their emotional communication was frank and simple. He allowed her to lag behind slightly and hadn't reiterated that he loved her, hadn't prodded her to catch up.

And so she relied on him, because he invited her to. Everything about him semaphored that he was an honourable, mature man in love.

'Sanae, silence please.'

Walking up and down the aisles created by the tables, Orla caught the Japanese girl's eye as she hissed a hurried question out of the side of her mouth. Orla already knew who'd attain a decent mark and who'd fail; Dominika's body language told her that the girl hadn't found time for vocab revision during her enthusiastic exploration of London's Russian club scene.

If Marek was a straight-A student, Orla could only award herself a C. She knew how to overhaul her grades: give up the struggle and let Anthea keep the journal.

This weekend, with no Marek around, would be a test. Orla would mark it with rigour. She'd stay away from the internet. She'd stay away from Beatrice Gardens.

Anything less would be a fail.

Disengaging herself from Skype, wondering at Juno's refusal to pick up, Orla heard the heavy uneven tread of the doctor descending the stairs.

'So?' she said expectantly, stepping out into the hall and wrapping her cardigan around herself, pulling the sleeves over her fingers in a gesture from childhood. 'How did you find her?'

'Mrs Roxby-Littleton is in excellent shape.' He didn't break step, forcing Orla to trail him down the last flight to the front door. 'Hope I'm as good when I'm her age.'

Orla had always considered that phrase to be patronising, particularly so in this doctor's case. Carrying three extra stone and with a fruity boozer's nose he wasn't as good as Maude at *his* age. 'You talked about her agoraphobia?'

'Obviously, as that's why you dragged me out of the surgery

on a freezing Friday evening.' This doctor had evidently missed the Bedside Manner tutorials. 'I've left her the leaflets. Tricky business, agoraphobia, although I have some experience with it. I'd suggest exposure therapy, seen some marvellous results, but this all has to come from her. I'll gladly refer her to a psychiatrist, try and get to the root of it. But . . . '

'Right. It has to come from her.' Orla nodded. She'd feared this. It *wouldn't* come from Maude; since that long chat on Wednesday night Maude had avoided mention of her problem, not even answering when Orla told her she'd made an appointment with her GP.

'I'll leave this with you.' The doctor pressed a folded piece of paper into Orla's hand as he wrestled with the door, wheezing. 'It's a prescription for anti-depressants. Mild ones,' he added, as Orla's eyes grew huge with alarm. 'SSRIs.'

'Is she depressed?' Orla wished she'd phrased it differently: a more adamant *She's not depressed*.

'It takes many forms.' The doctor stood back as Orla took charge of the door and freed him.

'What's an SSRI?'

'Selective Serotonin Reuptake Inhibitors,' recited the doctor, raising his voice against the efforts of the noisy street. 'Look 'em up. Oh, and try and persuade her to try exposure therapy. She won't be dancing up and down the high street any time soon but there's no reason she can't take the first steps. She'll need a stout ally in all of this.' Without a goodbye, he turned away and trudged towards the crossing.

'Thank you,' Orla called after him, her gratitude lost in the thrum of cars and buses and hurrying feet. She closed the door and leaned against it. Talk of anti-depressants scared her: the little blue capsules Ma had taken after Da's death made a cardi-wearing zombie of her.

A beep from her pocket signalled a text. Marek hadn't been in touch since a to-the-point *Just touched down* at lunchtime: she'd expected more ardent communication but he was busy, after all.

The text wasn't from Marek.

Hello stranger! Lunch? Dinner? A trip to the moon? You've got my number – use it. Rx
P.S. Hope you're behaving.

Behaving.

The word pressed Orla's 'pause' button. She stared at it, insulted, conscious of being talked down to. *If I'm 'behaving'*, she told Reece in her head, *I'm the only one who feckin' is.* Where was Reece's headmasterly tone when Anthea was shagging Sim in her tented boudoir? When Sim was going through the motions of a loving boyfriend, about to propose? And did Reece reprimand himself for covering up the whole sordid tangle?

Behaving.

Orla had behaved her entire life.

Reece is frightened I'll pounce on Anthea, use my claws.

Orla glanced down at her neat squovals, then grabbed her coat from the hook by the door. With her new acerbic inner voice, she thanked him for his earlier Tweeted tip-off.

Supping with client/chum Ms Anthea Blake tonight at our special place. #niceworkifyoucangetit.

She reckoned she could be at Reece's club in forty minutes.

Tackling Anthea as she sat across a table from Reece would answer Reece's finger-wagging question nicely: Orla Cassidy was *not* behaving.

In the whirlwind, the proposed test of her own character had been forgotten. Swallowing hard, Orla, her hand on the latch, paused. A sudden cacophony on the other side of the door made her leap away from it as if it were alive.

Orla knew only one person who simultaneously rang a tune on the doorbell and banged a tattoo on the knocker, and she was in Dublin. Opening the door a fraction, Orla saw a sliver of the high street, and a sliver of Juno.

'Surprise!' Juno said it limply, ironically, head to one side. 'Look who it isn't!'

'This,' said Orla, opening the door wide, throwing her arms around her visitor, 'does not compute.' Orla was dazed, and struggling with the feeling of being caught red-handed. She couldn't help but fret that some evidence of the sin she'd been about to commit stained her clothes or was caught in her hair.

'You look gorgeous! The fringe looks even better in real life!' Juno was examining her and finding no clue. 'Great jacket!'

'Come in. Come in.' Juno had appeared out of the drizzle like a genie and it took a moment for Orla's manners to catch up with the action. 'And welcome, Juno. It's been so long. And you look fab.'

Juno did. Her spunky crop, reinstated after the brief excursion into growing her hair, was an even brighter vermilion than

Orla remembered, and her emerald coat gleamed in the dim hallway.

'Come for a drink,' said Juno, bending at the knees, taking Orla's hand in both her own, just the way she always had when coaxing Orla into something nefarious, whether it be skipping double maths or setting fire to Fr Gerry's cassock. 'Come *on*! We need a chat!'

'Who's that with you?' Maude's voice drifted from the top tier of the house, sleepy, cracked, *old*.

'It's Juno, Maude. We'll be up in a minute.'

'Ah, the famous Juno!' Maude perked up a little.

'Hi Maude!' warbled Juno, her wide mouth open to show her pink pink tongue and her fluorescent teeth. 'I'm just taking madam to the pub and then we'll say hello!'

'Enjoy yourselves, dears.' A door slammed.

'Come on.' Juno was impish, sparking. 'There's a pub on your corner.'

'Not the Rose? Juno, it's like Fagin's den in there.'

'Great. London atmosphere. Come *on*.' As ever, Juno won and the two of them stumbled to the pub.

Kicking open the weathered saloon door, Juno muttered, 'I see what you mean.' The room had never been refurbished, so it boasted etched mirrors on the walls, flock paper, an ornately carved bar. But it had never been cleaned either, and its clientele had followed suit. The carpet beneath their shoes was sticky as they picked their way past men with over-long slicked-back hair and chain smokers' complexions to where a barman, liberally sprinkled with tattoos and sporting a belly that confirmed his love of the product he sold, awaited them.

'I think a clean glass costs extra.' Orla studied the map of filth around her vodka and tonic as they found a corner table as far as possible from the football match on the bellowing wide screen. 'But what the hell. Cheers!' She smiled conspiratorially at Juno then lowered her glass. 'What is it?' Juno looked haunted. 'OK.' Orla put the glass down. 'What's this about? You have much the same face on you as when you borrowed my new boots without asking and threw up on them.'

'I wish it was that innocent.' Juno downed her drink in one, grimacing at its aftertaste. 'Now listen. I have a preamble.' Juno launched herself into a patently prepared speech. 'There's something you need to know. About me. I've come all this way to tell you, so please, please don't judge.'

'If you're trying to scare me, you're doing a grand job.' Orla's tone was deceptively light. Horrified by the escapade Juno's appearance had saved her from, she was in no position to judge anybody. 'Just feckin' tell me.'

'I'm in love.' Juno's cat eyes turned liquid, and her wry wide mouth turned up in a smile that was too gooey for her wry face. 'I'm in love, Orla, and you have to know and you have to approve and you have to love him as much as I do.'

'What?' Orla said it loudly, crisply. Had they time-travelled to an era before Himself, before Jack, when this pronouncement could be good news?

'And he's here.' Juno nodded to somebody beyond Orla's back, and Orla swivelled to see a tall man with a dandelion head of brilliant white hair stand up in a far corner and make his way towards them.

'Rob?' Orla frowned at the sudden appearance of yet another Tobercree native in this godforsaken boozer.

'Yes, Rob. My Rob.' Juno beamed at him as he made his way through the swaying, malodorous pub crowd.

'Hi,' Orla held out her hand. 'How's things?'

'I'm good.' Rob, crisp and clean and modish in this spit and sawdust interior, looked from one woman to the other. 'Am I allowed to join you?'

'Join us, please.' Orla watched him drag his stool nearer to Juno, as if she were magnetic and he an iron filing, analysing her face as if committing it to his memory.

Rob had looked like that at Fionnuala, Orla recalled, on their wedding day. Orla had been a bridesmaid; Juno, as sister of the bride, matron of honour. There had been cummerbunds and gypsophila and Fionnuala's horrible, horrible crinoline. 'This is a bit of a surprise.'

'Typical Orla understatement.' Juno didn't return Rob's gaze, she was studying Orla. 'This wasn't planned. We know how it must look. It hit us both like a lightning bolt.'

'At the very same moment,' said Rob, treading on the tail of Juno's sentence. 'Wham!'

'Wham,' echoed Juno fondly.

This cheesy Juno was disconcerting. 'How long . . . ?' Orla pointed from one to the other vaguely, uncertain what to call their affair.

'Five months. Since . . .' Juno turned to Rob, clasped his hand in hers and smiled, 'July the twelfth at quarter past five.' They both giggled, school-kid conspirators.

That was about the time Himself had been promoted. Orla recalled gripes from Juno about being left to her own devices, with neither a husband nor a confidante to call her own.

'We bumped into each other in town, outside Bewlay's café.' Juno tripped over her words. 'Rob was—'

'—on my way home from work.'

'I was getting new crowns done.' She tapped her front teeth at Juno. 'Like them?'

'They're great.' Her old teeth, slightly gappy, had been cute.

'We chatted a bit, then Rob said—'

'Let's have a coffee,' said Rob.

'So we popped in to Bewlay's—'

'—and our lives changed,' said Rob, his gaze unwaveringly on Juno.

Feeling very much the third wheel, Orla raised her glass to them, then lowered it halfway, uncertain of the etiquette around adultery.

'Juno wanted to tell you. Didn't you, darling?' Rob looked for, and got, an affirmation from Juno, as if asking his mummy if he could have more cake. 'But there was never a right time.'

'I've been bursting to confess but—' began Juno, cut off again by Rob.

'Not *confess*. We're not doing anything wrong.'

'Well …' Juno looked as if she might contest that, but instead she chucked Rob's cheek like a child's and said, 'There was never a right time. And I know you're fond of,' – she looked at Rob apologetically, as if swearing – 'of Himself. I've been terrified of you finding out. You think I'm a bitch, don't you?'

'I don't think you're a bitch. I think you're an adult and you can make your own decisions.'

Even if one of them is to embark on a love affair with a frankly dull man who left your sister when she was pregnant because he had to, for Jaysus' sake, 'find himself'.

Orla trusted Juno not to put innocents at risk for the sake of a fling, so there had to be more to this story and Orla didn't care to hear it in the Rose.

'Come on. Back to mine. Cheese on toast, wine, chat. Yes?'

'Oh *yes*!' grinned Juno as if she'd been promised a guided tour of the hanging gardens of Babylon. 'I've missed you so much. And I want to hear *all* your news, too, yeah?'

'Yeah.' Orla led the way, privately qualifying that 'yeah'; Juno didn't need to hear *all* her news.

Chapter Twenty-Seven

Despite the fug of her new affair, Juno was sensitive enough to despatch Rob to their hotel for part of Saturday so she could have some time with her oldest friend, just the two of them.

'Well,' she said eagerly, as they walked together along the Embankment, self-conscious tourists, 'what do you think?'

'Of Rob?' Orla stared out at the lazy Thames. 'I've met him before, Ju.'

'Yeah, but he was just my sister's husband then. I mean, what do you make of *us* together?'

'Um, he's a nice guy. Quiet.' This wasn't nearly enough to satisfy Juno, Orla knew, so she added, 'And he's wild about you, anybody can see that.'

'Can you?' Juno did a short, impromptu Riverdance. She was the antithesis of Orla: sketchy, nippy, *thin*. 'He's so *nice*, Orla. I never appreciated that in a man before. He's sweet to me. I think about him all the time.' Juno stopped walking, stopped swinging her Union Jack carrier bag. 'Do you think about Marek all day too?' She'd skirted around the subject of Marek, wary of pushing too hard, but was obviously eager to learn more.

The wind dashing her hair into her face, Orla said, 'It's

different with me and Marek. Because, I've just lost Sim. Yes, *just*,' she insisted at the flicker of dispute in Juno's eye, 'and it's complicated. Not as complicated as you and Rob, admittedly.'

She booted the conversation back to Juno's end of the pitch. Her own reluctance to enthuse about Marek dismayed her. She'd never been a gusher – in the early days with Sim she'd been just as circumspect – but she could feel herself keeping it in. Perhaps she was waiting for it all to go wrong, for Marek to agree with Sim that Orla wasn't worth the trouble.

Quite when she'd grown so cancerously pessimistic, Orla wasn't sure.

'Our relationship isn't complicated.' Juno spoke with the certainty of a woman wilfully in the wrong. 'I love him and he loves me back. Simple.'

'Oh come on, Ju. It's not so simple for Fionnuala, is it? Or Himself. Or Jack. Or your niece.' They seemed to have agreed without saying so not to use Poppy's name, as if they were on a daytime chav-spat show.

'Do you hate me for this?'

'Not this again! If I did hate you, would it matter? I'm not one of the people who could be hurt by it, so it's not my opinion you should be worried about, Ju.' Orla caved at Juno's crestfallen expression. 'And of course I don't hate you. I couldn't. Mainly I'm scared for you. *All* of you.' *Except Rob*, she silently qualified.

As if obeying a secret signal, they both turned away from the river, companionably knocking into each other as they meandered towards the boxy bulk of the National Theatre.

'He's very calm,' said Orla eventually, feeling she should throw Rob a bone of a compliment.

'Oh, so calm!' Juno grabbed the scant praise and ran with it. 'He's like a rock.'

Glib, serene, Rob verged on the plastic. He was new, with no philosophy or history about him, as if unwrapped fresh every day from cellophane. Orla had never known what Fionnuala saw in him, and for him to lasso the younger sister's heart too was incredible. She didn't hate Juno for embarking on an affair with Rob – they'd been through too much together for hate to gain a foothold between them – but she did wonder at her lack of concern for the innocent parties.

'You should see our hotel. It's pants.'

'You usually head for a Four Seasons.'

'Rob has no money,' boasted Juno. 'And I don't care!'

'But Rob's a managing director of his family firm,' Orla pointed out. 'Why isn't he rolling in it?'

'It all goes to *her*.'

Shocked that Fionnuala, for all her faults, should be *her* and not *my sister*, Orla said evenly, 'I suppose that's fair. She's bringing up their child after all.'

'Oh of course it's fair. Like I say, I don't give a hoot. I'd live in a tent with Rob.'

'A Gucci tent, maybe.' They toiled up the broad steps of the National, eager for a hot drink and a respite from the slate-grey skies. 'I can't help thinking, Ju, why you didn't look further than your sister's ex.'

'I wasn't looking at all,' protested Juno, pushing a plate-glass door. 'This found me. It overwhelmed me. Nobody in their right minds,' she said with confidence, 'ignores love when it comes along.'

*

Bridling from the indignity of the doctor's visit, Maude was elusive that weekend. She granted Juno an audience and liked her very much – 'Such spirit!' – but she dismissed the affair, to Orla, as 'karmic suicide'.

The joy of female friendship with your exact peer, a joy almost forgotten, was balm for Orla's troubled mind. 'Sunday afternoon already,' she wailed, much as she'd bemoaned it every weekend back in their teens. 'There's so much dumb stuff still I haven't told you yet.'

'I know,' agreed Juno. 'I have about eight hundred really important but stupid things I haven't told you yet.'

Orla was glad they'd reached 'dumb stuff'. Cherry-picking what she could and couldn't tell Juno about the fallout from the valentine was exhausting. Her friend was ignorant about the internet shadowing, the vigil in Beatrice Gardens, the determination to hear the truth from the journal.

'Shall we skip the National Portrait Gallery?' Such lowbrow behaviour was tempting and very 'them'.

Juno prevaricated for a moment. 'Nah. Let's go in. I've always wanted to see it and besides we've done that too many times, sat in the pub instead of actually *doing* something.'

Orla felt time speed up; she needed to maximise each second with Juno, a walking talking encyclopaedia of Orla's past. Her gestures mirrored Orla's, both women used the same upward inflexion at the end of jokes, trotted out the same silly voices when putting words in the mouths of strangers who passed them. It was *fun* being together.

'I liked the modern portraits,' declared Juno as they lingered in the gift shop after their tour, picking out postcards. 'When everything changed, and everything was *new*.'

'Give me a Tudor every time.' Orla disagreed partly to provoke, partly because she'd stood for an age in front of Elizabeth I, transfixed by the detailed splendour of her brocade gown and her pale demi-smile. The Queen held flowers in her white hand but, according to the printed guide, the posy was painted over a coiled serpent. Responding to Juno's impatient *Come on, you eejit*, Orla had reluctantly moved away, touched that she and a monarch born five hundred years ago should have something in common. It gave her hope, that she, too, could superimpose a posy over her own serpents.

Orla had found much to empathise with in the faces of the women on the high walls. She saw stress and effort and the strain of waiting, and of loss. Until this year, Orla had been juvenile, despite her degree, her responsible job, her mortgage. Avoiding real setback until her thirties now seemed like a fluke. Sim's death and its aftermath had changed her forever; she knew about grief and she knew about surviving it. She understood more; her suffering had made her useful.

Paying for a postcard of Iris Murdoch, a present for Maude who adored the author, something occurred to Orla.

'Juno, how did you get away from Himself for a whole weekend?'

'Visiting you.' Juno shrugged, as if she'd been in the grip of a higher power at the time. 'It's the only reason he'd accept for staying away overnight. I've visited you before. You *begged* me to.' She punched Orla's arm. 'Sorry to drag you into my mess. I was visiting you the weekend Rob and I spent in Kerry. The first time we, you know.'

'Too much information.' Orla held up a stern hand.

'But I have been trying to visit you, haven't I? You've been aloof. Yes, that's the word. Aloof.' Juno carried on hurriedly, over the words Orla was trying to frame. 'It doesn't matter. You're recovering. You have to do it your own way. Just come back to me at some point, won't you? I might need you. I might need you soon.'

Parting with a long hug at the bus stop – Juno worriedly scrutinising the map on the shelter the way Orla had done back in February as a London newbie – Orla hoped that the affair would run its course before the casualties began to pile up.

Whoever ran things – Ma's white-bearded God or even just some minor celestial civil servant – had a genius for timing that infuriated Orla. Her forty-eight hours with Juno had been an unexpected treat thrust at her, but it had coincided with what should have been Maude's first two days on medication.

The unopened bottles in Maude's bathroom early Sunday evening told their own story.

'Maudie . . .' Orla waggled them at Maude shaking out the duvet in her oddly angled loft bedroom.

'In case you missed the list of side effects,' said Maude, as the duvet sank fat and downy to the bed, 'I'll recite them. Nausea. Headache. Diarrhoea. Dizziness. Dry mouth. Loss of appetite. Sweating. Insomnia. Stomach cramps.' She beat a pillow soundly, as if it had insulted her. 'Not my idea of a good time.'

'Nor mine,' agreed Orla. 'But you won't get all of them. Or perhaps any of them.'

'And you know this how?' Maude swept past Orla, forcing her to leap out of the way. She began to bang about in the kitchen, stowing pans with unnecessary vigour.

'Are you at least doing the yoga breathing I showed you?'

'Breathing in through my nose and out through my mouth? Yes. I sound like a Grand National winner.'

'Good. Because when we start the exposure therapy—'

'The what?' Maude looked as if Orla had suggested bestiality.

Orla had planned to introduce this idea slowly, and cursed her heavy-handedness. 'I looked it up. Apparently it's the most successful treatment for agoraphobia. You prepare by using techniques to help with the anxiety attacks – for example, medication, breathing and meditation – and then you move on to taking a very small trip.'

Maude shrank back against the worktop, a frying pan held like a shield in front of her.

'Just a walk, a few hundred yards, and I'd be with you the whole way and you'd be in charge so we'd go as far as you were able and there'd be no pressure . . .'

'You're pushing!' Maude threw the pan into a cupboard.

'Sit down. Here. Come on.' Orla guided Maude, who was surprisingly cooperative, to a kitchen stool. 'We'll do it at your pace. Message received.'

'Good. I know best in this matter.'

That was up for debate, but Orla let it lie. 'Will you *try* the tablets? Just for a couple of days?'

Maude hesitated, her lips twisting this way and that. 'Oh all right,' she said, half exasperated, half fond. 'Bring me a glass of water and I'll take the first one now.' As she popped the pill into her mouth she asked, 'Are you hanging about to make sure I don't spit it into a potted plant?'

'I'm hanging about,' said Orla, putting the kettle on,

'because I like you very much and I've barely seen you this weekend and I don't have to be at Marek's until late because his plane gets in at ten thirty. I'm going to surprise him by being in his bed when he climbs into it.' This would delight Maude and take her mind off the tablet.

'How romantic.' Maude beamed, as if it were she who had a passionate reunion pencilled for later that evening. 'Will you strew the bed with rose petals?'

'Does anybody really do that?' Orla wondered how to get her hands on sufficient roses at short notice and decided against it. She'd only end up with petals lodged up her behind.

'Arthur did.' Maude smiled. 'We were the only people we knew who slept in the nude.'

'Goodness gracious me, Maude Roxby-Littleton!' Orla looked outraged, then laughed. 'How do you know? Perhaps everybody slept in the nuddy but nobody let on?'

'True. Shall we open a bottle of wine?'

'You've just taken a pill.'

'Exactly. I need something to take the taste away.'

It was an ideal day, thought Orla. A little bit of Juno, a little bit of Maude, and later on a great chunk of Marek. She wrestled with the cork in the bottle, ignoring the lessons from history that wine plus a late night with her new lover would equal bear-like yawns in front of her class tomorrow.

They deserved this wine. Maude was, to use the favoured parlance of every tabloid, facing her demons and Orla had come through her cold turkey and proved something vital. Saved from a horrendous lapse by Juno on Friday night, Orla had completed an Ant-free weekend. No Googling, no urge to see Anthea in the flesh, no weeping over the journal.

Orla felt for the first time in a long time that she could defy her obsession.

'Your friend, Juno, is full of life.' With a resigned air, Maude accepted the small glass Orla had selected for her. 'Hurtling towards disaster, though.'

'Don't,' grimaced Orla, walking to the eaves window that gave her a pleasing view of roof after rainy roof.

'And taking a lot of souls down with her. Can't you get through to her?'

'I tried.'

Orla hadn't felt able to express herself too strongly: Juno's real fear of her censure had troubled her. Had Sim felt constantly judged when they were together? She knew, from experience babysitting nieces and nephews, that if you told a child repeatedly not to do something they would, inevitably, do it. Perhaps her loftily high expectations of Sim had contributed to his last, spectacular failure to meet them.

'She's so utterly in love. I can't believe it's the real thing with somebody as insubstantial as Rob.'

'There's no accounting for taste. Particularly in bed.' Maude's glass was empty and she looked at it as if it had personally let her down. 'Keep an eye on her. She's doing an unwise and cruel thing.'

Just as Sim had. At least Orla now knew the reason for Juno's inexplicable empathy with him. She thought of Juno, rushing to the airport with Rob, savouring the last hours of their freedom to be a couple, and looked at the slight figure now up from her chair and inching towards the wine bottle. Loving people turned your skin inside out, so that the world was full of sharp edges and potential hazards. Orla wouldn't countenance unhappy endings: Juno *would* come to her senses in time; Maude *would* vanquish the agoraphobia. And she would find a way to love Marek honestly.

When her father was diagnosed with his last, horrible tumour, the Cassidys had chosen to believe that the combined force of their love would beat the cancer into submission. They had been wrong. Orla promised herself that she would get Maude through this process of recovery. Who else but she could be the 'stout ally' the doctor had prescribed? Tutting as Maude refilled her glass, Orla saw Maude's recovery as a thread that extended into the future, pulling them both irresistibly with it, until they were out the other side, past Juno's lovestruck madness, past the agoraphobia, past Anthea Blake and past the journal.

Marek jumped back in the dark, knocked his head on the bed's headboard, swore loudly in Polish, switched the lamp on and gasped. 'You!'

'Me!' laughed Orla, holding out her arms. 'Oh, Rabbit, your poor head!'

'Never mind my head.' Marek slipped between the covers and glued his body to hers. His grin was unstoppable, as if his face wasn't big enough to contain it. 'You're crazy, Irish.'

'But are you pleased to see me?'

'I am very pleased to see you.'

Orla had slipped in the front door as his taxi jolted along the mews, despite having hours to spare after leaving the tiddly Maude.

Her cold turkey had turned out to be a purely circumstantial fowl: once freed from Juno and Maude, Orla, like a strict dieter offered the keys to a patisserie, had binged. Standing on the corner of Beatrice Gardens, out of the jurisdiction of Anthea's security camera, Orla faced a truth.

I'm an addict.

She'd read enough misery memoirs to tick off the symptoms – the need that built and built until it was unignorable, the sweet release of meeting that need, then the crashing realisation that the sweetness was momentary. Now that she'd dashed across London to Anthea's darkened house, Orla was awash with guilt and shame and stupefaction at her own rat-in-a-maze behaviour.

Most ruinous of all, she knew she was jeopardising her relationships for the sake of another fix.

A silver car, gleaming and almost noiseless, had interrupted her soul-searching. Nipping behind a pillar, Orla saw it glide to a stop outside Anthea's house. The driver jumped out, another eager courtier, and held the door open.

Orla concentrated. She'd have only as long as it took Anthea to disembark and climb the steps to study her.

Anthea wore a soft woollen blanket, in a moody lavender colour unknown in Primark's palette. Her red mane was dishevelled: she'd obviously dozed on the way home from recording the ITV medical drama she'd Tweeted about.

Rehearsing Lady M AND filming Second Opinion today. Send Lucozade!

The contrast between the sleepily dishevelled woman and her freezing, disconsolate sentinel couldn't have been greater. The front door closed with a clunk and Orla put her forehead to the rough stone of the pillar, shaking, waiting for the anger and the unhappiness to pass.

'She has everything,' whispered Orla. Her desire for the journal clutched to Anthea's chest was endlessly rechargeable, as was her inability to claim it.

The night had melted. She raced Marek back to his and won.

And he was pleased to see her.

But then he didn't know where she'd been.

Chapter Twenty-Eight

Da was a vague presence, a benign bundle of memories, but sometimes Orla remembered him so vividly that she could smell the pipe smoke that always curled about him, and hear his introspective chuckle. She had a sensory flashback now, as she queued in the post office to mail the last wave of presents home.

Da had been a safer port than Ma. Orla's mother believed that children should speak up in company, pushing Orla forward when fearsome relatives visited. Da would let his smallest girl hide behind his legs, safe from the grown-ups and their non-stop questions about how old she was and what was her favourite subject and wasn't she the image of her mammy? Da understood. With him, all five Cassidy kids felt like only children; Orla's shyness had been part-and-parcel of her Orla-ness, not something to be corrected.

And as quickly as Da's essence appeared, it receded, leaving Orla with tears in her eyes: a Daddy's Girl with no daddy.

Pulling herself together, Orla looked about her. Perhaps Maude's exposure therapy could start with a trip to the post office. Really just a chaotic corner of a convenience store, it smelled homely, of cooking and people, and was two minutes' walk from the book shop.

A small parcel fell from her pile and she squatted to pick it up. By its size and weight she judged it to be the Enid Blyton books for her niece, Niamh. These stragglers probably wouldn't reach home before Christmas, but Orla couldn't bear to leave anybody out. Word had got out in Tobercree that Orla wouldn't be home for Christmas, but her plea of 'No presents please!' hadn't; each morning brought a fresh batch of brown-paper packages that she guessed would reveal themselves on Christmas morning as a slag heap of novelty slippers and talc.

The Cassidys didn't do minimalism, particularly not at Christmas.

The queue inched forward as the frontrunner turned away from the counter. Slight but erect in a raincoat devoid of the merest insolent crease, George passed her.

Orla put a hand out, and he stopped. He smiled, creasing his faded eyes.

'Hello there,' he said.

He smelled of pipe smoke: perhaps he'd prompted Orla's reverie. 'Could I have a word, George? I'm Orla, by the way.'

'I felt you deserved an explanation.' Orla watched George's face as he took in her story. He'd suggested the chip shop for a cup of tea as they granted a discount to pensioners. There is an Irish expression, *gregging*, which means a smell or sight bringing on ravenous hunger: it's fair to say the smell of fish and chips was gregging Orla.

'It wasn't the real Maude speaking when she shouted at you.'

'I was rather surprised.' George was as restrained as his outfit. 'I admire the lady greatly.'

'I'll let you into a secret. She misses you coming in to see her.' Good thing Maude couldn't hear all this, thought Orla, or the old lady would slap her in the face with a battered hake.

'Does she?' George pressed his lips together. 'This is all a great shame, then, Rola.'

No point in correcting him again. She'd already been Oola and Only. 'It is. But there's hope. Have you ever heard of exposure therapy?'

Unsurprisingly, George hadn't. Orla filled him in, noting the strained look on his face, as if he'd seen something he shouldn't, a flash of knicker or a bra strap.

'Is this really any of my business?'

'Yes,' said Orla emphatically. 'Because you can be part of it.' She ploughed on, dismayed by his look of faint distaste. 'Once I've managed to coax her out on a few short journeys, perhaps you could ask her out to dinner again? Or for a stroll? It could be an incentive.'

'But what has this to do with me?' George looked affronted, eking out coins and piling them on the table. 'I'm sorry for your friend, very sorry, but really, to talk about, well, it's not proper.' He stood, belting his coat even tighter. 'I wish Maude all the best but I have troubles of my own,' he said. 'Goodbye to you, Nylon.'

Sim's journal

27 November 2011

O called. I was in the mood for friskiness but she wanted me to measure my arms. This can mean only one thing – Ma Cassidy is knitting the dreaded Christmas jumper. There is another life out there that I can have by clicking my fingers. A life where the Christmas jumper comes from Christian LaCroix. I just can't click my fucking fingers. Not yet, anyway.

'How did this creep up on me? It's next Tuesday! How am I going to get through it?'

'Christmas didn't creep up on you, Ju. It's beautifully predictable, the same date every year. Take your head out of your hands, lady. You're making my computer screen look like Sky News coverage of a Middle East hostage situation. You've still got a few days to wriggle out of Christmas Day at Fionnuala's. Make some excuse.'

'But it's the only way I'll spend Christmas or at least part of it with Rob.'

'Is that so important?'

'Yes, actually. I'd like to spend Christmas with the man I love. It's not such a big ask.'

'Is Rob looking forward to sitting around a turkey with his ex-wife, his daughter, his lover who's the ex's sister, and his lover's husband and his lover's son?'

'Jaysus, my life is a bad soap opera. He's very cool about it. Rob's very cool about most things. That's one of the reasons I love being around him. He soothes me.'

'Maybe he's enjoying it.'

'Nah, no way, that would be *weird*. He's just very capable, very calm.'

'Fake a headache on the day. That's what Deirdre does every time she wants to get out of something. Everybody knows she's pulling a fast one but nobody dares say so.'

'But then I'll miss Rob.'

'This is circular. We're back at the beginning again.'

'Himself is looking at me sideways. He knows something's up. He can smell the sexual satisfaction I radiate.'

'Be careful, Ju. Don't rush into anything. Think of Jack.'

'The best thing for Jack is a happy Mammy!'

'You know what I'd like? A special elixir that locks everybody's emotions down the instant they fall in love.'

'I would refuse to take it.'

The room felt quiet after Juno said goodbye, called inevitably away to Jack and an interface between a white sofa and a jammy hand. When Orla had first arrived in the little L-shaped flat she'd been aghast at the non-stop intrusive noise that leaked in through every window. Now her ears automatically blotted out the urban opera: now the flat was too quiet.

Quiet can be a euphemism for lonely: that certainly applied here, with all Orla's personnel otherwise occupied. Juno was in a whole other country. Maude was dozing upstairs. The twentieth was the day Ma put up the tree and ladled it with far too many decorations. And Marek was working overtime, pitching in with 'the lads' to meet a Christmas deadline.

She imagined him in a hard hat, breaking a sweat. She knew he'd be as good at knocking down walls as he was at negotiating deals. Orla's fingers itched: she'd like to knock down a wall herself. Physical graft might distract her.

Maybe, she thought, *it's just Christmas*. The season to be cheerful is equally the season to be lonely, after all. For somebody who generally liked – and, growing up with a mass of siblings, had occasionally *craved* – her own company, Orla was doing her best to avoid herself, picking up and putting down a magazine, pulling together a haphazard sandwich and leaving it uneaten, cleaning a bathroom that was already spotless.

The television was no help. Eight zillion channels and nothing worth watching. Orla's iPad, now joined by the laptop, was imprisoned in a distant cupboard out on the landing, her tiny flat's version of Siberia. Technology couldn't help.

If only she could fast-forward to Christmas. She would be grounded then, distracted, surrounded by people, *her* people, with much to do. It would be another anniversary ticked off and survived; her first Christmas since Sim had died.

It wasn't as if their last Christmas together had been joyful. He'd acquiesced to a plan that had dismayed her, but if they'd known it would be his last Christmas, perhaps Sim could have withstood Lucy's maternal thumbscrews, her *we never see you, darling, can't we have you to ourselves, just you, at Christmas lunch this once?*

Belatedly, a penny dropped.

His protestations against Lucy's selfishness had been far too baroque all along, and his disappointment at missing lunch with Orla's family had struck her as false. A year on, the truth rose to the surface, decomposed and rank.

When Sim had come to Orla on Christmas night, an hour later than promised, he was fresh from Anthea.

It shouldn't sting so much.

But it was Christmas! Once again, Orla was full to the brim with feelings she couldn't put anywhere. There was nobody to rant at, nobody to shake and ask, *How could you?*

Off to Siberia she went, where it was cold, and the climate suited her better.

*

The Madonna and Child on quality paper was by far the most tasteful of Orla's crop. She stood the card from Reece beside Ma's garish blue-eyed, blond-bearded Christ, along from Juno's naked Santa, and the handmade pop-up cracker from Niamh. On second thoughts, she moved Reece's card in front of her brother Hugh's traditional family photo shoot: the sight of that many braces and glasses and fat knees was un-festive.

'Happy Christmas from all at Reece Dodds Artists,' read the printed message. He'd added a personal scribble. *I hope all is well. I'm here if you need me.*

Orla took a moment to digest that. In her place, Juno would toss the card away, choosing to read the innocuous words as both manipulative and condescending, but Orla had a more complex reaction to Reece, which was hard to pick apart.

This didn't translate into wanting to speak to him. For now, she was happy to keep him at arm's length. She spotted a smaller, more untidy and less legible P.S. in the corner.

I've got a present for you. Hope that's OK. I'll be away over the festive season (thank goodness) so I'll be in touch after New Year. X

Orla made a mental note to send him a card in return.

Tinsel dripped drunkenly from the classroom's centre light. Some of her students had already flown home before this, the last day of term. Orla sympathised when Abena burst into tears because she wouldn't be tasting the Christmas barbecued goat this year, and invited her to Ladbroke Grove.

'You are kind, but I am going to Sanae's house. I will cry a lot but she says she does not mind.'

Japanese Christmas cake sounded nicer than the dense aromatic leviathan that glowered annually on Ma's sideboard: according to Sanae it was white sponge mounded with strawberries and cream. When Natalya spoke nostalgically about Poland, Orla visualised the twelve courses she described, the candles in a dark room evoking the star of Bethlehem, emphasising the mystical, symbolic aspect of the meal. A little heavy on the herrings for Orla's palate: she was relieved that Marek had opted to go British with his menu.

'I know what Marek buys you for Christmas,' said Bogna in a sing-song, *wouldn't you like to know* manner.

'And I'll know too when I open it on Christmas Day.' Orla was not a peeker; she'd never joined Deirdre in the traditional pre-Christmas rummage at the bottom of her parents' wardrobe. She preferred to wait patiently and relish the anticipation. She also ate her greens first and always said 'thank you': if Orla was a friend of hers she'd get on her nerves.

It was the last Saturday before Christmas and the three Maude's Books musketeers stood around, ready and waiting for the Christmas rush Maude had prophesied.

'See?' said the proprietor, proudly, when a man came in and purchased a Peter Rabbit anthology, closely followed by an elderly lady who bought all three of their Barbara Cartlands. 'Told you so.'

'Look!' Bogna pointed into the foggy street. 'George.'

Hurrying by, George tipped his hat at the brightly lit shop, his gesture landing on no woman in particular.

'Why does he not enter any more?' Bogna scowled at his receding back. 'Silly old fart.'

'I scared him off. It's my fault, not George's.' Maude watched him too. 'Don't call him a fart, dear.'

'He *is* fart, though,' insisted Bogna.

Silently, Orla agreed.

Chapter Twenty-Nine

Her tiny flat felt crammed, as if there were hundreds of people in it, even though there was just the four of them.

With the decadence of pre-revolution Russian aristocracy, they drank champagne at breakfast time. Christmas's magnifying glass made everything bigger, shinier, sparklier. There was food on every surface, a glass in every hand and the air was charged with bubbling good humour.

Singing along to carols on the radio in his touchingly out of tune baritone, Marek wore a clean white apron over his chocolate cashmere jumper. Even in an apron, Marek looked dashing, as if about to leap on a horse and gallop to a duel. Perhaps it was the hair. Orla was a little over-keen on Marek's hair, to the point of envy. It flopped just so, whereas hers flopped just wrong.

When he and Orla met each other's eye, they shared a sense of excitement that wasn't to do with the packages under the tiny tree.

This day was a step forward. The feeling Orla had in the National Gallery – that she was officially older now, more mature, more *useful* – had lingered. Marek, laughing his deep joyous laugh at one of Maude's absurd tales, brought out something fresh in her, a depth of character she'd never utilised in a relationship before. They'd gone up a gear.

There was no way to entertain that happy thought without remembering the one woeful failing that threatened to blot out all her virtues. With Sim, *he'd* been the problem. Orla had been the eye-roller, the tutter, the forgiver as he carried on being profligate, indolent, star struck, vain and, naturally, adorable. Now it was Orla's turn to be the problem partner and the role chafed.

Particularly as Marek was unaware of the problem. She passed him, and he paused his endless whisking, beating, dicing and cursing to grab her for a bear hug, nipping at her ear. Her scream delighted him.

In a raspberry cardigan with swooping sleeves, Maude tweaked the table endlessly, primping the napkins, turning the silver candelabra she'd dug out to its best advantage, placing a mini poinsettia at each place setting. The pops of scarlet burned against the starched white linen cloth, ironed, incredibly, by Bogna the night before.

Vocal about her dismay at the choice of venue, Bogna had threatened to boycott lunch unless it was at the mews. 'Why squeeze us in crappy flat when you have fuck-off house?' had been her reasonable question.

Marek's reply – 'We're eating at Orla's' – was so final that even Bogna's prodigious belligerence wouldn't tackle it. Orla had only told him about Maude's agoraphobia because of the impossibility of taking her out on Christmas Day; he'd immediately begun to plot the logistics of cooking a three-course turkey lunch in such an abbreviated kitchen.

'Christmas in Poland is about eating together, or visiting. It's about family, and friends, and your neighbours,' Marek said as he stirred the gravy, sexily. (Orla had discovered that the

310

simple application of an apron made Marek's every move sexy. He had peeled potatoes in an erotic fashion earlier, and she could hardly wait to see how he boiled carrots.) 'We don't place such emphasis on gifts as English people – and yes, Orla, yes, *Irish* people, I don't need another lecture about the war of independence.'

Bogna, feet up on the sofa while the others toiled, shouted through, 'Ha! You scare her, Marek! Now she worries your present is rubbish.' She downed her drink. 'Champagne!' she shouted.

Marek took a deep breath in.

Sexily.

'Counting to ten?' asked Orla.

'A hundred,' said Marek.

'Happy Christmas Ma!'

'And you, musha, and you.'

'Did you like the place mats?'

'Oh, you know me for place mats! They're stunning! But you shouldn't be wasting your money on me, Orla.'

'I can hear everybody. Are they all OK?'

'Sure, they're grand. Although Deirdre has a migraine. She's in me bed. She'll force down a little turkey later, she says.'

'Will you kiss the kids for me?'

'I will. They're all playing with their presents. It's a mad-house. Is Mark there?'

'No, because he doesn't exist. Marek's here, though.'

'Feck off. I'm too old to be learning foreign names. Say merry Christmas for me.'

'Mum, gotta run. Sheraz just came in.'

'Sher-who?'

After a brief chat and a ticking off for leaving his son at home at Christmas ('He's fine! He's stock-taking!'), Sheraz left and the action sped up.

Pots belched steam, the oven yawned like a hell-mouth, Maude lit the candles and Marek bade them sit.

The feast was ready.

At Marek's request, they all held hands. He said a short grace in Polish. Before he let go of Orla's hand he squeezed her fingers, and she felt a perfect peace soon chased away by the clatter of cutlery, the handing round of sauce boats, the wordless exclamations of pleasure as all four of them fell on the food.

How different the table looked at the end of the meal. From a glamorous still life to a boneyard of crumbs and napkins and a toppled glass, it was a testament to the meal.

'My compliments to the chef,' said Maude, sitting back, exhausted and dabbing her lips with a napkin.

'To the chef!' Orla lifted her glass and threw some wine on her own face. *Classy*, she giggled to herself as Marek dabbed it off. She was tipsy, and liking it, her body languid and her mind taking a day off from its hamster wheel.

The journal was missing – that's how it felt, even though she'd never owned it – but for today, at this candlelit oasis, she could bear it. She could put off the scheming until tomorrow. She could even feel confident that one day she *would* own it: a feeling that was elusive at best.

The silver Tiffany bangle jangled at her wrist. 'Bloody

handcuff,' Bogna had said. Orla liked the gentle heaviness of it, the way it circled her wrist but didn't grab. 'Thank you for my pressie,' she said, leaning in to Marek's shoulder.

'You said that already. A few times.' Marek had looked tense as she'd opened it, only smiling when she screamed, 'Tiffany! Feckin' Tiffany!'

'A man who's good at gifts,' Maude murmured approvingly, sipping her coffee. 'Unusual. Worth hanging on to.'

'Next year, Maude, I'll get a little something from Tiffany for you as well,' said Marek.

Next year.

Orla shut her eyes as Marek and Maude chatted. He was perfectly at home with Maude: he'd grown up around his grandparents, he told Orla, and appreciated an older person's perspective. His deep rumble and her silvery rise and fall were like a lullaby.

Bogna's return from the bathroom, in full magnificent warpaint and wearing a dress composed mainly of holes, broke the mood. 'I told you,' she began combatively, 'I go to meet gang.'

'No, you didn't,' said Marek, calmly. The sort of calm that seaside towns experience before a gale destroys the pier. 'In fact, you promised you'd stay all day.' He was concentrating on her face, Orla could tell, trying to ignore the outfit.

'For god's *sake*!' Bogna was unselfconscious about her tantrums. She threw her head back and sagged at the knees, her whole body telling Marek just how boring, bossy and *old* she found him. 'It's Christmas. I don't want to be here. No offence, Maudie.'

'None taken,' said Maude equably. She enjoyed Bogna's displays.

'Bogna!' began Marek, before snapping his mouth shut. Orla had squeezed his knee under the table. 'I insist that . . .' She squeezed a little higher.

'Bogna just wants to be with her friends,' she said

'Well . . .'

'You are young one day. Remember that day?' asked Bogna, her head wobbling archly.

'I remember it well. I was at work that day,' said Marek. 'I was helping to bring you up that day.' Another squeeze of his thigh, and a change of tone. 'Oh, go, you monkey. But don't get too trashed, please. I like you all in one piece.'

Bogna swooped and kissed his head, almost laughing out her gum at his surprise. 'Happy Christmas, stupid brother. And you,' she nodded at Orla. 'Marry him, please.'

As the door banged behind her, Maude looked on Orla's ketchup features with fond humour. 'Subtle as a wrecking ball, that one. Now. Let's start on the clearing up.'

Sly old fox, her offer was made with transparent disingenuousness. She knew Orla would refuse all offers of help. 'You don't know where anything goes, I'll be quicker doing it on my own,' she flapped, echoing Ma. Despatching Maude to her flat for a lie-down, and Marek off to the shower, Orla set about the pots and pans, impressed with how speedily she could wash up when sex with Marek was on the cards.

The bedroom smelled of her favourite mimosa bath gel. 'That was a quick shower,' she said approvingly, kicking off her shoes. Marek lay across her bed, laptop open in front of him. Even in her sugar pink towelling dressing gown he was desirable and she felt a sucker punch of desire.

'What are you . . .' She guessed halfway through the

314

sentence and the sherbet sweetness of the tableau soured.
'... looking at?'

Marek spun the laptop so she could see the screen. *ANT FACTS*, it proclaimed boldly at the top of a spreadsheet.

Orla saw her own words, raw and dumb in the tender lamplight. *ANT CALENDAR*, she read, above a font that looked, through tears, like dancing gnats, but which she knew to be a list of Ant's public appearances and some private ones. *ANTSITES* was a bullet-pointed index of web pages.

But *SPOTTED* was the worst. It was a list, only two-strong but damning, of the vigils she'd kept outside Anthea's house, the most recent only nine days earlier.

Marek regarded her patiently.

A defence along the lines of *that's private* was possible but, Orla knew, pathetic. She remembered now that she'd left it open on the bed, almost daring the truth about her stinky pastime to emerge. Sinking into the wicker chair she aimed her clothes at when undressing for bed, Orla said limply, 'So now you know.'

'Why?' Marek pushed out the word and stood up. 'I had no idea. You kept all *this*,' he gestured at the computer, 'from me. How many lies have you told me?'

'No important ones.' There was a whine in Orla's voice she didn't much like and tried to iron out. 'This is the only thing I've been dishonest about. Because I'm ashamed.'

Marek snorted, like a horse. He looked down at himself, noticed the embroidered pink towelling and tore off the dressing gown as if was dusted with itching powder.

Orla averted her eyes; she didn't feel entitled to look at his

315

body, the body she'd craved all afternoon. 'Sorry.' She wished the word had more syllables, so it would sound weightier as he crossly tugged on his jeans and forced his head through the neck of his jumper.

'Sorry enough to stop?'

This was no time for fobbing him off. 'I have a problem, Marek.'

'Yes, you do.' His face was alive with energy, his eyes black and bright. He looked healthy and she could feel him slipping away, leaving her to her disease.

Orla stood, urgent now, to match his demeanour. 'Try and understand. Watching Anthea—'

'*Stalking* Anthea,' said Marek crisply. 'The word for what you do is stalking.'

'No, it's . . .' Orla stumbled on the term, so long held at bay. It was an ugly word, dull and knobbly. 'I stalk,' she said wonderingly.

Marek's brusque assessment triggered an epiphany. She saw herself, in an unflattering flash of light, through his eyes. Her rational plan to win the journal was anything but.

'Listen,' Orla fanned her face, hot with the realisation of her own lunacy, and the repercussions it might soon have, 'I don't want to *stalk* her and I don't want to keep secrets from you, but . . .' another word she tried to avoid barrelled towards her, 'it's an addiction,' she ended quietly. No use to deny the dark buzz that standing outside Anthea's house gave her, even while it corroded her self-respect. She had something in common, it would seem, with junkies and alcoholics, with the flat-nosed wino singing up a Christmas Day storm in Sheraz's doorway.

'What do you get out of it?' Marek was tying his shoelaces, sitting on the very edge of the bed.

'In a way,' began Orla, knowing how this would sound, but unable to phrase it any other way, 'I'm doing it for us.'

Another snort, as if almost amused. 'Run that by me again,' said Marek. 'For us?' His eyebrows were invisible, somewhere up in his tousled, damp hair.

'Look, I know you hate to hear his name but Sim was—'

Marek held up his hand and interrupted. 'You're wrong. I don't hate to hear his name. I am not such a monster of arrogance that I need you to forget him. It's the way I hear his name. The way he comes between us.'

He nodded; he was done; she could carry on.

'OK, well, whatever.' The nod had brought out Orla's inner Bogna. 'This year has been so, so *awful*, Marek. And I can't get over Sim in a linear way. From the outside it must look messy, but I've been doing my best. I loved him, after all. I just need one detail tidied, put to rest. I need the journal. I *need* it.' She banged her chest. 'It will fix me.'

Marek winced. '*Fix* you?'

'Since reading the valentine, I'm broken,' said Orla, sorry for herself, and for him: under his silverback blather she discerned his confusion. And hurt. 'The journal will sort me out. If I can read – just once – about what really happened, get my head around it, stop feeling as if I'm unloveable, monstrous.'

'*Moje złotko.*' Marek stood and took a step towards her, his eyelids heavy with compassion. He stopped short of touching her.

Orla cursed the two feet of carpet between them.

'If it's about the journal,' he said slowly, 'why hang about outside Anthea Blake's house? Why not walk up to her and ask for it?'

'I will, I will.' Orla shook with the need to impart this. 'I haven't because, well, I just couldn't but I will.'

'OK.' Marek snatched up her phone. 'Call her and ask.'

'On Christmas Day?'

'On Christmas Day.'

'I don't have her number.'

'Reece will have it.'

'He won't give it to me.'

'He'll damn well give it to me,' said Marek, with certainty. 'Go on. Call. And this all ends. And you and I are fine, like you say.'

He was offering her a way out, a resolution.

A thought surfaced and waved: if she'd shared this with Marek earlier he'd have smoothed out her thinking, applied logic and muscle. This conversation would not be happening and she'd have read the ill-fated journal by now.

Orla looked at the phone, hating it more than the carpet. Marek thought in straight lines. She thought in woozy circles. It was clear cut, his solution, and it would work.

But she couldn't do it. It was terrifying to even consider it. She'd built Anthea into a monstrous, fabulous creature, far larger than her outline, superhuman and worth a hundred Orlas.

Marek threw the phone to the bed with force, so it bounced. 'You won't talk to Anthea. You enjoy the process. You're locked into an insane relationship with her that she doesn't even know you're having.' As Orla shaped her lips for a protest, he barked, exasperated, 'I've seen the spreadsheets!' He hung his head.

Orla covered her face with her hands. She knew he was big-hearted. She knew he was a man who would always want to do the right thing. If she could throw herself on his mercy, he wouldn't walk away. But throwing herself on anybody's mercy was alien to Orla's self-sufficient nature. She waited for his next move.

'I don't want to fight with you,' murmured Marek.

'Me neither, oh, me neither.' Orla grasped at the life-line.

'Are you still in love with Sim?' Marek glared at the thread-bare carpet, as if trying to see past it and down to the book shop.

'What? No.'

Orla hadn't examined her feelings for Sim in a long while. If she was frank then, yes, there was still love. There always would be: she saw the truth of Maude's analysis back when she'd opened the valentine. But she didn't love him in the way Marek feared.

'It's not about him.' Marek's head remained down, but his eyes raised and met hers sardonically. 'I know that sounds unbelievable, topsy-turvy, but it's not about Sim. It's about me. And how I didn't see what was happening. And why he should prefer her to me.'

Orla stabbed at her eyes with blunt knuckles, appalled at displaying her pitiful fears in public. She sensed an irresolute movement from Marek: she knew his instinct was to comfort her. She sighed, a ghastly groaning wheeze, when he didn't approach her. *I've lost him*, she thought, and an ache like a ravenous mouth began in her stomach.

'You humiliate me,' said Marek. He was quiet, controlled. 'I was second best. I put my pride to one side. I told myself that this woman is worth it, is worth anything. I told you I love you. You didn't hear me, Orla. Instead you moved me back, not to second but to *third* place behind some actress.'

'I did hear you.'

'Then why ...' the sudden increase in volume shocked them both. Marek snapped his mouth shut, and turned away as if he couldn't bear the sight of her. 'I am straight with you and you make fun of me.' He whirled to face her and closed the gap between them. They were close, nose to nose, but he didn't tone it down. 'I don't have to stay.'

'Go then!' Orla could shout too. 'Go on, disappear at the first sign of trouble!'

Shaking, their breath mingling, their faces almost touching, this would be the moment in a movie where they would kiss passionately, and have explosive sex.

It wasn't a movie.

'I have never,' said Marek deliberately, 'known anybody as infuriating as you. You hold me at arm's length and beckon over your shoulder. And I know that's a mixed metaphor. I'm Polish, for Christ's sake. And you lie to me. You keep me in the dark. You are not a good person to have a relationship with.'

Eastern European candour again. Orla couldn't argue: he was the second man to feel that way. 'If I'm so horrible,' she said, suddenly sixteen, 'why not dump me?'

'Dump you?' Marek stalked away, hands on his hips. Orla missed the closeness of his face, angry though it was. Now he was on the other side of the room, looking as though the expression she used had exploded, stink-bomb-like, under his nose. 'I'm a grown man, I do not *dump*. I think love is precious, even if you do not.'

That incendiary word again shining in the midst of all the ugliness. Orla became very still. They were nearing the apex of the argument. What Marek said next, what she said next, would be very important.

'You have to choose, Orla. You should choose life. You should choose me,' was what Marek said next.

And Orla said nothing.

This was a crossroads in a dark wood. How she wished that Marek could see through the gloom how she needed and admired him. And loved him.

Why had she never told him? She'd never even used the word in her own thoughts. Yet it was the only word that did justice to the complex way Orla felt about him. *What would it have cost me to tell Marek I loved him?*

To say it now would be cheap, as if she were desperately lobbing everything that came to hand to make him stay. It was too late to tell him and, besides, this was patently, obviously over.

Because he was an honest man and she tried to be an honest woman and any promise she made would be false. Orla couldn't just abandon a quest that had come to define her. She couldn't promise not to pursue the journal.

Orla knew that, deep in her bones, as certainly as she knew she loved him.

'That's my answer?' Marek's voice bled out of him. 'Silence?'

Orla shut her eyes. He was her favourite thing to look at

but she couldn't bear the wounded astonishment on his face.

'I thought you were a woman. But you are a child.'

Marek left.

Orla had a shower and went to bed.

Chapter Thirty

Maude had heard the raised voices, she said, cutting off Orla's tearful reportage the next morning. 'I heard the door bang behind him. If he's got any sense, he'll be back.'

Beyond the sitting room windows, Ladbroke Grove was back to noisy normality, as if keen to underline that no piffling Messiah's birth could interfere with its mojo for long. Within the flat, yesterday's sparkle had dissolved, supplanted by a funereal hush as if some person, not just a love affair, had died.

Despite her dejection, despite the acid burn of regret in her stomach, Orla found a strange relief in her dilemma.

It was out in the open. Her darkest secret had been shoved, blinking, into the light and along with the expected shame there was a sensation of something suffocatingly tight being unlaced. Orla could breathe out at last. Marek *knew*: what happened now had a momentum all of its own, but at least he knew and there was no further need to lie.

'It's a tradition!'

'I never heard of such a tradition,' scoffed Maude. 'The Boxing Day walk? It doesn't exist.'

'OK, I admit, it's a brand-new tradition. But I need some air, Maude. I'm stale. I'm going off, like that fudge Sheraz gave us yesterday. Please.'

'No, no, no. I'll take my rotten meds, and I'll practise my yoga breathing but I'm not putting my nose outside. Soon, dear, I promise, but not yet.' Maude returned to her book, glasses high on her nose, with finality.

By nightfall, Orla had stowed the phone on a high shelf where she couldn't see it. It was too painful to continually check its little screen for a light, for his name, for rescue. She placed the bangle beside it, back in its box. It was impossible to wear it now that the pact implicit in its perfect circle was null and void.

Anaesthetising herself with Boxing Day television, glad of the tiptapping tread of Maude overhead, Orla had a bizarre revelation.

Bereft of Marek, far from home, still denied the journal and its cruel comforts, she was, somehow, immune to the call of the iPad.

She examined that word: no, not *immune*. She could sense it teetering just outside the glow from the campfire of her consciousness. But she could withstand it.

There was barbarous irony here. Before the argument, the addiction had brought a double pressure to bear on Orla: not only had she to withstand the lure of her fix but she'd had to hide her withstanding of it from Marek.

A hope flickered valiantly, a candle in the arctic of her new situation. *I can do this*, she realised, giving herself the assurance she hadn't felt able to offer Marek last night. If she ditched the unhealthy habits, if she *deserved* him, then maybe Marek would come back.

New Year's Eve was key. She'd work towards that. With his

usual sensitivity Marek had divined that it was a time heavy with significance: Orla knew this had prompted his elaborate plans for their first New Year as a couple. He wasn't the sort to let her down. If she could hang on until then, keep her fingers from tapping that dire name into a search engine, keep away from Primrose Hill, Marek would come back.

He wouldn't let her down.

'Simple things,' was Maude's prescription. They would apply themselves to simple pleasures, unfussy and modest in scale. This would nibble up the days, help them to pass, as the future unrolled in its relentless way. 'We'll get through it,' she said briskly, as she settled down on Orla's sofa, fussing with a fluffy shawl around her shoulders. She groaned as Orla unwrapped the boxed DVDs. 'This is not a *simple thing*, Orla. I want it minuted that I consider this to be a bad idea.'

'*Whisht*.' Orla threw her a Terry's Chocolate Orange. 'And have you taken your tablets? All of them?'

'Yes. You *whisht*.' Maude mispronounced it, neglecting to prolong the *sh*.

'It's starting.' Orla turned up the volume.

The irony of standing over Maude to ensure she took her medication wasn't lost on Orla. Her own mind played tricks on her every bit as elaborate as Maude's did. As they sat like bookends on the sofa, Orla could, if she chose, see them as two loony old dears walled up in this house, but such tabloid reduction was too broad: *we're two complicated, troubled women doing our shambolic best*.

'Oh, there he is,' breathed Maude.

Sim was in the very first scene of *The Courtesan*. They saw his back as he strode the length of a gilded corridor, his buck-led shoes noisy on the wooden floor. He rapped at an ornate door, twelve feet high, and it opened on to a pistachio green and sorbet pink salon. It was ravishing, and when Sim turned to face the viewer, so was he.

Oh Sim, thought Orla with that old inflexion she'd aban-doned with the valentine. He was half smiling, his eyes knowing.

He was alive.

Orla wanted to throw up. She felt Maude's eyes on her and made sure nothing of her turmoil was visible. It was close to unbearable to see Sim and yet she devoured him, reminded of the heft of his shoulders, the lilt of his walk, and, when he spoke, the playfulness of his voice.

'Mother!' he shouted. 'Don't you have a kiss for your son?'

And again Maude's eyes bored into the side of Orla's head as the camera pivoted to find Anthea emerging from behind a screen, fastening a diamond bracelet about her wrist. 'My pre-cious boy, you're home,' she said, in a voice that slithered and rustled like her silk gown. 'I've missed you.'

'This is too much,' muttered Maude, reaching for the remote control.

'No!' Seeing Maude jump, Orla repeated the word more gently, took the heat out of it. 'No, Maudie. Let's keep watch-ing.'

Not up to the marathon of a whole series in one slab, Maude fell asleep during episode three.

Four hours in, Orla was drunk on Sim. Denied the journal, his performance was all that was left of him that was new: after

326

the final credits rolled there'd be nothing more. That would be it. Resurrected on her screen, he walked and talked and laughed ... and kissed.

Sim kissed almost every female in the cast. He kissed them like he'd kissed Orla: with plump greedy lips, a palm either side of her face, a swooning noise deep in his throat.

Some of the girls were recognisable – one Orla recalled from the Dublin fringe scene – and all were striking, in that changeling way of actresses. Orla fidgeted, enduring a physical flashback of how plain she'd felt among Sim's theatre gang. Frothy, mercurial, they were women who could rock a scarf as a bandeau top, wear a top hat wittily to dinner. Orla knew they gossiped about Sim's little country mouse, wondering at the mismatch. Orla had never fitted in.

I never brought that up with him. How odd that felt at this remove. Why hadn't she? *Because he'd pretend it wasn't so.* The answer was immediate.

The production made a dress-up doll of the Comte: See Sim in powder blue riding gear! See Sim in a brocade dressing gown! Once an episode, without fail, it was See Sim in the nude!

His bottom, his legs, the powerful muscles of his back such a surprise after the clean lines of his clothed torso, were all too familiar to Orla. She squirmed slightly at the unexpected nip of desire. Post valentine, Orla had carefully neutered Sim. On television, condensed, posed, bright, he was ravishing.

The infamous, shocking love scene between the Comte de Caylus and his mother led to a riot in Orla's mind. As if her head were held in place by a torturer's vice she watched Anthea bite Sim's shoulder as she bucked in orgasm.

It was obscene. No other viewer would share her opinion;

the scene was tasteful and erotic. But for Orla it was pornography, their sex tape.

While they filmed, Orla had been miles away, complacently preparing herself for a proposal. She half expected the camera to pan to her, in Tobercrec, going about her dull business as the village idiot.

The critical acclaim, hysterical though it was thanks to the glamour of his early death, was deserved. He was compelling, intriguing, and a beauty to boot. Sim – and Orla had never truly appreciated this – was a good actor.

But that was all he was.

Orla recognised each gesture, each glance, each tic. When the Comte walked by the river, stripping a flower of petals and dashing them into the water, he was *her* Sim, insofar as he could be called that now.

Why didn't I know he was always acting? Sim was a ragbag of learned mannerisms. There was nothing organic about him. How hard he'd worked on himself, on the creature that was Sim Quinn, always self-aware, always an eye on the mirror. He'd put all his energy into this creation and it had worked perfectly: Sim was envied, adored, lusted after, just as he'd wanted.

But that was *all* he wanted.

There was no core to him. No real Sim. Left to his own devices by self-regarding and ambitious parents, Sim had constructed himself out of pretty odds and ends he'd found. No wonder he betrayed her: he had no idea that he shouldn't.

Orla cried for the little Dublin boy who'd surmised that the way he was wasn't good enough.

I loved you, she told the screen. *You could have been real with me.*

To live and die without ever being known seemed to Orla like the saddest prank life could play on a person.

It was light when the final credits, with their RIP dedication, rolled. Orla had been quite wrong to mourn the end of her relationship with Sim. There had been one twist left in their road.

She pitied him.

Chapter Thirty-One

Climbing the ladder, Bogna was in vintage form. 'Up bloody ladder to put tinsel up, then up bloody ladder to pull tinsel down. And no overtime for working Saturday after Christmas. You are bloody slave pusher, Maude.'

'Slave *driver*, dear,' said Maude, holding the ladder while Bogna groped at the decorations.

Orla stayed out of Bogna's gravitational pull. Any innocuous snippet about Marek could wound: best to avoid the subject even though she longed to ask *how is he?*

Eventually, Bogna mentioned him quite naturally. 'At least coming to work gets me away from bad-tempered sod of brother,' she muttered, buttering herself a piece of toast.

Maude and Orla exchanged looks. 'Is he a bear with a sore bum?' asked Maude, hyper-casual, placing a guide to Oslo on the shelf upside down. She often recycled Bogna's more colourful gaffes.

'No. He is bear with yeast infection,' scowled Bogna, throwing herself full length on the sofa with her snack. 'Try and cheer him up when you see him, Orla. Give him ten out of ten blow job or something.'

'Lovely,' whispered Maude with a frown.

'Just off upstairs for a sec.' Orla flew to her flat, emboldened by Bogna's vivid scene-setting of a miserable Marek who hadn't mentioned the break-up. Maybe it wasn't a break-up. Maybe it was a break.

It felt like a break-up.

Not stopping to examine that, Orla scooped up her mobile and called Marek's number. She sucked her lips until they disappeared, not thinking, putting off any such common-sense activity until he picked up.

There was a heartless click and the outgoing message told her Marek was busy and invited her to leave her name and number. Many times he'd picked up halfway through and she'd smiled at the contrast between the curt recording and the big cat purr of his real-time *'Moje złotko!'* Now she wondered if he'd seen her name and diverted the call.

'Um, hi, how's, you know, things? Er, yeah, so this is strange, isn't it? Us not, you know, speaking. Just wondered if you're OK, but you probably are. Probably better off without me! Ha! I'm fine. Well, not fine. No, not fine. I'm, well, I'm a bit, you know and oh yes! Actually, yes. My *stuff*, Marek! You've still got some bits and pieces of mine. I could drop round to collect it, no fuss, just a quick hello and I'll be off, 'cos I, you know, need them and—'

Another click cut her off.

'YOU FECKIN' IDIOT!' Orla roared at herself, flinging away the phone, clamping both hands to her head. *My stuff?* The 'stuff' she'd left at the mews amounted to a toothbrush, some shampoo and a paperback: that call had made it sound like insulin and a fortune in Nazi gold.

Perhaps he'd smile. Perhaps he'd understand.

And then what? Back to square one? Marek was too sensible a man to visit square one more than once.

'Poppy was the worst. I mean, I felt worst about her. Rob's her Daddy, after all, and I'm her Aunty. She was so cute all day, playing with the wrapping paper instead of the presents. She made me feel sick with guilt.'

'Did Jack like my pressie?'

'The, let me see, what was it? Oh! Yeah! The painting kit. He *loved* it, Orla. He's already painted you a thank you card with it. And I couldn't even look at Himself. Or Fionnuala. She was making cow eyes at Rob all day. Desperate, feckin' *desperate* for a reunion.'

'Poor Fionnuala. How was Rob?'

'Well ... serene, actually.'

'Odd.'

'Pleased, even. A bit. As if he was, oh *yuk*, Orla, he *enjoyed* it.'

'Ah.'

'Ah, indeed. If my poor mother had looked under the lunch table and seen his foot up my skirt she'd have died on the spot.'

'That was a bit risky!'

'Yeah.'

'Was it ...?'

'Weird? Very. I mean, hello! These people are family.'

'How can I say *I told you so* without sounding like a complete cow?'

'You did tell me so and you were right. When he walked in I thought, *how do I stop myself ripping his clothes off*. But as the day wore on I avoided being alone with him. I hid myself in the yard at one point instead of snogging the gob off him in the utility room.'

'What now?'

'We've arranged to meet tomorrow. He's booked a hotel room.'

'For unbridled nookie?'

'I'm going to end it.'

'What? Are you sure?'

'Are you doing a U-turn on me?'

'Not in the least. I'm delighted. It was guaranteed pain, like asking to be punched in the face. It's just that your change of heart is very sudden.'

'As sudden as the way I fell for him. He's a symptom, Orla. Christmas Day is good for soul-searching.'

'Hmm.'

'It's like time switches off. The world puts its feet up and *thinks*. Rob's in love with love. And worse, he's selfish. I'm no better. I know you've been kind about it, but I've behaved abominably. I've had a close shave and I'll have to spend the rest of my life making it up to Himself and Fionnuala and Poppy and Jack without them even knowing.'

'You really *have* woken up. Welcome back, Sleeping Beauty!'

'Rob was a sticking plaster over my marriage. I got things the wrong way round. I should have sorted out my home life first. So wish me luck getting rid of Rob. He's a rubbish kisser, by the way.'

'How the mighty have fallen.'

'And then tomorrow when I get home from Rob I'm going to talk to Himself.'

333

'Work things out. I'm glad.'

'No. I'm going to ask him for a divorce.'

Three days until their New Year date. Three days' radio silence from Marek. It was sinking in.

Orla had shed her pride. She wanted to roller-skate to Marek's door and collapse on his step. The fantasy ended there: she couldn't conjure up a speech to win him back because their showdown had been inevitable and any rapprochement would simply start the meter running to the next one.

It was becoming real, their estrangement. She'd refrained from filling Juno in on this latest hairpin bend in her love life. She'd tell her after New Year's Eve; if Marek kept their date there might be nothing to tell.

The bangle gathered dust on its shelf, already sinking into the chintzy landscape. She envisioned herself clicking it shut around her wrist on New Year's Eve, the way Maude visualised herself sauntering along the High Street.

Maude was on best behaviour still, visualising like billy-o, knocking back her tablets, yoga breathing loudly three times a day. Orla envied her discipline: Maude wouldn't have made that absurd phone call. She could only hope that Marek chose to be charmed by her teenage gabble, but she could visualise all too well his face as he listened to her message, as he wondered when, if ever, she would do justice to what had happened between them.

'Orla, dear!' Maude called her down to the shop. 'Something's come. By courier. For you.' She pointed to a bulky package. Her look of excitement slithered off her chin when she saw Orla's face.

The ornate European handwriting on the label, so quaint in comparison to the more modern British style, was Marek's. Orla didn't have to open the package to know it was her 'stuff'.

'At the risk of stating the obvious,' said Maude, on Sunday night, the eve of New Year's Eve, '*ring him*. That's the second time you've moved Professor Plum diagonally and you know that's strictly forbidden in the rules.'

The simple things that she and Maude were taking pleasure in had started to look similar to boring things. Orla couldn't care which Cluedo character dunnit while Marek was at large, assiduously not getting in touch.

'I did call him, remember?'

'I mean call him and talk to him. Tell him how you feel. Be honest, for heaven's sake.'

Maude wouldn't suggest this if she knew about the systematic lying, the addictive behaviour. 'I think Miss Scarlett did it. With her knicker elastic. In the lean-to. It has to come from *him*, Maudie. He's the one who left. He either wants me or he doesn't.'

'Poor chap,' muttered Maude, rolling the dice. 'He has to do all the heavy lifting, doesn't he?'

If Marek stood by his word, if he was the man Orla thought he was, if the new year was truly going to be, as he'd put it, *their* year, then he'd be back tomorrow.

When she would tell him that she had withstood the allure of Anthea Blake and the journal.

Sim's journal

31 December 2011

Only a few hours to go. I am NEVER spending new year in this madhouse AGAIN. Mum's right. The Cassidys ARE mad.

Chapter Thirty-Two

It was the last five hours of the old year. A careful shower was in order, with neurotic grooming. Orla must be smooth of leg, glossy of hair, exfoliated, moisturised, perfumed.

The Trafalgar Square jaunt had been carefully planned. A cab was a must, Marek had said: he intended to drink a little too much. He'd pick her up at nine and they'd have a drink with Maude, who planned to ignore New Year as she always did – 'too schmaltzy' – before setting off for a late dinner in a W1 restaurant.

'Anywhere will do,' Orla had said.

'Somewhere special. I've booked already.'

Then they'd make their way to the square on foot. 'I'm bringing whisky,' Marek had promised, 'in a hip flask.'

'I'll bring my hand-warmers.' Orla had neglected to say she'd bought them *en route* to Beatrice Gardens that second time. 'If we hold hands it'll warm us both.'

'If?' Marek had insisted that they kiss on each of the twelve chimes, before travelling home on the tube.

'There'll be vomit,' Orla had warned.

'We won't care,' Marek had said.

Blow-drying her hair, Orla clung to the fact that he hadn't cancelled these elaborate plans. The doorbell would ring at nine o'clock. They would step over the threshold of 2013 together.

As she painted her wan face, a memory intruded on Orla's

artistry. This time last year, she'd applied her make-up just as carefully, only to sob it off later. She paused, only half her cupid's bow defined.

BONG! The long hallway of Ma's bungalow as Orla approaches the spare room. From the sitting room behind her, the live broadcast has started its countdown to midnight. Ma is yelling *'Come on everyone! It's starting!'*

BONG! Hugh's newborn is bawling – still – in the kitchen. Orla throws her brother a sympathetic smile as he paces up and down the lino, hair on end and baby to his chest. Above Orla's head, a game of tag in the loft sounds like an infestation of child-size mice.

BONG! Ma yells 'How many is that? Three or four? WAKE UP AUNTY ANNIE, IT'S NEARLY MIDNIGHT!' Stepping over Hugh's eldest mastering 'Danny Boy' on her new recorder – 'Keep at it, Niamh!' – Orla speeds up. She needs to wrap her arms about Sim, nose his neck like a pony, reconnect. They haven't been alone since they arrived, not really, and he has the air of a man who needs to talk.

BONG! Conor and Martin, down from the loft, *en route* to the sitting room, knock into Orla, send her reeling. 'Watch it, lads!' The Cassidys are heading towards the chimes like fleeing wildebeest and Orla is the only one going in the opposite direction. The sitting room sing-song has begun.

BONG! Despite the spare-room door lacking a lock, Orla and Sim's drought must end. They'll make love. They'll whisper special things. The glue between them is tacky, and gives a little. Orla stumbles on a Barbie car pile-up, and pauses to place the pink plastic up on a shelf, out of harm's way.

BONG! All it needs is a chair up against the door handle, a swift hand down the front of his trousers and a few choice words in his ear; they'll be on that lumpy bed, between those manmade sheets, before Sim knows what's hit him.

BONG! Deirdre appears from the loo, in a personal mushroom cloud of Coco Mademoiselle. She grabs Orla by the shoulders and says, 'Aw, me little sis,' kisses her roughly on both cheeks. 'Happy New Year! You're going the wrong way, you dirty-looking eejit! Is that my top?'

'No,' says Orla. 'Happy New Year.'

BONG! On second thoughts, thinks Orla, almost at the door, primping her hair and smoothing down her skirt, we'll bypass the bed and just drop to the rug. That bed is noisy: even in this pandemonium Ma's Catholic ears will pick out rhythmic bedsprings.

BONG! She opens the door and steps into a dimly lit room (*Ah good! Curtains already pulled!*) and closes the door. The noise of New Year is suddenly turned down.

BONG! Sim is on the phone, he's talking, fast, head down but looking at Orla. His face is that of a Saturday boy caught with his hand in the till. 'Let's discuss this back in London. No, no, nothing.' He laughs, not the baboon masturbating laugh but a counterfeit one. 'Yes!' He says with artificial glee. 'Exactly! Ha, ha, ha!'

BONG! Orla isn't laughing, and the suggestive smile that's been on her face since she stood up from the Buckaroo board has gone.

'Who's that?' she asks, curtly.

Sim puts one finger up, mouths *hold on*, and winds up the phone conversation with, 'Gotta go! Yeah, you too. Bye.'

BONG! Down the hall cheering erupts. Squeaky baby voices, menopausal ones, gruff male ones, all mingle.

'Who was that?'

'Doesn't that baby ever stop crying?'

'It's a *baby*. Who was that?'

Fiddle music breaks out. Somebody's playing a jig. There is clapping.

'It was nobody. What's the face for?'

'Who was it?' Her lunge for the phone is clumsy. Sim, fresh from *Courtesan* fight lessons, dodges her easily. That he laughs makes Orla angrier. 'Stop it, Sim, and tell me.'

'It was Reece.' Sim shakes his head, as if in disbelief at all this silly fuss. 'Remember him? My agent? The man responsible for my entire career? Is it all right if I talk to Reece?'

'It was *not* Reece at midnight on New Year's Eve!' Orla grabs again, misses again. Sim's teasing giggle infuriates her. She wants to cry but doesn't.

She knows they won't make love. She knows that Sim will say, as he did last night, that he can't perform in the lair of Ma Cassidy. And when they return to her cottage he'll be too tired or in a mood.

There will be more calls, and they won't really be Reece either. Orla knows it's over but she doesn't have the courage to say it out loud.

Orla blinked, and set to with the lip-liner. She was done. She moved her head from left to right, unable to judge how she looked.

Half an hour to go until nine. The full-skirted black dress was fitted over her bust and upper arms: she felt held in,

340

supported but elegant. She'd piled up her hair, and could feel it rebelling. She unleashed a tempest of Elnett, and could imagine Marek wrinkling his nose at the smell of hair spray. Orla hoped she'd get to shake it out for him.

Her reflection was a little funereal: it needed something. She wondered if she should tempt fate and wear the bangle.

After all, she'd been 'good'. No internet searches. No late-night surveillance missions.

The moronic peep of her mobile stopped Orla mid-reach. Counselling calm, she extracted it from her bag. The screen told her, dispassionately, *Marek*. She grasped it hard, afraid to drop it, and pressed the button as carefully as if she were defusing a bomb. She felt sick to her stomach and as strong as an ox. 'Hello?'

'No, not you,' said a nasal female voice. 'Maude, please. I want to say Happy New Year.'

'Bogna? You're using your brother's phone,' said Orla, accusingly.

'Mine does not work here. Maude? Please? Chop-chop.'

'Here? Where's *here*?'

'Bloody Chamonix,' said Bogna bitterly. 'Bloody Marek make me ski with him. I miss all best parties at home. I hate snow. I think I have crab from barman. Now get Maude thank you.'

'Maude!' called Orla, laying down the phone and racing to the bedroom. 'Call for you!'

As Maude's murmured words drifted through the door – 'And Happy New Year to you too, Bogna dear. How about we make 2013 the year of no swearing?' – Orla clawed off her dress. Roughly wiping off her careful make-up, Orla didn't see her reflection. She saw instead Marek flying down a white mountainside, like a bird.

There would be no kissing in Trafalgar Square for them. He hadn't considered their arrangement significant enough to need a specific cancellation; ending the relationship had covered it, evidently.

Foolish! Orla chastised herself for feeling that his ski trip was somehow an insult to her; Marek owed her nothing and could do what he liked.

And so can I.

A shadow, like a bird of prey, fell across her. Orla rubbed viciously at her face. She knew what was coming to get her.

To imagine she could magic Marek back to her side by being 'good' was superstitious folly worthy of Ma. A new plan, direct and clean, arrived in her mind fully formed.

The bird of prey might well be swooping towards her, but she could struggle in its talons.

Maude, phone dead in her hand, came to the door and watched with a closed expression as her lodger pushed her feet into trainers and pulled on an old and well-loved hand-knit.

Moving fast, Orla put no effort into her cover story. 'A crowd from college are meeting in a pub in, um, Hammersmith.' She rifled a drawer for gloves. 'Don't wait up.'

Maude was already out of the door, and on the way to her own flat. 'Whatever you say, dear.'

'See you next year!' yelled Orla, winding a long soft scarf around her neck. It was Marek's: she'd never given it back.

Rushing down the stairs as if fleeing a forest fire, Orla exhilarated in the fresh, forgotten feeling of power. *How did I imagine that sitting passively in a cell of my own making would win Marek?* She stooped to knot a trailing lace, impatient at the delay to her flight out of the door on winged heels.

Orla was at the door now, a tingling anticipation surfing her blood. She paused to imagine the scene where she went to Marek and said, *see, this is what I did for you. I whupped my demons, faced Anthea, read the journal.*

The tingling sensation intensified, but it wasn't positive and pastel any more. The door remained closed.

As she'd urged Maude to do so many times, Orla was visualising. She saw herself at Anthea's illustrious New Year's Eve party, a guttersnipe attempting to scale the ramparts of a vast glittering palace.

She couldn't trump Anthea. Anthea beat Orla effortlessly, pilfering her boyfriend and trashing her next relationship without even being aware of it.

The door was as much a barrier to Orla as it was to Maude. Beyond it lay proof of her own inadequacy. She turned to slink away but jumped instead at the sight of a figure on the stairs.

Maude in a hat and coat was as unexpected as Maude in a spacesuit. Tugging on her gloves, her face sharp, Maude said, 'We need to be quick, dear, so why don't I answer the questions whizzing around your head before you ask them. Yes, I *do* know about the stalking. Marek rang me. He felt somebody close to you should know.'

Shame boiled briefly in Orla's chest. Marek had squealed. *No*, she corrected herself. *He passed on the baton.* Very 'him', very decent, and not the action of a man planning to return.

'And yes, I guessed that silly Bogna's call on Marek's phone would spark another sortie and, yes, because I know you rather well by now, I guessed that you'd run out of steam.' Maude, stiff in her outdoor clothes, looked bemused. 'That journal must be terribly important to you. I'm unsure about the wisdom of all this but you're your own woman. So, yes, I'm preparing to leave the house on the thirteenth anniversary of the last time I managed it because I think it's an excellent idea to challenge Anthea and put an end to this once and for all. There isn't another person on earth I'd do this for. Now. Have I covered everything? May we go?'

Even in the dim light of the hall's eco-bulb Orla saw the pall of stress on Maude's china-white face. 'Maude, the house rule is that only one of us goes bonkers at any given time so *whisht* and come upstairs.'

'Look at us!' Maude slapped the sides of her coat in exasperation. 'One woman who can't go out and one who can't stay in. If you truly, really want to have this journal in your hands and ask it these damn questions, then get on with it. Do it. Tonight.'

'You're angry.'

'I'm furious. Do you think life is so long that it doesn't matter if you waste some of it? I'm telling you, dear, from the other end of it, that life goes by in the blink of an eye. One moment you're playing hopscotch, the next you're married, then whoosh!' Maude clapped her gloved hands, her fine-boned face ardent. 'You're burying him. These years when your body works perfectly and your skin is like taut cotton don't last for ever and to waste them is blasphemous.'

'I won't let you do this.'

'*Let* me?' Maude skewered Orla with a blue eye. 'What gives you the impression I'm asking your permission?'

Chapter Thirty-Three

Their driver, his eyes superstitious dots either side of a bread-knife nose, was the runt of Kwikkie Kabs' litter. It was, according to the uninterested controller, the busiest night of the year and Orla and Maude had waited two hours for even this substandard banger of a car to turn up. 'She OK?' the driver asked roughly at a traffic lights, in an accent even Orla couldn't place.

'My friend's fine,' lied Orla, knowing he'd watched their halting progress over the few feet from hall door to kerb, knowing he'd been reluctant to take them at all.

The car smelled of jockstraps. Belted in on the back seat, Maude kept her eyes closed. Both hands, like little paws, clasped her handbag, the fingertips white with pressure. She was quiet now, her bombast replaced with an urgent tension that leaked all over the car.

'You all right?' whispered Orla. 'We can turn back.' All other considerations, even the journal, shrank against the horrible change in the Maude she relied on, took care of, loved.

They bumped over a pothole and Maude's head trembled on her thin neck like a Christmas bauble.

'She's sick, is she?' A flickering glance from the front as the cab rounded a corner like a runaway stagecoach.

'We don't turn back!' Maude smuggled the words past clenched teeth. 'We get the journal.'

The driver said, 'Is extra if she throw up.'

Directing him through Primrose Hill, Orla frowned at the change in Maude's breathing. Loud and shushing, like the sea, it was a parody of her yoga breaths. 'We're here.' Orla leaned forwards to guide the driver. 'Could you pull in by that lamp-post?' Orla put a hand on Maude's knee. Her friend was shuddering. 'We'll just sit here for a while.' There was no way Orla could leave Maude marooned in the big bad outdoors she so dreaded. 'You know it's a wait and return, right?' she queried the driver.

'Yes. Double rate,' said the driver, his charm equal to his road skills.

Across the road, number forty-nine was festooned with coloured lanterns, its curtains helpfully drawn back on an archetype of festive bonhomie. Pretty, happy people, having just the greatest time, threw back their heads to laugh at each other in a room made peachy by fairy lights. Against the window a table bowed in the middle beneath a still life of catered food. Champagne bottles stood to attention, ready to give their all, the popping of their corks a counterpoint to the Prokofiev, tasteful and unobtrusive, seeping out onto the street.

A far cry, thought Orla, from the soundtrack of last New Year – the latest boy band, traditional ballads, Niamh's squeaky recorder.

'Leave me,' said Maude, listing to one side and apparently unaware of it.

Orla put her arm around her, righted her. It beggared belief that they were here, that Maude was putting herself through this. She cursed herself for going along with it in the first place.

She should have withstood Maude. Hindsight again, her smug companion.

A taxi disgorged more guests. The door was opened by a tall man whose name flittered at the edge of Orla's mind. He had an open, fleshy face with a big, well-made nose. Tom Best! That was right. Anthea's co-star in her upcoming role, Macbeth to her Lady Macbeth. Greetings and compliments drifted over the road on the frigid air. He was doing Sim's job: if Sim hadn't died he'd be on door duty for his lover. The door closed, keeping the heat in, keeping the life in.

Maude stretched her torso, as if trying to clamber on top of her breaths, tame them. 'Go get the journal,' she croaked, the words eked out like a miser's loose change.

'I won't leave you, Maudie.' Orla took one of her hands, unhooking it from the handbag and wincing as Maude's hand closed over hers like a clamp.

The driver sank in his seat, broiling with animosity. 'She doesn't look right,' he said.

Newcomers scaled the steps and this time the hostess herself answered the door, in floor-length green velvet. Even from this distance, Orla could tell Anthea smelled delicious, as she theatrically embraced the chicly dressed older couple, even dropping a cute, ironic curtsey to the white-haired man.

The couple were almost through the door before Orla recognised Lucy and the senator. She recalled their Christmas card. *Regards, Lucy and Paul Quinn*.

How fitting that they should migrate towards Anthea, show her the cordiality always carefully denied Orla. She had always been an interloper. Orla shut her eyes against the rush of pain.

Not posh enough for his parents, nor cool enough for his actor friends. *Just* a primary school teacher.

Lucy appeared at the window, her hand hovering above the modish titbits. Orla blushed at the memory of the tacky New Year's party she'd subjected her son to last year.

The sitting room knee-deep in Quality Street wrappers, a sleeping infant on every lap, somebody scraping a fiddle, the kids Riverdancing, the dog darting out from under the sofa to snaffle stray After Eights. Everybody being exuberantly *themselves*. Orla remembered Sim's appalled groan when Deirdre lifted her skirt to showcase her new Christmas knickers.

Awful.

Although ... Ma had made the stuffing with red onions because she knew Sim liked it that way. Ma had hidden a selection box under the spare bed for Orla to find (and keep to herself). The man next door who'd lost his wife ten years ago was there as he was every year, and was welcomed, and given the best chair, even though he smelled of cats.

It was bright, suddenly, this vision of Ma's party. If Orla held it the right way up its lustre vied with the glitter ball across the road.

I like *Quality Street*, thought Orla. *And I* like *hearing Niamh demolish a tune. And I* like *the sticky weight of somebody tiny I'm related to asleep on my knees.*

'Twelve! Eleven!' The sash windows were thrown up in Anthea's house. Orla could hear kazoos.

A rasping sound escaped Maude.

The front door banged open and Anthea led a conga line of chanting revellers down the steps. She waved a champagne bottle, and there was an inaccuracy to her steps and a wildness to her hair that gave the game away about how much she'd drunk.

'Nine! Eight!'

The unruly line snaked uproariously along the pavement. Anthea veered into the road, bringing them all with her on a collision course with the stationary cab.

Maude was having trouble swallowing. Orla scrabbled for the bottle of water in her bag, shrinking down in the seat as the counting, whooping conga line approached the car on her side.

'Five! Four!'

'You!' bayed Anthea, squatting suddenly in her finery a few feet away and throwing out her arm to point the champagne bottle through the cab window at Orla. Partygoers piled up behind her, bumping against one another, screaming and tittering.

'Right. Bloody troublemakers.' The driver revved the engine. 'Out!'

Anthea scuttled towards them and squinted in at Orla. 'It was you, wasn't it? Outside my house?'

The laughter tapered off. Her guests looked at each other for enlightenment.

'Get *out*!' yelled the driver, one beefy arm across the back of the passenger seat.

'It's all right, Maude,' said Orla, trying to hold Maude's head up. It was slipping back, making her choke as if she were drowning.

'That's my stalker!' Anthea stumbled and shrugged off a woman attempting to put her arms around her.

'OUT! OUT!' The driver bared his teeth and banged on the back of the passenger seat with a balled fist.

'Nonononono,' chanted Maude, eyes still shut, her body straightening out like a plank in the confined space.

'We can't, this lady is, she's not well,' Orla coughed out words, unable to string a sentence together.

'Leave me alone!' screamed Anthea, thumping the car roof to an affronted and girly shriek from the driver. Tom Best tugged at her elbow as she bawled, 'I'll call the fucking police if I see you round here again!'

The word 'police' galvanised the driver. He jumped out of the car, barged Anthea out of his way and pulled open the back door. 'Out. Both of you. Now.'

Tom leaned in to help Maude. He was strong and decisive, and between them, he and Orla manoeuvred her on to the pavement, where she stood like a puppet whose strings have been chopped. The look in her eyes, open at last, was fearful.

'What's the matter with her?' Tom asked Orla, both awkwardly supporting Maude. Their whispered conversation had to compete with the squeal of the cab's tyres and Anthea's ongoing diatribe.

'Of all the people! Orla thingy! You mad bitch! Tonight of all nights!'

Focusing on Tom, Orla said tearfully, 'She's agoraphobic. She should be at home.' She was good in a crisis, but this one was beyond her: Maude was too precious for Orla to think straight. 'We have to get her indoors, *please.*'

Without a word, Tom lifted Maude into his arms and strode back across the road. The guests tailed him, watching him ignore Anthea who beetled alongside, insisting, 'She's not coming into my house! Put her down! I will not let you—'

'I have a sick old lady here,' hissed Tom. To Maude he said, 'We'll soon be indoors. Everything's OK. Hang on, love.' He threw a beseeching look at Orla over Maude's head.

'Please, Anthea,' said Orla, from the other side of Tom's bulk, as they reached the front door.

Entranced by these developments, the guests looked from Anthea to Orla and back again, as if watching a Wimbledon final.

Anthea glared at Orla, then something seemed to fall away and she said quietly, as if bowing to the obvious need to have this out in private, away from their audience, 'Oh, bring her up to my room.'

With a heavy angry tread she led the way.

Watched by the multitude, Orla kept her eyes front as she climbed the stairs, aware that the Quinns were part of her audience. The wallpaper on the stairs was familiar from the article she'd bookmarked and she recognised the wide bed under a tented ceiling dotted with stars where Tom laid Maude as gently as if he were putting a baby down for the night.

'I don't like her colour,' he said to Orla.

There was a tentative knock at the door and a plump woman with an up-do peeked her head around the door and said mildly, 'Tom, darling, what's—'

'For God's sake, Ann,' snapped Tom. 'Wait for me downstairs.'

The face receded, cheeks red, lips pursed.

Anthea prowled in and out of the en suite. 'What's the matter with her? Who the hell is she? Why'd you drag old ladies along on your fucking demented hobby?'

The bedroom was smaller in the flesh and as untidy as a teenager's.

'Twice I've seen you out there, madam. Twice. Never recognised you until just now.' She shook her head like a hanging judge.

'This lady needs water.' Tom, ignoring Anthea as profoundly as if she were a ghost only Orla could see, found a mohair blanket and draped it over Maude as Orla removed her shoes.

They should never have come, but now that they had and the escapade had taken such a terrible toll on the woman, Maude was Orla's priority. She rubbed life into her freezing hands with her own. *I'll die my thousand deaths later,* she thought.

Maude revived a little, her face warming up. 'Tell her,' she commanded in a weak facsimile of her usual voice. 'Tell her why you're here.'

'Yes, *do*.' Anthea's hands went to her hips. Her arms were sticks, like a child's drawing. 'I'm all fucking ears, darling.' She shook herself free of Tom's restraining hand. 'Fuck off, Tom, this is none of your business.' The tall actor recoiled, wounded, and left the room. Anthea looked at the floor for a moment then dashed after him, hobbling, one shoe off, one shoe on.

There was a hissed argument on the stair. Orla ignored it, fussing over Maude who, if not herself, had at least reached a plateau where her breathing was normal and her eyes open. 'Soon be home,' said Orla, adding a whispered, 'I know, I know, I get it, not without the journal,' when Maude stirred.

The overheated room was sluggish. When camera-ready, it was a harem of dreams, but tonight it was a mess. Hair extensions hung like roadkill on the outside of the wardrobe door. An open sachet of low-calorie cup-a-soup lay on the carpet, its dusty innards trodden into the pile, in vivid contrast to the feast downstairs. Dresses, some with labels still attached, were strewn on the floor like mating eels: Orla recognised the aftermath of a wardrobe crisis when she saw one. And who, she thought, keeps a weighing scales centre stage on a priceless rug?

Anthea did. This room told many tales about her and, for a stalker, was the holy of holies. So why did Orla feel nothing? No curiosity, no satisfaction. *I'll get this over with as quickly as I can, nab the journal, spirit Maude out of here.*

Anthea returned. She'd sobered up a little. Pulling off her other shoe she stood in a pile of cracker crumbs and said, 'Explain yourself. And then I'll call the police.'

The police were an insignificant threat to Orla. Orla ate worst-case scenarios for breakfast. Flustered, abashed by Ant's ferocious gaze, Orla cleared her throat. 'Right.' The dressing table momentarily distracted her. Anthea's arsenal of miracle skin cream had a value of hundreds of pounds. Orla always turned the page on the absurd anti-ageing claims of the glossy ads, but Anthea bought every snake oil on the market. Orla marshalled her thoughts, galled by her compassion for Anthea's desperate credulity. This was no time to *understand* the woman.

'I didn't mean to frighten you, Anthea. I thought I was being discreet.'

'Ten out of ten on that score,' snorted Anthea. With her

shoes off she was minuscule. 'My neighbour told me about the freak standing in the hedge.'

'Oh *God*,' mewled Orla, mortified at her dirty washing being passed from hand to hand. 'I'm sorry,' she said abjectly. This wasn't panning out well: who apologises to the bitch who stole their lover? 'Knowing about you and Sim drove me a bit loopy.'

Anthea teased a hairpiece from the back of her russet mane. 'Christ, that thing itches.' She tossed it to the floor. 'Is she going to conk out?' Scratching her scalp maniacally, like a chicly dressed Bedlamite, Anthea nodded at Maude.

'She has a name. Maude'll be fine when I get her home.'

'What do you mean you know about me and Sim? How could you possibly know?'

'He told me.'

'What?' Anthea turned Neanderthal in her incomprehension. 'He wouldn't. Unless he was a bloody fool. Which, come to think of it, he was, so . . . ' Anthea threw up her arms in exasperation. 'What can I say, kid? Welcome to the real world. I always take my leading man to bed. It makes the shoot easier.'

'You stole him from me.'

The platitude came out shakily. Orla held Maude's hand tighter for courage. Maude had elbowed her way up to a half sitting position, but she looked awkward, as if she'd landed there from a great height.

Speed this up. Get Maude home.

'I want an apology but I recognise I can't demand that from you. So, give me the journal, Anthea. I'm not leaving without it.'

The weak squeeze from Maude's fingers felt like a standing ovation.

'You're talking in riddles. Sim said you were off centre.' Anthea sat on her dressing-table stool, hunched over, legs apart, an ungainly pose for a woman in couture. 'I can apologise, if that's what you want. I see how it looks but it's just a bit of fun, shagging the co-star. A good clean fight and nobody gets any ideas. Sim certainly didn't.'

'He died loving you. His card said so. I know he was leaving me for you, Anthea, so please stop pretending.'

Orla's stomach lurched but she didn't collapse, or want to cry: the truth wasn't so towering any more.

Anthea folded her skeletal arms. 'Listen up, Tinkerbell. Sim did *not* die loving me. In fact, I was a pain in the ass. This is *not* a fair cop. So goodbye, and piss off back to whatever crappy postcode you came from.'

This was the woman Orla had envied. Had aspired to.

Her negotiating skills honed in Tobercree Primary, Orla's first rule was *Never back down*. 'I don't believe you. And I'm not leaving without the journal. You don't deserve it. This time last year you were on the phone to him. Sim's reaction to me walking in was classic – he laughed to halt your conversation, let you know discreetly that I was in the room without saying so, there was even a *me too* when you said you loved him. Sim made out it was Reece but only a lover calls at midnight on New Year. The entire trip he was cold and distant with me. I knew something was up. But I didn't press him because that's the way we rolled. Then he confessed all in the card, the one you advised me to burn.'

'You did burn it,' whispered Anthea.

'Nope.' Orla relished Anthea's surprise, grateful to Reece for keeping one of *her* secrets for a change. 'In it he told me he was in love with a woman I knew of, a sophisticated woman who could offer him the kind of life he wanted.'

Anthea shook her head, her eyes large. 'You poor little cow. Reading that after he died. That is *cruel.*'

'Sim didn't know he was about to die.' *Now I'm defending him? To Anthea?* 'Let's cut to the chase. I won't ever stare up at your windows in the middle of the night again. That's over. Because I can see what I came here for.' Orla pointed at the floor by Anthea's stockinged foot.

Beneath a knot of discarded and trampled Gucci and Prada and McQueen, a leather book cover peeped out.

'This?' Anthea tugged at it, and heaved it on to her lap. 'You want this? Jesus, you're petty.' She threw it over to the bed. It landed, fat and heavy, beside Orla, who almost recoiled at Anthea's instant capitulation.

Reaching out a tentative hand, Orla touched the tan-coloured hide.

Maude craned to look at it, then fell back.

Pulling the journal on to her lap, Orla had to drag her attention back to what Anthea was saying.

'Did he name me? Did he write down my name?'

Orla trotted through the memorised text of the card. She blinked. 'No, actually.'

'D'you know why, Einstein? Because he wasn't talking about me. I'm glad he confessed, though. I told him to. Yeah. *Me.* The whore of Babylon was on your side. Believe it or not, I don't like to see relationships fall apart. When you see a showbiz marriage that's lasted for decades, it means that both parties turn a blind eye to a little indiscretion here and there, but typically Sim had to take it further. He left his fingerprints on every bird in the production. That's why Sim was so pissed off with me, because I threatened to tell you when you came over. I felt you should know what you were getting into, being with a famous man. Dear God, girl, didn't you know your boyfriend was a tart?'

Orla didn't answer. She held the journal to her chest.

'After the traditional rehearsal bonk, I never went near Sim again. Guide's honour. Besides anything else, I couldn't spend much time with Sim because of the booze and the coke. I'm not going back to rehab, darling, not for anybody.'

'Explain why his parents are downstairs, then.' Rattled by the late realisation that the valentine named no names – Orla had been so *sure* of Anthea's guilt she'd rewritten it in her mind – Orla was glad to be back on solid ground.

'They came to the set and we met and we've been in touch ever since.' Anthea shrugged. 'They're starfuckers, I guess. I'm nice to them because their son died; sue me.' Anthea ferreted out half a cigarette from the debris on her dressing table and lit it. 'Do you want to know my real alibi? The real reason I couldn't be the *other woman*?' Anthea locked eyes with Orla and said glumly, 'I'm in love.' She hung her head, puffed at her bent little cigarette. 'It doesn't happen often but when it does I'm a one-man woman.' Anthea pressed her fingers to her temples and gurned to keep the tears at bay. 'And, as usual, it's a disaster. But you've met him. You tell me, how could I not fall for him?'

'Are you talking about Tom Best? But he's married,' said Orla.

'No!' Anthea drew back with feigned horror, then resumed her bitter tone. 'Yeah, doll, he's married. They're all spoken for. I'm a home-wrecking bitch, but I'm not *your* home-wrecking bitch.'

Like Juno said, you know love when you see it. Since Marek had left, Orla was hypersensitive to love and she saw it now in bolshy Anthea.

Absurdly, Orla *wanted* Anthea to be Sim's mistress now.

'This,' Orla tapped the journal, grateful for its bulk as the case against Anthea began to unravel, 'knows the truth.' She pulled it open and flicked through the pages, stopping at one near the end, her mind already fluttering at the fact that the paper wasn't lined, or yellow, as she remembered. 'Macbeth,' she said to herself.

'Yeah, my script.' Anthea frowned, puzzled. 'Sim had the binder made for me when I admired his diary on the first day of rehearsal. Cute idea. Now I use it for each new job. My name's stamped on it.' She leaned over, closed it and tapped the tooled gold letters spelling out *Anthea Blake, A Class Act*. 'How can it tell you the truth?'

'It can't.' Orla stood, held out the binder. 'You did. I'm really sorry, Anthea. Really, really sorry.' She was *wrong*.

Orla had built the last two months around her mistake, and sacrificed Marek on its altar. He was out of reach in the cold clean snow while she ploughed through all this mulch with a tipsy woman who fucked other people's boyfriends for 'a bit of fun'.

'No, don't cry. Very bad for the skin. People do funny things when somebody dies, I suppose,' said Anthea, assuming this new amiable persona as easily as shrugging on a blouse. 'As stalkers go, I've had worse.'

'I should get her home.' Orla gestured despairingly at Maude. 'Do you have a cab number?'

'My PA is downstairs. If she's not too pissed, I'll get her on to it.' Ant stood, stooped to look in the dressing-table mirror and played with her disordered hair. 'Good thing the bedhead look is in.' A few pats with a sponge, a flurry of brushes and powders and Anthea was presentable again. 'I should thank you. They'll be talking about this party for fucking *years*.' In the carefully lit mirror, Anthea looked ten years younger.

'Will you tell me who Sim was in love with?'

Anthea looked directly at Orla's reflection, her green eyes vivid in the glass. 'I don't owe you a thing.' She returned her gaze to her own face, smoothing her eyebrows with one finger. Orla wondered if Anthea knew the image was flattering, or if she really thought she looked like that. 'I have a suspicion,' Anthea said eventually. 'A hunch. But I can't share a hunch with you, doll, in case this madness starts all over again with somebody else who doesn't deserve it.'

'Does Reece know?'

'Ah, Reece ...' Anthea exhaled heavily. 'The keeper of all our skeletons in all our closets. Put it this way. I'd be amazed if he didn't. But, listen, if he hasn't told you then there's no point bugging him. Reece is all about damage control.'

Anthea shook herself and was gleaming again. Pulling on her shoes, she grew three inches and threw her shoulders back.

'Time to dive back in.' She paused at the door. 'I will say this, though, and that's the subject over for me. If *you'd* died on Valentine's Day, Sim wouldn't be tormenting himself. He'd have made a fresh start. You do the same.' She reached over, trailed a finger down Orla's jaw. 'In your own funny way, you're kind of gorgeous.'

The room was drab again when she left. A crystal knob on the wardrobe door fell off.

'Let's go home,' said Maude feebly.

Sim's journal

1 January 2012

This is going to be my best year ever!

Chapter Thirty-Four

To recap.
No journal.
No idea who Sim left me for.
No Marek.

From her chair at the end of Maude's bed, Orla watched the first sun of 2013 rise.

Odd how a sleepless night can train a spotlight into the mind's dingiest corners. Truths stand obvious in the glare, and of these three deficits, the third was the one that cast the longest shadow.

And losing Marek was all my own work.

The slight figure in the bed stirred, swallowed, turned, but didn't wake. Orla had helped a paper doll up the stairs a few hours ago, and sat listening to her sleeping breaths in case they petered out.

They hadn't. Maude had slept well while Orla kept guard. And now London woke up around them.

On her feet, groomed to her standard high level, vigorous in limb and voice, Maude was physically revived. Her erect bearing, her sprightly gait all seemed to say, *it takes more than a hideous trauma for me to have a lie-in.*

Emotionally, there was a noticeable shift. It was a

quieter Maude that padded about her Queendom, one reminded of her frailties. Orla caught her look of introspection at odd moments and had difficulty calling her back to their present.

For this, Orla unequivocally blamed herself.

The aftermath of New Year's Day was more dramatic for Orla. It was as if some reckless giant hand had torn off the roof, flooding her claustrophobic doll's house with light.

Orla's mistake about Anthea had been fundamental, but she'd come away from Primrose Hill with something. She'd learned that Anthea was a woman, and just that, for all the trappings of celebrity.

And she'd learned that if, as Orla had often wished, Sim had lived one more day he wouldn't have taken Orla back. Because Orla wouldn't have asked him to. The sages were right to warn against idols: Sim's feet of clay had gone all the way up to his neck during that last sexless, jokeless Christmas. She could conjure up, even now, the pea-souper of septic boredom he'd dragged from room to room.

And that phone call.

Her life since pivoted on that call. Her romantic history might be different if she'd acted decisively on her instincts by either ending the relationship or rushing to London to re-stake her claim.

Instead, Orla had put her fingers in her ears, carrying doggedly on with her backwater life. *I encouraged him.* Some observers might argue that Orla had told Sim *she* didn't love *him* long before he put pen to pink paper.

Sim's sudden death left a hole bigger than Sim: the vastness of Orla's loss had perverted everything, made her suspicions unthinkable, even sacrilegious. So she'd kicked them under the rug, where they festered.

As Orla tended to Maude, discreetly – Maude didn't care to be tended to – she compared their situations. In a moment of acute distress, both women had handed the reins to their subconscious. Negative thoughts had swarmed to the fore, looping and coiling, folding back on themselves until both women had created their own super-real alternative reality. In their looking-glass worlds, the absurd seemed obvious. Wall myself up in the house? *Excellent idea!* Stalk an actress? *Why, I don't mind if I do!*

Love would get Maude on her feet and out through the front door, to the corner, and, in time, beyond.

And it wouldn't go amiss for Orla. There was some straight talking to be done.

'Good evening, the Cassidy residence.'

'It's me, Ma, you can drop your phone voice.'

'Darlin'! What a lovely surprise. I was just rinsing out me unmentionables. This is much more fun.'

'*More fun than washing knickers*. They can put that on my gravestone.'

'How's the hols going? Getting out and about?'

'You could say that. Listen, Ma, I've been thinking about the future.'

'And?'

'And it's here. I'm staying.'

'Oh. Right. Well, I expected this, I suppose. Is it to do with Marek?'

'No. Well, I'd hoped it was. It's a long story. I'll tell you in

February. I've booked my flights. You have to put up with me, whether you like it or not, from the twenty-second to the twenty-fourth.'

'Are you codding me? That's fabulous, Orla. I'll have to air that duvet. And I'll get some Vienettas in. You can help me shop for a cardigan. We'll have a whale of a time! Can I help you with the fare?'

'Definitely not. There's something else I have to say, Ma.'

'Go on. Me loins are girded.'

'Your New Year's Eve parties are the best in the world.'

Christmas falling on a Tuesday made the college holiday two and a half weeks long – *too* long for a disappointed, regretful, lovesick Irish woman. Keeping an eye on Maude was a happy distraction, but Maude had rallied quickly, belying her age. That worrying tendency to drift had gone: Maude was back to her pin-sharp self, and impatient with Orla's concern.

'Bake a cake, dear,' she suggested shortly, discovering Orla yet again on the shop sofa.

'Wouldn't you like to do a little visualisation?' Orla used the kind of encouraging face she'd used when coaxing Year Two to eat their cabbage. 'Mmm? Maybe visualise going to the dry cleaner's?'

'I'd rather visualise you out from under my feet.'

Out came a recipe book splodged with grease, and a rusty scales and a buckled cake tin. Creaming the butter and sugar, Orla wondered if the resulting victoria sponge would be as delicious as one of Anthea's 'famous' cakes. It was funny, if she was in the right mood, how this would have genuinely exercised her mind until recently.

The seventh of January seemed an age away. She wondered if her students knew how two-way the classroom traffic was: she taught them English grammar and idiom; they grounded her and gave her purpose.

Orla was allowing lots of small truths to resurface and one of these was her pride in her profession. Teaching had never been just a job for Orla. She'd wanted to be Miss Cassidy ever since she'd first lined up her teddies and Barbies and called out the register.

Teaching adults had stretched her at a time when she needed fresh experience, something to baffle her pain, but now, as the dust settled around her, Orla felt the pull of primary teaching again, just as Marek had prophesied.

Instinct had mattered with him. He'd tuned in to her, *known* her.

With a whinny of regret, Orla checked the cake through the glass oven door. *Rise, you git!*

One thing was certain: never again would Orla allow anybody to describe her as 'just a teacher'.

The sales tempted Orla into Oxford Street. She bought a belt and a poncho thing that she regretted before she'd even left the shop, and possibly the nicest dress ever, a draped fuchsia knee-length design which she knew would have inspired Marek to whisk her out of it.

Such thoughts were useless, but they persisted. She looked about the coffee shop as she ate her post-purchase snack and gauged it as the sort of place she and Marek might choose. She likened the small biscuit which came with her coffee to the *rogalicki* he'd fed her the last time they'd shared a bed.

Marek had supplanted Sim in her *if only* daydreams. There

was a crucial difference between the two men, beyond the obvious ones of temperament: as Juno pointed out, 'Marek is alive!'

Juno felt that the breach could be repaired, but Juno wasn't in full possession of the facts. She knew that Marek had left after a row on Christmas Day, and she knew that Anthea had been absolved; one day, when Orla felt strong enough and there was enough wine in the house, Orla would tell her about the cause of the row.

For now, Orla relished the sensation of power returning to her limbs, of energy rising within her. She was transforming, as in a fairy tale, into another being, except she was transforming back into *herself*.

There was no word from Reece. The promised present didn't arrive. His attentions were turned off like a tap. Anthea and he must have talked. She imagined them knee to knee in a corner of their club.

Good, Orla found herself thinking. She was weary of wondering about Reece's motives, gauging his sincerity, querying whether their friendship was genuine or part of, to use Anthea's chilling term, 'damage control'.

It was obvious that Reece knew the identity of Sim's other woman. Orla could pick up the phone, badger him, start the whole cycle all over again, but she had no plans to. She'd had her fill of half-truths and hints, of being led through mazes and past distorting mirrors. Squaring her shoulders, Orla hunkered down for a lifetime of not knowing. She shouldn't care about the true identity of Miss X, any more than she should care about the hows, whys and whens of Sim's defection.

But she did.

She shouldn't miss Marek so much, when she'd only known him for a few months.

But she did.

Abena, Sanae, Dominika and the others regrouped noisily. They demanded to know if Orla had liked their presents, and milked her for every last detail of her Christmas.

'I know what you're up to.' She'd pointed to each one in turn with a ruler. 'Trying to distract me. Well, it won't work. Page fifty-eight, ladies and gentlemen.'

Their cheeky questions, their attention to her, their lack of attention to her, it all energised Orla. She was mutating still, sparks flying from her fingers, changing back to herself. It was a profound feeling, and warming. As she listened to Dominika read, faultlessly, an official pamphlet which would have confounded her a few months ago, Orla felt serene.

Chapter Thirty-Five

January was wet.

The sound of rain on window panes is cosy; sopping toes inside leaky boots on the way home from work less so. Orla vaulted puddles and forded the angry little rivers coursing along the gutters, eager to reach the warmth of Maude's Books.

Her thoughts tonight were not serene.

Lately she'd likened herself to a phoenix, rising out of the ashes of New Year's Eve to be reborn as an emotionally robust specimen. Her mutation was decelerating now. She whirled slower, preparing to land again, and she couldn't help but notice some new landmarks down there that weren't pretty.

It's terrible to know that, handed the ingredients for happiness, you simply opened your fingers.

Choose, Marek had commanded, black and white, just like his colouring. She'd chosen and, taking her at her word, he hadn't looked back when he'd walked away. There was nothing coy about Marek.

The happiness she'd found with him had been like a personal red carpet they could have rolled out into the future, insulating them from every stone in the road.

There had never been a sense of potential with Sim: after the first euphoria they'd begun counting down to the inevitable dwindling, despite what the *billets doux* in the hat box said. She'd thought Sim good at loving; turns out he'd just been good at writing cards.

Marek, however, was good – very good – at loving.

The window of Maude's Books glowed, and Orla quickened her step. 'It's times like this,' said Orla, shaking out her overwhelmed umbrella in the doorway, 'that I envy you agoraphobics.'

'Tea,' said Maude decisively, leaving her post at the till. 'Bogna!' she called, 'come out and say hello to Orla.'

'You're back.' Orla shook her wet Medusa tendrils. 'How was your trip?' She'd forgotten it was late-closing day, and felt ambushed. Would Marek lunch around the corner tomorrow, she wondered, before answering *of course he will*. He was a creature of habit. 'Did you get to like skiing in the end? That's most people's experience, isn't it?'

'I fall in love with barman,' said Bogna, flicking a feather duster over the erotica. 'From day two I do not ski. It is pants.'

'And your brother?' asked Orla, dropping to the arm of the sofa to wrench off her wet boots. That sounded airy, she hoped. Yes. She'd pulled it off. Definitely airy. 'How's he?'

'Why are you so interested?'

There was a full answer to that.

Because I love your brother. I can name it now – it's love. Perhaps I didn't recognise it because, poor me, I'd never truly felt it before. I regret not saying it to him. I regret withholding. I regret losing him. I love Marek Zajak. There, I said it.

The answer Orla gave was more succinct. 'Just wondering.'

'He is in bad, bad mood every day of holiday. Your fault. I don't know what you do to him but it cut him, deep down. I tell him: only way is get new lady double quick.'

Gee thanks, Bogna.

'On New Year's Eve,' Bogna carried on, feathers pointed accusingly at Orla, 'he gets drunk. Stupid drunk. My brother *never* does this. He make sick on balcony and stay in bed all next day.'

Even though she loved Marek, and wanted only the best for him, these details thrilled Orla. Her hope – a pathetic creature, grooming itself in the corner – did a little jig and its fur stood on end like a ruff. So she had some power over him, enough to make him drink to forget her. That could be construed as a start.

'After this he is in better mood. As if he vomit you up and is over you.'

Reappearing with a rattling tray of mugs, Maude was brisk. 'Nobody could get over our precious Orla that easily. And Bogna, dear, take care with your metaphors.'

'Tell him,' said Orla carefully, 'I said hello.'

'No,' said Bogna.

Wet socks squelching, a demarcation line of damp mid-way up her jeans, Orla hobbled upstairs with her mug.

She'd been waiting for Marek to make his move, but he'd made it long ago. More than once.

The bathroom filled with steam, all the better to obliterate the stupid woman in the mirror as Orla ran a bath that was slightly too hot.

Marek had made *all* the moves in their relationship.

*

'I've no Skype on the computer – Himself kept the snazzy one – so I'll describe the new flat to you.'

'Are you moved in already? I didn't send you a card.'

'No matter. Yes, as of the twenty-first January, 2013, I live at fourteen Zelda House, Sweeney Avenue. And I love it, Orla! I can't stop jumping up and down in the sitting room.'

'What's it like?'

'You know the block I'm talking about? The new build, yeah? We're on the third floor. As I look around I see magnolia paint, Orla, a *lot* of magnolia paint. And it's got that new-carpet smell. The communal hall has a bike in it which me and Jack *always* fall over. Hideous kitchen. And it's small. Small, small, small.'

'You and small don't really go. Your old en suite was big enough to host a bar mitzvah.'

'This whole flat could fit in there. It's plenty big enough for me and the little fella. And listen – I'm going back to work!'

'Come off it!'

'I swear to God. I woke up one morning, rang my old boss, you know, the randy little sod with the wig, and hey presto, I've got three days a week.'

'But you hated work.'

'You and your elephant's memory. I'm not going overboard, just the three days and Himself is paying for a childminder.'

'How *is* Himself?'

'It hasn't hit him yet. He thinks I'm playacting at being independent. He's humouring me, you know? Hoping I'll come to my senses.'

'I know what it's like to live in hope. Be kind to him, Ju. He'll be confident one day and then gibbering the next, in case all his hopes are false.'

'Is that what you're going through? Marek is coming back. I can feel it.'

'I can't. It's been too long. Things have changed.'

'D'you know what? These conversations belong to our teens. We don't need men, Orla Cassidy. We're strong independent women. Feck 'em.'

'I agree, we don't *need* men. But I *want* that man.'

'Oh Orla, you poor thing. This is like when Sim died, when you—'

'No, Ju. It's nothing like when Sim died.'

'OK. Sorry. Oops. Stepped on a corn there in me size eights.'

'Has Rob stopped pestering you?'

'Yes. At last. He's in bits. I'm toxic, truly I am. I never should have encouraged him. It fed my ego, that's all. And now I look back at the wedding, our house, all the Bang and Olufsen and the architect-designed conservatory and I think yuk! I'm ashamed, genuinely ashamed that I thought those things were important.'

'Don't be too ashamed.'

'Oh, I'm not. You know me. I felt ashamed for half an afternoon and now I'm over it. But I should have been honest with Himself. We weren't on the same page. He was in it for love and now he's hurting.'

'D'you know, you could be Sim talking about me!'

'God, yes. Oh, yuk again. I don't want to be like Sim.'

'Well, you're not any more. Sim didn't live long enough to

evolve. With a few more years perhaps he would have grown out of that feeling that there's a better party somewhere else and he had to find it.'

'Poor Sim.'

'Yeah. Poor Sim.'

Two weeks to go and cardboard hearts crowded shop windows.

For anybody close to Sim, Saint Valentine's Day was a grim anniversary, its significance at odds with flowers and bonbons.

For Orla, besides being an anniversary of his death, the fourteenth of February marked four years since they'd met, and the end of a year unlike any other, one in which she and Sim had gone through more drama with one of them dead than they had while both were alive.

After twelve months of change and revelation, Orla was in negative emotional equity: she'd found Marek and lost him again. The clean efficiency of her cackhandedness was impressive.

There was shelter to be found in daydreams. On the tube, she'd loll in her seat and plan their perfect Valentine's Day, the one they'd be looking forward to if she'd made the right choice at Christmas.

She'd cook: he'd appreciate it, manfully finish his plate, but be candid in his summing up. She'd buy him something small, elegant, definitely nothing 'themed' – no teddy holding a poly-satin heart for Orla and Marek.

'Even you, Orochi?' All the students, even Orochi who was infamous for his excuses, handed in their work on time.

374

'I like this exercise,' he said, his straight brows serious and beetle black. 'I am in love.'

'Aw.' Orla smiled benevolently. She'd asked the class to write a love letter: it was impossible to completely ignore Saint Valentine. 'I never realised how romantic you all are.' For Orla, this day was as much about gravestones as it was about roses.

I can change that. The thought let itself in without knocking. It didn't even wipe its feet. And once in, it made itself at home.

She was waiting, passive as a damsel imprisoned in a tower, for Marek to declare himself, to gallop over the horizon on a white charger.

What's with the passivity? There was no history of inertia in Cassidy women; if Cassidy men could get a word in, they'd dolefully confirm this. Orla had always been a do-er, a practically minded person who got on with it, whatever 'it' might be.

Sitting on the radiator, pretending to listen to Abena's letter, Orla experienced something that Pilates had promised but never delivered. She felt taller.

She was done with waiting around. Where had it got her? She'd sat back like a geisha when Sim had trashed her Christmas and New Year when she should have had it out with him. She'd kept her head down around Lucy Quinn in case she let slip with a *Jaysus* or a *feck* when she should have been the red-blooded Irishwoman her parents had brought her up to be. And now she was hanging around like a schoolgirl waiting for Marek to come find her.

Why should he?

How could Marek trust her with his emotional well-being? He didn't even know that she loved him. He didn't know that she saw through the sophisticated exterior to the vulnerabilities beneath. He didn't know that she wanted to protect him, just as he'd tried to protect her.

A road forked ahead of her. By taking the correct path, Orla could leave behind a lot of burdensome baggage.

'Please, are you listening?' Abena was affronted.

'Of course.'

'You don't look like you are listening. You look like you are making evil plot.'

'Please carry on, Abena.'

Abena's letter, to a man who owned a garage back home, was long, filthy and ended with her promise to 'bear many children and keep the house clean'.

'But you want to be a teacher when you go back!' Orla was dismayed at the collapse of Abena's feminism in the face of love.

'I do not tell him this,' said Abena, a guarded look on her face. 'He will find this out when he marries me and it is too late!' She cackled, all her chins bouncing, and the room cackled with her. Being loved by Abena would be like standing in the blast of a jet engine, thought Orla. She rather envied, and rather pitied, the garage owner.

Listening to the declarations of love from her pupils, Orla scribbled one of her own on her notepad.

Dear Sim, I forgive you, love Fairy x

Hale and hearty, Maude switched roles and became the nurse, watching her patient for symptoms. 'We're a week away from you know what, dear,' she said as the two of them shared a horrible cake that Sheraz had thrown in free with the weekly delivery. 'How should we spend it? It's horribly sarcastic, marking an anniversary of a death on a day when the whole world is celebrating love.'

'I have something I must do,' said Orla. 'Something . . .' She looked for understanding from Maude. 'Something *private*.'

'Very well.' Maude patted her hand. Orla loved the papery feel of her skin. 'I'm here if you need me.'

'Thanks, Maudie.' Orla knew that Maude had stepped in and shut down Bogna's planned Valentine's Day window display: she'd seen the tissue paper hearts in the bin. 'I'm going to mark the day in my own way.'

Sim's journal

14 February 2012
5 a.m.

Saint Valentine, you soppy bastard, I need all the help you can give me.

Chapter Thirty-Six

Pre-dawn, lamps lit against the mauve dregs of the night, the flat felt special, like a house on the day of a wedding. The sugar-coated valentine hysteria beyond the front door was not responsible for this electricity: it was of Orla's making; it was bespoke. She was nervous, exhilarated and quite terrified.

Click. Off went the radio. The avalanche of gooey requests she could withstand but a proposal of marriage via the good offices of the idiot DJ was too much.

At times like this, Orla wished she smoked. Her hands needed something to do. She'd risen far too early, because the occasion had seemed to demand it, but now she prowled her abbreviated set of rooms, wondering where she'd be and how she'd feel by the time the next dawn rolled around.

London roused itself and hit its stride, oblivious of her agitation. The tops of the buses that passed Orla's windows went from empty to half full to sardine tin. Motorbikes whined. The crossing signal cheeped. The drunk – still there, still drunk – sang.

And the doorbell rang.

Orla took the stairs slowly and pulled open the door. She'd never seen that many red roses in one place before. They bristled slightly, then moved to one side to reveal the smiling man holding them.

His smile drooped. 'Oh. I thought it would be—'

'Maude? Come in, George.' Orla stepped back and the man–bush hybrid bustled past her. 'This is a surprise.'

'I've been thinking. I'm a silly old fool.'

'No, it was a natural response,' said Orla. *This* was the stuff of Valentine's Day, not an email to Radio 2 requesting Celine Dion. At last, the real deal: the triumph of Cupid over logic. 'She's worth the trouble, I promise.'

'Does she like roses?'

'She adores them.'

'Will I be welcome? Did you tell her about our conversation?'

'That was between us. You'll be very welcome. Top floor. Knock hard.'

Watching George climb the stairs in his tightly belted raincoat – really, how did he breathe? – Orla was glad that Valentine's Day was working its magic for Maude, and rueful already about her eager belief moments before that somebody else might be at the door.

The phone rang. She believed again and overtook George in an awkward manoeuvre on the top stair.

'Orla, love, it's Ma. Are y'in bits? Are y'on the floor? Don't go to work today, love. I'll ring them for you.'

'Ma,' said Orla, eyes closed, leaning back against the dresser. '*Ma, Ma, Ma*. No, I'm not in bits. I'm happy, actually.'

'I said a prayer for Sim, and I lit a candle and Father Gerry gave out his name at early Mass. I'll go to the grave later.'

Shuddering, Orla thanked her mother.

'That's very sweet of you, Ma. I'm remembering him, in my own way.'

'Good, good. We won't see his like again,' sighed Ma.

One day Orla would tell her the whole story. But not yet. Ma enjoyed a nice anniversary. 'No, I guess not. Listen, Ma, I need to keep this line clear.'

'Why?'

In case he calls. In case this day explodes into a shower of sparks. In case it's my turn.

'Work, you know.'

'Oh. Right. Now if you get tearful just offer up a quick prayer to Saint Jude, patron saint of hopeless causes. He's your man.'

The phone trilled again, as soon as Orla pressed the little red telephone symbol.

'Juno. What can I do for you this fine Valentine's morn?'

'Just touching base to make sure you're OK.'

I might be, if the entire Republic of feckin' Ireland would stop ringing me.

'Thanks.' Orla softened. She was lucky she had women, strong decent women who cared, checking up on her. 'I'm on an even keel.'

'The first thought in my head this morning was Sim.' Juno let out a laugh/sigh. Or maybe it was a sigh/laugh. 'After all the bastard did, I'm sad about what happened to him.'

'Me too,' said Orla.

They left it at that.

Today had to be about the future. If Orla was to salvage anything from the carnage of the last twelve months then she had to retool them, affix a happy ending.

By now, Orla was generous enough to imagine that Sim would be happy to know that his last card to her, followed by a howling silence which wasn't his fault, hadn't broken her. If she spun the straw he'd left her into gold, then today could be her own wonky memorial to him: he hated wreaths, anyway.

With time to kill, Orla opened her computer. Who would have thought a morning could last so long? Cruising through on-line newspapers, Orla stopped dead at an unexpected image. Sour memories reared up; Orla had only recently reclaimed the internet and reassured herself that this was not backsliding, but coincidence.

VALENTINE SURPRISE FOR TOM BEST'S WIFE, smirked the headline.

'Oh no.' Orla read the copy.

TV temptress Anthea Blake proves that life mirrors art by stealing her latest co-star from his wife of eight years. Tom Best, 32, is pictured leaving Ms Blake's two million pound North London house in the early hours of this morning. From the look on his face, and Anthea's dishevelled appearance in what appears to be a negligee, they weren't learning lines. It won't be a happy Valentine's Day in the Best house.

'Oh. You're still here.' Maude stopped dead as she passed Orla's doorway. She was wearing lipstick, a first, and holding the sheaf of roses aloft as if it the Olympic torch. 'No work today?' She looked suspiciously at Orla, inspecting her face.

'I booked it as holiday. Ages ago.' Orla hadn't told Maude. Today was hers and hers alone. 'I have ... plans.'

Behind Maude, George stood patiently, politely, glad just to let her sun shine on him. All this and more Orla read in his face, and she admired his courage in knocking on Maude's door, and for facing down his cowardice about her condition. Orla needed affirmation today that love was muscular, that love can conquer, well, *all*. And here was old George, affirming for all he was worth.

'Are you expecting Marek to make an appearance?' There was anxiety in Maude's query, and protectiveness, and fear.

'No. Not expecting. Although it would be nice if he did.'

Maude and Orla read each other's invisible subtitles.

'I'll leave you alone,' said Maude, her subtitles spelling out *I love you, dear.*

'Thanks.'

I love you too, Maudie, said Orla's.

With five minutes to go, Orla had to force herself to stay in the flat. Better to leave on time. *Stick to the plan.*

'Orla!' Maude's shout up from the shop had a frill of excitement. 'ORLA!'

'What is it?' Orla's body trusted Maude. If Maude was excited then it would be excited too: a glissando swept up and down her spine.

'A recorded delivery package.' Maude was trying and failing to regain her composure. 'For you!' she added, then, 'do hurry up dear!'

Turning the sign on the shop door to SORRY WE'RE CLOSED, Maude tiptoed upstairs with George, who was baffled by the change in atmosphere but ready to follow his valentine like a spaniel.

Alone with the package, a rectangle wrapped neatly and anonymously in plain paper, Orla knelt. She took a moment. Her intuition was adamant that this was significant and these days she listened to her senses.

Orla tore the paper to reveal a box longer than it was wide. The cardboard creaked as she pulled back the lid and then the journal was as heavy as a bible in her hands. She ran a finger down the cord that bound the spine, and traced the words *Simeon Quinn, His Journal* sculpted on the cover.

'Hello,' she said. 'At last.'

A square envelope was taped beneath Sim's name. Its top edge jagged, it had been opened. The postmark was a year old and it was addressed to Reece at his flat above his office.

Orla laid down the journal and peeled off the envelope. A scrawl on the front, in Reece's hand, read *The silly bugger put them in the wrong envelopes. You got my valentine. I got yours. He died loving you. I hope this brings you some peace. Keeping it from you has destroyed mine. R*

Orla took the card out of the envelope and opened it, barely taking in the Picasso portrait of Françoise Gilot on the front, the one that had always reminded Sim of Orla. Without pausing to think, she read.

Fairy,

Very very late in life I've learned something most people (you included) know from a young age. I've learned why honesty matters. It's always been a theory up to now, but something has rocked the way I feel about you and my life and suddenly I get it. We can't go forward together if I'm not frank with you.

O, take a deep breath – I've been unfaithful.

Take another – it's not the first time.

But this time I fell in love. The others are hardly worth mentioning, purely physical, just me being an opportunist. I always felt like poo afterwards but this time I planned to leave you and make a life with somebody else.

I feel as if I've woken from a dream where I was standing on a ledge high above traffic. One more minute and I would have stepped off. But I didn't.

So, O, I've lied, I've made a fool of you, I've been a bastard over and over again. I need you to know all that and I need you to forgive.

This card is really one big question – can you forgive? Can we start again?

OK. Another biggie coming up. This affair – which is OVER – was with Reece. I don't know if I fancy men – I just know that Reece was a comet streaking across my sky. I have to tell you, in this new spirit of honesty, that the relationship was intense, life-changing, unexpected and a roller coaster but crucially it wasn't YOU.

I'll never, ever, ever lie to you again. I'm different now. This has changed me. I'll cut Reece off utterly. I've cauterised the relationship by letter, a brief and cruel one, and I have no doubt that he hates me now. I must live with that.

Do you still love me? Call me and tell me you still love me. Now. And while you're on the phone, tell me you'll marry me. This year. This month? Tomorrow, if you like. You keep me on the straight and narrow (no pun intended).

I want to be faithful. I want to be a good man. I want to be your man. It's finally clicked. We're <u>real</u>, Orla.

My life is in your hands, my beautiful executioner.

Sx

Orla re-read it, twice. Sitting back on her heels, she let the card slip out of her hands and looked up at the ceiling map of cracks and wrinkles.

Everything shifted.

Shadows lengthened and contracted as her perspective altered.

Sim's lover had been in plain view the whole time.

Orla had never considered Reece's sexuality. He was modern, urbane, private. He was a strut for others, with no apparent needs.

But everybody has needs, Orla corrected herself sharply. Every human being needs love. It's not a trivial need, it's not copyrighted to Hallmark Cards. Love is a natural resource, like sunlight or water, without which we'd all wither and die.

Any minute now the hatred should arrive for the Machiavellian man who'd denied her the truth, let her cry on his shoulder, turned a false mask towards her.

It didn't arrive, and Orla couldn't see it on the horizon. She'd woken up that morning with a large landscape in her mind, an appropriate panorama for what she had to do. To see today through, she needed to be brave, she needed to be philosophical. And now this package had dropped from the sky, and it demanded much the same of her.

There's no way to keep love out. Orla had fallen for Marek

before she was officially ready in much the same way as Sim and Reece had given in to their feelings about each other.

Everybody says yes to love. Everybody in their right mind.

The journal sat, fat and smug, on the floorboards. Orla opened it, heard the soft *flump flump flump* as the yellowy pages fell on one another. It was all here. Her life with Sim in perfect chronological order right up until the moment the clocks stopped.

His handwriting flashed by, hieroglyphics ready to give up their code. She was the keeper of the secrets now.

A feeling like a dove landing in her chest.

Orla turned to the last page. She read the date, then an impulse made her check her watch.

She was going to be late. Orla snatched up the journal and tore out of the door.

Her boots were purposeful. Head erect, arms crossed over the journal, the new landscape in Orla's head held: despite the clamour of Ladbroke Grove, she was on a wide beautiful plain and could think in a step by step, forensic manner.

Effortlessly she read between the lines of the second, last, *real* valentine.

You would have done it again, Sim. There is an Irish saying, 'What do you expect from a cat but kittens?' Sim was a pleasure baby who could deny himself nothing: he demanded gratification as his right. If he'd lived, he'd have gone on to fresh conquests.

She halted suddenly, a no-no on a busy London pavement. With a 'Sorry! Sorry!', she stepped to the kerb, to the side of a vast rusting skip. Orla opened the journal at its last page, read the entry. And smiled.

For what had Sim done after writing that plea to Saint Valentine to intervene? He'd set off to find Reece.

Orla's well-documented passivity had meant she'd never questioned just what an actor was doing outside his agent's headquarters at six a.m. He'd been heading for Reece's *pied-à-terre*, above the office.

You'd already gone back on your promise, Orla pointed out. *You were trying to intercept the card before he read it*. She thought of Sim, panic-stricken, trying to wrench control of the future back from the valentine, unaware that his future was only minutes long.

You hadn't changed, you couldn't. Sim was slippery, evasive, dishonest. And glorious and warm and irresistible. Lovable. A lovable man.

You and I should have been a fling.

Orla tossed the journal into the skip. The soft crash of its landing put an end to their dialogue. She didn't need to know the whys and wherefores. None of it mattered. It was a historical document. Everything she really needed to know she carried within her.

Orla crossed the road, dodging the traffic, confident that one particular Saint – and it wasn't Jude – would grant her special protection against the number seven bus bearing down on her.

Be there, she begged. Really begged.

Orla's blood pounded. The landscape in her mind changed slightly. Colour crept in, as when rain soaks the ground after a long drought. She'd been through the contemplation and reassessment, and now that it was time for action she couldn't wait.

Three quarters full, the café was quiet, the kind of quiet a library generates, except this was the sacred hush of man communing with food. Orla was the only female, bar the bored-looking woman who sold her two *rogalicki* and a syrupy coffee.

Orla stood by the chair opposite Marek. 'May I?'

He'd seen her come in, looking up from his steaming plate of something foreign, and kept his eyes on her as she pushed her tray along the counter and paid at the till.

Marek nodded and laid down his cutlery. He was properly silent: he wouldn't speak, this silence said, until she'd laid out her wares.

She'd remembered his eyes many times, but never caught the history in them, a fable of duty and loss and experience. And loneliness.

It had taken a while to interpret that last one. Marek had such stature and confidence. He was a strider. He asked for no favours. But he was lonely and he needed a companion, a partner, somebody for him to protect who would protect him in return. Somebody who understood him.

Taking a seat, Orla placed her cup and plate just so. She licked her lips. The urn hissed. Somebody turned the page of a newspaper.

Orla began.

'You don't have to say a thing. But you should know that I heard what you said to me. I heard it and now I want to say it back to you. I love you, Marek. If I've missed the boat, that's my problem but I need you to hear me. You don't have to answer me. That's not the point. But I need you to know that you are loved. And missed. And wanted. And here's a *rogalicki*, because I know you like them.'

Orla held out the small sweet crescent, its sugar coating gritty on her fingertips, to Marek, who hesitated then took it.

He broke the biscuit, dipped it in his coffee and bit into it before he spoke.